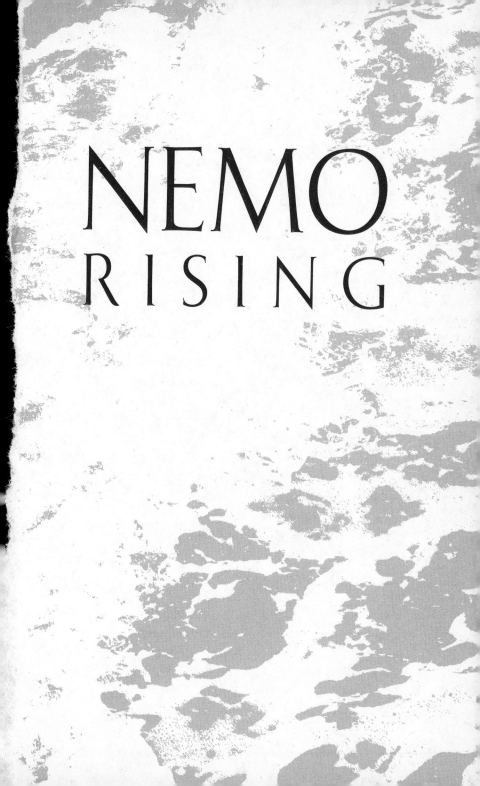

NEMO
RISING

NEMO
RISING

C. COURTNEY
JOYNER

TOR

A TOM DOHERTY ASSOCIATES BOOK
NEW YORK

This is a work of fiction. All of the characters, organizations, and events portrayed in this novel are either products of the author's imagination or are used fictitiously.

NEMO RISING

Copyright © 2017 by C. Courtney Joyner

A Tor Book
Published by Tom Doherty Associates
175 Fifth Avenue
New York, NY 10010

www.tor-forge.com

Tor® is a registered trademark of Macmillan Publishing Group, LLC.

Library of Congress Cataloging-in-Publication Data

Names: Joyner, C. Courtney, 1959– author.
Title: Nemo rising / C. Courtney Joyner.
Description: First edition. | New York : Tor Books, 2017.
Identifiers: LCCN 2017043430| ISBN 9780765376350 (hardcover) | ISBN 9781466851108 (ebook)
Subjects: LCSH: Nemo, Captain (Fictitious character)—Fiction. | Ship captains—Fiction. | Steampunk fiction. | BISAC: FICTION / Sea Stories. | GSAFD: Adventure fiction. | Sea stories.
Classification: LCC PS3610.O976 N46 2017 | DDC 813/.6—dc23
LC record available at https://lccn.loc.gov/2017043430

Our books may be purchased in bulk for promotional, educational, or business use. Please contact your local bookseller or the Macmillan Corporate and Premium Sales Department at 1-800-221-7945, extension 5442, or by email at MacmillanSpecialMarkets@macmillan.com.

First Edition: December 2017

Printed in the United States of America

0 9 8 7 6 5 4 3 2 1

For my wonderful and amazingly understanding family

For the beautiful lady in my life

And for Miles Hood Swarthout

Thanks for Standing Watch

NEMO

RISING

1

SKY DEMON

A punch of fast air shattered white vapor as the creature broke through the clouds during its descent, then flew at mid-altitude over the last fifty kilometers of ocean. There was no headwind to fight, and the moon reflected brightly across the always-moving details of the water below, allowing for perfect targeting.

Curving its wings, it picked up speed and dipped toward a freighter steaming for the horizon.

The writing was a child's, some letters scrawled together in an attempt at script, and the rest printed large and bold, including the date: April 20, 1870, with the "p" backward.

Horst couldn't help his smile, reading it through for the fifth time, eyes settling proudly on the words that were spelled correctly, and forgiving ones that weren't.

"Wievielen Malen können Sie das lesen?"

Krieg coughed his question as he reached for the coffeepot on the squat iron stove, then continued in English as guttural as his German: "All the day, you read that thing. You're not the only grandpa of the world."

"Her first letter not to St. Nicholas, and she's trying in English."

Krieg snorted. *"Eine zeitverschwendung,"* he said, pouring the last of the belly-wash coffee into a misshapen mug, his name painted on its side.

Horst said, "Your grandson made that thing. I've never seen you without it."

"Yah." Krieg drank, the wash dribbling as usual. "Because it's of use."

He wrung his coffee-soaked beard, then dropped a silver alarm whistle dangling from a chain and a Colt single-action pistol onto the small wooden table next to the stove. He settled on a crew bench, rolls from his hips swallowing most of it.

The bench groaned, but not loud enough to cover the hollow sound of the ocean slapping against the ship's iron hull. The wave-echo was a constant, but years as sea dogs made Krieg and Horst deaf to it.

A mess boy put out a fresh pot without a word, as Horst slipped his granddaughter's letter in one pocket, the pistol in the other, and hung the whistle around his neck. Krieg mumbled his standard warning about ducking below the crossbeam before starting up the stairs to the upper deck.

Horst always ducked.

The *Broomhilde* was the newest ship Horst ever crewed, and for him, taking the deck-watch meant time for admiration, particularly if she was under full steam, like tonight.

He'd gotten the habit of walking stern to bow as an apprentice seaman, stepping beyond the rail's end to that last bit of rigging; looking down at the waterline, seeing the cutting of the ocean, feeling the vessel's to and fro.

His hands traced the wood- and steelwork, memorizing every join, instinctively knowing when they were sure. It was Horst's connection with the ship that allowed him to sense when she was about to pitch; his nerves, stinging needles before an actual crisis.

Moving toward the stern, checking the worthiness of the lifeboat ties, Horst couldn't improve on *Broomhilde*. She was exactly as she should be at ten bells, with anchor chains coiled, cargo holds bolted.

He relit his clay pipe, listening to the gear-works heartbeat of the Day, Summers and Company engines. He knew he'd miss that pulse when he packed off. He checked his pocket again for the letter's comfort, continued to the opposite rail, then stopped, cocking his head.

There was something. Somewhere, in the dark. He listened, nerves taking over. Feeling the sting.

And then—the grinding.

The sound was low and mechanical. That groan of metal-on-metal, twisting before shearing, and rising, louder. Horst looked to the stacks. Their steam billowed, with no ruptures. No breach.

The groan became a steel scream.

He grabbed the brass amplifier crew call, blowing the whistle for the engine room. The scream around him intensified, beating the air, slicing his eardrums with a hot, invisible blade. He clamped his hands over his ears, squinting tight, trying to block something out. Anything.

The noise overwhelmed.

He threw open the hatch to the belowdecks, yelling to Krieg, *"Notfall! Alle Mann an Deck!"*

Horst made it to the rails, pistol drawn. Crewmen charged the stairs, rushing the deck, pulling on boots and pants, shouting orders that couldn't be heard over the sound.

Rifles were pulled from the weapons stores, ammunition slammed home. Others grabbed fire axes and sand buckets.

Horst pointed crew to either side of the ship as they brought guns to shoulders, taking aim at a calm sea.

Barrels raked the water's surface for a target. For anything. The sound, still louder.

Krieg and the Captain were last up the stairs, grabbing Horst by the lapels: it was his deck-watch. What the hell was happening? The metallic noise, the grinding fire, reached its crescendo. Krieg's glasses shattered.

The Captain's blood sprayed Horst like a burst of ocean foam as he was yanked high off his feet, a spiny prong jutting through his chest from the back.

The Captain was hurled a hundred feet through the air before rag-dolling, heels twisted against his neck, into the black water. And gone.

Crewmen backed off the rails, some falling to their knees. Horst swore and prayed with the same breath as the huge, manta ray–like creature roared past the ship, its dragon-split tail slashing wild, and gigantic wings blocking out the sky.

Then it circled back.

The men could feel speed and heat. More legs buckled, with just enough time to open fire.

The ray dove for the ship, fins guiding it on a blasting-hot stream of air, skin glistening as if polished steel, with brackish liquid pouring from open wounds around its throat and gill bars.

Its eyes were glowing mazes of color: red colliding with green in the orb, breaking into blinding white that lit up the deck.

Rifles flamed, bullet after bullet sparking off the ray's underbelly, then ricocheting back to the crew. Slugs lead-punched through chests, dropping the men as if they'd been Gatling-gunned.

They crawled blindly, bloodied and rolling, screaming their

last. Others kept shooting, the whip-tail tearing the smokestacks behind them, steel folding in on itself.

Horst dove out of the way as the stacks crashed to the deck, jagged edges chopping through planking to the holds below. Bursts of steam exploded out of the engine room, blowing plates off the hull, filling the air with spinning, hot metal the crew couldn't escape.

Fire and razors.

Krieg pulled himself to Horst with his arms, his legs gone, begging for something Horst couldn't hear, but understood. Horst pressed the barrel of the pistol against his mate's forehead. The sound of the ray turned the shot into a silent flash.

Men ran, pushing past each other for the lifeboats, tumbling into the water. Panic. The fins of the thing smashed through the masts, catapulting them over the side, log-crushing sailors frantically swimming away.

Horst stood defiant at the splintered railing, the ray diving directly out of the moon. He steadied his gun with both hands, focusing on an eye that kaleidoscoped white, orange, red.

The bullet pierced the glowing eye, liquid erupted, with the ray's head thrashing as if fighting a harpoon.

It collided with what was left of the ship, ripping down the middle, the tail hurling massive hunks of steel, sections of engine, sails, and the bodies of men into the ocean, all drowning together.

The *Broomhilde* heaved over, an explosion tearing the boiler room, gutting what was left of her. The blast was volcanic from the center cargo hold, black powder and fuel mixing, sending a plume of flame and smoke across the night.

Shockwaves followed, force bending the air, and murdering all sound for hundreds of miles. Finally, there were no more cries for help, or gunfire. Nothing, as the stern's edge was the last of the ship to be lost.

The ray circled wide, away from the wreckage, but close to the water, then climbed, wounded, toward the moon, before vanishing behind rolling clouds and smoke.

Death had taken less than two minutes. Left was debris, bodies floating, wide streaks of bloody oil on the water's surface, and a child's letter, carried across a rolling wake.

2

DEATH MESSAGES
AND DECLARATIONS

"How the bloody hell do you fight something that doesn't exist?!"

Ulysses S. Grant's question was thunder through the door of his personal office, stopping Efrem in mid-knock. He'd fallen twice, cutting his chin, while running the telegram upstairs from the White House communications room.

Efrem could hear a calmer voice: "Causing great havoc all the same."

"Are you pointing out the goddamn obvious?"

A Guard standing post in the second-floor corridor watched the twelve-year-old struggling: holding the red URGENT envelope, wiping his chin, minding the crease in his pants, then, lightly knocking.

Grant's voice was a rifle shot from the office: "No interruptions!"

Efrem glanced at the Guard, holding a Carbine and smirking, as someone moved on the other side of the office door, turned the brass knob, then opened it halfway.

John Duncan, the calm voice, stood before Efrem. "Son?"

Tall as the door frame, but compromised by an academic's stoop, Duncan sported a full beard on a thin face and thick lenses that enlarged blue eyes, which had no brows.

"Sir. A special communication, sir. Urgent, and special. Sir."

President Grant was by his desk, in a small alcove on the far side of the L-shaped room, topping a near-full glass of bourbon with branch water. He was a silhouette that didn't look in Efrem's direction. "When did it come?"

Efrem leaned in from the waist. "About three minutes ago, Mr. President."

Grant gave his glass a tilt to mix, then half-killed it. He stood by a large, rain-streaked window, and all Efrem could positively see was the back of his head, profile of a tight beard, and the lit end of a cigar.

"Too damn slow," Grant said. "And, it was never delivered. Understood?"

Efrem saluted, nodded, and saluted again. He tried "Yes, sir," but choked. Duncan gestured to his chin, silently telling Efrem to get bandaged, before shutting the door, and saying to Grant, "That's another one you scared to death."

"When I was a cadet at the Point, an officer would bark, I'd practically soil my drawers."

"A youngster," Duncan said, reading the message. "With no idea he was handling top-secret information."

"That ignorance makes him damn lucky. And trustworthy. Which country?"

"Germany."

Duncan put the opened URGENT envelope on a stack with the others. "With nothing pirated, ship destroyed, and all hands lost."

"In our shipping lanes. We might as well plant Old Glory on

the wreckage," Grant said. "A few days for a formal protest, then half of Europe will have their cannons aimed at us."

"I'm praying it won't come to that, sir."

"Then pray harder. Our harbors aren't big enough to hold all their warships—they'll be waiting in line to open fire, because they think us responsible for the sinkings, and then trying to alibi behind this half-brained lunacy of sea monsters."

Duncan said, "It's not that simple to dismiss," waited, and then, "is it?"

"Unfortunately, nations are punished for the transgressions of individuals."

Grant moved to the long table that dominated the office, stacks of CONFIDENTIAL folders littering its polished top, and grabbed one at random, breaking its black-ribbon seal.

"You believe these?"

Duncan chose his words: "Do I believe that they're an accurate record of the witness statements?"

"Stop dancing. You know damn well what I'm asking."

"Certainly not what you want to hear, but yes, I do."

Grant pushed the folder aside, knocking the last of his bourbon and branch. "Then you're a crazy fool, too."

"Mr. President, you wanted to know if I thought the sailors were telling the truth. For the record, I think they are."

"Well stated. For *my* record, they're probably all pissed as Lords, couldn't see a damn thing, and rammed some poor bastard's fishing boat, and that sank 'em both."

"Perhaps that explains one incident," Duncan said. "But that's skating thin. Sir."

"You're shooting credibility in the head if you side with this pile."

"Dying declarations. Precise details of the order of events in half a dozen languages."

Duncan caught Grant's dark scowl, kept a calm measure. "Is that the report citing a sea serpent?"

"What the hell does it matter?"

"The statement by the Swedish boson's mate, with the exact times? He was bleeding out . . ."

"The Captain of the Chinese freighter said a monster squid." Grant opened another folder, and another, scattering pages. "Of course, the Greeks claim a Cyclops, smashing a two-master with his fists!"

"Sir, all the reports have a common—"

Grant cut him off: "Want to run that one by the Secretary of the Navy?"

"I don't believe I would."

"See, there's *your* doubt," Grant said. "My worst imbibing days, maybe I've felt the spiders crawling, but I never saw a damn Cyclops."

Duncan was forward in his chair. "I believe those men saw something outrageous, and made truthful statements before dying."

Grant said, "I've heard my share of dying men, saying good-bye to their wives, or confessing their sins, some thinking they're about to walk the streets of glory, and some, not giving a damn."

Duncan said, "But they don't waste those last seconds to tell an outrageous lie." He picked up the red telegram. "The *Broomhilde*, her entire crew gone, courtesy of a giant flying manta ray. A Devil fish."

"Who claimed that?"

"Mess boy, fished up by a trawler, died of shock half an hour after rescue. That's nine vessels and crews, from five different countries, in our shipping lanes. Whatever the claims, we're pulling a lot of corpses out of our waters."

Grant said, "The world thinks we cut them into shark bait—and don't quote me."

"I never do." Duncan stood. "These aren't wild stories concocted to sell newspapers. And these aren't warships."

"I know where you're going," Grant's voice was a warning growl, "and it's deep water."

"So far we've managed to keep press away from the wilder details, but how long before one of these men makes a dying declaration to a reporter? You know what that'll bring."

"All these nations waiting for our play, and we're holding an empty hand. If Congress heard this sea monster guff, they'd have me trussed up in a straitjacket, which half of them want anyway," Grant said, waving the cigar. "Beware the drunken despot."

Duncan laughed to lighten the mood. "I imagine some representatives would be pleased."

"Carl Shurz'd be dancing a Missouri jig."

Grant walked back to the small desk in the alcove, his hands flat on its ink-stained, leather inlay. "Lincoln called this 'The Shop' because he could sit back here, the Senators around that table, take in all their horseshit, then find the truth of it. Solved the most impossible problems in the world, from this old desk."

"With your expert help."

"Hell's fire, it wasn't just me." Grant considered his next words. "Arrow-straight, what's going on at sea?"

"Want more theories you'll despise? That's what I can give you, as will every engineer or biologist we've got under Naval contract."

Grant held the whiskey decanter over his glass, thought better of it, didn't pour. "I have to make some kind of statement."

Duncan said, "There's one man who knows more about the mysteries of the ocean than anyone."

"Supposedly that's you, but you're claiming different."

"I'm a bloody novice by comparison."

Grant took half a cigar from his jacket pocket, lit it with a long match he struck against the fireplace. The fire was now just glowing embers and no comfort from the damp. Grant drew deep, letting the smoke curl. Not looking at Duncan.

"I do not want to hear that name."

Duncan said, "Five years ago, and the front pages were full of nothing but stories of sea monsters sinking warships from around the world. More people read about that than read about Appomattox, and he was responsible for that lunacy, and the panic it caused."

Grant said, "It was a goddamned embarrassment."

"Every Navy was his target. How many frigates did we lose, how many men?"

Grant regarded Duncan, mouth drawn tight. Frozen.

Duncan continued. "Who would know more about these current happenings, Mr. President? And perhaps, how to stop them."

"You're goading me, you son of a bitch."

Duncan agreed with a nod, but still said, "He is who you need."

Grant grabbed the bourbon, poured himself two fingers, downed it, and said, "Damn your eyes."

3

MADMAN OF THE SEAS

The paper tube contained two needle-thin metal rods. Stamped TOP SECRET: THE UNITED STATES OF AMERICA V. PRISONER #3579, President Grant had given it to Duncan an hour earlier, saying, "Maybe you'll learn something."

A blue-steel lockbox, with the same serial number, was waiting for Duncan when he returned to his small White House corner office.

He approached the box as a bomb that needed defusing, taking the needles, finding portals on the polished steel sides, then inserting them simultaneously. The sides dropped away in a mechanical flowering.

Inside were the sea-damaged journal of Professor Pierre Arronax, wrapped in preservation paper; a large, gilt-edged envelope; and a .52 caliber cartridge.

Duncan pulled a shelf from his draftsman's table, placed a chimney lamp on a hollowed space designed to hold it. From a false-bottom drawer came a Magic Lantern lens and bracket, completing the projector.

He held up the bullet cartridge and looked through a pinpoint lens in the center of the brass casing before fitting it onto the projector with a special clamp. Duncan dropped a calcium iodide pellet into the lamp's chimney. It flared as he adjusted the lens, sharp-focusing the micro-slides hidden inside the converted ammunition. The first image was the front page of *The Pioneer and Democrat*, March 12, 1865, now spread across his office wall:

HONORED SHIP DECOMISSIONED

The U.S.N. battle sloop *Constellation* has been decommissioned, according to the Department of the Navy, after serving her country well during the Conflict Between the States. The one thousand, four hundred, and fifty ton ship will remain at port in Norfolk, Virginia, where it will serve as a floating headquarters for Naval personnel.

Twisting the lead slug advanced the slides in their minichamber. The next, a communiqué, written in crowded rows of stick figures. Duncan put his glasses aside to read the "Dancing Men," never opening the copy of *The Union Standards of Codes and Ciphers* at his elbow.

There can be no doubt that the rogue terrorist Nemo/Dakkar is responsible. With this sinking, and the destruction of the U.S.S. Abraham Lincoln, a true revelation of his abilities to destroy our most fearsome warships would surely cause an unmanageable panic, and embolden our enemies.

With our Union troops still engaging Confederate forces, it is imperative that all attention and efforts focus on our victory, and that this rogue terrorist, his submarine-craft, and his actions, be wiped from public consciousness as soon as possible.

To that end, an exact duplicate of the U.S.S. Constitution *has been constructed in precise detail, to be moored at Norfolk, in place of the original, thus dispelling any further speculations about the destruction of the* Constitution, *Nemo/Dakkar, his submarine, or its abilities.*

Signed, George H. Sharpe,
Intelligence Secretary.

Duncan steeped Twinings at his corner stove, the model of a dirigible hanging above it, thinking about the man who cost the Navy so much. Drawings of sea monsters attacking, editorials by war correspondent Gideon Spilett, and E. Lime's grained photographs of carnage were the next projections.

Duncan's face was a clinical mask, studying the last micro-slide, courtesy of *The San Francisco Evening Tribune*. Front-page shouts of INSANE CAPTAIN CAPTURED! BIZARRE, SUBMERSIBLE SHIP DESTROYED! with a wild caricature of Nemo, defiant on the *Nautilus*, surrounded by ghosts of dead sailors, each in the rotting uniform of their own country.

Beneath, the single word: "Madman."

Nemo's body bent, then burned from inside, the limelight flaming, melting the micro-slides. Duncan doused it with tea, then opened a small window, pushing vines aside to let in fresh air and the first streaks of morning.

He gathered the scatter of Nemo's history from his desk. The gold envelope was marked by a dollop of red sealing wax, a signet "N" pressed into its center, circled by the words "Mobilis in Mobile."

The wax had been expertly cut. Duncan opened the envelope, taking out the parchment with Nemo's declaration of destruction in his own, precise hand: "To stop the war makers before they act; to destroy them, and their ability to make war, is the only hope for peace in this world."

4

THE DEVIL'S WAREHOUSE

The prison guard's temple was smashed with a wooden plank, sending him sprawling, the voices of the men around him beating him down even more. "Show us Nemo, or your tongue's gonna be hangin' like a slaughtered hog!"

He rolled, dazed, reaching for a leather sap he'd tied to a belt loop, the sap he'd used on them a hundred times before. Prisoners grabbed his arms, dragged him the length of the near-black corridor. He cried out, his shoulder separating.

They hauled to a stop, the Guard lying on his face, hair blood-sticky, mouth mashed against the frozen, stone floor. A patch of ice broke against his cheek, the slivers cutting his jaw.

Lyle, a prisoner with one arm not blown off by Union artillery, took charge by jamming a knee into the Guard's back, cracking bones. "You said we was too stupid to take this place, but we took it! Tell us where Nemo's at, or we'll do you like you done the old man."

Another prisoner threw in, "Only worse."

"But I didn't do nothing to—"

Lyle said, "Don't matter—you're wearin' the uniform!"

The Guard tried, "But . . . I . . . can't move nothing."

Lyle upped his knee, pressing his weight into the Guard's neck. The Guard managed to straighten his arms, reaching, fingers fumbling, for the sap. The others shredded his uniform jacket from the seams, ripping the weapon away, and pulling a large ring with only one key from a tucked pocket.

Two hard gut-punches from Lyle's only hand and the Guard was on the floor again, doubled into himself, yowling. "I know you're gonna kill me. But I got me some children. Little ones."

"We all do." Lyle was leaning in hot-breath close, his face a dark mass, blocking everything. "The only chance you got is, mebbe, he saves your life. He's the big secret of this place, and you don't give him up, your mama won't know who she's burying!"

The Guard said, "The last, the very last locker."

It was like the black recess of a caved-in mine, the prisoners feeling along the wall, until grabbing hold of an inches-thick padlock. Lyle sprung it with the key, freeing an iron chain threaded between rusting handles that were bolted to a cut section in the stone wall.

Lyle said, "They got him in a doggone crypt!"

"Grab hold!" was shouted, and two prisoners wrapped hands around the handles. Six feet high, it was a slab of solid granite, movable on a steel dolly, that rolled on a length of track in the floor. They strained the dolly backward, stone grinding stone, until the granite cleared the opening to a narrow but tall cell.

Rats stampeded from the dark, screaming.

Prisoners craned their necks, trying to make out the silhouette of the man in the back of the almost-tomb: on the edge of a cot, chin in his hands, wrists shackled. He cocked his head, and they could see his eyes. Two candle flames against a dark complexion.

He said, "If I'm to lead this, you'll follow my orders to the letter."

Lyle said, "It weren't so easy gettin' you out, sir."

"But now I am."

He regarded the men, the tatters of their military tunics over striped prison grays, then stood and said, "My orders only. There'll be no mutineers."

Lyle nodded. "We're with you, Captain."

"Then get that man up, before he dies."

The President's Coach skidded across the Virginia blacktop, the four-horse team fighting to stay true. Midnight rain slicked the Richmond road, water sheeting inches deep. Hooves pounded. Slipped. Found their way again. Kept running.

Grant steadied himself as the coach lurched, lit a cigar on a sconce mounted above the upholstered leather, then faced Duncan, who was sitting opposite. Duncan's hands went to the pair of Navy Six's mounted on the door, ready to draw in case of an assassination attempt.

Awkward fiddling, and then, "I'd never read Nemo's full statements before."

"So, you're impressed? 'When the tyrant has disposed of foreign enemies by conquest or treaty, and there is nothing more to fear from them, then he is always stirring up some war or other . . .' Plato. Stop wars by killing off the warriors. Nemo's debate has a thousand years on it, and that was his damn defense."

"His words became actions," Duncan said.

"Sinking our ships prolonged the war, didn't stop a goddamned thing. It never does. Kills our men, and he's sitting in a jail cell, not rotting in an unmarked grave. That's the only time I disagreed with Lincoln. He wanted that damn submarine-ship preserved . . ."

"And now, we need it."

"He wouldn't sign the execution order, thinking your Nemo'd reveal all he knew, his designs. That's what you think, too, making me the barbarian, right?"

"President Johnson took your side."

"They swore Johnson in with Lincoln lying dead upstairs. The only way he could've become president, by a bullet. Every order he gave was wrong, except that one. Nemo *should've* hung. And worse."

Duncan said, "The executive decision—never carried out."

"Because the fool got himself impeached, turning Nemo into some kind of martyr. And that makes a damn legend." Grant concentrated on his cigar. "Even to you. You honor him for what he built, instead of condemning him for what he did with it."

"I do know what he is, Sam, and why you've scheduled him to hang."

"Good-damn-riddance." Grant's voice trailed off.

Oliver, a thick-necked driver, side-cracked the whip, the team cutting through the storm faster. He felt the rear wheels careen as he swung the leaders wide, taking a far corner, and then pulled back. Careless handling. A lightning strike showed the barbed wire and sandbag barricade that blocked Canal Street, half a mile in front of them.

Duncan gripped his armrests. "One man, in one submersible, and governments quake. The power he had is terrifying, but now, he's a prisoner, and the *Nautilus* . . ."

"The spoils of war." Grant leaned forward, challenging. "I allowed you those files, and they didn't change your mind about this bastard?"

Duncan chose carefully: "It doesn't change what we need. This is the right thing to do, Sam."

"I haven't done it yet."

Grant focused on something beyond the rain, that Duncan couldn't see, his thoughts giving way to echoes: the distant Virginia thunder cracked like an artillery strike, mixing with the screams of the dying. Lightning was now the flame of cannons, the smell of the rain now sulfur and black powder.

The jagged silhouettes of warehouses that lined the blocks leading to Libby Prison passed by one after another, with Grant seeing them as a city he'd burned. "It's resurrecting the dead."

"Sir?"

"Rebuilding after a war. Johnson tried destroying every reconstruction measure, and damn him raw for trying. We've suffered deep wounds, and lost two years in the healing. I'm not going to be the President who let this country die."

"We'll need the world with us."

"Instead, they've got us in their gunsights." Grant looked to Duncan. "You know, enemies come from all quarters, John. How many advisors do you think I really trust? It's a damn small list, and you're on it."

Duncan said, "I'll always be frank with you, Sam."

"Your Captain's justified every insane action he's ever taken. That's the ego of a tyrant, and you swear we need him. Visionary?" Grant threw his cigar butt into the blowing rain. "Goddamn cutthroat."

Oliver pulled the team back, racing toward the barricades, reins biting gloved hands. The animals twisted, panicking their run, as the back wheels of the coach locked, fishtailing to one side, then stopping.

Grant didn't wait, throwing open the Studebaker's door, charging into the storm. "My blind granny can handle a four-up better than this!"

Duncan slipped the coach steps, upped his collar, and fell in next to Grant. They quick-walked to the wall of sandbags and barbed wire–strung crossbars that barricaded the corner where Canal and Twenty-First Streets met.

Two soldiers hefted another bag onto the pile. It tumbled forward, and Grant grabbed a burlap side. The one with the corporal's stripes said, without looking, "Obliged! These damn idjits got me runnin' ass-to-tarnation!" then stuffed his cheek with a chaw of tobacco.

"At ease."

The Corporal's eyes busted white, before a fumbled salute, and snapping to attention. Grant nodded to the barriers and troops scattered along Canal. "What's this for, soldier? And, don't choke on that mess."

The Corporal, who was too old for his rank, spit a brown stream. "Blazes, no one told nothing about you comin' into this, Mr. President."

"When did this take up?"

"Prisoners broke out the main cell block just after supper. Told us to secure the streets, in case they busted through the main gate. They're supposed to be sending reinforcements from Fort Independence. Sir."

Grant checked the Army Colt in the shoulder holster under his coat. "Need something from the coach, John?"

"I'll just stick close to you, sir," Duncan said.

Troopers moving onto Canal pointed and rib-jammed each other as Grant and Duncan continued through the gray curtain of water, walking the last block to Libby Prison. Grant's stride became a limp, a years-old injury dragging his leg. He peered out from under his hat as a jag of lightning lit the cobblestone street and the prison's main entrance. Rain guttered across his chest.

Grant spoke to no one: "The Devil's Warehouse."

Set away from the brickyards and businesses on Canal, Libby Prison could still be mistaken for what it once was: a food warehouse. The three-floored structure, hidden behind barbed wire–topped walls, conquered the block as a prison, but with freight wagon loaders, sales counters, and rusty signs welcoming farmers, reminders of its old purpose.

Grant said, "After the surrender, I came down to claim the body of a young Lieutenant. He'd showed great promise, but got captured, sent here." He wiped the water from his face. "Killed himself, swallowed his tongue. He knew we'd won, but couldn't wait out those last weeks 'til Appomattox."

"I'm sorry, Sam."

"We damned the gray for this place, now we're using it the exact same way."

"Sometimes the only difference is the color of the uniform."

As the storm rumbled off the Virginia Mountains, Grant regarded Duncan. "John, never repeat that in my presence again."

Grant's limp was worse as they moved for the front gates. Bedsheets, with JUSTICE FOR THE INNOCENT!, WELCOME TO HELL!, and WILLING TO DIE! scrawled in red, hung from the fourth-floor sills above the entrance, the corners tied to iron bars, the rain bleeding their message down the walls as if Libby had been gut-shot.

Grant said, "It doesn't look good for your Nemo, does it?"

By the Libby gates, Warden Kramer held the whalebone umbrella tilted against the blowing rain, eyeing Grant and Duncan coming down Canal, trailed by a small patrol. He ran a comb over his few hairs before striding down Libby's old cattle planks, umbrella up, hand outstretched.

Duncan took the greeting, but the jailer's attention was on Grant: "Mr. President, this is more than an honor that you're visiting," Kramer angled his umbrella over Grant and part of Duncan's shoulder, splitting the rain.

"But may I suggest coming back in the morning—or even

next week—and things could be more, uh . . . prepared to receive you?"

Duncan said, "Our business can't wait."

Kramer forced his fingers through the tangle of his wet beard. "We're in the middle of a situation, sir."

Grant said, "It's hanging out your windows."

"Containment is the priority, but I'm the one to guarantee your safety, Mr. President."

"I guarantee myself. Duncan, you're a witness. This sorry turnkey's off the hook."

"Stand clear!"

The shout came from a rough-made Gunnery Sergeant on a tall stallion, pulling an Ordnance Gun on brass wheels. Thick hands and a face like pounded beef, soldiers flanked Gunny, running together for the main gate, sabers in hand, surrounding the cannon.

Lightning cut, showing troops moving from the deep shadows beyond Canal Street, rain-soaked, checking rifles, before taking position along outside walls.

Grant stepped around Kramer. "I'm with the men."

5

DAKKAR

The dead man was in the center of the old loading dock, a bullet hole in his throat and a flowered baby's bonnet clutched in an arthritic left hand. Rain had washed away the blood pools, and his skin was starting to blue.

Above and behind, prisoners screamed for justice from the windows facing the yard. Faces beaten raw. Fists jutting through bars, hurling rocks and pieces of rusty chain.

Beside Grant, Duncan said, "Well, turnkey claimed a 'situation.'"

"He did, indeed."

They moved to the side of the gates as more troops made their way in, the last whipping a mule pulling a caisson loaded down with crates of Ketchum Grenades. A Private doled out one-pounders, setting charges and plungers, with Grant watching.

The men ran the rain, grenade in one hand, rifle in the other, taking scattered positions around the yard. A white-bearded sergeant had three Ketchums, juggling them like Indian clubs.

Grant said, "We'd toss a bunch over the lines, the Rebs'd catch them in blankets, hurl them right back. The boys'd scramble, they'd go off, taking a hand or a foot."

"Weapons have no loyalty."

Grant regarded Duncan. "That's what you're counting on with that *Nautilus.*"

Warden Kramer was last through the gates before they shut, tucking himself beside a wall scarred by bullet strikes from a firing squad, and decorated with a smiling pig declaring, *Nobody Beats Libby Pork!*

Kramer dipped his umbrella twice.

Troopers shouldered Carbines, sighting the windows for head and chest shots. Ammo was quick-passed, slammed home. Gunny smiled with broken teeth as he leveled the Ordnance Cannon on the massive double doors of the main building, then locked it off. A shell was breeched, powder tamped.

Grant said, "Hell, I didn't have this much firepower my first three battles."

A sniper ran in low, saluted Grant, then dropped to one knee beside him, pulling a Sharps single-shot from a leather scabbard. He steadied himself against a hay bale, while shielding the rifle's hammer from the rain with his palm. He was a farm kid, all thick hair and freckles, who declared his name as Billy Junior, after his grandfather.

Billy's kid-voice broke, squinting down the rifle barrel. "Mr. President, fifty feet's the kill line. Anyone crosses it, they'll not take another step. Courtesy of Warden Kramer."

"I tell you when to fire, son. No one else," Grant said.

"Chester!" was screamed from the barred windows, prison voices rising as the old man was dragged away by two troopers, the baby bonnet still in his fingers. A guard, ready and waiting for the body to be cleared, lit a torch from the common barrel, while another trooper, at his heels, hefted over-slopping buckets of coal oil.

Kramer caught an eye, twirled his umbrella as a Spring parasol. Trooper nodded at the signal, hurled the oil on the double doors leading to the cells, coating them. Torch Guard dove in, set the doors alight, then scrambled. The flames spat in the rain, then ate the oil in a burst of hot orange and wet, black smoke.

Grant put a match to his cigar with a flourish. "Nemo doesn't need a noose; he's going to choke off."

Mule-chested Gunny wrapped the Howitzer's trigger line around his knuckles, saw Kramer dip his umbrella, then yelled, "How you want to die tonight, you bastards? Roasted alive? Head shot, or bleed out like Chester? Your choice, and I'm fine with all of 'em!"

Shouts tore the windows, bottles tossed. The soldiers held their guns, ducking broken glass, looked to the Warden. The rain was sheeting, but the umbrella stayed put.

"Damn fools." Grant stayed on the burning door. "What the hell happened to surrender?"

A heavy blow from the prisoners' side split the burning double door from behind. Just inches. Then, another blow, exploding cinders from the wood, vaulting bits of fire into the air.

Guns stayed. Thumbs on hammers, rain bouncing off rifle barrels, highlighting them in the dark. More prisoner screams from the windows, and the Gunny tightened the Howitzer cord another eighth-inch.

The doors finally burst, burning pieces landing in the yard, sparks skyrocketing away. Captain Nemo stepped through thick, acrid smoke and the flames framing the doorway, smashing away burning wreckage with the chains shackling his wrists.

Nemo kept his hands open and weaponless before planting himself on the loading dock, directly in front of the cannon, looking down at the barrel's three-inch maw. His face was painted with soot-dried blood, his clothes singed and fight-torn. But he threw back his head, filling his mouth with rain, drinking deep, and smiling defiantly.

He said, "I am Nemo. These are my men."

The prisoners cheered, but Gunny's shout carried over them: "You make one hell of a fine target!"

Sparks from the fire turned to soggy ash, a gray cloak draping Nemo as he said, "To subdue the enemy without fighting is the ultimate skill, but you failed at that. So have we."

Grant said, "There's a canny son of a bitch."

His hand was on Billy's shoulder, whose voice broke again. "Just give me the order, sir."

Grant said, "No," as Nemo continued: "One of ours is dead, and we're prepared to take many of yours. The fuse is lit, but there doesn't have to be an explosion. If you'll hear me out."

Gunny shouted back to Nemo, "Them fancy words mean nothing but defiance of orders! You've all been told what to do, and fairly warned!"

Nemo said, "There's been nothing fair about the treatment of these men!"

Gunny raised his hand, barely, to let Nemo see the trigger line. Just enough. "If I scratch my nose or my ass, you're all dead! That's not a very righteous end for the famous Captain Nemo."

"I'm just a prisoner," Nemo said.

He made no visible moves, hands down and rain falling, but took in the men before him: a picket of Carbines aimed at his chest, others sighted on the cell windows, and all with the same eyes, wear on their faces, as the prisoners behind him.

Nemo said, "Bring him out."

The Guard from the cells was dragged through the smoldering doorway, a prisoner on each arm, and let go. He stumbled, catching himself before hitting the ground, keeping the troops back with a wave of his hand. Lyle was one of the prisoners, standing ready.

Rifles and bayonets jigged forward. Froze.

Grant was fixed. Duncan said to him, "That's the only man who can captain the *Nautilus*, sir."

"I'm aware."

Nemo called out to the yard, "The government can't be bothered with us any other time, but now I have your"—he nodded toward Grant—"full attention. This began with the murder of an old man, but we didn't revenge ourselves, although we could have—"

A clap of thunder cut his words, and the Guard scrambled for the pickets, rolling off the loading dock, landing hard. Gunny screamed, "Go to hell!" pulling the trigger line. It snapped in half, and coiled back, not firing the Ordnance Gun.

Nemo raised his arms, the chain between his wrists dangling over his head. "The threat of cannon, ultimately worthless—"

A slug ripped flesh, sending him spinning.

"Nobody make a damn move! Ease those weapons, that's an order!"

Rifle barrels went skyward with Grant's voice, guards and troopers stepping aside as he shouldered to the front of the picket. He stayed by the Ordnance Cannon as Nemo strained to stand, blood soaking him.

Nemo said, "The uniforms that separated each of you are just rags—"

A chant of "Justice" rose from the block windows.

"But you insist on still seeing these men as enemies, your prisoners of war—"

Lyle conducted the voices with his missing hand. "Justice! Justice!"

Grant said, "These men aren't just captured draftees, and you damn well know it."

Nemo got to one knee, saw the gold-scrolled Smith & Wesson that Grant was holding flush with his coat, barrel down. "Then treat them according to the articles of peacetime incarceration, not like animals! Food they can eat, ready medicine. They'll still be serving their time."

He struggled to stand, and said, "Find that much humanity, and it's a peaceful end. Answer with another bullet, you'll be repaid. A thousand times."

"Justice! Justice!"

"Every one of those hands? A weapon in it." Nemo pointed to the prisoners. "We got the key to the weapons stores. Our own grenades and bombs, to counter yours—black powder and dynamite now hidden on every floor."

Then to Grant, he said, "Ten prisoners for each soldier, and all aching for a chance at another war!"

"You're hiding behind these men, giving them your words."

"Speaking for them, General. But killing me won't stop the battle. Treat these men properly, for once? That's all in the world they want."

Gunny said, "We'll clear this damn place out, then stack your corpses!"

Nemo looked to Grant. "You've fought the ragtags, General. You know well how bloody this can get."

"Letting a dead man make demands." Grant fixed on Kramer huddled against the wall, and said, "Warden?"

Kramer said nothing, kept the umbrella steady. Grant looked to the anxious faces around him, washed in rain and sweat.

"The peace starts with you. These prisoners have to shuck their weapons first," Grant said.

Nemo half-smiled. "So they can be slaughtered?"

"So we know they can be trusted. And time's running."

Nemo raised his arms, the chains dangling. "Men, away from the windows!" Then, to Grant, "That's the best I can do."

The prisoners stepped back from the bars, hands with bottles and homemade bombs pulling in, but still chanting, "Justice, justice!"

Grant said, "Warden! You've the final word!"

Nemo, hand clamped on his shoulder wound, body swaying as he refused unconsciousness, looked at his own blood streaming. "One random shot and we're lost."

"Justice" chorused through the prison halls, and Grant's voice cut above the sound: "Warden!"

Kramer lowered his umbrella, then closed it, and shook it twice. That's when fingers came off triggers, rifles back to shoulders, grenades set aside. The last bit of rain was a scatter, the thunder someplace else.

Nemo collapsed.

Billy followed the Captain to the ground with his rifle barrel, hands shaking. He looked up to Duncan. "I had the head-shot, had it sighted cold, but my finger froze on the trigger. I couldn't shoot."

Duncan said, "It was the right choice, son."

"All these guns, and his only fear was for those men, not himself," Billy said, propping the rifle across his knee. "I've never seen that before."

Grant lit his cigar.

6

RED TIDE

Augusto was the youngest helmsman the freighter *Regina* ever had, and he couldn't be sure how long he'd been floating, letting the ocean carry him, since he watched her sink. Coughing out the sea, then gulping for air. Praying, holding onto the cameo of Stella Maris around his neck, forcing his arms and legs to move.

This stretch, from the Bay of Fundy toward the port of New York, was known for its deep trench, and near-ice temperature. But it didn't churn. Tonight it boiled: the ocean foaming, then, the attack.

Before the start of watch, Augusto imagined the other ships lost, filling himself with bravery, sailing the same course. It was also his twentieth birthday, and he'd rum-celebrated for hours, but the bravado lasted less than a minute. Picked up and tossed off the deck, his spine twisted as he smashed against the water.

Rolling in the ocean, the ship disintegrating around him, Augusto tried but couldn't see the thing that attacked them. Not entirely. Through debris and flames, he thought maybe a boat with a special weapon. Then, maybe, something alive. Prehistoric. Cutting the water fast, with huge claws. Razor-edged dactyls that butchered the crew, shredded the hull and cabins.

Screams, and chaos.

He fought himself for calm, and to stay afloat, stay moving. And think. There was a memory, in pieces, of holding onto a mast as a life preserver, cradling a dying shipmate with his free arm, as long as he could feel life in him.

The boy died, and he let him slip away, just before a swell tore the mast apart, pushing him under. He panicked his way to the surface, finding air, keeping just an inch above the water, thick with bloody engine oil.

With everyone dead, and surrounded by miles of dark nothing, Augusto needed to hear his own voice: *"Sì, questo è quello che devo dovuto fare . . . si . . ."*

He moved his arms forcefully, pushing with heavy strokes, eyes salt-burning, but strength coming from some hidden place. Maybe he could swim until he was picked up, or make it to a small island.

He swam harder, his mind full of what to say when he got ashore. First, he'd make a report to the Italian Maritime Board, then his father, at the Consulate General. Body movement was automatic now, his mind letting him be someplace else. Imagining a hero's welcome. A merciful dream.

He thought he heard a ship's engine: *"Io sono qui!"*

Blood erupted, flooding his throat, as his legs were cut completely through. No feeling. Everything below his waist, instantly gone. He saw his legs, still thrashing, held in the grip of a massive claw, then pulled under the water. A tasseled shoe bobbed up in front of him.

Below, a wide, saucer shape came up quickly from the ocean dark, open mandibles in view, just as the ice-cold of blood loss closed around Augusto like a shroud.

He saw the thing, and managed a breath.

7

IRON AND STONE

Gunny pulled the descending rope hand-over-hand, grunting with each pull, lowering the corn elevator to the cellar. Grant stood by the low wooden gate to the car, with Warden Kramer and Duncan flanking, and an armed guard crammed into a corner behind.

The lift creaked downward, allowing Grant a look at each of Libby's floors as they passed. Built for storing corn and grain, they now stored men chained in old harvest cribs. Rioters were marched in at bayonet point, laughing at their yard victory, slapping each other's whip-scarred backs, before being locked down again.

Lyle, catching a glimpse of the moving elevator as he was being reshackled, threw Grant a salute with his battle-missing right hand.

In the car, Kramer kept straight ahead. "See? These men are our sworn enemies, Mr. President, not disruptive children to be coddled, or bargained with."

Duncan cut in: "You forget yourself, turnkey. From what I've seen, it's a bloody miracle you're not having a riot every day."

"Libby is the way we inherited it from the Confederates, with a thousand new prisoners put in my charge."

"A lame-duck excuse." The temperature dropped with the descent, misting Grant's words. "This place is exactly as you want it, sneaking your orders with that damn umbrella, instead of speaking up like a commander. Something's rotten here, and I don't mean your floors or the food."

Gunny let the car slip the last six inches, banging to the bottom of the elevator shaft. "Apologies, sirs. Mr. President, welcome to the center of the earth."

Kramer opened the gate, and the air soaked everyone with icy damp and the stench of old, salted meat.

Curing barrels lined the granite-blocked hallway, while chains for carcasses dangled from the ceiling, all ending in large hooks for cows and hogs. Railroad lamps were hung on every third hook, casting the narrow passage in dim yellow.

Grant was sure the lamps were for his benefit, pushing them aside as he made his way through the cold, his leg, pain-dragging, his voice, bouncing off the granite: "Nemo?"

"The last cell," Kramer said.

Duncan coughed salt. "The last freezer, you mean. Have you done anything to make this place fit for men, instead of sides of beef?"

"That's where they attacked the guard." Kramer jabbed the spots of red on the floor with his umbrella tip. "Or maybe it's Nemo's."

Gunny laughed to himself through his nose. "We can but hope."

Nemo's still-shackled hands were raised, as an old doc, with gray beard and prisoner stripes, ministered the gunshot with shaking fingers. A lard candle was the only light as he pulled the last bit of catgut through the edge of the wound, then tied it off.

Grant stepped around the granite slab on the trolley, through the narrow cut, and into the once-cooler that was Nemo's cell.

Old Doc daubed the sutures, then tore clean bandages from a pile of shirts by Nemo's bunk. A Confederate Field Medical Kit, half the instruments gone, was open by his feet. He stood when he saw Grant, dropping a scalpel into a pan of pink water.

"Don't stop your work, Doctor."

Nemo rocked his head. "Yes—I have to be saved for the hangman."

"How did he fare?"

"Lucky, Mr. President. The ball was stopped by some pretty hard muscle. This is a tough man. Hope I did all right, haven't had a thing to do with doctoring since my capture. Guards dragged me down."

The Doc was wiping off the flop sweat with the back of his hand, and Grant noted the long-settled bruises from chains lacing his wrists and neck. He said, "I was part of the detachment you fought at Chickasaw Bluffs, sir."

Grant said, "You surely had us on the run that day."

Nemo stayed on his back. "Ah, former enemies shaking hands. If I'd had anesthetic, I'd say I was hallucinating."

Duncan said, "You're not."

"My pain already informed me," Nemo strained. "Welcome to my home, Mr. President. I'd stand to formally greet you, but, you understand."

"When's the execution?" asked Duncan.

Kramer jumped in: "Oh, Wednesday, at the high stroke of midnight."

Nemo said, "Your attendance will make it quite an occasion, General—Mr. President. I know the Warden's pleased as can be."

Grant didn't respond, letting Duncan say, "Condemned men don't usually spend their last hours negotiating for prisoners who're going to outlive them."

"It wasn't for your benefit. Did the good warden tell you what started the fracas? One of the oldest prisoners had a new great-granddaughter, and the baby wanted to meet her great granddad. But, this man, he denied it."

"A terrorist, who threw a bomb at Secretary of State Seward," Kramer said. "No visitors, ever. That was part of the handed-down sentence."

Nemo's voice gained: "The other side of eighty, and in despair, he climbs to the top of the old silo, waving that child's bonnet."

Kramer said, "I followed the judge's orders."

"Instead of talking him down, you had him shot in the throat," Nemo looked again to Grant, "by the same youngster who was guarding you, Mr. President."

Grant said, "And that boy's going to live with it."

Duncan shook the Old Doc's hand, easing him to the door. "Gentlemen, the President has private business to attend to. Kramer, I take it the doctor will be escorted to his cell, treated with respect? And that all agreements reached tonight will also be respected?"

Warden Kramer said nothing, just nodded to Gunny, who was stationed in the corridor with the guards. Before stepping out, he looked back at Nemo, the red spreading across his bandages. The wound brought a smile. "I hope you note that this man received medical attention, as required."

Kramer was gone, and Grant said, "You're not surprised I'm here. That's some arrogance."

"Actually I am, but a bullet's stopping me from bowing. I've attracted presidential attention before, but not while staring down a cannon. What of the engineer? Mr. Duncan, you wouldn't be wasting your talents thinking of a better gallows, would you?"

Duncan said, "This meeting can end as quickly as it started, with your death that much closer."

"My apologies; the pain, you know." Nemo casually adjusted the knot on his bandage, shackles rattling. "You're offering an alternative?"

Nemo studied Grant, when Duncan said, "In your expert opinion, what would happen if someone blocked free trade between all seafaring nations?"

"Undoubtedly, a war. Encompassing the world."

"Then you also agree, it'd be devastating."

"Yes, and good riddance." The shoulder tore at Nemo as he said, "A backward child knows the policies of governments follow the road of destruction. But you're familiar with my philosophy."

Grant examined the last stub of his cigar, tossed it into the piss bucket. "I can quote *The Art of War*, too, but I'm not here for a damned debate."

Nemo looked as if he were about to stand, even if he couldn't. "What are you saying to me, gentlemen?"

Duncan said, "Ships from every country are vanishing in our waters without a trace. The lanes are being strangled, and foreign nations are losing men."

Nemo picked up on Duncan's words. "Of course, the men are disposable, but the money lost is not. That's the usual thinking, isn't it? And they blame you for the losses, think the United States is responsible." Nemo regarded Grant for a moment, before, "Are you?"

Grant said, "That's a bloody stupid question."

"This is a country of warriors, General."

"We just buried over half a million. You think I want to dig more graves with another war?"

Nemo said, "The memory of conflict fades with the appearance of a new storm on the horizon, isn't that so?"

Grant stood, saying to Duncan, "I've given this son of a bitch all the courtesy I can stomach."

"I'm just a humble prisoner waiting for the hangman. What exactly do you expect of me?"

Duncan said, "Your expertise."

Grant rubbed feeling back into his aching leg, squeezing from his hip to his knee, words through his teeth: "Take your so-called submarine and find out who the hell's sinking these ships, and stop them. Dead."

Duncan said, "Complete your mission, and President Grant will sign a full pardon."

Nemo couldn't hide his surprise, even behind the bloody soot covering his face, as Duncan continued: "You'll be on the open seas, not rotting in a cell. Captain of the *Nautilus* again, and an official keeper of the peace."

Nemo's voice was in the back of his throat. "Using my own ideals against me?"

Grant said, "Ideals, hell. You're a bastard who perverted philosophy as an excuse to murder. No mistake, this is an uneasy truce. Very uneasy."

Nemo said, "See, that's your warrior's sensibility, General."

Grant came back: "You don't get to rest on an altar. You've got too much blood on your hands."

"If you're so sure of your doctrine, why, sirs, bother with me at all?"

"Because of your damn boat and your command of it. You've got thirty seconds to accept, or . . ." Grant snapped open the watch he was gifted on his graduation from West Point. ". . . forty-six hours and twelve minutes to hang."

Nemo said, "Not much of a choice, is it?"

Grant put the timepiece into a pocket beside the Colt six-shot. "Until this very minute, you had no choice."

The gun didn't escape Nemo's gaze. He said, "Buried in this tomb, I've dreamt of being back on the *Nautilus,* and more than once."

Duncan adjusted his glasses. "Is that an acceptance?"

"Let's say, I'd prefer to die at sea."

Grant regarded Nemo. "Get this mission accomplished, and your preference might take care of itself."

Kramer kept his umbrella purposely down, following steps behind Grant, Duncan, and the troopers who were walking them across the yard. The sky was clear, but fire ash floated from the old doors as the Howitzer was wheeled out the main gates, soldiers riding on either side of it. They all saluted Grant.

Duncan said, over his shoulder, "You'll be notified when and where Nemo is to be transported. Prepare him."

Kramer said, "I'm not pleased to kowtow to a prisoner."

Duncan said, "Your opinion was not sought."

"I'll follow orders precisely, sir."

"You'll do more than that." Grant clamped a hand over the wolf's head umbrella handle. "I'm sending an inspector, and if everything about this place isn't what it should be? You'll get a taste of the chains."

Kramer nodded respectfully as the President and Duncan walked to the Studebaker, troopers around them peeling off. Oliver held the door open, head down. Grant threw a look at the new wheel and climbed in, anger bending his back and shoulders.

In the coach, Grant said to Duncan, "I despise this was necessary."

"But will you engage Nemo and the *Nautilus*?"

Prisoner-made banners snapped in the breeze above Kramer like laundry on the line as the coach turned off Canal, soldiers saluting its passing. Gunny was beside Warden Kramer, waving the umbrella, saying, "Drunken, arrogant reprobate. And a god-damned coddler."

Gunny rubbed his hands over his swollen, broken knuckles. "What about that Nemo? I'd love to go a round or two with that strutter before his leaving."

Kramer tapped Gunny's chest. "He's still a prisoner until we hand him over, and so must obey all rules set down by his captors."

"That'll do," Gunny said.

Nemo's wound was soaking blood again as he tore open his bunk's hay-bag mattress. Ripping with both hands, piles of moldy grass stuffing were scooped and tossed. Then, digging into a corner, he snagged a golden sea horse between his fingers.

Two and a half inches in length, with an *N* snaking around its twice-curved tail. Nemo wrapped the creature in a stained bandage scrap, slipped it in his boot.

8

PROFONDO ROSSO

The torn skin and muscle was washed with warm water, the exposed pieces of bone dried before Perini tore off his rubber apron, reached for his rosary. He gently kissed the wooden cross before hanging it around his neck.

The funeral parlor was at the end of a short block on Mulberry Street, between the barbershop and men's haberdashery, its window display a deluxe child's coffin, the glass spotted with fingerprints of kids who dared to tag it.

Bishop Falcone stepped from a covered buggy, followed by two younger Priests. Even at two o'clock in the morning, Mulberry was shoulder-to-shoulder crowded, all trying for a glimpse of His Excellency under the gas streetlights.

The parlor door opened before the Bishop could reach it. Perini, bald and fat, bowed, then led the Bishop silently past the viewing room, to corpse preparation.

The Bishop moved among the porcelain tables, where the remains of a dozen sailors were on fresh towels, name tags attached to the larger body parts. He read the names, then paused where two heads lay on their sides, both young men, eyes taken by crabs, mouths still screaming-open.

"*Perché mostrare questo?*"

"*Per la giustizia, l'eccellenza,*" Perini said.

One of the Priests had turned away, crossing himself. "Why do you ask His Excellency for 'justice'? For what? An accident? To bring him here is a terrible joke, an insult."

"Father, I beg all pardons, but your eyes needed to see this."

Perini moved to a table, where a pulled-apart sailor was lying. "My nephew Augusto, his mother's name tattooed on his arm. Palermo-born, never a bit of trouble in his life, until he reached the waters of the United States. The Navy didn't even bring the boys here, but a fisherman who found what was left. And not American, but Sicilian."

The Bishop said, "*I nostri fratelli, il nostro sangue.*"

"Sì, our brothers, our blood. The *Regina* isn't the first Italian boat to be lost. Six 'accidents' in that many weeks. Hundreds dead, and the United States hides their face—*come un vigliacco*—claim no responsibility, even when it happens at their doorstep. That's the insult."

"*Non si tratta di una questione per la chiesa.*"

Perini gestured to the scattered human wreckage. "Begging your pardon, Excellency, these boys would have made their lives here, but they were slaughtered. We're the strangers in this country, so no one listens. When you speak, you carry the power of Roma."

The Priest said, "Do you truly know what you're asking? The burden His Excellency must carry?"

Perini lowered his head out of respect, handed the Priest a thick envelope. "I do know. There's a letter, one of these dead boys, his father is an official—*funzionario del governo*—but thousands of miles away. You're here, Excellency. You can be the voice of the dead."

The Bishop repeated, *"La voce dei morti,"* looked to the Priest, and then, "We'll try to be heard."

Gunny pressed his back flat against the cold stone, hunched down, but keeping the rifle across his knees trained on Nemo, who fought to tighten his shoulder bandage with chained hands. The candle next to him was burned to a wick in a puddle, surrounded by scorched newspaper clippings and letters, some still curling in the small fire.

Gunny said, "All that's happened, makes you feel pretty damn special."

"I'm still alive."

Nemo tilted his head, as if playing a violin, making room for both hands and their shackles, trying to get his fingers around the linen, to pull it. "I don't suppose you'd care to assist."

Gunny held out the rifle. "Got this brand-new Remington roll-back. That kind of help?"

Nemo managed to tie the bandage. "What you have are very specific orders, regarding me."

"You never talk like nobody else around here. Where do you hail from anyways?"

"The world. Are you familiar?"

Gunny moved, a bayonet hanging from his belt scraping the wall. "All your fancy smart-ass, and you just don't get it. This is *my* house." He tossed a moldy burlap flour sack at Nemo's feet. "And that's your'n."

9

DEAL WITH THE DEVIL

"My leg's deader than Julius Caesar. Run over here!"

Efrem dropped his telegrams, charged back down the second-floor corridor to the old pantry steps leading to the White House cellars and War Room. Grant was near the top, leaning against the wide door frame, his right leg stiff in front of him, as if bound by an invisible cast.

Efrem offered an arm and shoulder, and Grant hauled himself up, throwing his weight against the boy and soaking him with his raincoat.

"The damp, no sleep, and no supper. Bad combination." Grant almost added "bad bourbon" to the list, but thought better of it. What was churning wasn't old whiskey, but gutted anger he couldn't tamp down. And now, his leg wasn't cooperating, as he pulled it along, muscle-stiff, with his right hand.

Efrem said, "My Nana, she falls asleep in her supper."

He wanted to gulp back his words as soon he said them, but Grant laughed quietly. "I'm not there yet," he said as they managed the top step, then the hallway. Grant forced his locked knee, bones loudly clicking.

Grant said, "Sounds like a Peacemaker cocking."

"Begging my asking, sir, is this from the conflicts?"

"Horse-throwed. Years ago."

"Not by Cincinnati!"

"Never. My first year at the Point, the seniors put me on the worst hammer-head they had, teach me a lesson." Grant nodded toward a half-curtained window, and the breaking sunlight. "What are you still doing here?"

"My shift ends at half-past dawn, sir. And then, that's all."

"Clarify your meaning."

Efrem stubbed at the edge of the red carpet. "I was let go on account of getting that message to you late."

"You did fine. I'll let them know."

"I'm thanking, sir, but I don't think them operators take to a colored in the telegraph room. And I never was too good on that job, because there's nothing to it."

"What jobs are you good at? Look at me."

Efrem finally brought himself to President Grant's eyes, saying, "My Pap's the best of the blacksmiths in Washington. And, sir, I know horses. Even hammer-heads."

They reached The Shop, Grant now standing straight, taking the stack of red-enveloped telegrams from the secretary's table by the door. He sorted them, rain still dripping from his cuffs and coattails. "You've got a lot of messages to deliver before reporting to the stables."

Efrem was surprised: "Sir?"

"Don't make me give an order twice."

Grant gave Efrem an affirming nod before shedding his raincoat, water spattering, and making his way to Lincoln's old desk in The Shop's alcove. His leg was now bending a tad, just allowing him to lean across the desk's leather top and dash an order on Presidential letterhead. The only sound was pen scratching paper.

"Mrs. Grant will be up soon."

"Should I see about breakfast, sir?"

Grant signed, nearly tearing through the page, underlining his name with a final stroke. "That's not your job. Get this to Mr. Duncan. You've got one minute."

Efrem was out the door as Grant brought himself to the butler's tray, and the bourbon. He poured, beating down pained fatigue, and then fixed on the Mathew Brady photograph of the U.S.S. *Abraham Lincoln* that hung in The Shop's far corner.

Morning shadows waved across the formal portrait of the crew, at Attention on a Tennessee River dock, ready to board their ship. It was a large print, under glass, and all the faces, young and old, were finely detailed.

Faces of the drowned, shadows blinking their eyes.

Grant, his leg still leaning him sideways, raised his glass. "Gentlemen, I made my deal with the Devil, and I can only apologize," he said before hurling the glass against the marble fireplace, jags and bourbon spraying the floor.

The sack over Nemo's head was double-knotted around his throat, every breath bringing the burlap into his mouth. He coughed traces of rotten flour, while Gunny pushed him from behind, the Remington barrel jamming his ribs as they walked the prison corridor. He kept his hands folded, instead of clawing blindly ahead of himself, taking each step with purpose.

Gunny said, "Walk to the right, or crack your skull."

The burlap moved with Nemo's words. "It's another eleven feet before we turn, since we're now in the first-floor corridor, leading outside. This isn't a maze to me."

Gunny shoved with the rifle. "Do what I say."

Smoke and coal oil residue pasted the sack as a thick fog, letting Nemo know he was at the burned-down doors to the old loading dock. He stepped through, kicking charred pieces out of the way, as he felt for the dock's edge, then stopped.

"You thought this is where I'd break my neck?"

Nemo blind-walked the edge of the dock to the steps at the far side, then took them to the ground, saying, "I won't be accommodating that idea."

Nemo cocked his head, listening to Guards slop buckets of soapy water across the yard, washing off ashes and blood. Nearby came the scraping sound of chunks of brick and broken bottles, tossed by the prisoners, being swept away.

Gunny's fingers dug in tight on the back of Nemo's neck. "That's a new start, like nothing never happened. Like you didn't do nothing for them prisoners."

"It irks, but you're to take me out the gates, to my ship. Not to the gallows."

A cannon fired outside the gates. The echo slammed back into the prison yard, sound pile-driving wall to wall, rattling windows and dusting plaster. The sound punched Nemo, too, but he remained perfectly still, hooded, with hands folded. No reaction.

Gunny let his pride out: "*My* gun. No misfires this time. Blow this whole place to smithereens. You and all the scum you stood up for."

Nemo couldn't tell if Gunny was about to shoot, but said, "Is all this supposed to make me bow my head? If there were no thunder, men would have little fear of lightning. Do you even understand what that—"

Gunny's mouth curled as he smashed Nemo's shoulder wound with the butt of the Remington, to hear him cry out. There was nothing. Gunny's eyes caught fire. He hard-swung the rifle barrel into Nemo's stomach.

Nemo took it, not bending, then managed through the hood: "Out the gates. Those are your orders."

Gunny roared, snap-pounding the base of Nemo's skull with a massive, balled fist. Knockout blow. He was pouring sweat, and yelling, "This prisoner was causing a threat, sir! I did what I had to."

Warden Kramer saw all from his office on the second floor: Gunny and two Guards lashing Nemo head-down on the back of a horse.

Gunny put a hand flat on Nemo's back, called out, "He's still takin' some air."

Kramer squinted through his cracked window, pushing his spectacles back, focusing on that movement, so if anyone with a badge asked, he could swear Nemo was alive when he left the prison. He tapped the yellow glass with his umbrella.

Gunny threw a quick salute toward the window, slipped the Remington into a scabbard before hefting onto the horse, Nemo, tied and still, behind the saddle. Kramer let Gunny clear the gates before picking up the fire axe beside his old desk.

He held it over his head with both hands, and counted. Waiting. Arms shaking when the distant cannon fired again, Kramer brought the blade down, the Howitzer covering the sound of tearing through floorboards, into a narrow hold beneath.

The axe was dropped next to his umbrella as Kramer kicked through the broken boards before reaching into the opening, up to his shoulders. Straining, he took hold of a cobweb-veiled baby's coffin.

Metal clanged from inside as he wrenched the coffin around

old nails and the floor's splintered edges, pulling it free. He dropped against a never-painted wall of his office, wiping the sweat from his eyes on his sleeve, the small, heavy box beside him.

The task done, the Warden allowed himself a satisfied smile, patting the coffin's lid.

10

COMBATANTS

The burlap raw-scraped Nemo's face as he shook his head, forcing himself back to consciousness, with the eyeless hood tight around his throat, half-choking.

He tried stretching feeling back into his limbs before standing. His ankle shackles had ten inches of chain between them, threaded through an iron ring in the floor, and it snapped taut with Nemo's moving, locking him down.

The car jerked to one side, wheels crying steel-on-steel, as the train rounded a curve. It was a violent motion, and Nemo judged he could use it, bringing his cuffed hands up, feeling the slack in the chains, determining freedom of movement.

Gunny's voice was next to his ear, coming through the hood. "So, back from your dreams? Your skull crack open in there?"

"How close are we to my ship?"

Gunny said, "Close, and you'll be delivered 'cause them's my orders, but they don't say nothing about your wellness when you get there. You think I'm just a jackass in blue. Know how many professional fights I've won? How many men I turned to mush?"

He swatted Nemo's chest with the rifle barrel. "If you cause me fear of my life, I got every right to defend against a violent prisoner."

"One that's been shot and chained," Nemo said, feeling the train's speed, and the gun pressed against him. Making calculations.

Gunny's snicker was even closer. "The best kind."

Nemo dropped his head, chin-to-chest low, planning his moves before jerking up, head-butting Gunny under the jaw, punching his teeth through his bottom gums. Blood fountained from Gunny's mouth, and across the burlap hood, as Nemo grabbed hold of the rifle barrel, pulling it from his hands.

The boxcar tilted wildly to one side, taking a sharp mountain curve. Gunny stumbled, falling into a wall, spitting teeth and foam, words tangled together. "Your laughter's my v-victory!"

He drew the bayonet from his belt, charged, lost footing, then charged again, washed in his own blood. Nemo adjusted his hands, holding the Remington from the middle, giving weight to both sides like a fighting staff, then swung wide at the sound of Gunny's moves, forcing him back. His blind moves were sure. Precise.

Nemo's masked face followed Gunny's movements, sensing them, as Gunny kept to the walls of the car, climbing over hay and lumber stacks to the loading doors.

Nemo moved from only his waist, on guard, his feet planted, filtering out the sounds of the train's brakes and couplings to hear Gunny's moves and be ready to defend or deflect.

It was a discipline he'd learned: mind-mapping what he couldn't see, as he'd done before, navigating through deep-ocean canyons miles below the water's surface. Nothing but pitch black, with only instinct to guide him.

Nemo listened, then made a choice, lowering a shoulder and tightening his hold on the rifle, cued by the drag of boots on the wooden floor. Near, and just to his left.

He gave it three heartbeats, letting Gunny come as close as the point of the old bayonet, then smashed into his chest, the rifle's butt splitting bone. Pounding Gunny off his feet.

The boxcar swayed, hefting Nemo to one side, the rifle on his shoulder. He upended the gun, pointing straight down at the shackle chain between his ankles. Thumb on trigger, he searched blindly with the barrel, catching the front sight on the chain links. He fired, blowing them apart.

Nemo spun off from the bench, cuffed hands keeping the rifle over his head. Gunny made a move, stabbing wildly with the bayonet, holding it, from the elbow-bend in the blade, as a stiletto. The steel point caught Nemo's arm. Quick jet of red, and a cry through the hood, but not of pain.

A battle yell.

Nemo's legs were a blur, pounding gut-blows into Gunny, doubling him forward; whip-fast moves of an ancient fighting style. Nemo rocked back on his heels, taking a stance in the center of the car, then cleared the perimeter around him with a swing of the rifle.

Gunny lunged, blade slashing.

A scissor-move to the jaw hard-spun him into the boxcar wall. Blind-hooded, Nemo didn't stop, kicking Gunny to the corner. Left foot, then right, then left again.

Gunny screamed bloody spit, ripping with the bayonet. Stabbing. Nemo dodged instinctively, the blade sparking off the rifle barrel, then knocked away.

Gunny swung hard, raging without a weapon, his giant-knuckled fist pounding Nemo's face through the hood.

Nemo took the blow, angling his body into a perfect round-house, his legs snapping out like arrows fired from a crossbow. The kick's force hurled Gunny off his feet, propelling him across the car, twisting in the air, before crashing against a rail tie and rusty iron. Bones shearing.

Gunny stayed to the floor, agonized. The shapeless, burlap face loomed over him, close and sticky with blood. He tried his words with a split tongue. "You going to k-kill me now?"

"The blade."

"B-but you can't see . . ."

Through the bag, Nemo's voice: "Not in a way you can comprehend."

Gunny pulled the bayonet from a hay bale where it had stuck, then gripped the socket-end, angling the narrow blade toward Nemo's stomach, less than an inch away.

"Do you want worse? Take that chance," Nemo said. "I'm now showing the mercy you don't deserve."

Gunny pressed the bayonet into one of Nemo's cuffed hands, the steam-hiss of locomotive brakes filling the boxcar. The train jerked back, stopped, as Nemo jabbed into the rope, shredding the knot with the bayonet's point. Freeing himself from the noose, before ripping the burlap sack from his head.

He pulled it up and off, bloody sweat coming with it. Caked with grime, his face was swelling, but Nemo drew a deep breath, feeling his small victory over the pain.

Nemo's eyes adjusted from total darkness to the spears of light sneaking through the boxcar's side slats, and showing up the fight wreckage: crates, barrels, and Gunny, all kicked apart, or caved in.

"The key," Nemo said.

The bolt on the car's side door was thrown, and the inside soaked white as it was pulled open. Duncan stood on the rail platform, bleached by the sun behind him, a Derringer aimed into the car, saying, "I expected something like this, but wasn't sure who'd be standing."

Nemo held his cuffs in front of him. "All of this was in defense."

"I believe it." Duncan looked to Gunny, gun on him. "Sergeant, are you aware right now? Aware of your situation?"

"Y-yes."

"Release the prisoner. Your duty's finished."

Gunny's head shook. "Traitorous w-worms," he said as he worked broken fingers into his pocket, his tongue lolling from the corner of his mouth.

"Work faster," Duncan said. "And only produce the key, or a bullet is bound for your eye."

Gunny said, "That's a lady's gun, f-fit for a soiled dove, n-not a man!"

"I'd wager Mr. Duncan's a dead shot," Nemo said. "No matter what the caliber, or intention."

Gunny inserted the key into the tumbler, opening the jaws of the Adams cuffs. They dropped to the floor, and then Duncan said, "The shackles. It appears you've already had what-for to the head, so you're probably a tad confused."

He took a folded letter from his jacket. "The commuting of Captain Nemo's sentence, signed by the President of the United States, and rights of his release under federal probation."

"I ain't never confused, that's my trouble." Gunny opened up the shackles, a jag of pain cutting him, as he said to Nemo, "Look out them doors, traitor! You counted on us to be b-burned down and buried, but we ain't! You hate this country, but we're better than you!"

Nemo swung the Remington, smashing it in half against the post beside Gunny's skull. "You burned yourselves down."

He dropped barrel and stock into Gunny's lap before stepping over the metal ring that held his chains, moved to the car's open door, and into the bright Norfolk day.

Prying off the shackle restraints and kicking them aside, Nemo said, "All of this destruction, because brothers fought brothers. You should ponder that."

Gunny daubed his tongue with a wet rag. "What in hell's 'ponder'?"

Duncan kept the Derringer leveled as Nemo swung onto the handholds, landing on the freight platform alongside the rail spur. They got out of the way of a Sheffield handcar, carrying men and lumber to what was left of the Norfolk passenger station.

Duncan dropped the pistol into a coat pocket. "Actually, it isn't mine."

"That speaks well of you."

"I appreciated the bluff about my marksmanship."

Nemo said, "Necessary, given the situation." They followed a path around the station, past wagons-for-hire and teamsters loading them, to the street, where bombed-out storefronts lined the block with new ones.

Ashes and fresh paint, side by side.

"The resilience amazes me, as much as the butchery," Nemo said. "Despite relishing this fresh air, it feels as if I've traded one set of chains for another."

"You're always welcome to return to Libby, wait out tomorrow, enjoy a last meal."

"That's General Grant's caveat."

"Your ultimate freedom depends on how well you take command—"

Nemo finished: "According to your demands."

"You accepted certain conditions."

"I'm afraid my conscience bullies me into doing only what's right."

"An enviable conceit." Duncan let the words settle. "The President believes I pushed him into a terrible mistake; a good thing he didn't see any of this. So, your hand-to-hand training is in Kalari-paya-ttu? Did I pronounce that correctly?"

"It's not training, but an art. Governments are so thorough, even when they're blind."

Duncan said, "Given all that's at stake, I wouldn't underestimate your new comrades, Captain."

Nemo touched his bruises. "We'll see what the future holds, Mr. Duncan. For both of us."

The saber came down fast, heating the air, colliding with the edge of the King General battle sword, splintering steel. Franz Sigel shifted the Prussian-made weapon from right to left, slicing with its curved blade, keeping the gold-washed hand guard up and moving on the Lieutenant who was fighting back with the King General.

Another blow, splitting the King in two, knocking the Lieutenant off his feet. He raised his hands. "You've killed me fair, sir!"

Sigel helped him to his feet. "You did fine, boy, but your training's as antiquated as your weapon."

Sigel held out the curved saber, examining its polished surface for scars. There were none.

He said, "This steel is three times harder than what we could produce before. The edge, like a diamond."

There was a figure, distorted in the blade's surface. He said, *"Sei sempre pronti per la guerra, Generale."*

The voice was all authority, coming from the shadowed side of the gymnasium, next to the small boxing ring where Bishop Falcone sat in a chair in the front row. Two priests flanked him, but did not sit.

Sigel snapped a bow to the man he'd seen as a reflection. *"No, io sono pronto per la pace, quando si tratta."*

One of the Priests said, "*Grazzi,* General. Odd to hear our language with a German accent."

The Bishop said, "*Tutti dovrebbero sapere Italiano.*"

"I agree, Excellency. In the new world, everyone should be able to speak to everyone." General Sigel buttoned up his Union Army tunic. "My apologies, gentlemen, I had no intention of meeting you here."

The Priest said, "His Excellency finds truth comes with a lack of formality."

Sigel smoothed his hair and moustache with his hands. Bishop Falcone, overcoat tight to his clerical collar, regarded him with measured words: "Your country is preparing war with France."

"Germany is." Sigel moved to the Bishop, standing before him, hands folded. "Yes, sir. Weeks away."

"This will leave the Papal State vulnerable to King Emmanuel. Europe prepares to burst into flames, and a common, diabolic enemy has appeared. Who, or what, do you think that is, General?"

"Your meaning, in the oceans of the United States?"

"Killing our people. And your people."

The Bishop's gaze never left Sigel: "*Ma la colpa su una fantasia.* Monsters."

Sigel said, "But all the deaths, they're not a fantasy."

A finger snap, and the Lieutenant was at his side with a leather satchel. "From Otto von Bismarck to President Grant, informing him of Germany's official position about the sinkings. He holds the United States and its Navy fully responsible. Fully."

The Priest said, "You fought beside Grant, commanding more than—*trentamila.*"

"Yes, thirty thousand men of the German regiments, from New York to Indiana."

The bishop said, "You did it with honor, and '*scopo*'? Purpose?"

"I fought for the reunification of this country; I can't arbitrarily decide to destroy it."

"Would Mr. von Bismarck?"

Sigel gave some pause, before, "Your Excellency, what is the position of your government?"

Bishop Falcone said, "Even on the edge of civil war they're willing to confront the United States. As a Papal State, or unified, Italy will not be a victim of these assaults. Our congregations here are outraged. Their families, slaughtered by the very country they've adopted. A betrayal."

Sigel said, "We don't know what's happening in the U.S. waters, Father. We don't know who."

"Or what? Monsters, or men?"

"We can't add to hysteria," Bishop Falcone said, "but, this is to be a place of promise, and God's blessings. If it becomes something hellish, demonic, then the Mother Church is the defense for all."

Sigel said, "I'm sure the answer isn't demonic."

"Blood is spilled, either way," the Priest said. "There is a Heavenly plan at work, testing men and their faith, and the world must be ready to react."

The Lieutenant followed the Bishop's eyes as he raised a jeweled finger, pointed to the elaborate sword in the gymnasium corner, and said, *"Anche il male creato dall'uomo può essere demoniaco."*

Man-made evil can be demonic also.

11

RUST AND BLOOD

The sound of Nemo's footsteps changed.

The cobblestone streets had ended, and the wood planking of the Norfolk Harbor wharf had replaced them. A flock of gulls broke from a far piling, and he watched them dip before they angled for a strip of ocean he could barely glimpse between a sail maker's shop and a tavern.

The rows of buildings along the waterfront denied Nemo his view, but he tasted the salty-damp air, then soaked his lungs with a deep breath. His strides lengthened, quick-marching through an alley, with Duncan catching up, until they both reached the docks.

He stopped, taking in the shallow-bottom freighters and fishing boats, tied in their slips. Sailors worked the small craft on the first dock, and on the second the sails were coming down on a two-mast schooner. Orders were shouted, with all hands crewing together.

Duncan said, "You can deny it, but this is where you belong."

Nemo's eyes were set on the ocean.

He said, "No, Mr. Duncan. Out there. Beneath the surface."

A shriek of laughter, and they turned to some children play-ing along the water's edge, chasing around the remains of the old docks, now burned to the sand, crossbeams and pilings collapsed against each other as charred steel skeletons.

Nemo nodded toward them. "Do you feel any responsibility for the ships and men destroyed; perhaps their fathers?"

"What are you asking?"

"The battle of Norfolk. Fought a quarter of a mile out, your submersible against the U.S.S. *Virginia,* the cannons obliterating this part of the harbor. How many men were lost? You remember this, don't you?"

The laughing voices behind him, Duncan chose his words: "I designed a vessel meant to bring a terrible war to a quick end."

"And it failed in its noble purpose, failed miserably." Nemo turned from the running children. "Now, you understand a frac-tion more about the missions of the *Nautilus,* and my goals."

"Actually, I'm one of the few who always understood."

Nemo said, "Then we should get to your current situation."

"That's already turning into a worldwide crisis," Duncan said. "Beyond that horizon, not one vessel has gotten more than a hundred miles into our lanes before vanishing. And no two had the same port of call or cargo. You've been briefed."

Nemo said, "By your dossier, memorized and burned."

"Then you know the crews claim all sorts of 'sea monsters,' adding fuels to the fires of speculation, to put it mildly."

"Newspaper fictions," Nemo said. "But from what I've wit-nessed in my explorations, those deep-sea creatures seen, those testimonies, might not be outrageous."

"But they're problematic."

"What reasonable and intelligent man wouldn't accept such an explanation? Surely not the President."

Duncan said, "Your disdain's misplaced. No leader's accepting these wild claims, except to blame us, even harking back to your terrorism as an example. The truth is under the sea, which you will find, following a search pattern we devise, and reporting the true evidence of each sinking."

"To exonerate the United States?"

"Completely," Duncan said. "We've nothing to do with any of this."

"But in my proving, I'm to follow your plans, using only the evidence that you provide."

Duncan said, "I'm the one who has complete faith you'll use your best judgment in all situations."

Nemo said, "I can't tell if that's a warning or an endorsement."

"My advice is not to stray from the plans. For your own benefit."

"Or it's back to the hangman," Nemo said. "Unfortunately, there's a major flaw in your plan's conception. No part of this can be accomplished without the *Nautilus*, and I've seen no evidence of her."

Duncan presented a leathered billfold from his pocket that held a map made of pressed tin, its six hinged sections unfolding like a Chinese puzzle in Nemo's hands, his fingers tracing the punched surface with its coded shapes and ciphers.

"You know what that is?"

"I do," Nemo said. "I do indeed."

"Then you know it only functions with mechanics found on the *Nautilus*. We've taken great pains to make you part of this mission."

"I've never before met a government official who claimed to be an ally."

"At this moment, it's more than a claim," Duncan said. "And it's imperative that you succeed."

Nemo considered Duncan's words, turning the billfold over in his hands, looking as if he were about to hurl it into the Virginia surf, but pocketed it instead.

"Lead on, Mr. Duncan."

The livery was a mutt on waterfront row, common-walled with a rope-maker, and only suited for nags that towed milk wagons. Duncan worked the stable's large door, forcing bent hinges and rotting wood, until it opened.

Duncan said, "The United States government welcomes you to the fold, Captain."

They made their way past the stalls, swaybacks swatting flies with their tails, and Nemo saying, "Not what I expected, but then doesn't all American invention have its origins in a barn?"

"Your elitism's showing again," Duncan said.

He cleared the hay dust from his throat. "But then, I believed the *Monitor* and *Alligator* were great accomplishments until I saw your *Nautilus*. That's when I thought I *should* be mucking stalls."

Nemo said, "You improved on Dilleroi's design for the *Alligator*, and built truly workable submarines. You had to satisfy a government; I only had to satisfy myself."

Duncan pulled at the termite-eaten gate to the stable boy's closet. "I appreciate the buried compliment."

"Find what you like, it's just an opinion," Nemo said, spying four tall, perfectly groomed horses in a corner stall and draped in brown netting, making them almost invisible. "Fine military mounts, well camouflaged. And the weapons cache, under their tails?"

"Actually, I've been afraid to look," Duncan said.

He pushed aside the old stall's bridles and cobwebbed tack, then removed a piece of wooden slat, revealing a polished steel crank.

Duncan turned the crank quickly. "My world has always existed on paper, so this business is all new to me. An academic, not a commando, if you haven't gleaned that already."

"Grant trusts you."

"The President has his doubts, and if we fail, we could end up on a gallows together."

Nemo said, "I'd never make it to the thirteen steps. I've been incarcerated long enough to know when a rifle's trained on me. How many guards have you stationed outside this barn?"

"A precaution. That wasn't my decision," Duncan said, winded and still furiously cranking. "But your actions won't necessitate sniping, so, no worries."

"Just fingers on the trigger," Nemo said. "Your way of putting people at ease, I find very disquieting."

The cranking mechanism caught.

Nemo felt the vibration of meshing gears somewhere below him and took a step back as a section of the hay-sticky floor elevated, revealing gear-driven steel plates jigsawing into place. They shifted and locked, becoming a ramp to an open area beneath the stables.

Duncan said, "She's waiting for you, Captain."

Nemo walked the plank, footsteps on steel, down to the submarine pen that stretched beneath the Norfolk waterfront. It was a man-made cavern, completely enclosed, running from the shops and taverns directly above to the edge of a small fishing pier half a mile to the south.

The side facing the water and larger ships was hidden by an enormous curtain of heavy canvas, painted to blend with the dark shadows under the waterfront buildings. Perfect camouflage.

The submarine repair dock was a wide structure, designed to access any craft from either port or starboard, with built-in ladders and a bracing system to raise bow or stern for repair in the slip.

Walled chambers for a blacksmith, furnace, specialty glass, and metal works were set back from the dock, all fully stocked, ready for use. Large crates, labeled U.S.N. TOP SECRET were stacked six-high beside the chambers, along with open drums of scrap iron.

Duncan's expression was a melding of pride and nervous expectation. A schoolboy waiting to be graded.

Nemo gave a beat of recognition before making his way around the *Nautilus* for a captain's inspection. Each step was deliberate, singular, hands behind his back, as he walked the dock's circumference, taking in his creation.

The Cyclops-eye viewing port and jagged, retractable dorsal fin wafted above the waterline, but the submarine's monstrous characteristics that Professor Arronax had described in his diary were now rust-eaten openings and smashed, twisted wreckage.

The *Nautilus'* seventy-five meters had been torn by cannon and neglect. Her iron frame was a fractured skeleton, the riveted skin struggling to keep her famous cigar shape from breaking apart. The Navy had done a thorough job ravaging her, but the sea had picked over the corpse.

Nemo knelt on the dock's edge, reaching out to a split in the submarine's glass-domed prow, now riddled with bullet holes. A jolt of shoulder pain ripped him, his fingers smearing along the iron plating, coming back covered in bloody rust.

"The saber of the ocean," Duncan said.

"Of course, it would have been expecting far too much of the United States Navy to keep a captured vessel, only the most advanced in the world, shipshape." Nemo stood, wiping his hands. "Yes, too damned much."

Cincinnati jumped the fence, hooves smartly over the top rail, before landing at a full run. The Morgan Horse's legs never stopped: galloping through the air until perfectly meeting the ground again, then charging for the next obstacle. Grant stayed just above the saddle, knees locked and leaning forward, knowing the rhythms of his horse and reining Cincinnati's direction.

A half-minute behind, General Sigel and his tall Arabian made the fence, landing hard before he gave the animal his heels. Sigel had the reins tight, breaking the horse into a hard run, when a bullet tore a flank, blood jetting.

The Arabian screamed, legs collapsing.

They somersaulted across the wet grass, the Arabian's head twisting back, its mouth wide. Sigel dove out of the saddle, landing hard, just as the horse's side pummeled into the ground, water and mud erupting on impact.

Grant swung Cincinnati wide, then cut across the field that was the White House back property. He had the horse in a full gallop, keeping his head low, and body leaning away from the saddle.

Another shot. The sound of a high-velocity rifle.

Grant reined his horse quickly to the ground, legs properly tucked, and head flat to the earth. He leapt from the stirrups, rolled, and came up the other side of the animal, putting his arms flush across its neck and calling out, "Franz, you hit?"

Sigel stayed behind the Arabian's heaving belly, checked his Gasser pistol. "No, no—I don't think so!"

The Arabian twisted its neck around, fighting the ground, and Grant said, "If he bolts, you'll lose cover!"

Sigel leaned into the blood-wet horse, patting it down. Strok-ing and calming. A slug tore the ground an inch away. Back legs thrashed, violently chopping air. Sigel, pistol down, moved across the Arabian's wide body, got to its ear, and brought it to his mouth, letting the animal feel his warm breath. The horse settled.

"I can't see where the damn shots are coming from!" Grant said, scanning the far tree line that was the natural barrier around the White House grounds. Deep, fully grown protection in the Spring, but now winter-bare, offering no refuge.

"Mr. President! Sir!"

Grant waved off the Guards charging from beside the stables. "Stay the hell down, we can't spot him!"

He thumbed back the Navy Colt from his shoulder holster and took aim, but gray, winter light flattened out everything in view, making it indistinct and anonymous.

Guards broke from the greenhouse, running in low, dropping at the training obstacles and leveling rifles on the wooden posts. Again, the call, "Mr. President—Sir!"

Grant ordered, "On your bellies, and hold fire 'til we get a sighting!"

"At least now he's positive we can't see him," Sigel said, press-ing a strip torn from his shirt against the Arabian's wound, sop-ping it.

"Let him," Grant said. "Let the bastard get cocky. Give him long enough to spit, then fire three blind. Left, center, right."

Sigel fired three times then dropped back behind his horse. The return shots were a roar. Bullets punched mud, blasted the fence rails, and exploded a Guard's knee. But the rifle flame was just to the right of a tree break, coming from a tangle of scrub, the shooter's silhouette vague behind the bushes.

Grant rolled to one side, came up firing. Cincinnati stayed

down as Grant emptied his six, reloaded. Guards supplied quick cover, shots echoing for miles, then dying. Sigel pointed to the first trees, a shadowed movement.

Grant threw the Guards a signal and they opened up again, gunfire into the trunks and hanging branches. Union sentries on the White House roof laid down shots from their Springfields, the trees taking the slugs, bits of bark, and pine cones spinning away.

The shooter fired back from a new position, at the base of a Blue Spruce, rifle barrel peeking from the shadows.

Grant narrowed on him, using Cincinnati's neck to brace the shot. He fired once. Waited. The shooter's last bullet flamed wildly upward, breaking the treetops. Sparrows panicked from the branches, darting in all directions at the blast. Paint spattering against the sky.

Then, nothing.

Grant emptied his spent brass.

The Guards ran for the woods, covering both sides of the tree line, as Grant and Sigel stood, bringing up their horses.

Even as Guards surrounded, Grant checked the crease along the Arabian's left flank, "It skidded into muscle, but he's standing strong. I don't even think he'll take stitches."

General Sigel nodded to the trees. "Sam, there."

Grant watched the shooter's body being dragged through the mud by the heels, red spreading from the single bullet wound in the center of his chest.

A Guard, shouldering a rifle with scope, said, "That was a humdinger of a shot, Mr. President."

Grant holstered the Colt. "I want to know who the hell he was, and his fellow travelers. Living names, not just the dead man."

Quick salute as the Guard joined the others who were running into the field from all sides, barking orders and taking charge after the fact. Troopers laced the trees, plunging bayonets into bushes and shrubs, and setting loose howling pack hounds. The roof sentries rolled cigarettes, eyeing all, rifles cradled.

Sigel took the leather satchel from the Arabian's saddlebag before a stable hand grabbed hold of the two horses and led them away at a trot, with Rifle Guards quick-stepping alongside.

He said, "If he'd wanted to kill us, he could have."

"There's no way the dead one could have fired those first shots from that side of the field. There were two shooters, and he was the sacrifice. Always best to divide the enemy's attention," Grant said. "This 'attempt' was to see if we're paying attention to the coming storm."

The dogs yowled in unison, and Grant said, "The only thing they're going to tree now is a possum." He looked back at the gray woods, the dead man being rolled over, pockets searched. "Hell, spotters could have been in the trees all morning, waiting for my daily ride, and there's no fence on the far side of those woods."

"They'll start building it straightaway," Sigel said. "They may not have known my purpose here, but they knew I'd be riding with you."

"You're sure you're the one they were aiming for?"

Sigel smiled. "Didn't mean to insult you, Sam."

Sigel handed Grant the leather satchel, a spot of horse's blood smeared across it. "I made it clear to von Bismarck that I would deliver his communiqué, but I'd not act on it."

"Even if Germany and the other countries do?"

"I'm a General. In your Union Army. That never changes." Sigel patted Grant's shoulder. "We're both of us targets, Sam."

Grant said, "Hell, we've had bull's-eyes on us for the last thirty years, and these ships gone missing only make it worse."

"It was on every front page this morning."

"Like that dead bastard will be tomorrow."

Sigel said, "And a chance to stir this up even more—an assassin, motivated by sea monsters."

"We're taking action to trash this horse dung," Grant said. "Get some common sense back to the table."

"Mr. President, that would be your greatest achievement. Just be quick about it."

Grant laughed at his old friend's truth, before looking toward the White House.

Julia Grant, on the gravel walkway that curved from the stables to the old back steps to the President's office, was in royal blue from neck to ankle. She sidestepped her way through the crowd of reporters, guards, and White House staff. More guards gathered.

The First Lady kept her smile in place, and her damaged, crossed eyes for all to see as she continued to the edge of the lawn, her hand out to her husband. She was all pride and strength, but quick-walked to him.

Grant angled through the uniformed guns surrounding him, taking his wife's hand as she reached him, squeezing his assurance, and was about to speak when he saw the bundle of red, urgent telegrams tucked in the crook of her arm. "You tell me who gave you that bad news to deliver, and they'll be guarding the chicken coops by morning. That's not the job of the First Lady."

"It is when you ask for it." Julia smiled. "We've faced troubles before, and always together."

Grant said to his wife, "I thank God you're here," then drew her close.

12

INSIDE THE BEAST

The *Nautilus* was moving, and the Diver angled around its side, face covered by a celluloid cone, reed-thin tubing trailing from it to a device on the docks. Only twenty feet deep, the water was murky, silt rising from where the flat underbelly of the submarine rose and fell, stirring mud.

Pulling a small pontoon, a section of thin, plate steel lashed to it, the Diver swam to a gaping tear in the hull where a cannonball had blown through it. The wrecked area had been masked with luminous cloth, trimmed to exact dimensions.

The Diver fit the plate over the cloth, matching its sides precisely before bolting it down with a specialized wrench. Legs braced against the *Nautilus*, leveraging every turn, the plate was secured, the cloth filling in the seams around it like healing flesh.

The Diver surfaced.

Nemo's words were the first thing heard: "Of course it would have been expecting too much of the Navy to keep a captured vessel, only the most advanced in the world, ship-shape."

Diver climbed onto the dock, the other side of the *Nautilus*, pulling off the face mask and tubing.

Nemo continued: "Too damn much."

Duncan said, "We've been a tad occupied these past few years."

"Why avoid saying 'war'?"

Duncan sidestepped his words: "Despite obstacles, I made arrangements for the *Nautilus*' care."

"Not much of it."

"Captain, it's a true miracle the ship exists at all."

Nemo said, "Miracle? Who are you suggesting I be grateful to?"

Sara Duncan, in her athletic twenties, strode around the dock's side access where she'd been hidden by the submarine. Walking directly to Nemo with a greeting hand, water dripping from her hair and the man's red-striped swimming togs she'd tailored for her needs, she said, "Captain, this is a rare moment."

He wasn't what she expected, in torn and bloodied clothes, the beard and hair a tangled mask. She noted the purple bruises around wrists and ankles, the dirty bandage around one arm. This wasn't the great stalwart Sara had always imagined, but she kept her hand extended, her admiring smile intact.

Nemo took her hand, freezing his own reaction at the strength in her grip, or the figure she cut. She was a young, silly girl, obviously headstrong and therefore, to him, instantly dismissible.

Sara said, "I know all about you, this ship, all you've done. I know it as well as I know myself."

"That much knowledge would be rare in one so young. And very doubtful."

"I certainly didn't mean to offend," Sara said, breaking her grip, then pecking her father on the cheek. She was aware of Nemo's stare, as if examining a slide under a microscope, as she unhooked the belt of special-forged brass tools, freeing herself of the weight, tossing it aside. Sara was in constant motion, words and body never still.

"So, I don't know if Father told you how exciting, an honor, it's been for me, this work on the *Nautilus*. She's a wonder, and immodestly, we've made excellent repairs."

"Have you, indeed?"

"Trying to meet your standards, what I imagine they are, is an impossibility," Sara said, drying her arms, long bare legs, and brown mane. "But I just patched a huge hole in her side, by the starboard view port, and I hope you'll approve."

"Airtight?"

"The others have been, and this was the last major breach."

Sara fastened the towel around her waist. "You know how much artillery fire she took, but the lady's got strength. Every time I work on her, I find something new to admire."

"And now you claim she's seaworthy, thanks to *your* efforts? You and your daughter share some traits, Duncan."

Sara's face tightened. "No, Captain. My efforts kept her from a burial, but you'll have to bring her back from the dead."

They moved to the submarine, Duncan holding out a robe for his daughter that she didn't take. Nemo spied the small, boxed air compressor by the water's edge, the breathing apparatus, and multiple tubes leading from it. "One central air intake is more efficient. Interesting attempt, though."

A dock ladder led them to the *Nautilus'* outer deck, and what was left of the antennae on the conning tower, now bent in half, melted to the hull. Nemo picked up a piece of the scrap, favoring his wounded shoulder. "I was proud of the advancements I'd made in our communication devices."

"We saved what we could," Duncan said.

"After she was dissected and left to rot?"

Sara headed it off, "My father saw that a great deal was saved, Captain." She opened the primary hatch. "If you'd care to come aboard?"

"I've never been invited to board my own ship before."

Duncan said, "Want to know where you could be? Check your watch."

"One of your talents, Duncan. I thought I just heard General Grant's voice," Nemo said, looking into the pitch darkness of the hatchway. "I haven't lost sight of my circumstances, or the commitment."

Sara held out a miner's helmet with a kettle lamp attached to the brim. "For you."

The water made no sound.

No purr of liquid folding in on itself, no movement. Stagnant, as the lamp on his miner's helmet showed Nemo the algae-slick surface, and the smears of rotting salt that marked the ocean's highest point in the *Nautilus'* flooded interior.

He dropped from the mid-rung of the crew ladder into the waist-high murk, causing ripples to slop against the sides of the access corridor. Nemo could see fragments of damage as the light beam skidded about: hatchways ripped apart, fire-scarred walls, a steel support wrenched apart by an ammo blast, marked by crewman blood spatter.

He waded through the near-pitch, following the light to what was his formal dining room. More bits and pieces. Fine table, chairs, and china stacked, broken and molding. He picked up a bent fork, solid gold, and topped with the *N* insignia. Held it a moment.

Nemo tossed the gold aside, then pushed through the dark to the double doors at the opposite end of the dining room. Two

Roanoke bass swam around his legs as he reached the doors, grabbed the edges, forced them open. Breaking the rust, Nemo disappeared inside, with Sara and Duncan splashing their way in.

The library was the bow of the *Nautilus*; its far wall the submarine's largest observation port. The deeper room had taken on the most water, and Nemo was surrounded by piles of books, folios, and maps, some dry, others sea-rotten, loose pages floating.

His pride, the Brazilian rosewood bookcases, were just kindling, shreds of the library's elaborately woven seaweed drapery still framing them. On the bottom shelf, a stone crab waved his claws, defending the destroyed works of Shakespeare from Nemo's helmet light.

He grabbed a handful of sea charts from the water, hundreds of years old, on parchment, that were now sloppy mush. "You claimed to have rescued a great deal."

Duncan said, "And so we did, beginning with this ship."

"I'm standing knee-deep in your efforts." Nemo let the mush slide through his fingers. "Arronax stated this library, my years of work, would honor any palace, and he saw barely half of it. I'm not an easy man with compliments, but that had meaning."

Nemo splashed his way to the centerpiece of the chamber: the pipe organ, covered in white fabric protection. A specter rising from the mire. He pulled back the white, revealing the keyboard. "What did you use here?"

"Heated Caoutchouc spread on lengths of silk. My own formula, absolutely waterproof," Sara said. "I lined every repair on the hull with it, tried to protect what was in here with the leftovers."

Duncan made it a point: "Indian rubber."

Nemo said, "I'm aware of the substance, and the irony, but I'd gladly have sacrificed the music for my research volumes."

Sara said, "You haven't seen all we've done, Captain."

"What are you going to do about this mess, now that you claim she's airtight? Why haven't you emptied the ballast tanks?"

Duncan said, "Large pumps from the Navy should be here the day after tomorrow."

"There are internal pumps on board. We can rid her of this infernal swamp in an hour."

Sara said, "But there's no power."

Nemo turned, the miner's light stinging Duncan and his daughter. "I know you examined all controls, the engine room. Duncan, you must have had a field day."

"The most impressive configuration I've ever seen."

"Captain, we've repaired every bit of this submarine that we were allowed to," Sara said, shielding her eyes.

"Who stopped you?"

"The *Nautilus,* she holds many secrets." Sara rapped her knuckles against the closed steel iris of a large view port. "Locked, like everything else. She's your ship, and she'll only obey you."

Nemo said, "My creations all include special provisions to prevent military use, should they be captured by government forces."

"And yet, here we are." Duncan smiled through a neatly trimmed beard. "What are your orders, Captain?"

Floating pieces of his possessions slopping around him, Nemo said, "In spite of this careless desecration, the *Nautlius* is still an electric creature, with batteries stored. Stand fast, and learn."

Sara smiled, the light from her helmet following Nemo as he took a spiral staircase up to the bridge.

The Hindu god Varuna held the submarine's wall compass aloft in his four arms, mythic water animals crawling around him. Nemo fitted the golden sea horse from his boot into an opening beside the compass' casing, next to Varuna's head.

The spiny tail of the hippocampus recessed into the wall, becoming a small, curved switch. The sea horse's eyes fluttered dimly, grew brighter, then signal-flashed as stored power hummed from the lower decks.

Nemo stepped to the bridge's primary control podium, taking his rightful place in the Captain's chair, adorned MOBILIS IN MOBILE.

Settling into the bridge of his ship, Nemo checked the podium for damage. The sides were power panels embracing the station like the wings of a clergyman's desk, signal lights and blade switches crisscrossing them. Nemo set the switches.

In the library, Sara and her father took off their miner helmets, dousing the oil lamps as tubes in the ceiling and frosted globes along the walls fought to light. Coils heated. Some blew out, while power reached others, making them glow.

Illuminating the *Nautilus*.

The bridge's panels came to life in sections: lights first, and switches, sparking. Smoke. Then, lit, with indicators half-functioning.

Nemo engaged the flood pumps. The sound of the old water rushing from the *Nautilus* filled the submarine as the ports exhaled gallons of swamp back into the ocean.

Sara and her father moved from the library to the dining room, the swamp quickly receding around them. Swollen furniture, the slop of rotted books, all paste and pages settled in the corners as the water swirled into drains along the base panels.

Crabs skittered.

Nemo came down the circular stairs that connected the first deck with the bridge. "I see *Nautilus* has been made home to a catalog of sea creatures. They're to be gathered and set free. Mr. Duncan, I believe there's a *Carcharhinus limbatus* by your ankle."

Sara said, "Blacktip shark."

Duncan startled, Sara grabbing his arm, as he looked down

to find the baby shark, rolling in the last inches of ocean trapped on the deck. He picked the blackfin up by its tail, holding it away as it tried to snap.

Nemo said, "He's greeting you, Duncan. Now that you've met one species of shark, you only have three hundred and fifty to go. Until I discover another, of course." He stepped around Sara. "Get a bucket, assist your father." He made his way to a small alcove off the library, a door set back in the observation dome.

Framed in gold, smeared with muddy salt, the metal door was arched and decorated with a minutely detailed inlay of Poseidon breaking the waves. There was no handle, only a series of jewels set in a small circle.

Nemo pressed them in private sequence, ordering Sara, "Go below, check the pumps, clear any that are fouled, then prepare engines for inspection. I'll expect a complete list of repairs you've initiated, so I can isolate your mistakes."

The Poseidon door opened pneumatically, sliding into the wall. It hissed instantly shut, Nemo now behind it, before Sara could get out a word.

Duncan was at the far side of the submarine pen, tossing the baby blackfin, a scrape of oysters, and a tangle of silver eels into the water.

Sara hauled up from the *Nautilus'* primary hatch as Duncan made a choice about the twisting fish in the leather bucket. "These were in a lake by the crew quarters. More convenient than you catching them in the surf." He looked up. "So, what do you think of the genius?"

Sara climbed on deck. "He's a genius. That's all."

"His manner disappoints?"

"Let's say this has been a very unusual day, and he behaves accordingly."

"An understatement. You've already done a spectacular job, daughter."

"Not that he recognizes it." Sara climbed the ladder from the submarine's surface deck. "I despise the way he speaks to you."

Duncan saw a flash of Sara's mother, evident in his daughter. "Ease your temper. He's contrary, but I don't think the reality of all this has made itself clear, but it will."

Sara said, "I think you're asking a blind man to see."

"It's not that dire." Duncan regarded his daughter. "I've not been the father I should have been these last twenty years, so I'm not too sure I deserve your defense."

"You saw to my education, and that I got this chance."

"You've gone far beyond anything you heard in a classroom, and this 'chance' is no gift. You earned it." Duncan smiled, held up the bucket. "So, dear, *Nautilus* bass for dinner?"

Sara took her father's hand. "Father, it's not seemly, but take me somewhere with a great deal of whiskey."

13

THE VIOLENCE OF NIGHT

"I know you ain't got no dead kid there, not the way you're struggling that coffin into the wagon."

Warden Kramer kept his hands raised, fixed on the double-barreled Greener that was leveled at his middle. He glanced quickly up at the plaid-kerchief-masked face of the man standing just feet away from Libby's old loading docks, who was keeping the shotgun steady from a moon-shadowed corner, snapping out orders to Gunny:

"Down off that perch."

Gunny was leaning on the wagon's brake from his place on the driver's seat, trying to reach the pistol he'd tucked into the top of his boot. A swath of bandage covered his mouth and split tongue, gagging his protests into muffled nothing as he reached out with his left hand as if climbing down, while grabbing the gun with his right.

He wasn't quick enough for the man with the shotgun.

The blast tore through Gunny's shoulder, propelling him off

the wagon, and spinning across the backs of the horse team, then, hard to the ground.

The shotgun went to Kramer, saying, "He's stupid, but you ain't stupid, are you, Warden?"

"I like to think not," Kramer said.

"Not with all that money you stole; that takes smart figuring. And it's all gold, too. You should be proud as hell."

Kramer pointed to Gunny with his umbrella. "How did you know about this? About our getaway? Was it him?"

"He can't say nothing no way." The man in the kerchief stepped wide over Gunny, who was still twitching.

"All you got to know is, you were found out," he said, taking his place on the driver's seat, the shotgun never leaving its aim on Kramer. "I'm thinking it's time you traded that umbrella for a cane."

He let the second barrel loose, knocking Kramer back against a whitewashed wall, with LIBBY FOODS screaming in giant letters across it.

The wagon team bolted at the blast, and the man tossed the shotgun in the back, alongside the child's coffin, as he steered the running horses away from the prison and down a small lane, toward the reflected lights of old Richmond.

Kramer rolled onto his bloody side, crying out to Gunny, "You damned fool." Trying to raise himself to his feet, leaning on his umbrella, he snapped it in two.

In New York, the fireball lit Mulberry Street.

It was a silent flash, flames and balled heat, followed by the roaring blast of ten dynamite sticks as Bishop Falcone's buggy exploded.

The Bishop had settled inside for only a moment, with the young Priest asking, *"Qual è la prima cosa che dirai a Signor Grant?"* when they heard the ticking.

The young Priest grabbed hold of the Bishop's hand.

The fireball made them ashes.

The explosion hurled the coach's burning wheels into vendor carts and fruit stands, and propelled the horse, body twisting sideways, screaming through a store window, tail and mane in flames.

The cloth-covered rest of the buggy, instantly incinerated, drenched the New York block in a rain, filling the sky with debris and bits of flame that came back down to a smoking crater in the center of the street.

Grant pushed aside a stack of files on his desk, making room for Julia to set out the yellow-striped coffeepot and two cups with the Presidential seal. The sun had been up for less than half an hour, and the White House was quiet, their voices the only sound.

Julia poured and Grant splashed his face from a water bowl, saying, "Feels like I'm living on coffee these days."

"It's better than the alternative."

Grant moved the bourbon decanter. "Depends on your point of view, dear." He filled his coffee cup. "And the time of day. Don't read that."

Julia Grant had taken a newspaper from the desk, neatly folded to the second page, and started reading.

"The morning edition," Grant said. "A thousand people will be coming through that office door, and they'll all have seen it."

"What do you think?"

"I think my assassination's going to happen one article at a time." Grant drained the last of his coffee. "The man's a braying jackass, but he's not wrong."

FROM: THE NEW YORK
WORLD TELEGRAM

THE MONSTERS OF THE SEA ARE LOOSE ON OUR STREETS

> *Opinion by Gideon Spilett*
>
> *We have seen the dispatches; of the ships destroyed mere miles from our own ports, with crews slaughtered by mysterious creatures. This reporter devoted years following the travails of Captain Nemo, sinking ship after ship in his pursuit of peace at any cost, often using a sea monster as his guise. But now the blood has overflowed from our surfs and harbors, into our streets, with the killing of a representative of Italy, His Holiness Bishop Falcone.*
>
> *No matter who lit the fuse to the bomb, if this violence happens within our borders, our waterfronts, our oceans, then we are the ones who must bear the brunt of the world as it prepares to take revenging action for their loss.*
>
> *Defiance of the urge to battle is the lesson we never learned from Captain Nemo. We sentenced him to hang, without hearing his words: that man's nature will always lead him back to war, unless he denies the instinct, and lays down the sword and gun.*
>
> *Now those words have taken root in the very cities that were recently battlefields, and will be so again under President Grant, unless something is done to convince the world that we have less blood on our hands than we do.*
>
> *And no matter what the outcome, I will be on the front lines to report it.*

14

LOYALTIES

The Lieutenant threw the first punch. Sigel ducked it, then countered, with easy body blows.

Sigel punched twice, rocked back on his feet. "Your attack was too obvious; I saw it in your body before you moved."

The Lieutenant hard-countered, "I'll be more discreet next time, sir."

Sigel's hands were fast, hitting the young man's ribs, with more speed than viciousness, driving him into a roped corner against the buckles. Punches were the only sound in the empty gymnasium, bouncing against the walls, and back again, the Lieutenant taking the hits.

Sigel said, "Good exercise, though." He put up his hands. "Marquess of Queensberry. I have to give you time to recover yourself."

Lieutenant wiped his face with his padded gloves. "Thank you, sir. I imagine this is easier on the hands than doing it bare knuckle."

Sigel threw harder, knocking the younger man a few feet, then catching him before he fell, asking, "Just how old do you think I am, Lieutenant?"

"I meant no offense, General."

Sigel said, "I think a few minutes on the bag will be it for me."

"As you wish, sir."

They climbed from the ring, Sigel pulling off his gloves, handing them to the Lieutenant as they moved to a hanging bag in the corner. Sigel threw his first, much harder than his punches before.

The young officer took his place behind the bag, holding it steady, a distorted shadow of the two of them cast by the gymnasium's gas lights.

The General's shadow was enormous compared to the Lieutenant, who was actually noting the placement of the lamps. Sigel, head down, beat into the bag. Brawling an enemy, the Lieutenant absorbing the hits.

"Sir, you haven't commented on your meeting with President Grant."

Sigel said, "I'm aware of that," then threw another punch.

"I just hope it was successful."

Sigel laid quick blows. "It went well. It always does between us, as old friends."

"For now."

Sigel stopped. "What did you say?"

The Lieutenant peered around the bag's edge. "With all that's going on with the sinking ships, they say you might have to make some choices, sir."

Sigel said, "You're seriously forgetting your place, Lieutenant."

"Sea monsters? What kind of idiotic alibi is that?"

He stepped from behind the bag, noting a popped seam leaking sand, saying, "You have a lot of strength, General. Look here, what you've done. A lot of strength, but little sense."

The gun was in the Lieutenant's hand instantly. Sigel didn't react, but his eyes locked. The first slug hit his upper chest as he sprang on the boy, pounding him to the gym floor. The Lieutenant kept the pistol pressed into Sigel's stomach, even as his nose was being shattered by the General's fist. He fired again. Sigel rolled off, holding his stomach, red slicking the wooden floor, then, a final shot into the back of the General's head.

The Lieutenant grabbed a towel and pressed it to his nose before taking bottles of Fine Old Jamaica rum from a canvas bag and soaking the General's body. He tossed the black-glass bottles aside, letting them shatter the silence, then dropped lit matches on chest and legs. Instant ignition.

He stood back, arms folded, pleased with the burning, before using two more bottles to pour a trail from the corpse to the edge of the boxing ring and soaking the General's uniform tunic, hanging on the coat rack.

The Fine Old Jamaica was molasses-thick, its fumes biting the Lieutenant's nose as he tossed a burning handkerchief, spreading the fire along the rum, lighting ropes and canvas. The flames jumped across the gymnasium floor, the blue and yellow, racing.

The Lieutenant stepped casually to the wall sconces, blowing out each lamp, then opening the gas valves completely.

His moves were sure and calm, even as the flames from the ring climbed upward, becoming a pillar of fire behind him, reaching the ceiling. The gas filled the air, choking it, as he took the Prussian sword from the corner, and gave the General a last snap of his heels, saluting him with the blade.

He felt the gesture of respect necessary, before walking out the heavy, swinging doors, the poison filling the room with a snake-like hiss, the fire spreading across the walls, eating, windows splitting with the heat.

The Lieutenant's new orders were a folded sheet in his inside pocket that he read as he calmly walked. The sun was setting, and he was blocks away when the gymnasium explosion rumbled under the sidewalks, the gas lamp globes up and down the street blowing out as if they'd been shot.

He noted that final destruction had taken a bit longer than he'd expected, then lit a cigarillo and drew on it, while enjoying the fading echo of the blast. He kept walking, snapping open the orders, and reading Grant's name as target, a time, and a place.

Grant hard-ran Cincinnati to the end of the cobblestoned block, reining the horse in alongside a team pulling a steam-pump fire engine. The team pulled up, the crew scrambled with hoses, sand pails, and axes, to attack the burning remains of the gymnasium.

The heat was a cannon blast that slammed Grant, with Cincinatti rearing back, as the firemen and Bucket Brigade pounded down the last of the flames, the building's steel frame bending in front of them, then collapsing in on itself. The dying metal screamed, along with a last burst of fire, sparks, and heavy ash. Men dove out of the way, then soaked the ruins.

Grant controlled the horse, called out, "What about General Sigel?"

The Fire Chief ran over, hacking soot from his throat. "We've only one body so far, Mr. President. I don't know if that's the General or not, sir."

Two White House Security Guards charged their horses through the gathered crowd, followed by a cadre of troopers. Police maintained the line, the rubbernecks reacting to the rocking collapse of another wall. Security got to Grant as he dropped from his horse, pushing his way toward the body that was laid out on the flooded sidewalk.

The Guards kept their rifles up, creating a perimeter. Grant took no notice of them as he crouched next to the body. The hanging smoke, the smell of scorched metal and flesh were sickening battle memories to him but he couldn't react, show anything less than complete strength, while the crowd of onlookers choked into handkerchiefs. A young Fireman pulled away the rain slick that shrouded the face; what there was of it.

"Sir, there's another," the Fireman said, "but he seems to be a poor sod who was just walking by when the place blew."

Grant threw back another corner of the slick, revealing a seared right hand with a half-melted ring that represented the Union Army XI Corps.

He took the ring from Sigel's gnarled hand, the crowd around him growing, calling out, one woman slipping a flower into his lapel, as he made his way back to his horse, Guards trotting alongside. Grant's eyes were dead-focused straight ahead, the voices around him distant echoes. All senses lost to the heat, the stench, the thought of a fallen comrade.

A Guard called out, "Mr. President, we're to ride point, and alongside, sir!"

Grant swung onto Cincinnati. "Then do your damn job!" He broke into a sudden run with the Security Command scrambling to bring their horses around, and then, racing to catch up.

The clicking of the brass keys in the White House telegraph room was constant, and reminded Grant of locusts. He hated being there, with Operators bent forward, sending and receiving messages from a dozen stations, furiously decoding, but not saying a word to each other. Grant remembered when it was the old War Room library, preferring it that way.

Efrem, ready to grab the next telegram, jumped from the corner stool where he was perched. "Mr. President!"

The Operators turned, some bolting to their feet, as Grant stepped in scribbling on a tablet. "This goes out immediately, in Code Destrier. All operators are on active duty until I issue different orders."

Horace Prudent, scarecrow of an operations manager, took Grant's message with a stumbling, "Sir, am I understanding you, this situation, correctly?" and, lowering his voice, "Code 'Destrier,' meaning 'Great War Horse' preparations?"

Grant spoke to the room. "I will be available here for the next forty-eight hours. Any communications," he pointed to Efrem, "I want this man to deliver to me personally."

Then, the President was gone.

15

DEAD TREASURE

The belowdecks passageway was the main artery of the *Nautilus*, running its entire length, chambers on both sides, and ending at a fortified bunker that housed the ship's power supply.

All plated iron walls, its top curving up into the submarine's bow structure, the powerhouse had bundled pipes extending from its base, the legs of a brass spider, to carry pressurized steam to the engine turbines.

Its only ports were an envelope-sized window cut into its center, and a hatch recessed into the floor directly in front of it.

Nemo was turning the hatch's locking wheel, telling Sara, "Other side of the stairs, closer to the ballast tanks."

Sara got around the lower-deck access, held herself next to the curved railing. "Expecting an explosion?"

"You're to stay because I've ordered it." He opened the hatch, a radiant glow spilling out. She heard a motor as he stepped in and descended, carried by a small, mechanical lift, before the hatch sealed itself tight.

Sara charged the window, wiped it with her palm, and looked down into the bunker as the *Nautilus'* engines churned. Stalled. Churned again.

Nemo was at a freestanding control station, walled on all sides by the clear-fronted cells of the power generator. His back to her, she could only see him throwing a series of polished steel contact switches.

A flash of blue heat.

An arc of electricity blinded Sara's view, scorching the window from inside. She pulled a boat hook from the wall, jammed the handle into the hatch locking-wheel, strained it loose.

The hermetic seal broke, rushing air with the sting of burning ozone, as Sara lowered herself into the bunker, hanging for a moment by a brass fitting, then dropping to the thick linen mat that covered the floor.

Before Nemo could speak, Sara was cutting wires to the circuit board. Containment cells lost their pulsing color, their power, as one after another dimmed around the chamber walls, then went dark, the last fragments of energy drained off.

Nemo said, "My orders are to be obeyed!"

"You were shocked, about to collapse!"

"Shot, not shocked, and still carrying most of the bullet, courtesy of your government, which causes me great pain. What you saw was a spasm." He pulled an electrical mechanism, its glass conductors shattered and wiring melted together, from under the controller, and slapped it into Sara's palm.

"I was timing the melting point against the power surge."

"I only saw the flash."

"Which you wouldn't, if you'd stayed where I ordered. There was no danger. Except to my work, if someone interfered."

Sara said, "It seems I'm always apologizing for some gaffe, but, as you're raging anyway . . ." She took hold of a brakeman's switch handle, mounted next to a power cell, and pulled it back, as if she were stopping a locomotive.

An iron section of the wall swung outward, revealing a chute-trap littered with melted pieces of royal goblets, scepters, a princess' neck shield, and a battered, golden crown, its jewels popped.

Sara said, "The ship's fuel supply, or what's left of it?"

"Looting, Miss Duncan?"

"Captain, even you should appreciate how much has been done to make the *Nautilus* functional, while you were waiting—"

"For the hangman?" Nemo took the heat-twisted neck shield.

"Actually, this is another of your locked-away secrets, until just this moment." Sara picked the scepter from the rest. "The submersible that runs on treasure? Pirate booty, melted for fuel?"

"To the narrow-minded, it seems like fantasy," Nemo tossed the shield back into the treasure locker. "These are nothing, the leavings after the purities were extracted."

Sara said, "Then how, how does it work?"

"You haven't gone that far with your speculations?"

"When you were—captured—the newspapers were filled with them. Father made sure to read me every word."

"Before tucking you in, no doubt."

"Yes, I've dreamed about the *Nautilus* since I was a little girl."

"So now, you imagine she's yours."

"Just that I'd do anything to get her sailing again."

Nemo looked at her, holding the scepter as if she were about to give a royal decree, or cast a spell. "You put me in mind of the Captain of a pirate galleon, sunk off the Carolina coast. We were gathering fuel from the wreck, on the bottom about a year, crew eaten to the bones, and he was at the wheel, still clutching that idiotic bauble. Long-dead, but he wouldn't let go, so his hands came with it."

"You put the gold to better use than he would."

Nemo picked up the ruined crown. "One of the few inter-views I ever gave, a reporter from Guinea who seemed sympa-thetic to my goals, wrote a story about my desecrating underwater graves. 'The ghoul of the deep.' Did your father send you to sleep with that one?"

"No, sir," Sara said.

"It's always been easier to show me a monster, rather than look at any underlying reasons for my actions. Cleansing the oceans of man-made trash, putting it to practical use."

"They used the word 'genius' in descriptions."

"Usually with 'insane,' when they weren't trying to convince the world I didn't exist at all."

He tapped the front of a power cell with the crown's edge. "Those who saw our inner works were impressed with the stream of molten gold, instead of the energy being drawn through my own fission process. Arronax, at least, attempted a balanced view."

A point from the crown broke in Nemo's fingers as crumbling clay. "The pure metals extracted, the rest, harmless and back to the sand."

"A thousand dollars' of gold, and run underwater for two years?"

"Longer. Much."

Sara shook her head. "That's world-changing."

"No steam or smoke, because of containment. No toxins at all. The true reason I was imprisoned."

"Captain, it's the lives lost . . ."

Nemo added to the gold trash, recessed the vault back in place. "You're too naïve to see, it was my thinking that was the threat, not my ability to sink their warships."

"Your ideas, needed now."

He said, "The *Nautilus* is. I inspected your amateur efforts, some are decently effective, but I'm the only one who can rebuild her heart, and we've nothing but crude scraps. It won't do."

Sara half-smiled. "Captain, like you, my father doesn't allow failure."

Nemo said, "My ship took years to perfect, and a resurrection will not be instantaneous, despite your father or President Grant's panicked demands."

He kicked the melted circuit plate across the floor. "For your purposes, the *Nautilus* is useless. At rest is one thing, taking the sea, another. She can't withstand a voyage."

Sara pulled a strip of silverized gold from the scepter's handle and twisted it into wire before threading around the melted panel's contacts.

She threw a toggle, descending the hatch elevator, and said, "She's not going to keep you prisoner, or stop you from doing what you need to do. The wire's melting, and the *Nautilus* needs you up top, Captain."

The spines were jointed needles, with the edges of razors, and mounted on a spring mechanism that darted them out from the spheres at all angles. Sara stood by the objects lined up on the dock, as Nemo climbed from the *Nautilus,* then approached.

Sara nodded. "The parts you fashioned for her, from your own workshop on Vulcania, and still in their very unusual containers."

There were six spheres, each two feet in diameter, with the spines protruding from a spongy surface, and tags hanging from them, labeled CASE #3579.

Nemo stepped onto the dock. "All of these, confiscated, and used as evidence against me."

"How? None can be opened. When I found them, the spines jutted out, almost took my hand off."

Nemo was close to one of the spheres. "My special design, from the Japanese Roku fish. Were you speaking?"

"My father and I were discussing transport, and it was like those things attacked."

"Speaking was your mistake; the audio port is built into the surface." He leaned into the object, saying flatly, "Retract now."

The spines adjusted, pulling into the sphere's surface, then lying flat, creating a solid, outer shell. The others retracted, shells snapping into place, one after the other. Tin windups marching in line.

Nemo held his hand up to Sara, stopping her words. "They're equipped with a tuning fork that reacts only to my voice's vibrations. Another voice triggers their enemy defense, the spines of the Roku."

She whispered, "You don't know the trouble of getting these things here."

One sphere quivered, but the spines didn't eject, and Nemo said, "I did my job well, so the trouble was considerable. As I planned."

He stopped, taken aback at the sight of a painting in a gilt frame leaning against a crate, its subject masked with rubberized fabric.

Sara said, "I found it washing in one of the access corridors by the library, when I first came aboard."

"How much was damaged?"

"It wasn't," Sara said, "but I covered it, because I thought the unveiling should be yours. Alone."

Nemo's expression clouded as he picked up the painting with one hand. "This cloying gesture changes nothing about my assessment of your efforts." He picked up a sphere with the other.

"There's little hope these components weren't destroyed by Naval clumsiness, but I'll allow you to put up notices for crew."

He started back down the access ladder, careful with the

painting and sphere, and said, "Men I can rely on, for each position I designate. My decision, not your father's."

The hatch closed above him, with Sara on the dock, her hands balled fists, whispering, "Arrogant—"

She never got to add "bastard" before the razored spheres on the dock reacted to her voice, and sprung open.

16

HEARTS OF MACHINES AND MEN

Nemo grasped the sphere by its sides, where the razors would slice to the bone, and applied exact pressure, his shoulder burning, splitting it open as a hinged egg.

Inside, the specialty fuses and micro-gears for the navigation mechanisms were complete, the wiring undamaged. They were his most complex and minute work for the *Nautilus*, the electrics smaller than the wings of a fly.

Nemo's pride surged as he laid out the components in specific order, keeping his back to the painting between the arms of his Captain's chair, avoiding it, until finishing all preparations.

Then, as if hearing a familiar voice, Nemo moved to the painting. He separated the cloth from the frame at the edges, lifting the fabric as if it were a lace veil.

He always saw the eyes first, as if the rest of the face wasn't even there. Their perfect blue, with the specks of green around the iris, had been captured better than any dull photograph.

They were dancingly alive, and exactly as Nemo remembered them on their wedding day.

The painting fit exactly into the raised corners of the alcove above the desk in Nemo's quarters.

Hidden lights bathed it in white from the sides and below. Nemo took a step back from the image of his wife and toddling son in their linen blouses. He sat on the edge of his bed, his family smiling at him from the very desk where he'd designed his submarine.

He choked back his feelings, swallowing an old scream.

Nemo's hand went to a wall-dial, rotating it once, shifting the color of the cabin lights from white to red, the cocoa-skinned faces of his wife and son fading with the color change. Numbered diagrams appeared across their portrait, like emerging tattoos.

Still turning, the red lights became a deeper crimson. The family was now a large, multi-coded blueprint of the *Nautilus'* inner workings. The secret plans for the heart of the ship.

17

WATERFRONT

Sara was looking for the legless man.

A cold, Atlantic gust picked up her cape, allowing her a shoulder glance for the man in the small-wheeled cart. He'd been following as she went from tavern to tavern, tacking up notices for a "submersible ship" crew.

Propelling himself with wooden blocks in each hand, he pushed forward along the pier, his frock's coattail dragging. Sara had caught only glimpses: tangled hair over a face, legless torso bent forward, long arms in motion as if he were swimming.

He moved quickly, keeping tight to the shadows, then into a bit of light as Sara fast-stepped to The Cat's Skull, left crew notices, then waited in the doorway. Looking. She couldn't see him; just knew he was there.

"Hello? Can you say something? Tell me your name?"

No response. She started for Buzzard's Seat, and heard the blocks against the pier again, the squeak of the wheels. Buzzard's was the worst of the waterfront holes, shattered windows planked over, slits of light escaping along with sounds of broken glass and laughing screams.

She tossed a handful of leaflets into the air, hoping the wind would scatter them against this man, the white papers giving him up in the dark.

The leaflets blew across the pier, to nothing.

The man in the cart had wheeled through the alley on the other side of Buzzard's, found a place by the barrels stacked opposite its front doors. He drew one of two knives from a leather-tuck sewn into his coat sleeve, ready to throw, eyeing Sara as she went inside.

"Ye mariners all, as ye pass by! Come in and drink if you are dry. Come spend, me lads, your money brisk, and pop your nose in a jug of this!"

Sara tore old crew notices off the tack board, replacing them with the call for the *Nautilus,* as Whalers in the corner, passing a brown jug, bellowed to the rafters. Two of the Whalers, huge men with Maori tattoos mapping their faces, sang, and fixed on Sara.

"You got no idea what the hell you're about," an old Sailor said, leaning in close to Sara from behind, stinking of sausage and turned rum.

His words stuck to her cheek as a warm fog. "Me second sight's going, so I know you're holding some kind of secret about that boat."

She inched away. "Just putting up the notice."

"But there ain't nothing saying nothing about the voyage. What aren't you tellin'?"

"Come for the call, then, and see."

The rest of the crew in Buzzard's were made of stained leather, salt-hard rope, and low wages. Seafarers around the tables, having their drink, imagining Sara stripped. Or, wanting her to move from the board, so the barkeep could read the notice out loud, for those who never learned their letters.

She turned, meeting the sick yellow of the old Sailor's face. He pressed himself closer, hand vise-gripped around her arm. "Smile, and take joy in their song. Call me Jess, and pretend me your lover or your brother, just don't let go."

"And when I'm in my grave and dead, And all my sorrows are past and fled, Transform me then into a fish, And let me swim in a jug of this!"

The chorus of Whalers howled, with the two still watching. One slipped a straight razor from a pocket, letting the blade fall open against his decorated fingers.

Jess had Sara even tighter, "Start for them doors, and don't give nothing off with your eyes."

She looked to the bar, thinking she could grab a whiskey bottle with her free hand, and smash his skull. But she couldn't reach. Instead, Sara nodded, arm numbing, as Jess pushed her through the batwings, to the waterfront pier.

The Whalers leapt from their table, smashing whiskey jugs, and charged for the still-swinging doors. One with the razor, the other, bringing a revolver from his belt.

On the pier, Jess pulled Sara along as he ran, charging for a row of docked fishing boats. She twisted back, yanking down her arm and bringing up her knee, square between his legs. Sudden move to the sack, bolting him to the ground.

"Sweet Jesus' tears!"

Sara could see a throwing knife in Jess' shoulder, blood spraying around flat steel, as he rolled to his feet, then ran for the next pool of light from the pier lamps, showing up a net-maker's shed. Jess scrambled onto its falling-in roof, slipped, climbed over.

A Whaler stopped running, drew down the revolver, and fired, slugs sparking off a weather vane, missing Jess as he fell from the shed roof to a heap of rotting sail cloth. Just a dark shape now, tumbling away and gone, with a hoot of laughter.

The Whalers chased after, one of them yelling, *"Whiore hume!"*

"Maori. Means 'coward,' and I wholly agree," the legless man said, rolling toward Sara from behind the stacked barrels. "Any man who would use a woman as a shield."

Sara stepped back. He braked himself with his hands, then stood, stretching his long legs out of the false bottom of the cart. "You should retract your awe, Miss Duncan. You're working on the most advanced submersible ship ever imagined."

His hair came back from his young face with his hands as he said, "This cart's nothing but a sideshow trick, put to better use."

He opened his filthy overcoat, displaying the silver star of the Secret Service pinned to a leather inset by his waist, holding more knives and a small caliber weapon. "I am J. T. Maston, agent assigned to keep you from danger. Not an easy task, with your wanderings and attitude."

Sara said, "What—who sent you? You've been scaring me to death all night!"

Maston nodded toward the Whalers still chasing down the pier, "More than that lot?"

She spit her words, "So you're some kind of a damn Pinkerton?"

"A higher measure than that, Miss."

"An agent, is that a spy? What does that mean?"

Maston took a padlocked case from his rolling cart, handed it to Sara. "From your father. And the knife that released you from the rum-pot, from me. Quite a difficult throw, actually, to release, not to kill."

She struggled with the heavy case, cape billowing behind her. "Am I supposed to be impressed with all this bizarre circumstance? I don't believe a word of it!"

He rolled his shoulders, neck cracking, to stand at full height. "If you're thinking of chucking that into the ocean, I wouldn't. Neither your father, nor the mission would benefit. At least you know there's a protective eye on you. That should provide some comfort."

"It doesn't."

Maston kicked the cart off the edge of the pier, heard the splash, and said to Sara, "You're to install that device on the *Nautilus* immediately. Your father's composed a letter of instruction."

Sharp steel prongs were inches from Sara's face the moment she opened the stable door. It was deep-shadowed and dark when Nemo yanked her inside, bringing the pitchfork to his shoulder, a hand quickly over her mouth.

His look was fierce, but aimed toward the other side of the barn. Sara nodded, and the hand came down. She kept completely still; he angled the pitchfork and launched. It arched precisely, missing the ceiling by an inch before coming down in the hayloft, piercing its target.

Jess' scream was a scalded cat's as he crashed to the floor, his flailing hands grabbing for the prongs protruding from his shoulder blades. Cobwebs, hay, and dust from the loft rained after him.

"I knew a man who was good with a harpoon," Nemo said. "A bad-tempered fool, but he had abilities."

He yanked the fork from Jess' back, twisting for just enough pain, and said, "Explain yourself!"

Jess sat up. "Trying for some sleep, which ain't possible! I already been stabbed once! What the hell's all this? You a cop, or a stable boy?"

Nemo held the prongs at the Sailor. "I am the Captain of the *Nautilus*."

"Holdin' that sticker, you're lookin' like the Poseidon on my belly."

He pointed to Sara, who lit a shielded candle. "Perfect! More pain from that girl! She said there was some crewin', and got me cut tonight! Twice!"

"And I was almost killed, thanks to this creature!" Sara said.

Nemo pulled Jess up by the scruff. "Your chance to speak."

"A pair of humpers tried a robbery, and I took the young lady out of harm's way."

"Put me in it, you mean!"

"I imagine you're both culpable." Nemo regarded the Sailor. "Name your skills."

"Ship's carpenter since I was a pup, and know my riggings like nobody's business. Right? I need a doc, and strong drink."

"Step out that door, you'll likely be skinned." Nemo relaxed his grip. "And myself, shot. How many times have you been jailed?"

Jess was doubled over, blood lacing his side from his sliced arm, the prong wounds spotting his back. "Jail, or prison? And what countries do you count?"

"I've worn the chains myself. Sign on, your history on land is erased, but you'll obey the laws of the *Nautilus*. Break them, and punishment will be severe."

"Oh, I been keel-hauled," Jess said.

"I have no doubt. How many times shot or stabbed?"

"Shot three times, in Singapore mostly. I can't count about stabbed, but got cut anew tonight, and now, that damn pitchfork! Second time with a pitchfork, actually."

"What do you call yourself?"

He looked to Sara, then to Nemo. "Usually I go by Jess."

"The *Nautilus* is my creation, and the crew will be totally obedient to her needs. You prepared to accept these conditions? I need sailors, not dock rats."

"Paying off in gold?"

"You will be rewarded," Nemo said.

"Call the tune, and I'll be dancin' to it."

Nemo was in the far stable, saying to Sara, "I approve this man. Sign him on, patch his injuries."

Jess said, "Hold up, where's your ship at, this *Nautilus*?"

Nemo cranked open the stable floor to the dock ramp. Jess backed onto a hay bale, pain-wincing, but hooting a laugh. "There's *your* secret, girl! I knew somethin' like a bad dream would come out of tonight!"

The mirrors behind the curved lens spun pinwheel-fast, while Jess' voice blurted, scratchy and dim, from the small audio-horn: "I ain't never been in no goddamned iron turtle a-fore!"

Electricity glowed around the lens edges of the Phono-tele-Photo, a special communications device mounted on Duncan's desk. He sat before it, adjusting the power of the currents and jotting notes as Sara's face took shape on the mirrors from streaks and scrambles to a crisply defined image behind the lens.

He spoke into the microphone-horn. "You've always followed instructions well, daughter."

Sara's voice was clear in response: "We both know that's not true."

Nemo, standing beside Sara on the bridge of the *Nautilus*, looked directly into the sister device, its small electrical charges dancing erratically on the spinning mirrors, making the image of Duncan it was receiving from the White House a moving jigsaw puzzle, battling to come together.

Jess, on the stairs to the belowdecks, said, "Cap, I don't know how much more I can take in! This turtle's like somethin' from the moon!"

"Another world, indeed," Nemo said, then leaned into the jittering Duncan on the screen. "This device, my prototype, given to Arronax's secretary Conseil before my arrest. *Mine!*"

Duncan's image cleared, and he said, "Actually ours, after Monsieur Conseil's heart failure. Your plans, modified with my technology, and installed by my daughter. This is a true collaboration, Captain."

"On a device to use against me, for espionage," Nemo said. "Implanted on my ship, without my permission."

"Your mission demands constant communication. To that end, the *Nautilus* must sail by tomorrow morning."

"Or, we face our dual place on the gallows?"

"Don't think it can't happen!" Grant's voice was thunder through the speaker. "You've been given all you need, Captain! If you're not underway by sunrise, your ship'll be stormed, and you, taken!"

"Orders are forthcoming. Congratulations on your design, Captain. It will change the world," Duncan said, before the Phono-tele-Photo's curved screen blackened.

Nemo turned from his invention. "The voice of tyrants."

Jess said, "Somebody's got a tit in the wringer! Apologies, miss."

"It's how I'd describe it," Sara said.

Nemo looked at her. "I'm not fool enough to believe your father and Grant aren't listening still. You have a lot to make up for, Miss Duncan."

Grant was half in the office doorway as Nemo's last words came over the device, the speaker inches from Duncan, transcribing every word: "You and the dock rat are to the rudder cables, then to the crewing."

Duncan took off his glasses, rubbed the sleep away, "You heard it from our electric ears: final preparations. Nemo's a man of the sea, he's got to return, and mission accomplished, as planned."

Grant said, "The mission's gotten a hell of a lot tougher."

He looked out a corner window, frosted glass tilted, at cannons moved onto the White House driveway, shells stacked alongside, new troops riding in.

"There never was a time when there wasn't some way to prevent the drawing of the sword."

"I recall that speech."

"It's surely haunting me now—blood's been spilled not a hundred yards from here. And now, New York, the Bishop. These countries think we're slaughtering their own, and I can't blame them. If Nemo's mission fails, the gates of hell are wide open."

Duncan said, "I know that, sir."

Grant asked, "Does your daughter?" then placed General Sigel's damaged Union Army ring on the desk, beside the Phono.

18

INVADERS FROM ALL QUARTERS

The etched letters of the Remington Arms Company circled Fulmer's head like a crooked halo as he backed against a rifle case, thumbing a small roll of bills he'd just pulled from a denim front pocket.

A whiskey-voice hollered, "No American Confederate trash! Don't be tryin' that again!"

"It ain't as if you don't know where I am," Fulmer said, finding some Federal notes. "I'm good, I'm in."

The crates of repeating rifles and cases of ammunition were eight high and five deep against the cargo hold's rust-bucket walls, strapped and canvassed in, with narrow ways between them leading to the center of the hold, and the nightly poker game.

Fulmer snaked the crate-maze to the barrelhead, and the three players seated around it. Their faces, all pulped and scarred, were stories of sea voyages crewed, and battles continents away.

Red, nicknamed for the blood permanently swimming across his eyes, made room for Fulmer, slapping the young man on the back as he dropped money into the sparse kitty, then perched on some boxed handguns.

Red grinned. "From the young'un, all Union scrip."

He picked up the deck, and tried to shuffle with fingers that had been broken too many times, bending the cards. Fulmer took the deck, started to deal, peeling cards off around the barrel, the last landing in front of Tim, a toothless sot, shreds of an old front page slopping from his jacket.

Tim checked his poker hand, smacking his black gums. "A few years ago, we'd a been a sittin' duck for Nemo, and his underwater contraption, ain't that right, boy? A ship full of weapons? And you, alongside him, making us a target? Right? Did you aim the guns?"

Fulmer said, "The *Nautilus* didn't use guns."

Red dropped two cards, drew two. "How long you goin' to beat that horse?"

Tim's whiskey voice didn't let up: "They say Nemo's just hung in some Virginia shit-hole, is all. Must make our boy sleep easier, the man he turned over, finally gunnysacked."

Red said, "Pitched in as much as run your mouth, you'd be a damn sight better sailor."

"I just want to know what kind of man helps put his own captain in irons." Tim took his draw from Fulmer, saying, "You sided with a pirate, then went coward."

Fulmer fanned his cards, kept his voice level. "My reasons are my own, just like I kept my own for shooting any son of a bitch who approached when I was riding for the Pony Express. Why don't we bust open one of these cases, see if I've lost my aim."

"Been at the rum since breakfast, makes friends into enemies." Red threw down an ace-high straight. "But also, back again, so let's all have a little pull, and play right, since I've drawn the winnin' hand."

Tim swept the cards aside. "No point, because this Fulmer can't be trusted by nobody," then laid a curved Arab blade, with ivory handle, on the barrel.

"I'm callin' you a milkin' bitch of a coward, boy."

"And, not for the first time," Fulmer said, his body tensed, but making no sudden moves or letting his voice pitch. "You got one chance to use that Shafra, mate. Then I'll gut you with it."

Tim's hand was on the knife when the web wrapped around his neck, drawing in tight, a monofilament line garroting him. He choked out, sprawling to the floor, as acid sprayed him from above: searing his skin, peeling it from muscle, then bone, leaving a skull, with bits of dissolving cords in the throat, and burning hair curling.

The spider thing's mechanical legs were squat on a stack of rifle crates, its four-feet-across, blue steel body perched over Tim's corpse; a gargoyle high on a cathedral wall.

Red didn't move. Couldn't move. The nightmare crawled in front of him, jagged metal spurs on its eight piston-legs digging deep into the wooden crate, holding its position.

Its vaguely human head reminded Red of the shrunken one he'd seen in Ecuador, even as it rotated on a corkscrewed neck, tracking the enemies in front of it. An eyeball-lens centered the metal "face," jaws splitting just below it, opening sideways and revealing small, brass nozzles for the acid spray and webbing.

Fulmer dared a step, the thing reacted; internal gear works turning. He grabbed the Shafra knife. It leapt for him. He stabbed at its metal body, the legs churning wildly, spurs slicing, before he powered the knife's tip through a flexible piece under the spider's opening jaws.

The blade cut tubing and the thing misted acid, burning Fulmer's neck before he hurled it aside and charged the rifle stacks.

Smashing the lid of a case, splitting wood with his elbow, he ripped through oilcloth and grabbed a Remington repeater. An ammunition box collapsed with a single kick. Bullets were loaded in moments, the weapon cocked.

Fulmer sensed something behind him, whipped around. Two spiders, on top of a stack, blackened shapes against the cargo hold's lamplight, tilted forward on their pneumatics, jaws separating sideways and dripping corrosive liquid.

He shot both. Rapid fire.

One blew apart, the other spun into the air, a tin can off a fence post, coming down, the webbing springing from its mandibles as a membrane, before becoming strong cords. He shot again, the slug blue-sparking along the thing's side, but smashing a rear leg, then dove out of the way of the spreading web, firing the last slug that ripped the spider in half.

Gear works, congealed webbing, and shattered eye lenses splayed across the floor as Fulmer grabbed another box of ammo and cut around the stack of rifles to the center of the hold.

He kept the repeater at his shoulder as he had when coming down on the Paiute attackers of the Carson River Station, shooting from horseback at full gallop. His arms were crooked perfectly, absorbing the kick, as he fired with the rifle's lever action, the gun a part of him. But he wasn't aiming at men. These were odd machines, and the constant flame from the barrel was dragon's breath erupting, killing one mechanical after another, bullet-punching them into junk.

Rifle empty, Fulmer rolled out of the way as a crewman plunged into the hold from the top deck, screaming, a spider neck-clamped around him, soaking his face with acid. The corpse slammed the floor, the flesh bubbling into nothing.

Fulmer's voice was a raging howl, beyond words, clubbing the thing with the gun's stock, splitting metal hide and knocking it off the dead man. He reloaded the magazine, swung the rifle around, cocking the lever, but pulled up as the spider's webbing whipped Red's head and throat.

Red clawed at the fibers, the thing propelling itself to the back of his skull, spurs instantly digging into muscle, its leg-pistons locking onto his shoulders.

Fulmer leveled the Remington, blew two spiders on the floor apart, even as he dove for Red. But there was no shot to take, unless it was to kill his friend.

Red's cries for help were paralyzed by the spider's grip, and tears ran from his bloody eyes even as he reached out, taking Fulmer's hand, pulling him in.

Fulmer brought down all his strength on the spider, pounding, breaking off a steel leg, stabbing it, over and over, with the jagged end. He struck gears. Electricity sparked as the remaining legs started jerking without direction, the internals gnashing.

Fulmer clamped a grip around the thing and pulled as Red slumped over, unconscious.

Around them, mechanicals swarmed through portholes, dropped from upper decks, descending on webbing like marionette strings, their acid spray dissolving wooden crates to mush.

Their aim was deliberate, the nozzled spray eating weapons and ammo down to the brass, then spattering against the hot glass of the lamps hanging above the rifles. Whale oil burst from the lamp globes, the flames spiraling to the sloppy mix of dissolving wood and black powder ammunition.

Fulmer struggled to free Red from the mechanical, but the thing's legs were closing into themselves, springs tightening. Rifle-smashing one last time, he finally stopped the gears, then shouldered Red under his arms and charged for the crew ladder.

Smoke strangled the air, but Fulmer kept the Remington firing, picking off spiders attacking four at a time from shadowed corners. He reached the ladder, emptied a last round through mechanized jaws and out the back of a metal skull, took hold of the railing, and began his way up, balancing Red on his back.

Feet away, the weapon crates stacked in this hold of Her Majesty's Ship *Mariner* browned with the flames. Then, were engulfed.

A slop of fetid water and brined sludge poured over Jess as he worked to fit the oxygen net on the *Nautilus'* air generator. He wiped his face, spit out what he could as Nemo bent down to where he was lying under a crisscross of pipes and machine works.

Nemo handed him a long-bladed knife with a splayed end. "Corners first."

Jess took the blade. An inch from his nose were large panels made of a pinkish, almost translucent substance, veined ridges lacing it.

Jess slotted the corners. "This is flimsier than a whore's wedding dress; it ain't gonna hold no water!"

"That's not the purpose. Water collects on the surface as fish gills, when it washes back to the ocean, bits of air are trapped in the ridges, then pumped into the ship."

"So this turtle, she's actually got lungs and such?"

Nemo said, "If you've done your job correctly."

Jess side-crawled from under the pipes. "Guess we'll find out when we're under them waves, snakin' along the ocean bottom."

Jess brought the knife quickly to his chest, razored side out, his eyes fixed beyond Nemo into the lower-deck passageway, where the Maori Whalers hefted a riveted steel case, large enough to trap two men.

Their tattooed faces were demonic in the dim light, and they stopped in their tracks as they heard Jess say, "Captain, you brought some truly shitty trouble onto your ship."

Nemo's hands were instant motion, snatching back the blade, air-slicing a barrier between Jess and the Whalers. Even with his injury, he manipulated the knife with defensive artistry, causing the Whalers to lean off, their lips pulled back over file-sharpened teeth. Jess spit.

"We'll need harpooners for our quarry," Nemo said, "and these two can do the work of ten."

Jess took a large iron wrench, held it as a battle-ax. "But what about me, expecting a throat-cuttin'?"

"Any killing," Nemo chose, "executions, will be by my sanction only, according to the laws of the *Nautilus*."

"Oh, there's fancy comfort, that won't mean a damn when I'm cornered at the engine room."

Nemo angled the knife, and his words, at the Whalers: "Personal issues have no bearing on your duty, and if there is conflict, the punishment I mete out will be severe."

"Them two understanding all that blather?"

Nemo brought the knife down, a sharp blur, slicing open a pocket on a Whaler's coat, then grabbing a 9mm revolver from it. He asked, *"Matau?"*

The Whalers shrugged, bobbed their heads in agreement, before continuing down the passage, holding the massive case aloft.

"Cap, you know what a Nuckelavee is?"

"Of course," Nemo said. "The Scottish monster, from the moors."

"It don't matter if it's in Scotland or Egypt or on the moon, the worst of the worst, all slapped together and sewn up in a bag of flesh. That's them two."

"And yourself?"

"Innocent as a newborn babe compared to them. I don't have to talk their talk to know they're up to no good," Jess said. "I'll club one of 'em to jelly if I have to, and take my chance with the other."

A northerly current took the HMS *Mariner*'s lifeboat away from the sinking wreckage and last explosive blasts. Fulmer watched the strip of flames on the horizon fade to nothing, all color gone, before collapsing in the stern with his rifle and the boat's canteen.

He had eased Red onto the boat's middle seat, tucking his jacket under his head for a pillow. Red tried to say thanks, but Fulmer stopped him, not being able to watch the hanging skin left by the acid jostle and flap when he tried to speak. Fulmer prayed for Red's sleep, since there was no medical kit, no place for grog or a yellow-filled pipe; anything to cut the pain. Just sleep.

The acid sea spider that had done it to him was in the burlap sack, soaked with the blood of the crew, and tied off with Fulmer's belt. He tucked it under the bow, keeping the Remington cradled with him in the stern, so if there was any movement in the bag, a spasm or dribbling of acid, he could shoot it to pieces.

Fulmer was used to the ocean; it was his work, just like riding for the Pony Express. But he hated being lost, that frustration of not recognizing where you've been, or where you're headed. On the desert, trying to find his way back to an old wagon pass buried in a sandstorm, or on the water.

Except there's nothing as lost as drifting in the ocean on a starless night. That's where Fulmer and Red were, bleeding, and tonight, blind. Because the sky and water had become one, without a horizon; just blank nothing that surrounded them, and went on forever.

The cries for help that had him jump to his feet with the Remington weren't cries at all. But whistles, coming from a good ways out, but splitting apart, and dying as an echo over the miles of water, making it impossible to determine their original direction.

The whistles got louder, then steadied, and were followed by: "Hey, jackasses!"

Fulmer called out, "Easy on, we're here! Can you get to us?"

He heard something splashing in the waves, hands paddling closer. Chopping cold water through the dark. Someone coming in, but still couldn't see. Fulmer slapped at the water with an oar's blade, leaning over the side of the boat, reaching out as far as he could, toward the sound of more paddling and more swearing. Finally, the roof came into view, burned tin and wood, a piece of the *Mariner's* side cabin, with a voice behind it. "Jesus, boy, were you gonna let me swim home?"

Fulmer held the oar as a Cook from the *Mariner* swam around the edge of the wreckage, held on, and pulled himself into the lifeboat.

"You two didn't waste any time gettin' this for yourselves!"

Fulmer said, "We were loading people in, when a blast tossed us from the ship. Crashed in the water, lost all the supplies."

Cook said, "You got water? Real water?"

"The canteen. Who else is alive?"

Cook bent to where Red was lying, looked away from his face, found the canteen, and drank. He took too long of a sip, wiped his mouth on his sleeve. "Who the hell knows, and I could care less. When those little monsters came at us, every man for himself, right?"

Fulmer looked to Red, who had rolled over, and opened one eye, and said, "He saved me."

Cook reeled. "Jesus, I thought you were finding a place to dump the body! But I know you picked up some beauties before the whole thing went to shit."

Fulmer regarded Cook, glancing over at the Remington. "What are you talking about?"

"Diamonds. Cut diamonds, everywhere. Blues mostly. Scattered all over the hold, you just had to pick 'em up."

Red said, "From where? What is this?"

"That brought him back to life," Cook said. "You were so busy shooting them little windup what-have-yous, you didn't see no priceless shit they left behind? From their bellies, little cut diamonds. And you didn't help yourself?"

Fulmer grabbed back the canteen, checked the water. "I guess I was too busy."

"You got it comin' out of your ears, boy." Cook nodded toward the sack jammed under the bow point. "What you got there, Christmas dinner?"

Fulmer said, "I'm the survivor of a sinking, and I've been through this mill before. Lots of questions, and more doubt. That bag'll answer for me."

Cook was standing by the bow, the sea and the night just a field of deeper blacks behind him; if either man had stepped another foot away, they would have been impossible to see. Cook angled himself toward Red, who was still lying on his side but watching. One burned eye, and in incredible pain.

Cook said, "You still got that tattoo of the *Nautilus* on your arm. You're cattle, branded by Captain Nemo."

"I think I just saved your life, didn't I?"

"That was a chivalrous thing to do. That cowboy code, Pony Express? But you still didn't like paying your poker debts, that was the rumor around ship."

Fulmer said, "Again, I pulled you out of the water."

"Water, that's right. You're Pony Express, and I'm French Foreign Legion, but I was also a ship's cook, so you have no secrets. But we both know about water, and how valuable it is when you don't have it."

"More than diamonds?" Fulmer ventured.

Cook said, "I felt that canteen, you got barely enough for two for the next days, and no way for three."

Red said, "We should leave you to drown?"

"That makes more sense than sharing water with a corpse," Cook said, making an instant move with his leg, swooping under the Remington's stock, flipping it around, and catching it. In a single motion, it was in his hands and aimed perfectly between Fulmer's eyes.

"Half your water for half my diamonds."

Fulmer said, "That's my friend."

"You're a fool."

Red shoved the blade through Cook's back, between his last ribs, and into his lungs. He heaved forward, mouth surprised, his scream a choke of blood as he lurched across the lifeboat.

Fulmer stuck out a leg, tumbling Cook into the water, then looked back at Red, who still had the stiletto in his hand.

Red said, "Not—dead—yet, amigo."

Fulmer held up the canteen, sloshed the water inside. "Drink?"

19

FORTRESS

Maston pried open the baby coffin, its rotting lid splitting apart in his hands, and removed slabbed bars of gold and silver, setting them out in precise fashion before Sara. She stood by the table, an engraved map of the world under its glass top, holding her cape defiantly tight around her, not reaching for the gold set upon it.

He pointed to one of the bar's serial numbers. "Denver Smelting Works, which means absolute purity."

"Who'd you knife to get this?"

"Not a knife." Maston held a silver ingot. "The subjects were low-down thieves. I adapted their attitudes, confiscated this lot, and am now presenting it to you, as ordered."

"Did the 'subjects' know you had legs?"

Maston had been passed a message, nodded, and turned away from Sara, leaving her in the center of the city-block-long room with the precious metals, surrounded by the military.

Stifling hot, the room had been part of the Richmond Underground Slave Railroad, but was now a steel-buttressed stronghold, cramped floor to ceiling with weapon caches and all forms of field supplies.

Grant moved to Sara from a mapping station, advisors at his elbows, guards ready. He gave whispered instructions and bit off the end of a cigar before saying to her, "You reported the *Nautilus* as shipshape, and now you have your fuel."

Sara finally picked up a bar. "Yes, sir. Eight ounces could keep her underwater for a year."

He signed a sheaf of papers. "We don't have that much time." He handed them off to a faceless secretary. "Your crew?"

"The Captain trusts prison misfits, and anyone who's been shot."

Grant asked, "As much as he trusts you?"

Sara said, "That remains to be seen."

"Mr. Duncan."

Duncan lifted the map table's glass, placing a small tin Union Jack in the carved area indicating United States territorial waters. He rested his hands on his daughter's shoulders.

"Right there," Grant said. "A British ship's been sunk, with no known survivors. You'll be given coordinates, the first point of Nemo's investigations."

Sara's eyes widened. She looked to Grant, who continued, "You understand what this could mean? We're preparing our Navy to engage, and if the British attack first, it won't matter what the *Nautilus* can or can't do on its mission, it becomes a warship. *My warship*, you understand that as well?"

Sara said, "Nemo would never allow it, sir."

"He has no say."

Her words tumbled fast to Grant. "I'm sure there's some type of self-destruct mechanism, so any attempt to commandeer the *Nautilus* at sea would be useless."

"Then find and disable it. If the *Nautilus* is going to be a weapon again, it will be for our victory."

Duncan looked away from Sara, and she said, "I'll say it straight to you, sir. Nemo's impossibly arrogant and a martinet, but also a genius. I've never seen anything like what he's built, and I know he's figured a way that only he can determine his submarine's use."

Grant said, "You talk too much like your father."

"The *Nautilus'* discovery mission will succeed, and we will be exonerated from these attacks," Duncan said, taking General Sigel's Union Army ring from his vest. The melted areas had been repaired, and the ring's base made slightly larger, with a small stud extending from its side. "But policy is to prepare for the worst-case scenario."

"That's why this room, this place," Sara said.

"You're safe here, dear."

"That's a comforting word."

She regarded the ring. "You've never given me jewelry before, but this isn't that kind of gift, is it, Father?"

Grant said, "Belonged to one of our own, already dead in this fight. I can allow one minute for your consideration."

"Of what?"

Duncan pressed the stud, freeing a needle the size of a bee's stinger from the ring's side. He said, "The base, filled with a derivative of black widow's venom."

Duncan's words hung over Sara's puzzled expression, then he quietly added, "Dear, if Nemo gets out of hand, protect yourself first, always, but you're to use this ring, then find your way off the *Nautilus.*"

"You know that submarine as well as he does," Grant said. "I'm wagering you can captain it, if need be."

"I can't imagine—"

The stinger automatically retracted before Sara got out: "But I've never killed anyone—"

Duncan said, "No, not kill. It will render him—unable."

"Does that mean paralyzed? How can you ask me?"

"I know full well what I'm asking," Grant said, realizing that Sara's eyes and his daughter's were identically green. "And there's damn little I hate more, but the operation's now a combat mission, and you've been trained, and prepared."

Sara shook her head, as if to clear away everything she'd just heard. "Yes, only to get the *Nautilus* back to sea—which has been a privilege."

Grant said, "Nemo could be in league with the saboteurs behind this insanity, dragging us right into the fire. Don't ever lose sight of what he is."

"But I'm not a soldier! Nowhere near!"

Grant said, "But you'll be our eyes and ears at sea, and you might have to take action. Might."

Duncan took her hand, "Dear, we'll always be with you, that's why the tele-photo, but if you're not up to the rest, it's all right."

Sara said, "The tele-device was to observe and report!"

Grant sliced: "Forget our families' friendship. You're an appointed special operative for the United States of America, and your Commander in Chief is putting forth an assignment. And yes, you'll be in harm's way."

"Daughter, I believe completely the Captain will stay his course; this—stopping him—won't be necessary."

Sara took her father's words. "But we have to prepare for the worst . . ."

Grant relit his cigar. "The minute's done. What say you, girl?"

She looked to her father's wet eyes, then to the map's markings of all sinkings and latest enemy warship positions. "I understand what's at stake. It's bloody enormous. I just never thought I'd be the one with the burden."

"A hellish thing for sure," Grant said, "but it won't be yours alone."

Sara kept her eyes downward, but opened her shaking hand in agreement. Her father carefully placed Sigel's ring in her palm, and she closed her fingers around it.

Sara pushed the wall section from behind, stepping out of the passageway, into a red velvet corridor leading to the "discreet exit" from the House of Refined Delights. She ignored the pungent mix of opium smoke, lilac, and whore-whispers coming from side parlors, but kept her thoughts in the hidden fortress below, with her father, President Grant, and the gold weighing down her saddlebag.

The opium stung her eyes.

Once outside, the cool night hit her full-on, as a Mandarin boy handed Sara the reins to her horse. She secured her saddlebag, brought the stallion around, then rode fast out the alleyway toward the Richmond piers.

A second rider waited by an empty coach until he saw the last snap of Sara's cape, as she galloped away. He checked the pistol on his fast-draw rig, swung onto a tall Paint, and followed.

20

SWORD OF THE OCEAN

She saw the gun first. Blue steel, hidden by the folds of a duster, the weapon close to Maston's hand as he strode across the livery, sporting an odd, non-smile.

Sara kept her back to Maston, finished bedding down her horse. "Here to take the gold back, as ordered?"

"Just ensuring its security, and yours."

She treated the stallion to Virginia apples, patting it gently as it ate, before bringing the draping camouflage down over the stall. All the while, her every instinct was warning her about Maston, standing just three feet away, hand not moving from the gun. Sara's nerves were on the raw, and she didn't need his presence.

Finally, she said, "You've used the 'security' excuse before. I'm not buying."

"We all have our jobs to do, miss. I'm also to check on the readiness of the submarine-ship."

"Capable of that judgment, are you?"

"Simply report what I see."

"Yeah, simple." Sara shoulder-slung her saddlebag, cranked open the floor boarding. "My new ring? I have a bad feeling it's your creation."

"It's in your pocket now, so I'll assume you're allowed to hear this."

Maston stood aside, the walkway to the submarine pen shifting into place by his boots. "The President wanted that particular ring weaponized. No other, and he wanted it for a woman operative."

Sara said, "Don't call me that."

"I volunteered my design skills, for whoever uses it."

Sara walked the steel ramp. "Your talents, that's why the world's in this mess."

Maston's smile was for himself. "You might be thanking me one day."

He stopped at the bottom of the ramp, the *Nautilus* in its repair dock, bobbing with the rising tide, bowlines straining to be cut. The submarine's plated hull was armor-strong again, a new jagged prow in place, viewing ports glassed, and the melted conning tower reconstructed.

"Nothing else like it exists," Sara said.

Maston stood back, taking the giant craft in. "You could also claim that about Nemo."

Sara moved to the deck access ladder, defiantly shaking the saddlebag, the gold bars inside clinking. "So, what's Nemo stealing? We're giving him the gold for his ship, he can't wait to get out on the open seas."

"I'm not here about thievery."

Maston lifted the pistol from the fast-rig, keeping the long barrel pointed down. "We want to be sure he remembers his orders when he's underway. Giving Nemo a reminder of duty isn't a bad thing, Miss. Especially for you. Operative or not, you don't want to be trapped with a mad dog you have to put down."

The red beam hit the center-top of Maston's hand. A speck of light, then a muscle-deep burn. He cried out, spun with the gun up, as another, more intense beam struck: bolt of lightning, hammering him off his feet. Flesh seared, his duster on fire.

Maston's gun blasted into the pier, wood chips flying, as he dropped and rolled, tearing himself out of the burning coat. Sara hurled it into the water as the final laser burst scorched the ceiling boards high above them.

The red light, blinding.

Sara kept her head down, but could feel the beam's heat: the tail of a comet coming from below the waterline of the submarine dock, originating near the *Nautilus'* rudder, boiling the small patch of ocean that it passed through as it was fired upward from the ocean's sandy bottom.

The laser changed directions, hitting around the pen, burning holes through barrels, and fusing a stack of lead pipe. Sara quick-scrambled away, the beam's size narrowing to something almost wire-thin, moving as deliberately as a surgeon's scalpel across the wooden pilings, burning a circle into the planks around Maston.

It stopped. The flicking of a switch.

Nemo hoisted himself from the water onto the *Nautilus'* stern in a single athletic move, holding an elaborate rifle, with a stock made from the bones of a sea creature; like the rest of his *Nautilus,* the weapon was organic to Nemo, an extension of his body. He removed his breathing device, a small conch shell with flexible tubing, and said, "I would call this a success."

Sara said, "That thing—you could have burned us alive!"

"An underwater weapon using concentrated light, with more force than any bullet, and you were in no danger. My aim is always true."

Nemo adjusted the rifle's firing mechanism: a prismed lens on a brass slider fitted to a barrel mounted with multiple light cells that combined as a single beam. A battery on his diving belt supplied power.

He said, "Designed to fight off overly aggressive species of Elasmobranchii—"

"Sharks," Sara said.

"Among other predators."

Maston held his chest, leaned away from the burned circle. "I suppose you mean me, but I didn't need the demonstration."

"Thank Miss Duncan. This was housed in one of the Vulcania spheres, assembled, but never fired. I had to be sure of the laser's control, from widest to sharpest point."

"From shotgun to Derringer."

Nemo said, "A crude comparison, but not totally inaccurate. Except the power is far beyond your calibers."

Then, to Sara, "You have the fuel, as agreed?"

"Yes," Sara said, as she stood, shaken, "but I'm not sure now to hand it over. Of course, you could just take it anyway."

Nemo was at the access ladder. "I could, but I won't. Apologies if the weapon frightened you, but there's much you don't know."

He pressed the trigger, firing the laser a half-inch from Sara, cutting a rattlesnake slithering through the floor in half, its edge-cooked pieces rolling to her feet.

Sara blinked, handed Nemo the saddlebag.

Nemo looked inside at the ingots. "The only pure thing about our government," he said. Then to Sara, "This will take us far. You may report to your father that you've completed your job, and I approve, but the bizarre assumption that you're coming on this voyage couldn't be more wrong."

Sara said, "Wait—I've earned it, Captain."

"Whatever you imagine you've earned," Nemo gestured at the snake with the rifle barrel, "was just paid. The *Nautilus* is no place for a woman."

"I understand it was. Once."

Nemo gave Sara a cold stare. "You overstep yourself. Severely."

Nemo fired again. Short burst. At Maston, on his feet and reaching for the pistol with his other hand. He recoiled at the ray, tumbled against a piling.

"Agent Maston, your purpose is known, and despised," Nemo said. "The pistol stays, as you leave. I'm sure Grant will happily issue you a new one."

Maston got to his feet. "He won't be pleased about this, or your denial of Miss Duncan."

Nemo said, "The President's concern is our casting off, which occurs at dawn."

He was at the hatchway, with the saddle-bagged gold, and tossed Sara the conch with the tubed fittings. "My breathing device. Much more efficient than yours."

In the *Nautilus*, Nemo moved through the library, the shelves clean, except for a copy of Pierre Arronax's *An Encyclopedic Study of Deep-Sea Creatures* and some of his water-damaged sketches.

The furniture in the salon was mismatched, the pipe organ whined, and the gilt fixtures cobbled together; the trappings were a shadow of the old *Nautilus,* but this craft wasn't a swamped wreck anymore, and Nemo felt pride as he made his way down the main corridors to the belowdecks and the power station.

The small lift lowered him into the complete darkness of the now-dead station. The ship's heart, not beating. Cold. Nemo centered the gold bars on a fuel tray, then sealed the hatch as they heated.

The large containment cells immediately glowed, building, the pure metals breaking down in the chamber, converted into fissionable materials, feeding the *Nautilus'* turbines.

Soft light rolled through the chamber.

Nemo's wounded shoulder burned again as he regarded the bullet strikes on the floor, coming into view as the light around him grew stronger. He knelt by them. Just creases and punches in the iron, left by the slugs fired by government troops that tore through his crew, killing them.

The constant reminder.

Hunched there, Nemo reached beneath the freestanding controls, fitting in a voltage regulator from his Vulcania laboratory, no larger than a Liberty half-dollar.

The ship responded. Her heart, beating.

Nemo felt the same rhythm in his chest, as if synchronized with the *Nautilus*. An internal growl rose from the mechanisms, then became an assured roar of regained strength as the cells came to life around him, all blinding light and power.

Miles of water, with a lifeboat drifting through it, parched under a brutal sun. Fulmer stood mid-ship, balancing himself on the seat, while gently lifting Red to the side and pouring him under the small, continuous waves. The last days had been agonizing, as Red's muscles turned into dried paper beneath what was left of his face and arms. He tried to speak. To joke.

Fulmer watched the waves for a moment, then turned away before the body sank from sight.

He leaned back against the blood-washed seat where Red had been lying, and poured a few drops of fresh water on his tongue, closing his eyes against the bright afternoon, the absolute nothing around him.

Nemo put the laser rifle onto the special rack mounted on his cabin wall. The pressing of an emerald button opened a hidden wardrobe, his uniform hanging there, sharply pressed, "Mobilis in Mobile" gold-stitched on the breast pocket. He lay it on his bed before shaving over a portable sink.

Wiping off the lather traces, clearing steam from a mirror, Nemo's reflection wasn't that of a prisoner.

He moved to the large diagram of the *Nautilus* over his desk, rheostatted the ceiling lights, shifting from one color to another, fading the submarine plans and bringing the portrait of his wife and son into their place again.

Nemo said to them, "I won't forget my vow."

Jess pushed himself into a dark corner of the crew quarters, on top of the last bunk in a row, wrapping the garrote around his hands. He tensed, seeing a Whaler's huge shape, moving sideways through the hatchway.

Whaler's brass knuckles, with jagged spikes, caught an edge of light as he kicked bunks and checked under them, saying, *"Haere mai i roto i iti kirera!"*

Jess thought he heard "squirrel" in the language as he tightened the cord between his fists. Keeping dead-still, letting the Whaler get to the next bunk, which he'd stuffed with pillows, propped with blankets.

"Kierra?"

Whaler leaned down, spiked fist raised to crush sleeping Jess' skull. He pounded. Into pillows, feathers erupting. Jess leapt from the corner, whipping the cord around Whaler's thick neck from behind, pulling it taut.

Whaler clawed wild, prying Jess' fingers, trying to snap them. Elbows, hard-jerked backward into Jess' ribs. Bone breakers, as they both fell.

Jess landed flat, Whaler on top of him, his massive weight hard-pressing his chest into dust. Whaler jammed the knuckle-spikes into the cord, catching it, trying to shred, while Jess gasped for air but kept twisting the ends together, hearing Whaler choke. Losing his ape's tongue.

Jess felt Whaler's spit on his hands as he shrieked, "Kaatau!"

Kaatau, the near-twin brother, was in the hatchway with a machete. He took two lumbering steps. Stopped. His brother's face was becoming a death mask.

Jess yanked the garrote tighter, for emphasis, when he said, "He came in here lookin' for me, and you got that blade! Drop it, or his head comes off faster than a whiskey cork! Savvy all this?"

Kaatau watched the oxygen-starved purple crawl from the veins in his brother's neck, across his cheeks, his eyes rolling back.

"You ain't doin' nothing!" Jess yelled.

A commanding voice tidal-waved through the *Nautilus* via the crew call: "This is Captain Nemo. All hands report to stations. Ready to cast off!"

Kaatau looked to Jess, and said, "I savvy *that*," then dropped the machete.

Jess let it clatter before unwrapping the cord, now stained with blood from Whaler's mouth and nose. He kicked Whaler off, the massive body bending forward, choking for any air he could.

"You going to keep tryin' this shit?" Jess asked, wrenching the brass knuckles off Whaler's hand, then grabbing the machete.

"E kore ahau e matau." Kaatau smiled.

Jess fit the brass on his own fist. "So you're gonna try for my throat again, that's the right of it?"

Nemo's voice: "All hands report!"

"I'll have back, that blade," Kaatau said, not breaking his grin.

The ocean around the lifeboat was now miles of black, broken by diamonds that splintered on the surface as the currents rolled into each other, reflecting the night sky and breaking up the dull light of the moon.

Fulmer squinted at the pieces of light, using them to find the canteen that he'd lashed beneath the paddle stanchion, out of the way so he wouldn't be tempted to drink it all. He felt along the edge, and found the canteen, its sides sopping wet.

Fulmer yanked it free, water from the hole in its bottom soaking his hands. He drank from what filled his palm, slurping what he could.

He turned the canteen over, moved to where Red had been lying, the shreds of a bloody shirt still marking the spot. He settled there, taking his place, holding the canteen above his mouth to catch those final drops. The burlap sack, tied tight, was lying beside his feet, the mechanical thing inside still moving. Barely.

Fulmer listened. There was only the moving water, slapping the lifeboat, tilting it with a dip or small wave. The sky was clearing, clouds breaking apart, revealing more stars.

"Blessed are those who go down to the sea in ships."

Fulmer laughed, quietly, and then louder as he turned the empty canteen over. He'd never found any meaning in those words. Just something to say over the dead, and now he had to say it over himself. He laughed again at that, letting his voice settle across the water, and vanish, before thinking another thought. Before dropping his head to the bloody pile where his friend once lay.

The rising sun streaked orange as the flankers broke their horses down the waterfront pier, hooves clattering on the planking. Running full out, slipping rifles from their shoulders as they pulled up to the old livery, where the President's Coach was already tied.

They dropped from their mounts, and found positions around the pier as Grant and Duncan walked toward the last pilings, where Sara was standing, hurling bread to the gulls. Maston, hand bandaged and without a gun, stood watch from behind a stack of anchor chains.

The sun was higher now, the night erased, and throwing clean light across the rows of tall-mast schooners and small fishing boats casting off.

Fishermen pointed to Grant, waved their caps, as he marched for Sara, calling out before reaching her: "You should be on board; what about the launch?"

Sara hurled the last of the bread, letting the gulls fight for it. "Nemo declared me unworthy. The launch should be any minute."

Grant said to Duncan, "Your damn scheme's already going awry."

"He has a new weapon, by the way," Sara said.

Nemo was on his bridge, sea horse key in place, all indicators lit, all dials reading. He took his chair, his station, at the Captain's podium.

Specialized handlebars, rather than a ship's wheel, steered the rudders. Mounted at an angle, the touch on the bars was sensitive by design, allowing near-instant changes in the *Nautilus'* direction. Holding the bar steady with his left, Nemo slipped his right into a glove-like opening beneath the main indicators in front of him.

All fabric and wires, it manipulated hidden switches, reacting only to the specific length and spread of his fingers. Electric pulses confirmed identity as Nemo adjusted rudder tension, power flow, and steering with smooth movements of hands, as if playing a concerto. The electric nerves of the *Nautilus* were now his nerves, guiding every aspect of the submarine; man and machine, spliced.

Jess called out from the stairs, "Permission to enter the bridge, sir!"

"Granted."

Jess, sporting a uniform of sea denims, gave Nemo an admiring nod before moving to the control banks, all of which were preset. He squinted at the dials. "Looks like there's nothin' for me to do, Captain!"

"Responsibility is a gift earned. You've a talent for brawling, and decent with tools, but you'll need more to be First Mate. But, necessity dictates that's who you are. For the moment."

"Just as well; I ain't never sailed a turtle a'fore."

"And I've never had a first whose blood was pure rum."

"Then, we're both sailin' into uncharted waters."

"Just do your job, Mr. Jess. Preparing engines." Nemo switched power to the engine room. "All hatches ready for cast-off?"

Jess smiled wide. "Oh, yes, sir! All crew aboard!"

The Whalers charged both sides of the submarine pen, machete-slashing the ties of the large disguising canvas between the *Nautilus* and the ocean. The top hatch started closing. Whalers jumped for it, giant hands grabbing for the crew ladder, their great weight rolling them inside the submarine, moments before the hatch slammed shut.

Other crew moved onto the bridge, ragtags doing their duties as Nemo ordered, "All ahead, quarter speed, Mr. Jess."

Jess echoed the order.

Nemo felt a small burst of energy as the engines pulsed, gears engaged, and the *Nautilus* began moving. A glove-command opened the shutters covering the bridge's domed observation port, the iron plates folding back from the glass, as the *Nautilus* cut through the curtain into Norfolk Harbor. Out of hiding, they were now surrounded by ships, men, and an ocean, stretching wide. New sunlight flooded through portals on all decks, completing the feeling of the *Nautilus'* resurrection.

Jess caught the Captain with eyes closed, as if thanking for a prayer answered. It was a half-moment; Jess not sure what Nemo was truly thinking, and being met with a sudden glare. He snapped about, toward the open view ahead, standing a little straighter, ready for orders.

Sara, her father, and Grant were on the pier's edge, the *Nautilus* churning from the submarine pen. Splitting the waters with its amplified-swordfish design, it moved as a graceful living creature, not something clumsily man-made, its long shadow falling across every ship moored in the harbor, with crews rushing their railings for a look.

But Sara only saw Nemo, protected by the large glass dome, at his Captain's station and in command.

She repeated, "Unworthy."

Then she tore from her dress, clamped the tube-and-shell breather in her mouth, and dove into the water.

21

BENEATH THE WAVES

Sara angled herself in mid-dive, cutting deep through the ocean's surface, and propelling instantly forward with her arms and legs. Before diving, she saw how the water fell off the *Nautilus* at cruising speed, creating a wake, and swam to the right, keeping clear of the powerful draft while dodging sunken pieces of the old, bombed-out pier.

She knew the harbor from the months of work on the submarine, and kept her eyes closed against the burning salt water, but still expertly swimming ahead, seeing with her memory, the shell-breather working as naturally as her own lungs.

She pulled her elbows in, then glided with her lean-muscled legs, making good distance before going to the surface. Sara cleared her eyes, then dove, getting ahead of the *Nautilus'* bow, then straightened as if skimming the water, while the submarine passed, letting herself be pulled backward into its wake. She started swimming again, keeping steady against the current, while being drawn closer to the hull.

She challenged the wake with a strong breaststroke, literally swimming in place, so not to get yanked into the large propellers, but still maneuvering. She scissor-kicked as she reached out, trying to grab hold of one of the portals just below the submarine's waterline. The ones she'd retrofitted, and knew their location.

Fingers slipped. The wake gripped her stronger, yanking her toward the engine and rudder works.

Sara grabbed again, getting hold of a small view port as it moved past. She hung on, clinging, hands tight around the brass fittings, before hoisting herself up. Finding a grip on the hull's riveted surface, she climbed, rolling onto the top deck, raising a triumphant fist.

Duncan was at the farthest point of the pier, keening over the end, watching, then he waved both arms as his daughter stood on the *Nautilus*. The tiny figure that was Sara waved back, and Duncan's pride, and relief, were in his words: "That's the kind of courage you give medals for."

"Point taken. Now let's get her off that thing," Grant said. "No telling what Nemo'll do if she's seen."

Duncan's voice dropped. "Ulysses . . ."

The *Nautilus* was diving.

Sara's name was choked helpless in Duncan's throat as she scrambled up the conning tower, staying above the water, the submarine continuing its descent.

He squeezed Grant's arm.

Sara got to the tower's perch, holding onto a mounted telescope, whitecaps to her knees, and rising, before swan-diving into the rolling ocean. She vanished beneath, along with the last traces of the submarine.

"I knew this was riding to hell," Grant spit.

He barked to Maston, who was already charging for the small boats in the outside slips, "As planned!"

The fishermen, trained Navy in disguise, jumped into skiffs, oars chopping the water, quick-rowing to where Sara had been. They prepped cork life jackets, called her name through megaphones.

Maston's crew cast off, while atop a piling, a signalman flagged the frigates and gunboats anchored half a mile offshore to be "Armed and Ready."

From Grant's command, all action had taken moments.

Duncan was heaving, running fast as he could for the coach, Oliver, the driver, already bringing it around.

He got out, "Nemo, we've got to raise him on the communicator—"

"To tell him he's signed his own death warrant," Grant said.

Rescue boats formed a wide circle on the edge of the harbor, bows-to-sterns, tossing life rings, while Navy skin-divers powered under the water. Diving, coming up, forming a search grid.

By the livery, the Rifle Guards mounted. Grant and Duncan made it to the coach, Grant hoisting him in, saying, "Nemo's a lunatic, always has been."

Oliver snapped the team into a run, the Rifle Guards galloping alongside.

Sara clung to the side of the *Nautilus* like a remora on a whale's belly, feeling the vibration of the water being drawn into the ballast tanks. The submarine was taking on a rush of weight, meaning it was quick-diving at least another hundred feet, as the shallow of the harbor dropped off and the bow aimed for the ocean bottom.

She measured her breathing through the brassed shell, keeping herself flat against the hull while crawling forward on it, a foot at a time.

The *Nautilus* leveled, the engines upped their speed.

A sandbar shark swam in close, nudging Sara from behind, and she kicked at his sharp snout, sandpaper skin against the soles of her feet. Knocking him away.

A large, iris-formed hatchway opened mid-hull.

There was a burst of water pressure from the hatch, and then, a reverse force, as she was sucked into a vacuum tube, the iris closing down behind her. A frenzy of sharks swam in fast, mouths open for Sara, but missing, their heads butting against iron.

Sara was now standing in a polished steel tube, the cold water rapidly swirling out, warm air wafting in, before a glassed side opened, and she saw Jess holding a blanket.

He said, "You look like the spaniel what fell down the well."

Sara stepped into the Sea Exploration chamber that housed four other pressure tubes in cases, and all the *Nautilus'* diving technologies.

She pulled her wet hair back from her eyes. "Nemo, he really tried to kill me?"

"If he had done, you'd be washing up on the beach." Jess wrapped her shoulders. "You're here because the Cap knew what you could handle."

He snatched the shell-breather from the floor and said, "Dry off, you're ordered to the bridge."

In the harbor, Maston hauled a Navy diver into his flat-boat, the Diver saying, "Nope, she's gone."

Maston winced with pain from his laser-burned hand. "Your

meaning is, the *Nautilus* is gone, the ship. Not Miss Duncan. I have to be absolutely clear for the President."

The Diver had a mouth of brandy, then said, "You figure the phrasing. I took the emergency plan to be blow up the submarine with cannon fire, and if Miss Duncan's on it—"

"That's not for your conjecture, or comment."

The Diver laughed. "All I'm saying, if you're firing on the underwater boat, do it now, so we can fish out the bodies before the sun goes down."

Another drink, and, "It's too damn cold at night."

Sara cleared the last of the spiral staircase to the bridge, her voice catching as she saw a maze of fifty underwater mines, set between the harbor and the ocean lanes, surrounding the observation dome from all sides.

Bombs anchored by chains, challenging the *Nautilus*.

She moved past Nemo, and the helm, to the center of the glass dome over the bridge, its open curve magnifying all details around it. Rows of salt-rotten barrels, with cased explosives packed in chambers, were feet from the prow. They drifted close, almost colliding with the submarine.

"They're known as Raine's Kegs, and were very effective against Union ships," Nemo said. "A damaged bomb, Miss Duncan, almost as dangerous as a damaged man."

He then called out, "Track my actions, Mr. Jess!"

Nemo quick-moved the handlebars and glove-controller, angling the ship suddenly upward, ballast water jetting from side tanks, pushing the bombs back with their force. The massive submarine behaved as if spring-loaded, perfectly responding to his hand commands.

Jess scrambled at the valves, cutting water from the tanks, then re-flooding to level the ship's trajectory. The *Nautilus* was now moving arrow-straight, parallel, and feet-close to the bottom, the engines churning up fine sand from the ocean floor, fogging their view.

Through the swirling gray, a row of Confederate torpedoes emerged: giant, iron-clad insect cocoons, fluted, and chained together as a blockade wider than the *Nautilus*. Nemo knew them capable of blowing the hull of a destroyer, or a submarine, in half.

He said, "Blood in the water," through clenched teeth, then pulled back the engines. "Mr. Jess, cutting speed!"

Jess echoed the order to the lower decks, then said to Sara, "I've prayed never to see one of them bastards again, and there's a baker's dozen."

Nemo said, "Your attention, Mr. Jess!"

Behind Sara, the spinning mirrors of the Phono-tele-Photo pieced together Duncan's face on the screen, his voice crackling: "Daughter—Sara—is that you, you're all right?"

Sara didn't answer.

Nemo called out, "Side avoidance tactic!"

Jess said, "I ain't sure which that is—"

Sara charged the large railway hand switches on the other side of the bridge, watching Nemo's moves as he jolted the bow away from the blockade of torpedoes, but angling close. He threw a hand signal.

Sara pulled the switches. "There—now!" Jess grabbed hold, cranking back the stabilizing fins, so torpedo chains and triggers wouldn't snag against the hull.

Again, on the Phono: "Sara?"

Nemo starboard-set the rudders, passing the last group of mines suspended by their own buoyancy. Under his control, the

Nautilus had moved as gracefully as a dolphin skimming the waves, leaving the torpedoes behind.

He gave her a nod.

Sara let out the breath she'd been holding, and said, "Yes, Father, I'm here. And I'm well."

In the bunker, Duncan grabbed the Phono-horn as if grabbing his daughter, swallowing his panic when he heard her voice. "Dear, can you speak? You're all right? Truthfully now."

"I'm all right, honestly."

Duncan said, "Thank God."

"Hardly God."

Nemo's eyes sliced the Phono from the captain's station, his voice rising. "If you've built my device correctly, then the lens showed I was navigating your damnable mines. And now this ill-timed communication. Why this crude parlay, this game?"

Duncan was angry static: "You were charted safe passage, then attempted to drown my daughter!"

"Father—"

"Miss Duncan had nothing to do with it. I was forced to dive when I spied your Navy ships set as floating bombs."

Grant's voice: "What in hell are you referring to?"

Nemo said, "Your ships, General, rigged with explosives, forcing us into an undersea trap of mines—avoiding one, colliding with the other."

Grant, leaning across the map table littered with war strategies, exchanged a dark look with Duncan before speaking into the Phono-horn: "Those ships were to escort you to the shipping lanes. That's all."

"It's small comfort you weren't trying to sink the *Nautilus* in that obviously foolish way," Nemo said, his submarine now directly below the Naval ships laced with charges and impact detonators, hulls and rudders clearly visible through the observation deck.

Grant said, "*Your intentions,* Nemo. Now."

Nemo gave it a moment, then, "To reach the open sea."

Duncan's voice stammered. "A route was charted, you must adhere to it. As agreed. That's the safest passage."

Sara looked up at the ships through the glass dome, now seeming so close she could count the rivets that held them together. "We're passing beneath those frigates, sir, and I'm seeing cases of explosives, what could be timers, attached to the bottom of every single one. The Captain is right."

Grant said, "You're saying this on your own, girl?"

"I am, Mr. Grant."

Nemo said, "If the bombs aren't *Nautilus* intended, you've a saboteur eager to send your Navy to the bottom." He looked ahead at the ocean clearing before his ship. "You may not trust my motives, General, but you can trust my word. Your mission will be completed, one way or t'other."

Duncan's voice: "My daughter—what about Sara?"

"Stowaways aren't tolerated on the *Nautilus.*"

"Boarded, not stowed away," Sara said to the Phono, then to Nemo, "and I know this ship. Bow to stern."

Nemo was at the edge of the dome, a school of blue-striped barracuda swarming. "You've practical knowledge that might be of use."

Sara was whisper-close to the Phono: "Father, I'll remain."

"You're sure about this, dear? Truly?"

Sara touched Duncan's image on the screen before shutting the Phono's current, his face and voice breaking apart, repeating her name.

Her ringed hand hidden in the folds of the blanket, she said, "Captain, now you know I'm here of my own accord. And it seems I'm, somewhat, seaworthy."

"If that Secret Service agent had made one more attempt toward the *Nautilus,* I would've burned him to ashes."

"We were never together, sir."

Nemo let Sara's words settle, considering them. "I didn't know what advantage you'd take of the breathing device, but you did better than most." He called out, "Navigation!" and Jess handed Sara the relief map made of tin sections, folded into the leather wallet.

Nemo said, "Decipher that information. I'll determine its value."

A grin tugged at her. "Yes, sir."

"There's only one crew quarters on this ship."

Jess said, "I'll protect her modesty, Cap."

"Get into dry things. An ill woman suits no one's purpose."

Jess leaned in to Sara. "You've just been piped aboard, sis."

The barracuda broke ahead of the *Nautilus'* prow, its body turning, angling through deep water as a hawk whip-dives for its prey. Nemo, back at the helm, commanded the engines to full.

The images attacked Fulmer's exhausted sleep.

Eyes first. Huge. Glowing yellow. Fierce, and skimming just below the water. Hunting. The wake of a speared-snout breaking behind it. The sea animal moved faster, emitting a piercing cry before attacking, spines ripping through the frigate's hull, exploding a boiler. Tearing men in half. Screams and fire. In moments.

Red said it was "Nemo's beast."

Fulmer screamed from his dream, slashing wildly at the night. Heart racing, looking around the lifeboat for Red; maybe he crawled off? But he was alone. Dreaming. He shook himself awake, trying to clear his head, the freezing ocean air slicing him through his rags.

He thought he'd felt something that woke him.

The lifeboat heaved. Something smashing from below, tipping its edge. Waves slopped in, filling the bottom. Fulmer rolled to one side, grabbed the Remington, and pushed his feet off the middle seat, getting to the side of the impact. Another hit. Fulmer stumbled, with the boat tilting. Nearly capsizing.

Holding on, turning the rifle around, to beat the water with the stock, all ammo spent.

He saw it in the fractures of moonlight. Just glints from water beading: the hammerhead's sharp tail slashed the waves before its head turned and rammed the lifeboat from the side, against the flat of its head.

Fulmer swung at it with the rifle, catching some fin, bouncing off its hide. The eyes clocked up at him, one side of the skull, then the other, before circling the boat. Declaring its prey.

It hit. Again. Starting a split in the hull, water spurting. Fulmer jabbed, pounding with the rifle barrel, the tail snapping, cutting hands, sending the Remington into the ocean.

Another hit from the shark, popping nails in the hull. More water spurting through, the lifeboat giving way. Fulmer watched the tail and fin circle, diving, and swimming back.

Fulmer grabbed the burlap sack, pulling out the mechanical crab. The legs moved in jerking motion, the sensors not registering as the retractable jaws hinged open and the acid began to spew.

He aimed the stream at the hammerhead, burning its eyes, sending the shark thrashing. It threw itself against the lifeboat, twisting in pain. Fulmer held the mechanical in front of him as a weapon, still spraying. Burning more skin. Muscles melting from bone, and the hammer sinking away, fading under the water.

Fulmer collapsed against the bench, still holding the mechanical, gears and servos winding down. He flipped it over, popped out the small, cut diamond in its belly, and pocketed it.

Extending his arm, he looked at the tattoo as if he hadn't seen it in years: "Mobilis in Mobile."

The mechanical lying beside him, robotic insect-face staring with artificial eyes, Fulmer laid his head back and gave a hoarse war-whoop to a moon that was fading with dawn. And started to laugh.

22

LEPRECHAUN

The door to the net-weaver's shed shattered under Maston's heel, hinges popping. He stepped around, grabbing a baling hook jammed into the frame, looking for more green movement.

He'd seen it as he pulled his rescue skiff to the shore: someone behind the shed's one window, looking out at the harbor. A glimpse of a man sporting a green bowler, who ducked away.

Maston squinted through dusty shadows, at the spools of rope, some waist tall, lining the tar-paper walls. Iron pikes for net-stringing took up the center of the shed; jagged fangs emerging from the floor leaving little room for anything else.

The green moved.

Darting from behind a stack of cork floaters.

Maston snagged Mr. Lime's collar with the baling hook, jerking him off his feet as he tried for the window.

Lime twisted, squealing, with wild kicks into Maston's stomach, punching into his throat. Maston fell back choking, just missing the iron pikes. He hooked Lime again, yanked him down, then pressed his thumb and forefinger against the nerve below his jaw, crumpling Lime to the floor, the hook ripping his velvet-piped green jacket to the tails.

A notebook marked NEMO fell from the shredded lining of the jacket, and Maston pocketed it before dragging Mr. Lime out to the waterfront, and onto his horse.

Opium.

The House of Delights was heavy with a sweet haze that Maston shook off while following the beautiful Mandarin, an erupting volcano tattooed across her back. She cast a smile with her eyes and slid open the false wall, not even acknowledging the small, unconscious man slung about Maston's shoulders.

"Father, I'll remain."

Sara's voice scratched from the Phono-horn, then bounced off the stone walls, as Maston came down the steps into the bunker and sack-tumbled Mr. Lime onto a scrolled desktop, scattering a folder of Sea Battle Strategies. Lime didn't stir.

A few glanced, but everyone was about their business as Maston grabbed Lime's celluloid collar and pulled him forward, his head still drooping.

Duncan put his hand up to hide the sounds of Maston slapping Lime awake, while saying into the horn, "You're sure about this, dear? Truly?"

The Phono powered down, Sara's face mouthing good-bye, then dimming out. Duncan touched the blank screen. Beside him, Maston delivered palm, then backhanded hits to Lime's jowls. Sharp stings.

Lime bolted up, fists swinging. Maston dodged, instantly flattening him to the desk by the shoulders. Pinned down.

"Call off your damned beast!" Lime squealed, as Maston wrenched his tiny arm, elbow-to-jaw.

"He's twisting out my bloody socket!"

Grant said, "Stand down."

The words unlocked Maston, who propped Lime up like a souvenir teddy bear from a shooting gallery, making a show of dusting off his shoulders and adjusting his tie.

Lime squirmed from reach. "I expected better from you, General. We have a bit of history, yes?"

"You're almost costing us the Overland Campaigns?"

Lime was now sitting on the desk, legs not reaching the floor, shaking feeling back to his fingers. "I risked my life for those pictures, hiding in the back of that God-awful medical cart."

"Where you were discovered, photographing our troop positions," Grant said, while Maston pulled a spy camera, disguised as a jeweled tie clasp, from Lime's green-striped shirt.

"A simple record of innocent young men preparing for battle."

Grant said, "That you'd have gladly sold to the Confederacy."

"You'll recall, sir, I gave up my beauties before your siege of the Rebel stronghold. *Before.*"

"You feared I'd have you executed as a spy if you didn't. Now," Grant lit his first cigar of the day, "this morning. Explain."

"Merely following a stink," Lime said.

Maston handed the President Lime's NEMO notebook. He thumbed the pages, eyes narrowing, and said, "Elaborate, Mr. Lime, or the beast comes off his chain."

"It's you lot. Paying the shopkeeps to stay away from their waterfront. Sailors, got-up as fishermen, standing by, while the *Nautilus,* captained by a dead man, headed out to sea."

Lime threw a look around the bunker, at the chattering

telegraphs, the stored arsenal. "I couldn't begin to decipher the meaning of all these odd events myself, but I'd wager editors at the National Press Building would drool from their purses for my record of them."

"Any conclusions?"

"You're on the eve of war."

Grant said, "Wrong."

Lime's voice picked up, declaring the headlines: "Foreign lines and freighters sunk! Hundreds killed! Mystery fires and bombs, and now, a hostage journalist, surrounded by secret battle plans and assassins!"

Grant said, "That horse pie's sold papers before. The cuff links."

Lime straightened his arms, eyes rolling with sarcastic bother. "Tell me, please, Mr. President, do you believe your States would be victorious in a worldwide war? Especially with that magnificent submariner at your beck and call? I promise to quote you exactly."

Maston popped a small-lensed camera mounted on a silver link from the right cuff. Then ripped, taking hair and skin, a cabled shutter release taped across Lime's back through to his other sleeve, and left hand.

Lime winced. "Funniest thing, I'd read a dispatch that Nemo had been killed in a riot at the Devil's Warehouse. Quite a gruesome end, so it claimed."

Maston dropped the camera's mechanics, cables splayed, onto the desk, along with a Derringer from Lime's waistband holster. He split the pistol, emptying it.

"See, I could've shot your beast, but restrained meself," Lime said. "Not like the anarchists who decorated Mulberry Street with his Excellency, the Bishop. Or, is he coming back from the dead, too, like the good Captain Nemo?"

Grant said, "No, his Excellency won't be coming back."

"At least we have the truth of that, colored by Mr. Spilett's editorials. And your would-be assassin at the White House? There's been nothing but speculation."

Duncan said, "Still unknown, unless you have some clues."

Lime said, "I wouldn't be so foolish as to hold back information that important, not under these crisis circumstances. Do I get a taste of your legendary bourbon before facing a firing squad, or whatever torture you have planned?"

"Actually, I was considering you being of some damn use for once. Where's the film for all these devices?"

Lime said, "Hidden. Well. Before I was brutally attacked and kidnapped. Gun to my temple, you'll never reach my price for those beautiful pictures."

"Your price is what you extort," Grant said, exhaling smoke through his nose. "Keep your images, hold back your publishing. You said 'eve of war.' Wrong. We're in it. Now."

Lime pondered, "And the *Nautilus'* devilishly secret mission is our chance at victory?"

He was now standing on the desk, at his full four foot three, examining his destroyed green jacket and saying, "That sounds like a superb reason for me to go to press as soon as possible."

Duncan said, "With a great deal of blood on your hands."

Lime, seeing Maston towering over him, said, "That would not make me rare in this room."

"When the timing's appropriate, you'll get complete details directly from my office," Grant said.

"As in the Nemo 'death reports'?"

"I said *complete*."

"Me exclusively, no other scribes?"

Grant said, "You'll write a story for the entire world, spin the yarn as much as you dare."

"Oh, hellfire propaganda for your enemies to read? And just who are we fighting, Mr. President?"

For Lime, all sound then stopped. Everything shut out except the threat-edge of Grant's voice: "No speculations beforehand, but I'd say this situation's too damned important to sell off for a banner headline. Don't you agree?"

"Imagine." Lime clapped his hands as if breaking a trance. "The President of these United States trying to strike a bargain with me."

Grant's response was nothing.

Lime dropped his grin. "You've always been the warrior with a conscience, but I've a sour feeling if I don't bend to your proposal, there'll be hell to pay."

Grant flicked away his cigar's hot ash.

"And then some."

23

HARPIES

The sea laboratory was at the end of the *Nautilus'* lower deck, and graveyard-quiet. Exotic species circled their tanks, as Sara, now in a *Nautilus* uniform and with the poisoned ring in her pocket, worked a safe lock to a chamber door that was hidden behind a row of marine cages.

Nemo had given her the combination in Hindi, not allowing it to be written down since it was one of his personal secrets. Sara felt a twinge of pride. He also gave a time limit, that if she failed, "You'll be cast off in a raft with a day's provisions, and forgotten."

Sara bit her lip. Figured her translation. Spun the dials.

An Anglerfish tapped aquarium glass with its antenna as the pneumatic seal around the door split apart. Sara stepped through the casket-shaped opening, choking dead-stale air, eyes cutting the dim of the chamber, to see the Device against the back wall.

It was as Captain Nemo described: a mutated music box, three feet across, with a glassed front and six green tentacles framing oval sides. The demonic head of a Kraken erupted from the top, fanged mouth hanging open, and what looked to be the roll-cylinder for a player piano attached to the base by a series of awkward gears.

Shelved around it were all manner of battle sabers and rifles, with combat medals hanging from barrels or blades. Military tunics of every continent, some bloodstained, lay alongside the weapons, name tags on each.

Sara shoved crates of letters and family photographs aside to get to the device before unfolding the pressed tin from the bill-fold, the hinged pieces dangling as a strip that fit perfectly around the cylinder.

She wound a key, tightening springs. Rod-and-gear works clicked over the tin strip as the cylinder turned, each ridge and indentation on the map sections triggering a mechanism, just as punch-holes in a player piano's music roll brought a note.

In the box, a mariner's chart of the Atlantic Ocean popped up behind the glass, with paper harpies swooping in front of it on thin wires like a puppeteer's strings, and tearing apart a minia-ture freighter sailing the box's bottom edge. The intricate, ani-mated spectacle fascinated Sara, the tiniest details of the attacks all described and noted.

The harpies froze, wings paralyzed, as the Kraken's mouth dropped open, a paper tongue lolling out across the top of the Device, the exact latitude and longitude of each "Monster Ship Sinking" printed across it. And the death tolls.

Sara ripped the tongue away.

The waves rolling from the Humpback whale crashed against the *Nautilus,* the motion of its tons of animal weight churning the water into a tempest as it propelled itself easily with large pectoral fins. The whale cried out its high-pitched music before chopping the ocean, playfully diving, then coming back.

Making fifteen knots, the *Nautilus* cruised the surface of the Atlantic, splitting the calm, the Humpback alongside, its length a match for the ship, its tail wider than the submarine's stern. Turning onto its speckled belly scarred by failed harpoons, the whale dove again, swam under the hull, then powered to the surface on the other side of the bow, creating waves taller than the submarine, and spout-blasting water from two blowholes across the observation dome.

Nemo was at command in the dome, the highest point on the bridge, making notes in a dog-eared journal on the whale's movement and size, all beneath his own detailed sketches of a Baleen Humpback birthing a calf.

He'd brought the *Nautilus* to this place, following his internal compass, to find the herd, and this calf that had grown into a cow. His admiring smile nearly split his face as the beast stayed with the submarine, emitting a cry like teasing laughter.

"I dunno what you're playing at, Cap," Jess said, standing on the catwalk parallel to the engine control panels. "That thing'd crush us like a rotten egg."

"If that was its intention, but this species wants nothing more than to exist in harmony with the ocean," Nemo said. "The lesson for us all, if only man were smart enough to learn."

"You have little faith," Sara said.

"My faith is that man will always do the wrong thing," Nemo said, glancing at her and the Kraken's paper tongue in her hand. "There was a whaler who could look at that creature and know instantly how much oil could be drawn from its head. What could be boiled down, and what the bones would bring. He'd have it to the last dollar, but could never see it as a perfect example of how to live on this earth. To be one with the sea."

Jess allowed, "Sounds like a man what knew his business."

Sara said, "A fool, without insight."

"Both. A typical example of corrupted priorities," Nemo said, refining the sketch. "We will take a different tack, Miss Duncan. Something new to you, I'm sure. You entered the chamber?"

"Instructions in Hindi didn't help."

"I understood you to have a background in languages."

"I managed," Sara said, unfolding the numbers and positions. "That 'Flying Monster Box' gave precise coordinates, every single attack on a foreign ship. A perfect record. It's fantastic."

Nemo studied the Humpback. "Fantastical, you mean. Built by an illusionist who shared my feelings about war, joined my crew as a navigator. A citizen of Paris who became a citizen of the *Nautilus*, forever proud of his wild contraption. And you're correct about its accuracy, but we're not following those coordinates."

Sara said, "These are the attacks."

"According to a device fed information from a map fashioned by a government official. Those markings have nothing to do with the oceans, of how this world truly works. Look out there."

Sara watched the whale leaping ahead of the *Nautilus*, a graceful giant.

Nemo said, "Tagged as a calf by Professor Arronax and myself more than five years ago, to track its migration. Arronax died, I was entombed, but the Humpback became a perfect creature. What we all wish we were."

He stepped to the helm. "They have amazing memories: recognizing the vibration of the *Nautilus*' engines as our voice, our cry, and not the voice of an enemy. It's no accident I brought us to these waters. This is the Humpback's habitat. It's returning home, and that's where we need to be."

Sara said, "But the mission—"

"Will be accomplished. My way. In concert with the ocean. The Humpback will be our guide, despite your expression of disbelief. I have belief in that beast."

Jess said, "Good God at the bar, I need a drink."

Nemo dropped his voice. "You don't understand; you don't have to." He took hold of the steering, fit his hand into the speed controls. "Need another communication with Grant or your father?"

Sara looked to the Phono-tele-Photo's mirrored screen. "No."

"The coordinates from that fantasy box, they'll eventually serve a purpose," Nemo said. "As will you. Take the navigation station, map our course, and open your mind."

Sara engaged the submarine's direction trackers, brought out the sextant and charts. Beyond the glass dome, the whale circled away from the bow, and Nemo shifted the direction from the helm, a slight turning toward the animal, before pushing the steering bars forward, and announcing, "Diving, Mr. Jess!"

Jess said, "If you say so, Cap!"

He sounded the bells as the *Nautilus* broke the waves, bow down, following the churning underwater wake of the Humpback's enormous tail.

The Three Draw battleglass telescoped with a sharp snap of Grant's wrist. Looking across Norfolk Harbor, he focused with the center tube, clarifying the convoy of ships from the South Atlantic Squadron that were a quarter-mile out, the October sun showing up the war sloops and frigates to be as imposing as a steep, dark-shadowed mountain range.

Grant scanned ship after ship, adjusting to the distance and size of each craft, before settling on *The Black Heel*, a sister to the battle frigate *Pawnee*. Within moments, he'd sized up her length, beam, and cannons.

"Is it as Nemo claimed?"

Grant said to Duncan, "We've a half-dozen vessels, armed and ready, and I'm not spying any saboteurs swimming their edges, planting dynamite."

"That's not how my daughter described it."

"Sara said exactly what Nemo wanted to hear. It's what I'd do in her place."

"A bright girl," Duncan said, wiping the mist from his spectacles.

"And a natural mermaid," Grant said.

Duncan couldn't deny it, and laughed like a father.

A Marine Lieutenant by the docks sounded three short bugle blasts, signaling beach skiffs to the convoy. Duncan pushed his bifocals up his nose, to see divers towing the small boats from shore, duffel bags of equipment slung around their shoulders. After the harbor shallows, they leapt aboard, and rowed for the warships.

Duncan said, "Your orders. Thanks, Sam."

"I won't be played for a damn fool. This sabotage nonsense is Nemo's great delay tactic."

Grant tucked the telescope under one arm, opened his watch. "*The Black Heel* hoists anchor in less than an hour, leading the convoy, giving the submariner two miles. No matter what the *Nautilus* encounters, we can cross it with hellfire."

"Nemo carped about more distance between the *Nautilus* and our guns. He's sure we've tattooed a bull's-eye on him."

"That's his old song. Let him worry, maybe it'll keep him in line," Grant said, returning the glass to *The Black Heel*.

The divers were at the convoy, pulling dynamite disposal boxes from their duffels. They tethered them to the skiff bows before swimming under the hulls of the warships, long blades and wire cutters to defuse any bombs on their belts.

Grant sharp-focused on the ships and said, "Lots of men on this mission, John, and you're the architect. I know how heavy that can weigh."

"Simpler than that. I'm worried about my daughter."

"She'll make you proud."

Grant re-collapsed the Three Draw, thinking of the secret orders he'd drafted with the Secretary of the Navy, and given to the Captain of each ship in the convoy. They were executive directives for action in case of "worst-case scenarios," with the *Nautilus*, and he'd downed two tumblers of Old Kentucky before signing them. What he'd never do as a General—planning for defeat—now had to be considered as President.

He took a deep drink of ocean air, clearing the ghosts, when Lime howled: "Bloody ape! I'm not to be hurled about like the dirty washing!"

Grant and Duncan turned from the harbor, and were now standing by the Pleasure House's "Discreet Exit," flanked by Rifle Guards, as Maston dragged Lime by his suspenders from the other end of the alley, the toes of his green Brogues scraping cobbles.

The photographer's hands were cuffed behind him, his mouth never stopping: "Is this your 'oh-so-famous good word' in action? A joke, General! A blood-soaked one!"

Maston tossed Lime onto the back of his horse lashing the cuffs to the saddle horn with a leather strap. "Mouth shut, or your ankles'll be tied behind your ears."

Lime yanked on the strap's knot. No use.

Maston moved to Grant. "Sir, what about this leprechaun?"

"Sew him in a sack if you have to, but get all his pictures," Grant said, taking a match from his vest pocket. "Keep your eagle's eye on him, son. He's four feet of guile."

Maston tipped his brimmed Stetson, adding a small salute,

before turning from Grant, who struck the match against the House's window sill to light his cigar.

"Where's that damn fool with our coach?"

The match flared against the velvet-curtained glass.

Half a moment, and the tiny flame became something enormous: a reflection spreading across the window as a yellow-white tidal wave. Filling Grant's eyes.

The match dropped.

Grant darted a look toward the waterfront. Toward the feeling of sudden, intense heat. Of fire pluming from *The Black Heel*.

Then, the sound. A roaring force from the harbor, pile-driving Grant and Duncan against the wall like a huge, inescapable fist.

The battle glass heat-split, house windows shattered, and bolting horses screamed from the streets as *The Black Heel* exploded, its hull evaporating into jags, the crew caught in a tornado of fire.

Flames taller than the masts, longer than the decks, swept over *The Heel*, when a second explosion tossed its heavy cannons as broken children's toys and hurled flaming pieces across the water, snake-striking other ships in the convoy. Setting fire to sails, rigging, and men.

Another blast turned sailors to bloody mist.

Grant pulled Duncan to safe cover, as Guards ran in, keeping low, forming a barricade around them with bayoneted rifles. Bullets punched their chests, sending the Guards spinning, fingers on triggers, their Carbines firing wildly as they hit the ground, more sniper-slugs tearing backs and shoulders.

Maston fought his horse, spurs deep, and rode for Grant, who signaled him off. Burning ashes from the harbor rained, setting overhanging trees on fire as Maston galloped to a side street, Lime barely holding on behind him, screaming above the din of alarm bells and panic.

More shots sliced smoky air, pocking the ground around the horse's hooves. Maston broke the animal into a full run, clearing the alley as the last shots followed, rapid-fire.

Grant was still tight in a doorway, the shooting paused. Then, three shots in a row. And another pause. A feeling came to him. He recognized something as the echo of the shots died, and said to no one, "Miserable son of a bitch," before charging the alley, game leg dragging, and wrenching a Spencer repeating rifle from a dead guard's hands.

Shavetail, Grant thought, closing the guard's eyes.

Chambering a shell, he pressed himself against the house's bullet-scarred wall, the girls inside still screaming, and worked to its far corner. Oily-gray, billowing from the harbor, cloaked Grant as he brought the Spencer to his shoulder, scanning for the sniper.

Leaves from the burning trees were swirling pieces of fire he swatted away as he moved, before another explosion shook the ground, splitting the cement between the cobblestones. Grant felt the blast, sledgehammering his chest and legs, but stayed braced against the house, gun ready.

Searching for his target.

Beyond his rifle sights, he saw the waterfront through breaks in the smoke: sails-in-flames spiraling to the water, the heavy canvas trapping sailors swimming for shore. Drowning cries.

Another bomb, deep in the harbor, went off. An eruption; wreckage tossed-twisted into the air. The last of the ships and skiffs, pulverized, as the Fire Brigade and Marines swarmed the docks, hot shrapnel coming down on them in a torrent.

Then, four horses charged through the ashes and fire.

Oliver steered the President's Coach wide, careening to each side of the street, losing control of the team, the rear brakes sparking. The horses fought their rig, eyes wild, legs chopping at the sound of gunfire, shouts, and echoed explosions.

The coach back-tailed to one side, almost tipping, before slamming to a stop against a lamppost, as Grant made it to the front side of Pleasure House. He kept the rifle poised, infantry style, still looking for anything of the sniper.

Grant called out, "Ready to move?"

Feet from the coach, Duncan crouched by a storm cellar, knees to his concave chest; a folded scarecrow that had dropped from its cross. He grabbed his words: "L-L-Lord in Heaven, it's all—all—just as Nemo said."

Duncan looked up to see Grant, and stood, shaking, as the next volley of three shots tore Oliver's shoulder and hip, knocking him from his seat. Falling hard, wounds jetting red, a slug clipping off half his ear.

The flashes from the sniper's rifle came as darts of white. Grant dropped to a knee and fired at their origin point, his shots exploding an upper window of the abandoned building across the street. His target was actually the faceless man beyond the window's yellowed glass: a figure holding what looked to be the rifle.

Grant re-steadied, feeling as if he was aiming at a specter, wanting to see the shooter's eyes, or a uniform, but there was only a moving form. A shape, now farther away from the window; just dark, with no features. Grant leveled two perfect shots to its chest, hitting it. Tossing it backward, and gone.

It had been only minutes since the first bomb, the thunder of the blasts still bouncing off distant buildings and hills, but now settling into nothing, with no new explosions following.

Grant didn't trust the quiet. He stayed his position, rifle aimed, in case this was just the pause between attack waves, the trees around him still burning.

A sea wind was clearing the smoke, as Fire brigades and more troopers swarmed the waterfront, soaking the flames, and gathering the dead washing against the pier.

"Mr. President! Sir!"

It was the voice of a young Marine, leading a patrol zigzag through the alley from the opposite side. Grant didn't look back at them, didn't respond, his aim still on the upper window, a dagger of broken glass dropping from its frame and shattering on the street.

Then—nothing.

At that, Grant lowered his rifle, spat out the last of his cigar, crushed it under his heel.

The *Nautilus* was beyond the reach of the sun at this depth, having followed the Humpback whale into an enormous chasm that split the ocean floor seventy miles from the Virginia shore, and beyond the Continental Shelf.

The animal veered for its home, and now whirlpooling currents batted the descending submarine, water challenging iron, as it propelled into the sea canyon, farther into darkness. Electric yellow escaping from the observation ports barely illuminated a few feet around the ship, before dropping into nothing.

The deeper the *Nautilus* went, the more useless its lights, as if it were going blind.

At the Captain's Station, Nemo countered. Fighting the whirlpools with speed, keeping the rudders in a steady dive, and steering the black of the waterways. Anticipating every narrow turn, every outcropping of rock.

Sara, braced against the Navigator's station, the bridge sloping with the continuing descent, charts falling, noted depth, speed, and direction. The large wall compasses spun wildly, needles jigging north to south, then back again. Never stopping.

"We've lost all compass—"

"Conclusion, Miss Duncan."

"This sea canyon's magnetic rock."

"Correct," Nemo said. "But I know this place better than all of my prison cells. We're getting closer to one of the shipwrecks, even if you can't see it."

Something smashed the glass dome. Sara jumped.

Albino sea snakes burst from a nest in the cave wall like an exploding artery. Eels, as long as Sara was tall, swarmed the dome like they would a wounded enemy, moving flesh covering the glass, while striking with their large white skulls to kill it.

Nemo said, "*Eptatretus goliath*. Blind. Have never known sunlight. And when other species aren't available, they feed on each other. Like politicians."

He pulled back on the steering bar, shifting the rudders, braking the *Nautilus'* dive. "Release tanks one and two."

Ballast water powered from the front with an explosion of air, the bubbles foaming across the dome, driving off the swarm of snakes, and revealing nothing. A black void, as if the *Nautilus* were floating in space, without stars. Emptiness.

Nothing above, below, or ahead.

24

LIEUTENANT

Grant's two shots from the street punched the bulletproof leather-and-steel vest beneath the Lieutenant's coat. He tossed himself back from the window on impact, out of sight of the street, but still holding his sniper's rifle, as he slammed to the floor.

He'd trained to take the bullets, building the muscles in his chest so there'd only be a lingering bruise after the slugs hit his armor. He also practiced throwing his body wild, giving the impression of kill-shots.

Lying flat, he tasted the oily, waterfront smoke that clung to the cheesecloth he'd used to mask his face. Peeling the cloth away, oil-soaked bits sticking to his mouth, the Lieutenant hacked out residue that was rough-deep in his throat, careful not to lift his head up.

He pried the smashed slugs from the vest with his left hand and flicked them aside, the fingers on his right still crooked around the trigger guard of the Vetterli Swiss rifle. Stretching, shoulders still to the floor, he dragged the weapon to him, laying it flush to his leg.

Light, despite a long barrel, he'd gotten very comfortable with the Vetterli during his training. But comfort never guarantees the oneness that the Lieutenant sought, the gun's becoming the assassin.

The White House had been good practice. Bringing down the horses, but not the men, then laying sniper fire that sent guards scurrying in wrong directions, while making good an escape after killing the decoy shooter. He felt a twinge of pride about that work, about his skilled precision.

Today, he'd sniped as planned, complimenting each convoy time-bomb explosion with a dead soldier, the ejected brass from his rifle scattering on the floor around him like loose change falling from his pockets. The shooting behind Maston's horse was the challenge: just missing, but striking close enough so the animal would feel the hot lead spatter from the ricochets, and keep running.

Belly-crawling, the Lieutenant's second position in the old Confederate Post Office was a frosted, side window that overlooked the end of the street. He rolled into the window's corner, still keeping low, checked his rifle, and listened to the echoed voices from below.

A young man called out, "Mr. President, sir!" Then Grant thundered, "Get to the damn water! Lend a hand to those that need it! Now!"

Grant's voice gave the Lieutenant a picture of a blind dog barking from a porch; a hunting animal once, but now old, and ready to be put down. Snickering behind his teeth, rifle propped on his knees, he raised his head just enough to peer over the windowsill, catching a glimpse of the President's coach.

Oliver was sprawled beside it, flames from the burning convoy dancing in the blood pooling around him, while the horses tugged at their rig.

He watched the Marines break from the alleyway to the

docks, as Grant and Duncan moved for the coach. Easy kills. Grant's stubborn leg was now jammed out straight, unbending, and a shoulder drooped. He untangled the coach reins, his face mapping his pain, then tossed them onto the Driver's seat.

The Lieutenant pressed stock-to-shoulder, keeping the rifle barrel down so the blued steel wouldn't catch a glint of sunlight, giving him away again. He froze in this position.

Grant, staying behind the horses, reloaded his Spencer from a dead Guard's ammo belt, before working his way toward the lead stallions of the team. Duncan crab-walked to the rear of the coach, where Oliver was lying, his moans now flecks of blood staining the corner of his mouth.

The Lieutenant watched Grant over his rifle barrel, keeping a bead on his temple, as he struggled from behind the horses to the side of the coach. Grant looked to the window he'd obliterated, for a sign of movement, of anything. The Lieutenant didn't even breathe. Just kept steady aim from his second position.

Grant held his rifle up, as he had before, squinting through his sights, shifting his aim from windows, to alley, to livery stable. Nothing. The street was now still, with only the last burning leaves from the trees drifting to the gutters.

At the window, the quiet was total. The Lieutenant listened to his own heartbeat, muscles tight, and straining to not pull the trigger. Not yet.

Satisfied with the silence, Grant reached for the coach door, the Spencer casual on his hip, and nodded to Duncan, who slipped long, thin arms under the Driver's shoulders.

The Lieutenant leaned forward through the frosted window, Grant's head perfectly in his line of fire.

He released his breath.

The first shot blasted a hole a foot wide in the wall, next to the Lieutenant's head, almost grazing him, as Grant fired repeatedly from the street, sweeping the second floor of the post office. Firing, cocking the lever action, spent shells spinning from the Spencer's chamber. Firing again.

The Lieutenant ducked, eyes tightly closed, slugs tearing the room, sparking off an iron radiator, pulverizing old plaster, exploding a mirror into shards. He grabbed a piece of mirror, angling it beneath the window to catch a bent-reflection of Duncan hauling the Driver to the coach.

Duncan threw open the door, then awkwardly pulled the unconscious Driver in with him, slipping, legs tangled, while Grant continuously fired, just as an infantryman keeps an enemy pinned to their trenches.

He stopped shooting, the barrel of the Spencer repeater burning hot, to reload the magazine.

The Lieutenant leveled the Vetterli from the window, as Grant shouted, "I got the four-up! Use the door Colt if you need it!" before pulling himself onto the Driver's seat, his game leg dangling.

The Lieutenant fired, ripping the coach's side, sending chunks of lacquered metal flying. Grant brought the coach around, the Spencer next to him. But he didn't grab for the rifle; he stayed the horses, wrapping the reins around both hands, the leather cutting deep, as the team fought to bolt.

The next shots blew apart the coach's side lanterns. Grant didn't flinch, didn't look back for the shooter's face. He snapped the reins, moving the team as one, before breaking them into a full-charge gallop, away from the burning waterfront.

The Lieutenant cursed the old dog handling the horses, and wanted a real showdown with Grant. A real test. But he was following his strict orders, and fired his last, the bullet striking the back of the coach, leaving a gaping hole where the Presidential seal had been.

The target he'd been aiming for.

25

DARK WATERS

Five thousand fathoms deep, the shapes of the sea canyon walls had become invisible. The rock face was there, all harsh cuts and boulders, but unseen in this ocean-black. Fighting the void, Nemo held the steering bar hard-to-starboard, angling himself as if his muscles were pushing the *Nautilus,* toward something only he knew existed in the miles of darkness beyond the front portals.

The one sound throughout the ship was the steady echo of the engines. A distant pulse. No violent waves punching the hull, or whales calling. No crew voices. Grave-quiet.

The running lights shut down.

Sara hung to the struts beside the navigation station, hoping for a tiny reflection in the glass of a compass; any hint of light to adjust her eyes. But there was only the black. She could see nothing.

"Closing shutters, we're running dark. No lanterns, no light until further orders!"

Nemo's command roared out of the dark to the crew call as

gears engaged and steel plates rolled up from the *Nautilus'* deck on hinged arms, fanned out like playing cards, then interlocked completely around the observation dome, coffin-sealing the glass with a metal clang.

The air on the bridge was now thin and hot as Nemo ordered, "Engage the prow, Miss Duncan."

Sara felt her way in the dark, measuring her steps to get bearings, turning on a heel, facing the other side of the bridge that was all pitch corners and alcoves.

"You rebuilt the ship, you know the levers! Now!"

Sara moved forward, hands out, trying for a throw-switch, feeling along the panels and counting them to the place she knew the prow control was.

Jess' hand clamped on top of hers, moving it to an iron hatch wheel mounted on the wall. "This one's tougher than a fiddler's bitch."

Fingers laced, they pulled back on the heavy wheel with all strength, straining, rotating it once. Below, a turbine whirled. Then, the sounds coming from the bow: iron fighting iron as the grinding of metal and the thunder of rock being pulverized filled the bridge.

Boulders pounded the shutters from outside, smashing at them, sending anchor bolts flying. The grinding was louder. Metal screamed. The noise avalanched through the submarine as stones tore against the deck and bridge, the vibration shaking its steel skeleton, echoing in the pitch-black decks and hatchways.

The Maori Whalers stayed to the curved walls by the engine room, knives out, as other crew stumbled blindly past them, the sounds surrounding them as if the hull were being gutted. Some panicked for a life-craft. Anything. Another threw his feet to the wall, and held a tattered Bible to his chest. Posed, ready for death.

Sara stood in the bridge's center, the pounding of the steel, the metal slamming, coming at her from the complete darkness. Closing in. Inside a kettle drum. Near-deafening.

Nemo steered a straight course, steady in the dark, and ignoring the cacophony, as if he were immune. Staying fixed, knowing his ship, and what furies she could stand.

His voice carried over the noise: "The prow's designed to slice through a frigate, or chew away the stalactites blocking an underwater cave. That's what you hear. You dreamed of what it's like to be on my submersible boat"—the grinding and crashing were reaching a crescendo—"this is the reality."

Sara kept her hands over her ears. "My God, it's like being buried alive!"

"No," Nemo said.

He turned the bar, upped the speed. Sara felt the *Nautilus* shift beneath her, move into a strong current. The pounding of the boulders eased. Rocks hit the shutters with less force, bounced to the hull, with smaller pieces rolling off. The outside sounds muffled to scattered thuds, and the grinding gears halted, stopping the iron saw-blades of the prow, but the bridge was still dark.

Nemo had waited to speak. "I've been buried alive, Miss Duncan. In dungeons around the world."

The iron shutters folded back from the dome, retracting into the decking, revealing the water's darkness being broken apart by a distant glow of blue light, soft and above the surface.

He said, "It was nothing like this."

Nemo kept the bow upward, toward a current that was a distorting wave through the dark water. The bow pierced it; the running flow of an underground river. Freshwater fish suddenly darted across the dome, their silver scales a reflecting rainbow,

coming from nowhere as pieces of white swirled in the currents
carrying them; illuminated snowflakes dancing.

Nemo said, "There's Heaven, and you were nowhere close to
death."

Sara reached out for the dome, fingers brushing the glass,
the white just beyond her touch. Her feeling of the dark tomb,
the dread, now gone as Nemo said, "Sailors believed these pyrite
flakes were sea sprites. They weren't far wrong. Surfacing!"

The river fell away, the waters a bleeding wash of colors as the
Nautilus surfaced into the mammoth cave, stabilized, and shut
down engines.

Sara shielded her eyes. The glow she saw from below the surface became like blue sunlight emanating from the wet cave walls
around them: cool, but very bright.

Nemo spoke via the crew call. "All hands on deck for inspection and repair!"

In a hatchway, the Maori Whalers leaned against a store-
room door they'd broken down with their shoulders, passing a
bottle of medicinal brandy, cork life preservers from the stores,
and a snapped-in-half harpoon strewn around their feet. Nemo's
voice repeated in Swahili: *"Mikono yote juu ya staha!"*

The Whalers shrugged, an empty brandy bottle rolling from
between their knees. They sheathed the broad knives they'd used
to split the liquor case, and finished off their current bottle, shattering it against a bulkhead, before standing.

26

BLUE FIRE

The Cave of the Blue Fire was a massive natural cathedral at the bottom of the ocean, supported by volcanic rock arches growing from its walls, with veins of pyrite decorating their surface, like wide strips of stained glass.

Phosphorus rain from the cave's ceiling was the fire's brightness, becoming blue as it flowed through the arches' centuries-old lava pores, lighting the pyrite from inside, before waterfalling into the underground lake where the *Nautilus* was anchored.

"C'mon you sneakin' bastard apes—pull it!"

Standing on the bow deck, the Whalers followed Jess, jamming thick arms around a piece of stalagmite; a huge stone fang stuck between the saw blades of the submarine's prow. They held it firm, to give Jess a clear target for his double-sided pickax. Jess swung. A hard blow, skidding off the stone, sparking its edge.

He dropped the pick. "That didn't mean a kiss to a salt maid!"

Nemo grabbed the pick, told Jess, "Take hold!"

Jess crouched with the Whalers, letting them see the small-caliber Colt he had stuck in the top of his boot, before grabbing at the prow's iron teeth and pulling them back. Just enough. Nemo brought down the pick with great force, smashing the rock to pieces that he pried from between the iron with the ax handle.

He tossed the volcanic rubble into the lake, breaking the shimmering surface, before vanishing under the liquid mirror.

Jess said, "Cap, I thought this place was just spit 'n' legend, but these damn rock spikes is real enough!"

Nemo slapped the ax back into Jess' hands. "It's all real, Mr. Jess, and I want everything cleared in fifteen minutes!"

Jess said, "If them's the orders."

Nemo stepped around a crewman who was dipping his hand into the swirling blue and coming back with fingers covered in bits of light. He grinned at his captain, then got back to tightening the bolts around a hatch.

Blue Fire had been claimed by explorers a century before, and described in a seaman's diary that had washed ashore in the Caribbean. Assuming it close to the islands, others had tried finding it, but failed. Miserably. Money and years gone, they wrote Blue Fire off as another grog tale. Of course, they didn't have a submarine. Nemo allowed himself a brief smile, some pride, at that thought.

He looked to the crew. "We've made it to Blue Fire, gentlemen. A place most of you have only heard whispers about, but we're here, and it took the *Nautilus* to bring us. You've been told this mission's about monsters. It could all be rummy piss, or it could be something real, but no matter, we're going to be living under the sea. That's the only way, and some of us might be dying there. If you're not ready for that, say so. We'll put you ashore at the next land crop."

Work stopped. The crew threw glances. Crewman with the pyrite hand said, "But if we stick, we get paid our full?"

"You'll get full wages. And more," Nemo said.

Jess piped, "Provided you live, you sod!"

The crew laughed, as they knew, and Jess cleared the deck of volcanic rock, saying, "Fifteen minutes, sir!"

"This was most definitely not our route," Sara said, using hand-holds on the narrow deck from the conning tower, her eyes taken with the blue fire. "It's incredible. But where are we, the center of the earth?"

Nemo said, "Spiritually, not far from it. We're fathoms deep, in an air pocket. Perfectly safe."

"I'm not afraid," Sara said. "We were guided by your hump-back?"

"To his habitat, which I knew was very close to here. But we're also more than a hundred nautical miles closer to the site of the British steamer's sinking. That's the mission, isn't it? Our purpose?"

He checked the iron plating protecting the side portals and fins, the hinge works and mechanics, and said, "Your repairs are holding."

Sara said, "I didn't imagine we'd have to blindly break through the wall of a cave."

"The stalactites blocked our entrance, and our progress."

Nemo started around the port side to the stern, the pyrite in the water outlining the ship with a rope of light. "You have an annoying habit of interpreting every comment as a criticism. You need to correct that."

Sara unfolded the paper tongue, the coordinates wrinkled across it. "You didn't follow any of this, you avoided it. Why send me to that box?"

Nemo said, "So you'd see the traps they've laid. Those coordinates, they've been set down for me to follow without question. Your father assumed I'd use that device to navigate this voyage, but when I saw that map of the attacks, I recognized they followed a direct path."

"Yes, to the European shipping lanes."

"To Brigand's Trench."

Jess looked up at Nemo's mention, but Sara didn't notice his reaction. "I've never heard of it."

Nemo said, "Like this place, a legend that's true. It's not been charted, but anyone who truly knows the history of the oceans knows it."

Sara still held the paper, letting it cover the poison ring she now wore on her right hand.

She said, "And we're going to this place? All of the attacks are still in the European shipping lanes."

"There's deliberation at work. The route we're expected to follow, those mines that were set. For us? Or to destroy the harbor? I don't know who's behind all of it, but they've made a study, they know the oceans," Nemo said. "So, we must counter expectations."

Sara said, "Against the unknown forces."

"If it's a government, one is as bad as another; they can devour each other, and probably will. I am happy to stay beneath the waves while the world burns."

"Even if we find a common enemy?"

Nemo said, "I leave that conceit to Grant and your father. That's why they have a Navy. My enemies belong to me alone. We're to find answers to the sinkings and be done with it."

Jess and a burly crewman, head shaved, eye scar-lanced, pulled iron shutters from the doored slots around the dome, knocking out their twisted bolts with a sledge. The crewman grabbed the iron, about to throw it.

Nemo's voice boomed. "These waters don't want our trash. Scrap goes below. Mr. Jess, timing for the repairs?"

Jess said, "Soon!"

Sara said, "Take the bolts from the sides first, then pull the plates. They'll line up better that way."

"Well, surely sounds like she knows," Jess said. "Get to it!"

Bolts and plates were pulled. Sara crumpled the Kraken's tongue. "Beside the fantastic box, there were uniforms. Pictures."

Nemo measured his words. "What's left of the crewmen who gave their lives for the *Nautilus*."

"Is that what you expect of us?"

Nemo said, "We'll be taking the river out the other side of this cavern to the ocean, and the direct path of the British wreckage. Given the tides and drift, I calculate we'll be within a mile of what remains. You should prepare yourself for the worst."

"I don't think you could sound more ominous," Sara said.

"It's the truth of what we're doing."

"You're not afraid."

"Death will not be a surprise to me; I can't speak for anyone else."

Nemo and Sara were now standing on the far stern of the submarine, over the propeller and rudder works, and watched the last of the iron shutters being bolted, the sections aligned by the crew.

He said, "Look at these men."

The blue light of the cave cast no shadows, and to Sara they were specters moving about the deck; hazy in this cave, with the indistinct features of dead men.

"They're not who signed on when the *Nautilus* was created. Those were idealists, these are seafarers, following orders for pay. Most running from the law, or worse. You didn't agree with my dictates, but this is the crew this mission demands."

Sara said, "They'll take any risk for money?"

"You sound like you're on a jury, making judgments. There's something to be said for the purity of the mercenary. Motives are always clear."

"And I had to fight my way on board."

"True," Nemo said, "because you have something to prove. You've studied my ship, you want my acceptance. Which means you're the one crewman who might actually understand why, and what, I have to do."

Sara accepted the grudging compliment, acutely aware of the poisoned metal band on her finger.

The pain from Grant's shoulder was a wave, breaking down his side to his hip, where his leg was unmoving. The weight of the Spencer rifle was too much, and he'd taken the pistol from the coach's door pocket. He raised it with both hands, aiming at the glass insulator above him.

The shot killed the glass, its pieces flying, and cut the telegraph wire from its pole. Whipping wild and singing, it landed in the wet grass next to Duncan, who was putting on gloves. Grant fell back on the coach steps, exhausted, as Duncan snapped the lid on the portable dial-telegraph, attaching the fallen wire to the terminals, gingerly screwing them down.

Grant put the gun beside him and looked out at the blue-green of the Virginia hills, the smokeless sky, and the long stretch of road where he'd pulled the coach over to give the Driver water. Duncan filled a bullet-dented canteen at the bend of a cold-running stream, and Oliver coughed out most of it, but managed a swallow through the dried blood sealing his mouth.

Barely alive, Grant thought, watching him. *But enough to make the ride home, and be buried.*

It was a judgment he'd made too many times on the battle-field, and today had been as bad as any he'd fought. He took a heel of the water from the canteen, wishing it was bourbon, as Duncan set the telegraph's alphabetic dials.

The horses fed on the tall grass edging a road rutted and broken with artillery craters. Grant was trying to remember who had bombed this county, who had given the orders, when Duncan said, "We're connected, Sam."

"Tell Mrs. Grant that we're safe, and coming in."

Duncan flipped the brass needle on the sender, indicating each letter, the coded words sparking.

"And the message to the vice president." Grant rubbed his eyes with his fists. His words were the last things he wanted to say. "We're on full war footing. Every member of the cabinet should be ready to report at sundown."

A message chattered back. Duncan read: "They want a location, to send a special detail."

"Naturally. Turn this into a damn parade. We'll be in Washington in a few hours. No detail. But start preparing the airship."

Duncan reset his glasses on his nose. "Really?"

"Norfolk's in flames, and we haven't got a clue." Grant wiped blood from his hands; the Driver's, the soldiers' in the street, all mixed together. "I hate this, but if Nemo's got the oceans—he's an arrogant son of a bitch—but if he's got the oceans, then we need the air. It's the only way to see who's gunning for us."

Duncan stammered. "P-P-Perhaps—everyone?"

"My friend," Grant looked up, "if that's really the answer, then God help us."

Duncan said, "Duncan's Folly will fly at last."

Grant said, "Hell, I got Congress to pay for it."

Oliver moaned from the backseat. Grant set a pillow, with

Mrs. Grant's needlepoint, under his head, calling back, "Is every-body straight?"

Duncan closed the portable kit. "All orders sent."

Grant said, "We're burning daylight."

He relit the stub of his cigar, taking in the artillery craters, the Virginia grass struggling to grow over scars left by kerosene and gunpowder.

"Surely not the 'Conflict of States.'" Grant stiff-legged him-self to the driver's seat, keeping the rifle and pistol with him. "It's the whole damn world."

27

PREPARATIONS

"Hold the stock with your right hand, looking beyond the transmitter down the barrel, to the ruby chip. That's your siting."

"I've shot with my mother, but this driftwood—it feels strange."

Nemo said, "The shoulder stock's the back of a shark's skull, the thickest part. The barrel support, the spinal column. The laser is where the dorsal fin would be."

"All of the sea," Sara said, holding the rifle precisely, the shark spine thin but very strong to support the transmission barrel, its slight under-curve perfectly fitting the metal cradle holding the laser-source.

Adjusting her stance in front of the library's observation portal, she brought the barrel slightly toward the center of the curved glass, as its protective copper shield opened to miles of murky, blue-green Atlantic.

"After your declarations, I never thought you'd be teaching me about a rifle."

"I've never denied the use of force for the right purpose. Adjust the light source. Bring the cradle all the way back, to understand its function."

"I've seen this gun in use, remember?"

Nemo said, "Then this should be simple for you. Make the adjustment."

Sara slid the cradle and light cells back to a spinal knob that was the weapon's rear sight.

Nemo said, "Different positions control the laser's intensity. You have to travel through the portal glass, and the water, to your target."

"Which target?"

"Not living. Stay absolutely still," he said, securing the cradle, light cells, and focus lens with the twist of a small knife.

"Now. Fire."

A bolt of electric red from the laser traced the water before dropping off behind a coral reef and vanishing as broken pieces of light. A squid rolled from the coral, tentacles curling, then propelled itself away, squirting a cloud of ink.

"You disturbed his slumbers," Nemo said, upping the front of the barrel. "Again."

Sara fired upward, the laser traveling clean: through the water, breaking the inky cloud, and splitting a bank of thick seaweed. Fish scattered, the beam making it nearly to the surface, forming an impression around the bottom of a floating object.

An indistinct, waving shadow.

Nemo kept Sara's finger on the laser trigger, setting it, until the bow and stern were completely outlined by the sharp-edged beam, as if the boat were made of burning red sections. His hand came off the rifle.

"According to the fantasy box calculations that craft should be from your British steamer. And we're here in one day instead of three, with no government vessels trailing."

Sara lowered the gun, laser cells dimming. "My God—"

Nemo took the weapon. "Not designed exclusively for destruction. One of the many differences between what we create on the *Nautilus* and the rest of the world. You've seen the vessel, maybe there are survivors, maybe it's a drifting ghost, or something to lure us in."

Sara looked to Nemo. "Are we going to approach?"

"Yes, but my way."

The hatchway for the rescue orb was belowdecks, next to the power source, recessed into the stern. The hatch opened with a swift turn from Nemo, the double iron door opening to reveal a polished steel ball, large enough to house two people.

Nemo said, "As you'd claim, another of the *Nautilus'* secrets, the steel pressed in the forge in Vulcania. A magnetic rail ejects it spinning into the water, creating centrifugal force that speeds it along. There are rescue supplies on board."

"The power of friction," Sara said.

Nemo locked the hatch. "Friction or fiction?"

"Captain, one thing I've learned on this ship is that my eyes will tell me only half the story."

Nemo said. "Better to be prepared than surprised."

Troopers fell in behind the President's coach miles before the White House, two of them leaping from their horses, grabbing the coach's back handles, with guns out. One of them covered the blasted-apart seal with his body, not wanting an enemy to see that vulnerability, or the bullet holes around it. The other climbed the coach roof, scrambling not to fall, and took a prone position, bringing his rifle around on its sling.

Around them, the others ran their horses faster, trying to keep pace with the president's team. They called out to Grant, as if not believing he was driving; asking if he was injured, asking, again and again, if they needed to take over.

Grant waved them off, pushing the team to take a sharp corner without skidding. He caught the turn, keeping the horses running sure, as they had been for hours, with a reins-snap, quick-pull, and release. Always in control.

Before this day, Grant hadn't driven a four-up since his last visit to his parents' Ohio farm, but the old skills, of knowing the animals and their moves in harness, that control, had returned. So had his skill with a Carbine.

The feeling in the Norfolk street was as if he were at Palo Alto again, his troops spread along the Rio Grande, shooting through dust and cannon smoke at the revolutionists. The instinct of battle, and how to pull a trigger, had come back, too.

The coach ripped over railroad tracks, wheels catching the ties, then landing. Grant played the brakes as the team circled wide to a dirt road along the tracks leading to Pennsylvania Avenue. His eyes followed the guidelines to the bridles, steering the animals with precision.

Flatcars stacked with girders and barrels of cement were on the siding that Grant passed, thinking the materials looked exactly like what was needed for a new gymnasium.

Grant didn't know if General Sigel had even finished the journey to be buried in Germany, but there was already new steel and fresh-cut wood to rebuild the place where he'd been assassinated. The ground now clean and bloodless.

Reconstruction, he thought sadly, running out the last stretch. Soldiers fought to keep up, as if protecting him these last few blocks. Coming in from the side, oil torches spitting fire, Color Guards rode with the coach, a bugler announcing Grant's arrival.

Just what he didn't want.

The streetlights around the White House were lit, with more torches tied beside the lamps, giving off huge circles of yellow, forming their own barricades behind the barbed wire that blocked the sidewalks. Two Howitzers stood sentry on the front lawn.

Grant tossed his cigar, pulled the coach off the road, cutting down a grass slope, to a gravel spit from behind the stables, to the far side of the White House grounds.

He didn't slow, keeping the same gallop if he was dodging enemy shells. More Guards leapt for their horses, others ran to follow, as the coach careened toward the stables.

Grant halted by the greenhouse with a single, skilled motion: braking, and the horses pulling up. He grabbed his rifle and pistol from the boot, dropped from the seat and walked for the green- house's double-doors, leg dragging, but making it. The Guards rolled from the coach roof, landing with their rifles. Some bruis- ing knees, all coughing dust.

"Mr. President—"

Grant said, "There's a wounded man in the back, take care of him!"

Grant stopped, and looked to the back balcony stretching along the White House second floor, and saw Mrs. Grant at the railing, holding up a bottle of brandy. And a relieved smile.

Grant said, "Let's get this the hell going."

Duncan climbed from the coach, brushing himself clean, as the soldiers pulled the Driver roughly from the seat. "He made it this far, gentlemen, let's give him a fighting chance."

Other riders rode in, voices shouting for the president, as Grant and Duncan stepped through the greenhouse double doors, letting them shut behind them, then automatically lock. The works clicked over.

A voice from outside said, "We don't have access!"

The doors were plate steel, painted to look like termite-rotten old pine, with vines growing across it via wire ties, and leading into a long, clay-walled tube, lit from the ceiling.

Grant and Duncan heard their own footsteps and another sound coming from the tube's end. Rhythmic. Pumping, with a low whistle.

Echoing back to them from an open door leading to a cellar that stretched dark in all directions, the sound was mechanical, but with the touch of something familiar. And human. Huge lungs drawing in air; a sleeping giant breathing.

An instant flash of hot light from the cellar blinded them, followed by a cloud of burned magnesium and sulfur.

Maston handed them both blue-paper sunglasses. "Sir, I didn't know when you'd be arriving, but thank God you're here."

"'Thank' isn't the right word." Grant put on the paper glasses, saying, "All orders have been met?"

Another flash.

"I'm not completely privy, sir," Maston said. "If I might, I did see everyone assembling in the executive room, and sir . . ." He held out a large folder, sealed around the sides. "This is from Mr. Colfax. He assumed you'd be coming down here first, check on the progress. Just in case."

Grant took the file. "And?"

Maston looked to Duncan, who was slipping on his sunglasses, and said, "They've also followed all of Mr. Duncan's instructions to the letter regarding construction. Claimed to, anyways."

Duncan adjusted his glasses, modestly nodding, but Grant said, "I sure as hell hope so."

———

"General, certainly glad you survived the melee," Lime said, pouring new powders into a flash pan set next to his camera, both on tripods, and facing the other side of the cellar, toward the breathing machinery. "I didn't think your friend there would let me make it without another beating, but here I am. Not quite big as life, but still here, eh?"

Lime cackled, slipping on his dark glasses, framed gold, and dangling around his neck on a chain. He checked apertures on the studio-folding camera, the price still on its bellows. He attached a cable plunger to camera and flash, then set off a bigger burst of light.

"A little yellow," Lime said, "but, it'll have wonderful detail."

He bowed toward Grant. "Despite the manhandling, I owe you a debt, sir. I even had time for new equipment, to celebrate our little arrangement."

Grant said, "Just honor it."

"Oh, yes." Lime brushed sprinkles of magnesium from his new green shirt, reset his trouser crease. "You'll be telling me what to print, and when, or I'll face a bloody firing squad. That's motivation enough."

"But isn't it coincidental," Lime pointed to the other side of the cellar, "that all these secrets take place underground? Or under the sea?"

Lime hooted through his nose, the voice of a crow. Behind him, the machines continued their breathing, drawing air and exhaling more rapidly. He set his camera. Ignited the flash pan. Still brighter.

He said, "When these are on the front pages, General, the entire world will be envious of your United States and your wondrous toys."

Lime quickly pulled the exposed negative plate, replaced it, then brought the camera to a corner, taking in all of the secret apparatus with its short lens.

His voice was almost singing: "This creation of yours will soak the hearts of your enemies with fear. Just like Captain Nemo. You really should have Mr. Spilett write it up that way."

Grant tore his glasses off. "What about your damn spying?"

"Your man got every single picture I took of Nemo, the *Nautilus,* and the waterfront," Lime said. "And destroyed my specialty cameras. So, did any of Norfolk survive?"

Grant ignored this last, turned to Duncan. "Mrs. Grant's waiting. In five minutes, we'll be buried in half-guesses and ignorant battle plans for all this insanity, and I need to speak to someone."

And then, to Maston: "The Leprechaun stays until we're gone."

The White House was on high-alert.

Guards patrolled the lawns, and a wash of light from their lanterns spilled into Duncan's corner office, throwing shadows across the submarine diagrams on the walls. Slicing them into sinkable sections.

Duncan sat at his desk, back to the submarines, teakettle boiling, and the Phono-tele-Photo coming to life.

Fingers moved expertly over the dials, finding optimum signal strength, before he spoke into the receiver horn. "Sweet, it's your father. Can you hear me? Nemo, are you getting this transmission? This is Duncan, calling the *Nautilus.* The situation's changed, and I want to talk to my daughter, know that she's faring well. This is Duncan."

From the horn, there was only static. Duncan poured tea,

took a Derringer from his desk drawer, checked the ammunition before tucking the small weapon into a vest pocket.

He tried again, "Sara, this is your father," then sipped his tea, "if you can hear my voice, please come back."

The only answer was a distant, electric hum.

28

GHOST FROM THE MIST

A polished-steel meteor, shooting across dark ocean instead of a summer's night sky, the rescue orb rotated wildly, creating a whirlpool of water-energy propulsion, after its launch from the *Nautilus*.

Inside, Sara's stomach was upside down. Then, jolted to the left, thrown forward, and set straight. In seconds. Her seat gyroscoped to remain level as the rescue orb sliced water, always turning and spinning.

"My spine's—coming out my back, or my front. God, this is miserable."

It was the first thing she'd managed since Jess strapped her into the chamber, positive the centrifugal force was pushing her stomach beyond her skeleton.

"You have a gift for exaggeration," Nemo said, piloting the orb with foot pedals, swooping around a reef, then jolting upward again. "I haven't been at this helm since before my capture. Needs adjustments, but I'm satisfied. Be ready for rescue."

———

Fulmer hadn't seen Yellow Scarf, or his men, climb into the lifeboat. They were just suddenly there when he woke. And then, he wasn't even sure. Fulmer couldn't believe his senses now; his nightmares were becoming more and more real, and he didn't know, couldn't figure, where and when they were bleeding into his thinking. Taking it over.

But he heard Yellow Scarf's voice: "You ain't dead."

Yellow Scarf turned from the lifeboat's bow, jabbing a machete at "*Mariner,*" painted in blue, and peeling off the bow's side.

"Your ship's dead, but not you. Cut your eyes, feed them to the seagulls, you don't speak about it. Where are to be, all the guns? Special bombs? I know you had the weapons, so where did they sink?"

Words dribbled over rotten gums, in an accent from a distant coast, Scarf leaned into Fulmer. "From here! Point it out!"

Fulmer whispered, ". . . can't . . . see . . ."

"You got your hand again!"

Fulmer tried. He moved his arm, the first time in hours, muscles crying, as he brought his hand to his face, prying open infected eyes, digging away the salty paste sealing the lids. A Berber's scimitar at his neck, pressing harder, was the signal to put his hands behind his back again.

Scarf said, "Now, tell me. Something."

Eyes cleaned open, Fulmer saw the night was starless, the moon just a gray disc, fog settling through it. Slammed forward, jaw gouged against an oar cradle, his wrists were retied, with knots yanked tight.

"You've got to speak!"

Fulmer stayed silent, hunched over the bloodstained burlap sack, now between his knees. The stink from the sack was constant, and Scarf had waved off looking inside, moments after taking the lifeboat and threatening to kill if he didn't show where the *Mariner* sank. Now the sun was gone, and he was still pressing about the *Mariner* and its hold.

Scarf said, "The *Mariner*. Everyone's drowned-ed, but we find you, in rags, holding onto a bag of shit. Could be your rescue, us, but you have to tell where to dive for the guns. Fair trade, your life. *Adil ticaret*, yes?"

Ocean salt had thick-coated Fulmer's tongue, streaming acid down his throat, burning away anything he could say.

Scarf spit out, "Is this some kind of—loyalty? To the dead? Or, you're just *geri zekali*? No brain left?"

Fulmer half-smiled. He knew delirium was soon taking him some other place; his senses had been broken by the sinking, by rolling, night storms, and then, boiled to nothing by a punishing sun. His mind would escape. Leaving him behind. And he smiled, because there was no stopping it.

Scarf backhanded Fulmer's smile, "Listen! You can even have some money. Understand this?"

Fulmer nodded, wishing he was Red, on the ocean bottom, wafting in the currents. The pirates were going to kill him. He knew it, and wasn't afraid. Your mind has to be clear to be afraid, to make sense of the pain, and they'd scuttled the lifeboat of a crazy man, trying to get his secrets. He'd have laughed, but his throat was too raw.

"What are you protecting? You're us. A wanderer of the seas nobody cares for," Scarf said, scraping Fulmer's face with the blade, catching skin on its edge, wiping it with his thumb. "Want to die, or lead us to the sinking? Maybe get rich."

The Berber clamped hands around Fulmer's skull, locking him, and Scarf angled the machete to strike just above his shoulders. A clean cut, the blood fountaining straight into the night air, and Scarf thought at least he'd have that kill to keep his crew in line. This blank-eyed Fulmer, this *piç Kurusu*, serving some purpose.

Other pirates yelled and whistled, each brandishing a broad knife, pistol, or breech-loading rifle. Dangling on the lifeboat's sides, crammed together from stern to bow, they started a low chant: laughter, becoming thumping words in Turkish that Fulmer didn't understand. But that excited Scarf, so he stretched the blade higher.

It was the moment Fulmer was to be overwhelmed. Chanting. Stomping. The blade, showing against the moon, about to guillotine. Voices louder, and surrounding him. All eyes and open mouths. He was supposed to break, but how would that happen without feeling fear?

Thumping louder: *"Ölüm en iyisi! Ölüm en iyisi!"*

Fulmer's mind was somewhere else, watching the water around the lifeboat beading: grease on a hot skillet. The energy coming from just below. Something rising. By fathoms, then feet.

Scarf's rage screamed over the chants, the machete coming down as a massive, rolling wave jolted the lifeboat, its curl tossing the bow into the air, bodies thrown from sides and stern. Shouts in a dozen tongues.

A cannon blast of water hitting the lifeboat. Sudden and powerful. Water churning, as something from the deep raced to the surface, off the bow. Fathoms, then, feet closer.

The ocean boiling with its friction.

The rescue orb exploded through the surface, catapulted into the air by its own force, shedding waves from its sides like showers of fire, then coming down again. A meteor crash landing on the ocean, cutting furrows of water.

Fulmer threw his head back, laughing without a sound, and

around him, all color and movement from his delirium. His mind swimming. Hallucinations. Had to be.

The huge polished-steel orb, spinning wild, swamping the lifeboat, then bobbing over its own wake before rolling onto a calm stretch of ocean, and stopping, as solid as new cobblestones.

Feet away, pirates beat against the waves, choking their way back to the boat, panicking to its side, screaming for help. Grabbing hold. Scarf yelled an order. No moves to anyone in the water, but keeping weapons on the large steel ball, floating, its top and bottom rotating fast, stirring water energy around it.

Fulmer, hands still lashed, watched, doubled over on the burlap sack, his eyes clouding again, but trying to believe what he was seeing: a seam splitting through the orb's middle, revealing an invisible door the way a scalpel slices flesh. Skin folding, and the opening suddenly there.

Fulmer grinned at the thought of whatever emerged from the ship's door and onto a metal gangplank that was cranking from the orb, ending just short of the lifeboat's bow, a few inches above the water with a hooked chain dangling its end.

The orb's mechanical sounds stopped, leaving only the lapping water and rising north winds.

Scarf used his machete as a pointer, calling out in a familiar way, "Hey! Are you the Ocean Monster? *Canavar okyanuslarin?* That's what I think you are! Can you show it?"

Nemo stepped through the opening, shark's skull at his shoulder, fittings on the laser set to full power, the red glowing. He didn't let the weapon drift as he spoke, looking at the guns pointed at him, the fog thickening around the men in the lifeboat aiming them.

"Evet," Nemo said, acknowledging Scarf's Turkish. "For you, I'm the Monster of the Ocean."

"Who else would build something like that?" Scarf said. "I didn't know you were a real thing, but who else would build it?"

"Your prisoner, he's coming with me. That boat is yours."

"All of this, for that sack?" Scarf jabbed Fulmer with the machete's rounded side. "But he hasn't told me the good of what he knows."

Fulmer coughed salt, let his eyes wander; watching it play out. Nemo nodded in Scarf's direction, and said, "I don't think he could tell you his father's name."

Scarf laughed. "Yah, if he knew it!" He switched hands with the machete, but kept it next to Fulmer's head. The Berber stood by with a battle hammer in his fist.

Nemo said, "Are these the leavings?"

He was steady in the orb's entrance, watching a deadeye pirate vulture-perch on the lifeboat's stern, keeping a Chinese Match-lock Musket leveled, throwing knives bound to his leg.

Scarf, always smiling: "What is this you're saying?"

"That I've seen a thousand pirates, from a hundred countries." Nemo eyed four more around Dead Eyes, all with revolvers of different makes, and war axes. "The Chinese rifle, how many of those did you find floating? Three of your men have German Army pistols as sidearms, one of the others is Spanish."

Scarf said, "You talk like these are guns of yours."

"Despise something, you get to know it well. I'll wager all are from the ships sunk in the Atlantic these last months. How many have you raided?"

"Unlike you, monster," Scarf said, "we didn't put a single ship on the bottom. But, you're *efsane*," he searched for it, "the legend."

"You picked over the bones, you've had your fill, and this man can serve no purpose for you. Don't be foolish."

"Foolish? My men, they could eat your liver for breakfast. But why? And what purpose the half-dead one serves to you? Or her."

Fulmer kept his head bowed, but cocked it at Scarf's words, glancing over to see Sara standing at the orb's split-open entrance, on the metal gangplank behind Nemo, the chilled fog wrapping them both.

Scarf said, "It's just the two of you, and us?"

Waves had picked up with the wind, the orb and lifeboat moving with the ocean's roll, almost colliding. The gangplank dipped under the chop that crashed against Nemo, the ocean pulling back and hitting him again in the chest. But he stood defiant. Ignoring the waves and assessing his target, the one with the machete and yellow headscarf.

For Nemo, this small piece of ocean wasn't just cold, black water between their crafts, the fog bringing more chill. This bit of ocean was a hidden corner of every prison he'd ever been in, every yard where he'd fought. And Scarf was the one you had to challenge, and put down.

He saw only that, even with Scarf offering, "We have a mission, too. We have to dive. Your crazy ball, seems like it's perfect for us, so we'll buy it from you. And the gun. The girl, we won't even try. She's yours. *Onu boğazından vurdu, sonra onu ateş açın.*"

This last was said warmly, like an invitation, Scarf sure that they wouldn't completely understand.

Sara stayed close to Nemo, said quietly, "If you didn't get it all, the one with the knives is going to kill me first."

Nemo tightened his hold on the shark spine. "I wasn't sure about their priorities."

"You never put down that crazy gun? Okay, it's all yours. Everything," Scarf said, pulling Fulmer's still-lagging head back, his eyes closing again. "And this. You can have this mess, and we part. As friends."

Scarf eased toward the bow, out of the sight line of his men, saying, "We're sea dogs, yes? Have to try these things, but you win. Just like these ships that are going down. Talk to sailors, they say it's monsters. Even some of my own men. But I've heard it before. That's what they always called you, Nemo, yes? In my village, your underwater boat was a dragon. I don't know what they'll call the silver ball!"

All the while Scarf spoke, the others moved around the boat, taking their strategic positions. "You're not the one sinking these ships, are you?"

Nemo said, "Not this time."

"How many times did they tried to hang you, and you still alive? Good to know, if I ever get caught because some *ölü piç* wags a tongue."

The laser sliced, from Nemo to its target in the pirate with the knives. Two burns: one heating the blade, to toss it aside, the other through his eye. Cooking in the socket, sending him over the stern in agony.

On the gangplank, Nemo swung the rifle around, hitting Dead Eye's rifle, exploding the gunpowder in its pan, the hammer and works blowing back into his face, dropping him, blood jetting through fingers.

Through the fog-gray, pirates threw knives and hurled battle-axes. Sara batted a knife away with a medical kit, the other blades skidded off the orb's polished steel. Nemo fired, burning a hand, and jaw, to exposed bone.

Others dropped behind the lifeboat's bench, unloading revolvers. Wild slugs and ricochets. Sara ducked into the orb, Nemo dove to the gangplank, firing through the top of the waves rolling into him, cutting the water before cutting chests and throats. The shooters now firing into each other in blind pain.

Nemo burned the blood and flesh of Scarf's men, as easily as Scarf's machete decapitated. Screaming into the waves, or bleeding across the boat, holding themselves, as if they could repack their pouring insides, before collapsing into freezing water, eyes open and surprised.

Fulmer stayed bowed over, happily. Hands lashed, bearded face to the lifeboat hull, his mind was relieving him of the chaos, separating him, as weapons fire traced the air and blood sprayed his face. He didn't know whose, or see the man fall, but there was no panic. No reaction. He fixed on the warped lumber of the hull, edging forward, away from the Berber. Carefully.

More blood, and a wave, soaked him. He moved again.

The Berber grabbed Fulmer's collar with one hand, the battle hammer raised in the other. In a single motion, Fulmer brought his entire body backward, rolling onto his shoulders and kicking the Berber in the chest with all his might. Slamming him with both legs.

Berber was thrown, grabbed a knife from Dead Eye's sheath, and charged, leaping the length of the lifeboat for Fulmer. A red beam of light slit both his eyes. They drained. He dropped. Fulmer wrapped his knees around Berber's neck, squeezed together to choke his cries, then twisted. Breaking his neck.

Fulmer imagined that he was smiling, rolling to his side, relaxing his legs, letting the Berber go slack between them. No threat now, just dead weight. An anchor. His mind at drifting-ease during all of it, Fulmer's heart hadn't even raced. The strength was something outside of himself.

He stood, hurling himself into Scarf, knocking him over the side of the boat, the hull keeling into him, cracking bones. Puncturing his temple. Red bled across the yellow as Scarf choked on the swells, filling his lungs with brine before pulling him under. Fulmer stumbled forward, still trying to see through the fog, see who was coming next for him.

Sara stepped, wincing, over Berber, steadied herself against a coiled rope soaking with blood and cut Fulmer's wrists free. She took his hand, leading him to the gangplank where Nemo was standing with the laser, the beam lacing straight into the sky then breaking apart against the highest clouds, scattering as red stars.

"Up to the heavens or across a man's throat," Nemo said, not looking at the lifeboat battlefield. "Their choice, and always this result. Now, we'll see if your survivor has any worth. I doubt it."

Sara said, "These dead thought so," as Fulmer snatched up the burlap sack, tucked it under his arms. He tried to say something to Nemo but his throat wouldn't allow it.

"Pirates, trailing the wrecks to scavenge, killing anyone who hadn't drowned. And this scalawag is the only living witness," Nemo said.

"Is this man known to you?" Sara got her question out just as Fulmer was knocked by a gust of wind, tumbling over a pirate body, and her catching him. He squeezed her hand in thanks.

"He reads familiar," Nemo said, "but the one in yellow could us give us more accurate information."

"He's dead. You followed your own plan, through the caves, away from the Navy, or my father, using your weapons. It worked, Captain. This man will help the mission."

Nemo's eyes were set on Fulmer. "We'll see."

Fulmer was on the bow of the lifeboat, steadying himself against Sara, the boat dipping as she shouldered him to the orb's steel gangplank to make the crossing between the two crafts. The wind picked up, the waves getting steeper.

Nemo said, "You have an idealized idea of what this is all about, Miss Duncan. Even who the enemy might be. That's dangerous."

Sara said, "More than this? I'm sprayed with blood, too. Bleeding. This was a battle, Captain. Thank God, you won."

Fulmer was now on the gangplank, the burlap tied to his belt loop. Rain started. Broken glass in the harsh wind. Nemo stayed the orb's entrance, watching this man, then finally extending the laser rifle for him to take hold of the stock. Using the shark's skull to steady himself, and pull closer.

He took a step, hand reaching.

A curling wave splayed across the steel plank, with Scarf's hands ripping out of the water from below, grabbing Fulmer's legs, jerking him down, head slamming on metal. Jet of blood, before pulling him off the gangplank into the ocean. Another wave crashed. Larger, fed by the rain, twisting the gangplank, with Sara holding on. Calling out over the storm.

Beneath, violent darkness.

Churning water whipped Fulmer from side to side, like a shark shaking life from its prey, as he tried to swim against waves, inside the storm waves. And behind him, Scarf's hands wrapped around his throat, holding and choking him from behind as they both sank from the surface, the storm ripping the surface. Rain punching.

Both men sank deeper as they fought. Twisting, with Scarf wrenching Fulmer back, hands tighter around his throat, cutting the last of his air.

Prying Fulmer's mouth open to strangle him with ocean, the last of Fulmer's strength, gone.

He didn't see Nemo diving through the waves, swimming for him, and grabbing Scarf around the middle, pulling him away. Fulmer could only feel Scarf's fingers weaken, start to slip. The water punching from all sides. A rip current grabbing hold, taking the three men deeper, and the storm bringing up silt from the bottom as an erupting cloud, choking the water. A moving, swirling blindness.

Scarf let go, and Fulmer turned, falling back, the water carrying him. Trying to move his arms. Or legs. His breath gone. Eyes rolling to white, even as Sara slipped herself under his shoulders, carrying him toward the surface. Pulling with all her might.

Fulmer drifted down, his body cold, and waiting for the warmth that would precede death. Beyond him, Nemo and Scarf still struggled. Becoming two silhouettes in the currents. Drifting farther away, hidden by the storm. By the cloud.

Through the churn and stinging salt, Fulmer could barely see Nemo push the rifle strapped on his back into Scarf's face. Under his chin. Sara swam harder, bubbles flowing from her mouth and nose, powering to the surface.

Fulmer looked down. His last. Into the swirl. And saw a red dagger of light, punching through the top of Scarf's head and to the water's surface, followed by a spreading curtain of blood.

Fulmer choked his air as Sara broke the waves, carrying him to the chain hanging from the orb and hooking him onto it, the heavy chain taut through crashing water. Fighting the waves, and the storm, she hauled herself from the water and set the winch to pull Fulmer aboard the orb. The burlap bag still tied, safe whether he was alive or dead.

29

SPIDER

The bourbon was warming, but with just the right edge of feeling, that moment of satisfaction, for Grant, that the bath would always be warmer, and the two could mix together, inside and out.

It was all he wanted to think about at this moment, lying back in the tub, with Julia Grant on a chair by the vanity, the sheaf of telegrams and special letters in her lap, a glass of claret in her right hand.

She flipped the pages, murmured to herself, not ready to give an opinion. Grant turned the hot tap for a moment, then cut it off, precisely, settling back.

Julia looked up at her husband, shaking her head. "For an easy man, you can be very particular."

"About my pleasures, and you, and the children," Grant said, draping his face with a wet washcloth, letting the water run through his beard and down his chest, across battle scars. He took a blind sip, a bar of soap floating past his belly.

"The fate of the world, all bundled here in the upstairs bath. If I don't reduce the enormity for just a moment, goddamnit, I'll break."

"You've never shirked your duty, husband. Even now." Julia, her brown hair uncharacteristically loose, held a telegram at arm's length, and said, "This might be the last private time we ever have."

"Don't ever voice that, dear, I can't stand to hear it," Grant said. "You've read those latest?"

"There isn't a single message that doesn't imply you planned all this to draw them into a war."

"Not-so-carefully implied."

Julia said, "Even with my eyes, I can read between the words," and put aside the file. "And Norfolk's gone."

"The frigates certainly are." Grant sipped. "God knows the waterfront's burned to hell. I'm getting more details before midnight, but I was there, so . . ."

"So you already know. What about this Nemo?"

Grant said, "He warned of sabotage; I thought it was a blind. We have no idea where he is, or who he might be challenging."

"To set all these countries aflame."

"He could tip us into war, or save us. I thought I was getting a rogue submarine, and I ended up with just a rogue." Grant sipped quietly. "I hate like hell not knowing; how can I plan a battle?"

Julia's voice gently trailed with her question, "And you have to plan a battle, Ulysses? Or a new war?"

"Goddamn, I wish I knew which, but it has to be something. A defense. An answer, for all this craziness. That was the whole point of saving Nemo, to give me some bearings. God, how many attacks have we faced in the last week? We're still wounded from the war, and we're going up in flames. How the hell do I stop it, or fight it?"

Grant wiped water and sweat from his face, reached beside the tub, poured some more bourbon, and his wife said, "Thrashing like a mule in quicksand."

"That's it." Grant smiled. "My father had a way with words." He sat up in the tub. "Did you see Gladstone's note? I don't know how he slipped it in."

Julia pulled the letter with the Royal Seal. "Mr. Gladstone is being an alarmist. England would never take up arms against us. They wouldn't dare."

Grant said, "He's saying I can't bet on a damn thing with Victoria. That's what that Summit at Sea is about, to decide any moves against us."

Julia said, "And planned so there'd be no chance of you attending."

"Those Kings and Kaisers know I can't be there. The accused doesn't get to plead his case," Grant said.

"So they can plan *their* attacks," Julia said. "Gladstone risked something, telling you this."

"Every country that lost ships, they're building a damn catastrophe, and he knows it."

"So I guess you're going to have to use your wings."

She got up, sat on the edge of the tub. "That machine's been breathing, or whatever you want to call it, since you sent the messages."

Grant said, "I thought I'd have to tell you."

"No, just like you didn't have to tell me about the shootings."

Grant said, "Someone's really pushing us." He took the last of the bourbon in his glass. "I never imagined I'd be holding a rifle that way again."

Julia lowered her head. "You were under fire."

Grant said, "I'm sorry, dear. It's an old story for us, and I know I only have so much luck."

Julia fought tears. "The warrior's day never ends."

Grant said, "You said something like that the day I proposed."

"To remind myself about your duties."

She went to the window, lowering the lights next to it, to see the glow of torches and machines coming from below, the lights surrounding the greenhouse. In the quiet, the sound of the machine's operation, its breathing, echoed from the cellar and traveled across the grounds.

"Getting to that summit is the only way."

She turned to her husband. "No matter what side Nemo takes, or whatever he finds, you have to show your face to the world."

"I always feel like I'm preaching to the choir; I never have to explain anything to you."

She said, "Remember, you're not a shavetail anymore."

"I'm reminded constantly. All my life, I've never been as frank with anyone as I can be with you."

Julia smiled. "And your reputation's for plain speaking."

"Among other things."

Grant put his empty glass beside one of the tub's clawed feet, looked to Julia, standing at the window, the lights from below reflecting behind her.

"Those little eyes of yours. Everybody thinks they just see each other, but they see everything."

She smiled, "Always."

The Whalers swung reinforced boat hooks, coming in from the side, to catch the edge of the rescue orb as it rolled onto its rails from the sea entrance. The velocity too fast, the rush of water, all powering it into the *Nautilus*. They ran alongside, grabbing at it as they would a ship's line, snagging handles on the orb's middle with the magnetized hooks and pulling back against the ball's momentum with their combined strength. Feet braced against the submarine's grating, slowing, braking it on its short track like a runaway mining car.

A steel-enforced net brought it to its final stop.

The seal split, the top sections unfolded. Jess brought Nemo and Sara from their seats, as others hefted Fulmer, not moving, from a small place behind the orb's controls.

Fulmer's skin was bluing, his infected eyes closing again, but Nemo said, "Supposedly, he's breathing. Get him to the laboratory."

The crew made quick work of strapping Fulmer to a battle litter, running him down a passageway to the stern and lower decks. Nemo and Sara followed. Silent. Soaking wet, carrying the laser and the burlap, leaving footprints of bloody seawater behind them. Battle weary.

Jess held out a blanket for Sara. "This is gettin' to be a habit."

Nemo said, "You'll need this, too, Miss Duncan," handing Sara a *Nautilus* key: a silver dolphin, in mid-dive. She held it as if it were a posthumous medal of honor, and followed the litter.

Jess produced a bottle of brandy and shot glass from his peacoat. A sly move, and he was proud of it, saying, "Takin' liberty, sir, but it must have been a hell of a thing up top."

"Does this mean you've been in my quarters?"

Jess said, "No, sir. Never. This here's from the old stores. It's not Napoleon or nothing."

"We've got foul weather blowing in for the next two days at least. Set special coordinates. My brandy's off-limits, but you can distribute that fairly among the men, as I'm sure you will."

Jess turned on his heel. "Aye, sir."

"And Mr. Jess, have a burial detail ready. Within the hour."

The silver dolphin opened a wall that had broken the sea laboratory in two. Folded back, it revealed the other half of the *Nautilus*' laboratory: a place of two worlds and two sciences. One side, all modernized sea cages and study tanks. The other, an operating amphitheater that was a never-finished Victorian puzzle.

An examination table, surrounded by glass tubing and bubbling chemical tanks, was it center, gold sconces illuminating its far corners with elegance against iron walls dented by bullet strikes from the *Nautilus'* capture.

The table was spotted with blood, the old stains as dark as the knots in the wood. Beyond the table, a jungle of wiring laced the edges of the domed-iron ceiling, spools running to freestanding energy arcs throwing off power. Other wiring was in tangles about the room, along with wrecked components. Pieces of steel and specialty glass, in labeled boxes, with dates of the failed experiments.

To Sara, the different equipment in the lab, the conflict of old, new, ruined, and unexplained technology was the epitome of Nemo: an always-fighting brilliance, looking backward and forward simultaneously.

The crew rushed the litter past the spotless chrome and glass, to the examination table where a full complement of oddly twisted surgical equipment was laid next to it.

"Those knives and clamps are meant for creatures with all number of lungs, not just two."

Nemo crossed the lab, the Whalers hefting Fulmer from the litter. The table tilted forward, large steel bands snapping around from beneath, flexible belts locking Fulmer's ankles and wrists in place, the table's balance wheels automatically setting a position for surgery.

"Stop being goggle-eyed, Miss Duncan. It responds to the weight of whatever's put on it."

Nemo was at a washbasin, sterilizing his hands. "That device was created for subjects that won't be still. If your survivor had a dorsal, you'd understand completely. Sterilize. There's a pharmacy kit in the far cabinet."

Nemo tore open Fulmer's shirt, ordering the Whalers, *"Mab-wana, nyuma yako posts,"* then to Sara, "You're dawdling; do you want your survivor to die? That would represent a great deal of wasted effort. Take the bio-carbonate. It's the first syringe."

Sara opened the kit, and the syringe was exactly as Nemo said. She moved to Fulmer, chest exposed, blood wiped away, with Nemo pressing on his breastplate with both palms, massaging the heart.

"You had two years of medical college," Nemo said. "When I stop the massage, inject the carbonate into the sack around the heart muscle. Around, understand?"

Sara drew the fluid, watching more color drain from Fulmer's skin, his blood gathering purple around the tips of his fingers, swelling the veins on the top of his hands. His breathing and circulation, shallowing to nothing.

Sara said, "Sir, you're aware what's happening . . ."

"The important thing is, are you? Now!"

Sara jammed the needle into Fulmer's chest, just missing the breastplate. Not all the way in. Nemo punched the syringe, driving it farther into Fulmer's chest cavity, pushing the plunger down completely, snapping its tubing in half. Nemo yanked the broken glass away, pulling out the needle. Blood spurted.

"What eye movement?"

"None." Sara's fingers were on Fulmer's wrist, feeling for a pulse.

Nemo said, "His throat!"

Nemo grabbed two wire coils attached to the base of an electrical arc, and unfurled them to the table, the ends bare and wound around small copper flats. He hung them on the side of the table beside Sara, now with both hands on either side of Fulmer's neck, lightly feeling for an artery.

"Reactions? Don't rely on your touch!"

"I don't have any choice, Captain. It's there, and very faint."

Nemo tossed a pair of gloves to her, rubber strips sewn along the fingers. "Your studies were only with western medicine, a common mistake. Go to the arc, and throw the red switch, on my command."

Fulmer's eyes moved, searching beneath sealed lids.

Sara called, "Captain!"

And then there was the faintest sound: ". . . death . . . ?" before his head cantered to one side, mouth open, jaw slack, and tongue swelling white.

Nemo slapped the copper flats to Fulmer's chest. Sara threw the switch at the arc, hammering with a measure of electricity. The creatures in the lab churned at the blast; reacting to the ozone searing the air, the voltage skidding over the water in their tanks.

Another charge. Like a lightning strike.

Fulmer seized forward, body lurching against the steel bands, then falling back. Again. Then again. Three intense jolts. Nemo signaled Sara off, and stood back from the table, watching Fulmer's hands and feet. Beginning to flex.

Sara, about to speak, but Nemo cutting her with, "Could be delayed nerve reaction. There's a heart monitor with amplifier by you."

Sara placed the small probe, a glass half-dome, on Fulmer's chest, tube and wiring to a battery-powered speaker. Nemo turned up the current until the lab was filled with Fulmer's loud, steady heartbeat.

Sara delighted in it. "Your design?"

"For the heartbeat of a whale calf after surgery, or the flow of blood from the two hearts of the Hagfish. But this works as well," Nemo said. "His life's been saved too many times today, none of which will make a difference if we don't get him fed. Wipe the muck from his face."

Sara wet down Fulmer's face, dabbing away dried blood and salt, cleaning out his eyes. They opened for a moment, and he moved his hand, to glance hers.

Nemo said, "He was close to dying, probably thought you're an angel."

Sara said, "Exhausted and a mess."

"It was a near-death delusion, but understandable given the circumstances. Open his mouth."

Sara smiled at the almost-compliment. Nemo hung a bottle of milky liquid from a stand, and she opened Fulmer's mouth for Nemo to insert a rubber tube from the bottle into his throat.

"More magic medicine?"

"As long as he doesn't choke." Nemo checked the flow of the liquid. "My own recipe for whale calves, when the cows have been slaughtered. Should work on your witness."

Sara looked down to Fulmer, who was deeply asleep. "He gets to rest. Do we?"

"Not yet."

"Why is this man my witness?"

Nemo was at a tank, pouring in seawater. "Because the government has a theory about these monster sinkings, and he's to verify it."

Sara said, "He could give us information to any theory, including yours, if you'd like to share it."

"I wouldn't."

"Captain, you do seem to know him, recognize him at least."

Nemo said, "Our history's unimportant. Hand me that sack, he risked all for it."

Sara picked up the burlap bag from beside the table, instantly reeling from the stench rising from it. "That smell, God, some-thing's dead."

"It is indeed." Nemo cut the burlap with shears, rotten threads pulling apart, followed by a dribble of brown. "Pure whale oil, directly from the animal's skull."

"You can buy it," Sara said. "Is that what he was protecting?"

"Hardly."

The burlap split completely, and the Sea Spider dropped into the tank. Piston-legs frozen, metallic body scarred, seaweed and flesh still caught in its claws. Its eye hung by a thin, vein-like wire, with antenna snapped off clean.

"I'm not sure what I'm seeing." Sara squinted through the side of the tank at the thing turning lifelessly in the water, then sink-ing to the bottom. "A crab, but I've never seen a species like it, I don't think."

Nemo said, "Not a species, Miss Duncan. A machine."

30

ANOTHER LAUNCH

"Do you know what that is?"

Maston was surprised at Duncan's question. "Sir?"

Duncan said, "That box. Any ideas?"

"Well, to me, it looks like it could be a bomb."

Maston was in the doorway of Duncan's office, hat-in-hand, as if he was a beau come calling for Sara. Duncan used his bifocals to point to the tall, metal box on his desk, next to the Phono, and surrounded by stacks of rolled charts and half-folded maps.

"A bomb. One of my first thoughts, and many would agree with you." Duncan rubbed the exhaustion from his unshaven face with his palms. "You're perceptive, in your way."

Maston kept his eyes averted and words low. "Well, I have training."

"That's the Nemo file, and my opening it started all of this. Papers. Reports and memos. That's what government is, young man. Papers that instruct others to pick up weapons."

"That actually sounds like some of Nemo's philosophy."

Duncan regarded Maston for a beat. "It's someone's."

Maston said, "Sir, I've been ordered to write a report about Norfolk."

"You were there. Tell the truth."

"I don't know all of it."

Duncan said, "What are you asking me for, Mr. Maston? Everything's completely out of my hands."

His voice was as measured and folded as the maps and blue-prints he took from the walls, jamming the leather satchel with paper. "For me, the worst is that I haven't been able to speak to my daughter."

Maston said, "Inflation's almost completed."

"So we'll be leaving straightaway," Duncan said, turning up the signal of the Phono-horn. "Nemo, this is Duncan. I need to contact my Sara."

No response. Nothing heard in the office at all but the bouncing back of the mechanical breathing from the greenhouse cellar and the sound of crowds and horses gathering outside.

Duncan said, "The signal's falling off somewhere. I checked weather reports, at least a day old, but they may be having rough seas. I have to keep telling myself that excuse."

Maston responded as if Duncan were speaking a foreign language. "Yes, sir, a storm would do it, I guess, but these new machines are all a mystery to me."

"But you understand guns, which I don't." Duncan let his voice trail, allowing a little fog around its edges. He spilled water from his teakettle, fumbling to relight the stove fire, the cool demeanor he had when alone now frayed and nervous in front of Maston.

"Sir, I'd like to volunteer to go along on this mission," Maston said. "I feel like I failed by not being with Miss Duncan."

Duncan regarded Maston "You didn't fail."

"She's on that ship, and I should be there with her."

Duncan took a folded tin map from his top drawer, slipped it into the satchel's side pocket. "No one holds you responsible."

"I was given an assignment, I failed."

"You designed the poison ring for my daughter."

"And showed her the best way to use it, yes, sir. That's part of my job, and I'm dedicated to it."

Duncan said, "I'm aware of your accomplishments."

"But this wasn't one of those. I was to be the watchful eye, which means I should be on the *Nautilus*. Now. I'm not afraid to get my hands dirty, when it's asked of me. I complete my missions, and I need to complete this one, see it through," Maston said.

"What about your other duties here?"

"The Leprechaun, uh, Mr. Lime, he ain't going anywhere, and he'll be doing exactly as the President ordered."

Duncan said, "Well, I'm sure of that."

Maston breached the doorway, saying, "They have Army and security officers. I genuinely feel my place is with you and the President, but it has to be requested for me to be assigned."

Duncan's words dragged on the floor. "I've never been shot at before, never been in any situation like this."

Maston said, "I surely have, sir, and more than once."

Duncan said, "I'm still shaking."

Static burst from the Phono. A distant sound. Duncan immediately went to the dials, trying to find the signal again. Anything stronger. Silence. Duncan's expression darkened with more frustration, his tall frame almost bent in half by an invisible weight, leaning into the horn as if climbing inside would bring Sara's voice.

Nothing. Not even static. Duncan straightened.

Maston said, "Sir, I know I can be of use here."

He peered over the tops of his glasses. "With all that's happening, your presence might be a soul comfort, Mr. Maston. Consider yourself requested."

Cincinnati was on his hind legs. Back arched, eyes wide and white, with nostrils flaring and kicking wild, after the blinding flash of powder. Rearing. Hot magnesium flashed again as Grant and Efrem kept hold of the bridle, easy with it, and brought the horse down, Grant calmly stroking withers and sides.

Efrem stayed close to Cincinnati's bobbing head, ears twitching around, speaking quietly. "Apologies, sir, but this is truly scary for him; he's never seen nothing like this. Or, heard nothing like this."

The mechanical breathing was still a constant echo from the greenhouse, and Grant said, "Scary for me also, for the same reasons."

Grant traced the scar of the sniper's shot on Cincinnati's shoulder, the hair around it a lightning slash across his onyx coat.

He said, "Healing, and damn well."

"Honest, sir, the stuff the veterinarian used just wet the hair. My papa's salve, that's what made him heal up so fast. I didn't ask no one." Efrem looked down at his boots. "Am I let go from the telegraph room?"

"Son, you worry about losing your job more than a senator. I'll be gone these next weeks, keep taking care of the old boy. Your way. And bridle my daughter's new paint; I don't want him ill-tempered. You know how."

Grant put a folded envelope into Efrem's pocket. "For your grandmother."

Artillery flashed. Four charges going off as silent fireballs, but it wasn't artillery, only camera pans. Cincinnati twisted at the yellow-white, snapping his head away from the corral fence post.

"He can stand the sound of cannon, but not the flames." Grant tossed Efrem the reins. "Take him to the other side," he said, before turning to the greenhouse. "Lime!"

Lime, in double-breasted emerald, set the last of four cameras and flash pans in a semicircle around the greenhouse, focused upward at its hinged open glass roof and the enormous dirigible that floated within it.

Grant started for him, a different person asking for a signature on special orders, or "one last question," as he walked to the first row of cameras and flash pans.

Schuyler Colfax, Grant's Lincoln-resembling vice president, fell into step next to him. "Ulysses, I've prepared all statements, and the cabinet's ready to act in your absence."

Grant said, "I'm sure they are. Just don't let 'em act like the hogs got out of the pen."

"This has already turned into a county fair." Colfax put a hand on Grant's shoulder. "Are you positive about doing this, this way? Your signature above a formal letter of protest is more than sufficient."

Grant said, "I'd prefer it if it wasn't so, but you're wrong. They're serious about a first strike war, and a letter won't speak for us. Hopefully, the airship and me will impress the hell out of them so at least they'll listen to the evidence."

Colfax tried, "Ulysses, as your vice president, I'm officially advising you: don't take this unorthodox approach. If nothing else, your solo crusade's going to be damn hard to defend to the press, not to mention Congress."

"That's actually what I'm praying for," Grant said. "Schuyler, if they wanted orthodox, they should have elected the other fella."

Grant broke away. He was feeling the Washington damp.

That bone cold that defied the torches lighting the lawns and stables, and always seeped in. Grant lit a cigar, and thought about his children. A flash went off, scorching his view.

Lime called out, "The President Weighs His Options! Superb!"

Lime's cameras were scattered, capturing it all with a flash burst. He rushed between tripods, switching out negative plates, then setting off three more bursts as the greenhouse pumps shut down their breathing. The dirigible sleeve was now inflated, an American flag stretching across it.

"Well, there'll certainly be no doubt as to your identity." Lime snapped off another picture.

"Exactly the point." Grant regarded Lime. "You understand why all your pictures have to be seen in every country?"

Lime said, "I've telegraphed newspapers around the globe, sir."

"These aren't your stinking spy photographs, the quality of the work—"

Lime finished Grant's thought. "Must be superb. These images are your warning shots to your enemies, and I've done them more than justice."

He turned the camera, adjusted the bellows, and took a picture of the gondola, the flash plan lighting it completely. "From every angle, the world will see your air fortress and tremble at its coming."

Grant said, "I've made too many deals with scoundrels without knowing how their loyalty's going to fall. It's not to my liking."

Lime said, "General, you can always depend on my fear of you."

Grant said, "That's wise. You're going to set a special camera."

Mounted soldiers rode in behind the greenhouse, handling guidelines for the balloon, its sides expanding as it cleared the now-opened glass roof.

The riders took position, six on each side of the balloon, handling the lines like roping a steer, bringing the inflatable from its hiding place, across the back lawn, and positioning it over the two-tiered, cast-iron gondola for Grant and his crew.

A cigar-shaped ironclad with dual propellers at the bow and stern, its crown was a tank turret, with riveted sides ventilated by gun ports and small bomb doors.

Duncan ran the lawn, giving instructions to crew to attach the gondola and balloon while he checked the locking of the metal frame to the inflatable, the sleeve grasped by steel claws from the gondola's rim. And then, the tying down of the balloon itself at more than a hundred points.

All hands worked furiously to secure it, with other staff handing off supplies and weapons to be packed in the gondola's cabin. The riders formed a circle around it all, cradling their rifles and watching.

"The first, true Presidential ship of the skies. You must be very proud, sir."

Julia had filled his pocket cigar case with his very best, and Grant lit one, the flame toward Duncan, saying, "That's the man responsible, not me."

Horace, scarecrow of a Telegraph Manager, stood in an ill-fitting coat, holding a lockbox with both hands, shifting nervously. "These are the latest communications, Mr. President. All foreign intercepts."

"You shouldn't be handing this to me in the open."

Horace shrunk. "I know . . . this is very . . . very sensitive material, sir. My sincere apologies."

Grant said, "You apologize too much. Not a good quality in one of my staff."

"No, sir. I'm sorry."

Beyond the back lawns, reporters and mechanical crews

racing the sky ship together, Efrem rode Cincinnati the length of
the far corral, running fast inside the fences. Grant's attention
was there. Separate from all of the other activity, all the other
business. Just running.

Grant said, "Starting now, young Efrem's out of the telegraph
room, takes care of horses and that's it. No more handling communications. That makes him a target for kidnap."

Horace said, "I understand, sir. Very, very wise."

Sledgehammers cracked heavy bracing. Crews knocked the
lumber from under the iron gondola, the balloon holding the
command center aloft.

Duncan took a step back, and a breath, to enjoy his pride.
He'd only seen his design on paper, and now it was real. He faced
Grant, and threw him a mini-salute.

It was the only military gesture Grant had ever seen Duncan
make. He returned the courtesy, saying to Horace without looking at him, "Every communication reaches that ship. Every one."

"I've made all arrangements personally, Mr. President," Horace said, bowing from the waist, his shirt bunching. "It will be as
if you and I were in the communications room together."

Grant's eyes narrowed, his response a curl of smoke from his
nose. He was aware of the pistol under his jacket, the government
secrets under his arm, and wished like hell to be night-riding
with Efrem.

Maston stepped between Horace and Grant. "Mr. President,
I'll be providing extra security for this mission."

"Sounds like a fit to me, son," Grant said. "Let's get the hell
out of here before I come to my senses."

The dawn was colder than the night before, but all preparations
were met.

Julia Grant stood on the White House balcony, the doors to The Shop open behind her, with curtains drifting. On the railing was a tumbler of bourbon, and below, her husband, before the dirigible, addressing the swelling crowd of reporters and cabinet members. Lime's cameras flashed with his words.

Onlookers pushed and shoved beyond barricades, the soldiers holding them to the barbed wire and sandbags of the White House drive. Their voices rose, cheering Grant as he assured everyone that the United States would vanquish this new, unknown enemy.

Julia heard, "There never was a time, in my opinion, some way could not be found to avoid the drawing of a sword. That is my mission. But, if forced to fight, we will, and we will be victorious, as our cause is just, our hearts pure, and our will unbeatable."

Grant waved to the exploding flash pans and roar of voices. Julia's smile was brought by all the quotes and images since West Point, made famous by the man she shared her bed with, that a newspaper declared was, "The warrior who will charge, when no one else is willing, putting duty above everything, except his devotion to family."

She told him his sentimental streak would get him killed, that he'd be shot trying to save a picture of their children. Ulysses laughed. He couldn't deny a truth.

Julia bit her lip as she watched Ulysses climb into the gondola, its heavy iron doors sliding shut, and trying not to think this would be the last glimpse she would ever have.

The crowd cheered its loudest as soldiers guided the dirigible, releasing tether lines on command. Each cut of a line brought whistles and applause as the airship rose over rooftops, the flag painted across it taking up the sky.

Julia didn't fight tears. She picked up the bourbon and raised the glass to her husband as the President's *Aero Force Ship Number One* gained speed, propelling into a violent sky.

31

TWO SHIPS

The *Nautilus* cruised through a tangle of a coral beds, stretching for miles, the rudders snapping apart pieces of its red and orange rock like ribs from rotting skeletons. The submarine's wake churned it all into watered dust, spreading as a cloud behind it.

Nemo was in his quarters, sitting at his desk beneath the luminous portrait of his wife and son, the steady throb of the engines accompaniment as he wrote in a leathered journal, hundreds of pages thick.

My dearest Valanda,
I've been labeled insane by so many that my ritual of writing every night would certainly add to those claims, but expressing myself to you is the only true soul comfort I have, as I struggle to return the Nautilus *to her former glories. Her purpose is being stained by this government mission, hunting for a villain whose techniques, I admit, are intriguing me. But what of his*

motives? I can hear your voice now, dear, telling me to find my own truth.

I will never forget the oath I made over your grave, to ultimately destroy the war-makers and their weapons. That goal remains pure, even if the journey to it seems, sometimes, to be compromised.

This tortures me, but as the one person who knows my heart best, I ask for your forgiveness, and love, so I can endure.

I shall always be your loving husband,

ਡਾਕਾਰ

Nemo checked the watch on his wrist, then moved to the side-view port, sliding over the magnifying dome to see the petrified Roman trade ship just beyond the *Nautilus'* bow.

A sunken ghost, the ship's regal shape, oars, and a single seafarer's helmet had been preserved in the cold currents for a thousand years, fish swarming about the mast instead of tattered sails. Nemo had marked its position with a trident, topped with *N*, as his own navigational guide.

His view was suddenly blocked by a swirling orange cloud of destroyed coral, broken pieces spinning, crashing against the port's outer glass, breaking again.

Nemo ordered into the crew call, "All engines, full stop. Farming crew report, that means you, Mr. Jess!"

Jess, arms folded, stood outside the crew showers, with Sara toweling off behind the modesty screen. Jess whistled, kept his eyes averted, as Nemo marched the spiral stairs to the lower-deck passageway, heavy boots on iron and a voice from the dark before he could be seen.

"You didn't hear the call, Mr. Jess?"

Jess squinted at Nemo at the far end of the passage, and said, "Well, I'm protecting sis' virtues, sir."

Nemo faced Jess. "I know Miss Duncan's quite capable of protecting herself, and I'm sure you're enjoying your view. Mine was just corrupted."

"I'm not gettin' you, Captain."

"Didn't I leave you in charge on the bridge?"

"Yes, sir. We're on mechanical pilot. As you would."

Nemo said, "Do you know how long it takes a coral reef to grow? You destroyed one in seconds. We're part of the sea, not intruders!"

Jess said, "But them spikes in the cave—"

Nemo's voice was thunder: "A reef's a living thing, not frozen rock! Your lack of education continues to be a problem, sir. That's to be corrected."

Sara stepped from behind the screen, into the passage, lacing her boots as Nemo said, "You as well, Miss Duncan. You want to see this."

The reflected light from outside the *Nautilus* washed back into the diving chamber, forming a pattern of moving starfish across the ceiling and the polished steel access tubes that were filling and draining water.

Sara held her diving helmet, examining its skull shape, glassed eye sockets, and metal breathing fittings along the bridge of what had once been a snout.

She said, "Nature and Nemo always prefer flesh and bone. Another shark?"

Nemo pulled on his deep-water suit, made from the under skin of a manta ray. "That's large blue tuna, actually. Two skulls

split, retrofitted, and joined together. Nothing stronger to withstand the pressure. The air's recycled through gills of my creation."

Sara said, "So you improved on nature. Again."

Nemo said, "Always impossible. This is simply using what the
sea allowed me."

"You don't never get tired of speeches, Cap," Jess said, wrig-
gling into his suit. "When my ol' dad worked his place, I don't
remember him wearin' a fish head for a hat. But I'm game."

"I'm sure your family history would be enlightening," Nemo
said, fitting Jess' helmet, snapping down the neck-plate. "But it's
not pertinent. You're on probation for the reef, Mr. Jess. Remember that as you gather our food."

Sara said, "I've read a great deal about your undersea farms.
The newspapers were full of them."

"I know." Nemo handed Sara her gloves, also of manta skin.
"Idiotic speculation, most of it, without vision. We're here for
practical reasons, which is the best way to experience anything.
This journey's promising to be a long one, and this is our oppor-
tunity to harvest the crops without bombs or guns."

"Do you think we'll be attacked?" Sara asked, securing her
helmet, eyes large behind the glassed sockets.

Nemo tied a harvest sack to her belt, then tied his own. "There's
a chance, but we can travel where no one can follow. Which
means a great deal of time on this turtle, Mr. Jess."

Jess spoke through his bone faceplate. "A man can get used to
anything, Captain. Given enough drink."

The Whalers opened the steel chambers. Sara stood perfectly
still as ocean filled the tube, waiting for the power of force that
drew her into the *Nautilus* from outside. But the reverse was a
pressurizing with the outside, then the tube opening, so she could
slide easily from the submarine to the ocean floor.

Free-falling, like in a dream.

Sara landed, the heavy boots bringing her to the sand too quickly. She compensated with fast athletic moves, stretching legs and balancing, then drawing herself together, fighting the weight of the ocean, millions of tons above and around her, trying not to slow. She stood straight as Jess and Nemo followed from the submarine's belly, bringing up heavy silt.

Jess twisted, legs kicking, and landing in the sand on his back. He tried rolling. Struggling. But the weighted shoes tangled in long strands of seaweed and rocks. Sara glided to him with long swimming-like strides, reaching him in moments and pulling him to his feet. A jellyfish he'd rolled across pulsed around him and away.

Jess said something in his helmet she'd never hear, fogging his faceplate. Then squeezed her hand.

Nemo watched, then raised his hand with the laser rifle, signaling the *Nautilus*. Lights flared on: the running lamps around the submarine's side, the lights within every view port, and all the recessed lamps from bow to stern.

The lamps spread electric white-yellow in a glowing wave that worked through the water to show the expanse of ocean floor beyond the sunken Roman ship. A torch in a cave, showing the way.

Sara and Jess were standing before the farm beds.

Traps of lobsters, cold-water shrimp, and rock crabs were mounted on pikes topped with the *N* that staked Nemo's farm. Around the pikes, sea cucumbers twisted from the sand with clams growing in beds around them. Sea lettuce, blooming pink coral, and red seaweed stalked like palm trees were planted in rows but had grown into each other, carried by fish and crabs.

But the abundance stretched father than the *Nautilus* threw its lights. Nemo opened the lobster traps, Sara and Jess bagging the largest, tying them to a pike, before gathering the cold-water shrimp, scooping hundreds.

He wrapped his hands around the pike for a moment. Barnacles had scarred it, but it stood straight, his steel initial, that he'd forged in Vulcania, marking his achievement.

After these years, he didn't know if the farm would be growing, destroyed by storms, or buried in sandy decay. Until he saw the petrified, carved bow of the Roman ship. If it was here, proudly the same, and not washed away, then he knew the farm would be here as well.

A great white knifed just above Sara, before diving and swimming back, closer. Nemo rifled a low-level beam, hitting it along the pectoral, turning it suddenly away; not reacting and never stopping, just moving in a new direction. Looking for something easier.

Sara gestured her thanks to the Captain, and tied more sacks before pulling the nets around rows of rainbow-striped water fruits. Jess pulled sea cucumbers from the sand, tiny brine shrimp bursting from the holes after the cucumbers, like New Year's confetti.

Jess batted the brine away, and Sara laughed, then looked to Nemo, moving for the Roman ship, its sides now covered with strips of green and yellow boa seaweed, long leaved and flowing.

Nemo approached the ship as a serf would approach a throne, his body telling his respect, moving through the tons of water surrounding him. Rifle lowered, he regarded all of the ancient ship's history in its bow carvings, and the small pieces of color surviving along the hull not eaten by ocean parasites. Centuries later, the dignity of the craft was still there, and he was swept up by it.

Watching Nemo, Sara wondered if he was seeing his own future there, ragged and petrified on the ocean floor.

A sudden current bent the light from the *Nautilus*, throwing a beam toward the ship. Highlighting a movement in the hull, something behind the seaweed layers that flapped over the split in the hull. It moved again. A twisting, black eel.

It was a moment she caught: of muscles curling under reptilian skin, and ten feet between its head and its tail. The tail slashed from a rot-hole beneath the mast, then vanished inside the wreck, the eel coiling into itself, ready to strike.

Nemo had turned his back to the ship, to gather catch nets of lobsters and sea lettuce. Sara stopped her gathering, dropping her bag, the crabs escaping sideways.

She moved, springing herself forward as fast as she could from the soft bottom, diving boots and the pressure holding her, calling out from instinct, but only hearing herself inside the bone helmet. Trying for Nemo. Before the eel ripped from the hull and seaweed, its massive mouth open, both sets of jaws unhinged.

The Moray struck, mouth and skull colliding with Nemo's helmet, snapping back at his suit, its hooked teeth tearing into it. Air burst. Explosion of bubbles, tossing Nemo back, the laser rifle falling.

The eel snapped back, circling around Nemo as if it was eating its own tail. Forming a noose with its body, drawing in tight around Nemo's ribs.

Gasping for his controlled air, Nemo dropped to his knees. The eel wrapping itself. Tighter around him.

Sara dove for the animal, her body turning, stabbing with her fishing knife into its open mouth, the blade jamming through its tongue and beyond its jaw.

Blood smoked the water. The animal corkscrewed in pain, its body twisting, breaking Nemo in half. Water began filling his suit. Nemo closed the ripped opening with his fist, sealing the manta skin. Holding his breath, and fighting the pain of the water pressure, his bones near-cracking.

Blood teared from Nemo's eyes, but he would not scream, as he made out Jess grabbing the pike, then running for him. Pulled by the water, sand churning, Jess struggled to get close, raising the pike as a harpoon.

He fought the weight of the water, cried out for double his own strength to bring the harpoon down.

The eel's skull separated from the tender point where it joined the body, Jess pushing the pike's N and prongs into its flesh, twisting the metal. Shredding its muscles. The thing reared back. Blood, a fountain, from its mouth as it snapped at Jess, whipped at him with its tail.

The ocean seemed more blood than water, with a cloud of silt churning through it, forming a thick curtain.

Jess slashed the curtain with the pike, bringing it down again, through the same tears and farther into the eel, prying it back as if he were moving a boulder up a hill. The thing's head separated from its flesh, the body stiffening with spasm, then becoming a loose ribbon. Sara slashed to free Nemo.

Pieces spread apart, floating on a dark red wave, as Sara swam with Nemo for the *Nautilus*. He instinctively grabbed harvest sacks and a net of lobsters, snagging them before the submarine vacuumed them back into the dive chamber. Absorbing them.

All lights from the *Nautilus* were still on, now pink through the bloody water.

Jess had one knee on the ocean floor, catching his breath himself, as if he'd just had a barroom brawl. Instead of as a harpoon, he used the pike as a walking staff, getting himself to his feet and starting for the *Nautilus*.

The laser rifle was settled on the bottom, and Jess got a toe under the butt, kicked it upward, and grabbed it as it spun through the water, slinging it over a shoulder. He also picked up a sack of lobsters.

Jess looked back at the Roman ship, half of the eel draping across the bow, staining it red as it poured out its last.

The Whalers pulled Nemo and Sara from the Sea Exploration chamber's diving tubes, snatching their catch nets, throwing them over shoulders. A gush of ocean waved in after them, then drained back. Nemo leaned against the wall as Sara unlocked his helmet. He drew in a heavy breath, stretching himself as if getting his skeleton back into place. Aligning his chest and lungs. His breath came, and Sara handed him a canteen.

Jess said, "I'd think you'd want somethin' stronger than that."

He was climbing from the last chamber, the Whalers throwing him an eye, not moving to help. One of them had his fingers on the long blade hanging from his belt, ready to pull it.

Nemo took a controlled drink of water and said, "Peddling your spirits again, Mr. Jess?"

"I just know what works for me, sir."

Sara said to Nemo, "That suit tear alone could have killed you."

Nemo said, "But it didn't, something to consider, though, the use of the manta skin." He turned to the Whalers, *"Chukua samaki hii jikoni kwa ajili ya chakula cha jioni."*

"Jioni? I knows that one. Dinner," Jess said, tossing the helmet to Sara. "Them two'd cut your head off quicker than piss in the lake, but they know their stew."

"Colorfully put," Nemo said. "They shall be in the galley tonight. My sea gardens, I planted a hundred others across the Atlantic and Pacific. When this monster hunt's over, that's the work I'll return to."

The Whalers snatched up the nets, and Nemo had the laser rifle, examining the bones for damage. He looked to Jess and said, "Good work today."

He turned to Sara. "Miss Duncan, this area is to be shipshape before you leave. Report in an hour for further duties."

Jess held out the pike, a string of eel flesh still hanging from the steel initial. "Don't forget your weapon, sir."

Nemo took it without a glance or nod and stepped from the chamber. Jess struggled with his suit, trying to pull his arms free, when Sara said, "You saved his life."

"Take hold of me arm, Sis."

Sara stressed her words: "You saved his life."

Jess' arms were tangled, and he said, "He's the captain, that's what I'm supposed to do. You got in there pretty good yourself. How'd you know to use that blade?"

Sara said, "He barely acknowledged it."

Sara freed him, and Jess said, "You're mixin' us up with the Navy what spends as much time pinnin' medals on each other, as they do on the water. We're crew, Sis. You do what you do because it's the job."

Sara said, "That eel was no machine."

"I can't follow what that means, Sis. But, you need a drink more than any of us."

Sara, knowing she spoke out of turn, but feeling reduced, separated her words evenly. "He is a cold bastard."

Jess hooted, "But he's the Captain."

The dirigible pilot wore his vanity on his lapel as a series of small, jeweled stick pins from the Weldon Balloonists Society, the Academy of Aeronautic Pilots, and several others. He had the kind of face that was perfect for a portrait, but showed nothing useful at all in terms of experience. His eyes were like a doll's.

He identified himself as, "One of the Prudent family of

Philadelphia. We've been quite active in ballooning for two generations, and have advised several governments."

This was all before he shook hands with Grant, Duncan, or Maston, and took his place in the pilot's chair at the dirigible's helm. Prudent said to Duncan, "My being here was a precaution of Vice President Colfax, given the import of this voyage."

Grant said, "We're aware of the import."

The airship cut through colliding black clouds, rain bullet-striking the arched front windows by the helm, with Prudent saying, "It was felt, as this is the maiden flight of Mr. Duncan's design, and with this storm, someone of experience should be at the helm. No offense meant, sir."

Duncan peered over the top of his glasses, which Grant knew was his sign of contempt. "Oh, no offense taken. Actually, I couldn't agree more."

"I've only barely inspected the craft, but you seem to have done an interesting job," Prudent slowed the air speed. "Not all choices I would have made, but interesting."

Prudent set direction from the pilot's station with a Captain's wheel as if traveling the Mississippi, its upward and downward propeller controls hanging from the ceiling like boat whistles on brass chains. Thick, bleeding rain from the passing clouds covered the glass that encircled the gondola, along with its gun ports.

High winds shoved the dirigible, as waves roll into a two-mast schooner. The air was the ocean, the airship, fighting high water.

Grant flicked cigar ash. "Well, I said we're on a righteous mission. I hope God in his Heaven sees it that way, keeps us in the air. Or better."

Top-secret paperwork was spread across a small, leathered desk, with an ornate top and cigar cutter. Duncan was beside Grant, unrolling navigation specifics. It was a true office, befitting the

President, with upholstered comforts, paintings on burnished walls, and weapons mounted along the baseboards.

Two Rifle Guards were stationed at the gun ports, with Maston standing by at the iron-shuttered side windows, with openings to drop grenades.

The Phono-Phone had its own corner alcove, with the navigation equipment. A rack that once held rifles now held telescopes of all lengths and swung out from the wall for instant access.

Duncan said, "If Gladstone's coordinates are primarily correct, we'll reach the meeting within a day easily, provided we can negotiate the weather."

Thunder rattled the windows, coming through the iron gondola as a scream in a cave. The ship weaved, but still climbing, propellers chopping heavy clouds. Prudent brought the speed up, adjusted the dirigible angle with the hanging chains like boat whistles.

Prudent said, "I'll get us through the storm, sirs."

Grant looked down at the city through a short-spyglass portal, with great magnification. The clouds were shifting, showing up pieces of Washington, half of streets, below. He could see the faces looking up at the ship, shielding eyes, and waving through the rain before running, laughing, to their front doors. They'd seen the President.

The storm's gray-black seemed to be the fog of cannons, the thunder bringing Grant memory slashes. His words were for himself: "Not on my watch. No one's going to strike this city."

"Duncan, we had a purpose to stop this war before it starts. That's why Nemo, that's why all of this. What about the attack coordinates? I'd like to tell these crowned heads I inspected the sites personally."

Sliding open a floor panel, Duncan stood back as a projection device corkscrewed out of the floor, its lens pointed to the ceiling. Duncan fit the maps underneath it, saying, "The meeting's only a few miles into international waters, so we're following the attack pattern as our route."

The projector threw the image of the maps across the curved ceiling of the dirigible, the planetarium view from corner to corner, with the exact position of the sinkings and the route to the conference outlined in separate colors.

"An improvement over my office viewer," Duncan said. "These are the same coordinates we assigned Nemo."

"The route he's not followed." Grant took his cigar from mouth, and stayed fixed on the ceiling and what was shown across it. "You can see every foot of the direct orders that son of a bitch's ignored."

Duncan said, "We have the air, the *Nautilus* has the water, so there's no movement an enemy can make that we won't know about."

Maston absently flashed the laser scar on his hand and said, "Find that iron ship of his, I'll find a way to board it. Mile underwater, don't make a difference to me."

Violent thunder broke. An explosion in the sky; sound from nowhere felt through the airship as rain blew in through the bomb doors.

Duncan said, "Young man, I'd just like to know it's still sailing, in one piece. And my daughter's safe."

Maston's words were a rush of, "My intended meaning is we'd get Miss Duncan back in our protection. That *Nautilus* ship is powered by our gold, that's reason enough."

"You delivered the gold, and that's a credit to you," Grant said. "Son, you're waiting for another chance, but don't get too eager to charge. Hold back."

"Mr. President, the Secret Service works for you," Maston

said. "At this moment, you can't be taken hostage, and there isn't a ship in existence with the cannon to reach us."

The airship jostled, the storm roaring, and Maston held onto a side railing, his gun rig and holster showing.

Grant said, "Maybe we won't be taken down by a cannon."

"You're safer here than anywhere on earth," Maston said. "Just give me an order, sir. Any order."

Duncan turned to Prudent, pointed to the chart, everywhere above him. "Pilot, you can interpret all this?"

"We're breaking the clouds, coming over the storm, Duncan." Prudent looked to the projected charts. "Quite easy to read. I'll set our course, gentlemen."

Grant bit down on his cigar, quietly laughing. "Sometimes I ponder you and Nemo as brothers. At least half. To build all this."

"Design it." Duncan shook his head. "You know I'm just an academic, not a pilot. Or submariner. Or genius."

"Take some damn credit," Grant said, relighting. "You created this airship, and all that's in it, to do some good for your country. That's a hell of a thing. You've done yourself proud."

Prudent wiped his glasses on his sleeve and said, "It is a good ship, actually, and is probably suited for the job of finding this submarine."

Fulmer was dead weight, leaning forward, arms across Jess' and Sara's shoulders as they hauled him down the bottom deck passageway to the crew bunks. The copper plates had burned his chest, leaving small, scarred rectangles, and his jaw lolled to the side, almost open, the way a corpse at sea would be found.

Jess said, "I seen worse, but haven't smelled worse. That why Nemo won't have him in that laboratory?"

"The Captain said his work required secrecy, and he didn't want this man waking up and interrupting him."

They stopped. Jess breathing hard, adjusting Fulmer's arms around him, and saying, "He always needs his damn secrets. You know that. As for wakin' up, I don't think that's happenin' anytime soon."

Sara pulled herself farther under Fulmer's shoulder, stood straight. "But he'll wake."

"Not doubtin' it for a second. And when he does, he's got you to thank," Jess said, hauling Fulmer along. "That'll be your acknowledgement!"

Sara smiled at the jab. "Okay, now I owe you a drink."

"Tell you what, wish I'd been with you to fetch this one from up top."

Sara said, "No, you don't."

"Even if it meant takin' on another Moray," Jess shouldered the hatchway open. "I hate bein' buried under all this water. Feels like drownin' without the dyin'."

Jess and Sara dropped Fulmer onto a bare mattress without his stirring. One of the Whalers sat in the quarter's dark corner, watching, as Sara pulled open Fulmer's belt.

Sara said, "Lend a hand. We're not on our honeymoon, you know, we have to see if there are any other injuries."

Jess said, "Who knows what was feedin' on him, but they probably spit him out."

Jess shifted himself, his back to the corner, showing the Whaler, again, the pistol in his boot as he leaned over Fulmer. "We going to be burnin' these?"

Sara said, "We'd be doing him and us a favor."

They yanked off the rags of pants and shirt. Something clinked to the floor. The slightest sound; lighter than a coin bouncing off a plate. Sara bent down to a glint of blue light under the bunk. A spit of reflection, thin as a razor's cut. She reached for it, fingers stretching, to grab the diamond shard.

Jess put the bottle of milk beside the bed, and jammed the rubber tube into Fulmer's lax mouth, saying, "I'm doin' the dirty work, and you're findin' buried treasure!"

Sara put the shard in her pocket, saying to Jess, "Just keep him quiet. If he wakes, give him some. Just one swallow, Jess."

The laudanum was an amber bottle that Sara handed to a grinning Jess, who said, "I know about restraint, Sis. Even done it once, maybe twice."

Jess looked to the Whaler as Sara stepped from the quarters, the hatch heavy-swinging shut. He hadn't moved. Or possibly, blinked. Only staring.

Jess said, "You keep on waitin' it out, and we'll all get rich off this turtle ship. Then, maybe, we'll have a different kind of fight. Savvy?"

Eyes that didn't move was the answer.

Nemo stood before the bridge's large portal, all blue-green moving before him, with darts of silver from schools of fish swimming in the *Nautilus'* running lights. Colors becoming other colors, this quiet beauty of the ocean.

"Still my serenity," he said to Sara.

"We haven't seen much serenity lately."

"There it is, nature's perfection." Nemo turned from the ocean. "But for this journey, it's been more blood in the waters than anything."

Sara said, "I feel like I've been through a war."

"You have. I expect brutality from mankind, but what we've

found, this mechanical monstrosity, opens new doors. I've seen much in the oceans, and odd rumors can become stalwart legends in the retelling."

"Like this submarine being a sea monster?"

"The speculations of newspapers, and penny dreadfuls, and always concocted fantasies."

Sara said, "Except in this case, yes?"

"You're like a child who's delighting their parents made an error."

Nemo set the automatic piloting system, engaging the mechanics. "Our destination is the next sinking in the so-called official reports, but following my route. If the wreckage exists, we'll be on it very soon. To sort out more of this strangeness."

Sara took the blue diamond from her shirt, held it up between her thumb and forefinger.

The security blades from the Vulcania cases were recessed, and Sara stood by the laboratory hatchway, breath held, quiet, as Nemo opened the case and removed a tray of specialty tools. He replaced the case under the examination table where the sea spider's tank rested, alongside surgical and dental instruments.

Nemo laid out the tools specially forged in Vulcania, saying, "It's wise you didn't speak, Miss Duncan."

"Remember, I've seen those hidden blades spring out of the sides and top. Very clever, Captain."

Nemo said, "A Moorish design, several hundred years old, but suited for our use. Your assistance, here."

She moved to the sea spider, approaching as if it were about to leap from its tank where it floated.

Nemo lifted the thing from water with surgical tongs, laying it on the examination table, its claws held tightly closed with vein clamps. Cloudy water streamed from its piston legs and hinged jaws, but it remained still. Mechanically frozen on the long, wooden table, stained with blood and dividing the lab in two.

Sara watched Nemo in his worlds, the Victorian and the futuristic, performing a bizarre autopsy on a mechanical animal: a sea insect that wasn't real.

He pried the mandibles with a curved blade, exposing tubing inside. "That mouth construction is a tube and nozzle works, spraying acids of some kind. Brass and porcelain, very well crafted."

Sara looked over Nemo's shoulder. "God, but for what purpose?"

Nemo took a scalpel. "Here's a way to find out," he said and slit the thing's belly. Whale oil bled from the cavity, along with a corrupted, liquid jelly, revealing a series of gears and servos attached to hair-thin rods and balanced flywheels within flywheels.

Nemo said, "That's your machine."

"This could have been engineered by you."

"No, this work might be beyond even my abilities."

Nemo pressed a servo with the scalpel's edge, fully rotating a robotic eye from the side of its body, searching the room, and a claw to struggle against its clamp. Another servo, and the mandibles locked open.

"These constructions, they're the most delicate mechanicals I've ever encountered, superior to anything on the *Nautilus*. Remarkable."

Sara was now conscious of the living eyes in all the tanks surrounding, watching them, rotating on muscles and not mechanics. She was looking about the lab, from creature to creature, when she said, "So, you admire it."

"Respect, and I'd be a fool not to. These eyes actually transmit visual information, and it reacts automatically."

Sara said, "So it can think."

"It reacts, and surely better than a God-made crab."

Nemo scraped the shell of the thing with a jeweler's saw, rubbing the shred between his fingers. "The works and legs are steel or brass, but the body's something else. Near flexible, but like living tissue."

Sara said, "This thing scares me."

"Turn it."

Sara flipped the crab over, revealing the diamond-shaped opening, saying, "Is that the power conduit?"

Nemo said, "I see no other sources."

"Then, here's the power."

She dropped the blue diamond shard on the table, next to the spider, peering into the chest cavity as Nemo held it up, inserting the blue piece into its back. She knew it was a machine, formed like a living thing, but seeing its works, the oil-slimed interior, made her look away as if watching an amputation.

Sara said, "The last time I was here, you were resurrecting a man."

"One of your exaggerations, but marginally appreciated by someone who doesn't have a license to practice medicine. That was sea doctoring, Miss Duncan. This is mechanics," Nemo said, placing the diamond. "A secure fit."

Gears clicked, then moved, teeth meshing. Turning the rods. The spider sprung to life, snapping its clamps and spraying the last of its acid from its jaws. Nemo pulled Sara away from the jet, the acid soaking the sides of an aquarium, melting the seals around the glass.

The spider leapt from the table, legs propelling it to the other side of the lab.

The aquarium tank burst, sending its fighting squids tumbling to the floor. Tentacles latched onto Sara, her arms, the things crawling up her body to her throat.

Nemo pinned the spider with his boot, prying the diamond from its back. It scuttled for the hatchway, all eight legs collapsed. Gears and rods, slowing. A watch winding down. Stopped, its acid dripping.

"Close your eyes!"

Nemo called out, then showered the fighting squids with salt, bubbling their flesh, burning the soft underside of the tentacles, loosening their fierce grip. Nemo peeled them back, the suction cups pulling her skin, then giving way.

"Did it draw blood?"

Sara brushed her arms clean, felt her throat. "No, I don't think so."

"All right, that poison they carry is not to fool with," Nemo said. "Now, how does this mechanical draw energy from a diamond? Our own metal converter takes up a quarter of this ship. The technology is truly beyond my approach."

Sara wiped her face of salt and ink, Nemo's mind and attention having completely shifted. "So what to do, admire that thing for its workmanship?"

"This thing," Nemo spit the word, "is going to answer every question that's been asked, and a thousand others besides."

"By dissection, I hope."

"On the contrary. We're going to make sure it's in perfect running order."

Sara patted down the sucker marks reddening along her arms. "Why? You could build a thousand of those in your sleep."

Nemo said, "Flattery doesn't obscure that you're missing the larger issues. There's purpose to this, amazing sophistication, and that's what we have to discover. Your watch begins in less than ten minutes. All engines steady, at night speed."

Sara was at the hatchway. "Yes, Captain."

Nemo said, "Miss Duncan, you're very capable, but you should never struggle with a Humboldt squid."

The red marks on Sara's arms were worse. "Oh, really?"

Nemo kicked the broken glass of the squid tank out of the way before cradling the sea spider with the tongs. "Only newborns, but they have tendencies, and fighting only made things worse. Those specimens will have to be replaced."

She watched Nemo, the Victorian side of the laboratory wide behind him, gently lay the mechanical, taking great care, on the examination table. Then set to work, surgical instruments in hand.

He looked up and said, "Understand the nature of the animal, and you'll know how to respond."

Sara descended through the *Nautilus* decks, following the circular stairs to the bottom passageway and its steady, glowing hum of the power generator. She paused on the bottom step, one of many she had repaired and rebolted, to let her eyes adjust to the faint yellow haze in the dark.

She peered into the machine's view port at the gold conversion generator, the switches and systems she'd rewired. All of the work done—bringing the *Nautilus* back from its grave, saving the iron corpse while Nemo was rotting in a jail cell—was hers. Following her father's plans, she repaired, and nursed, and healed, with rivets and torch throughout, always respecting the creation, even while improving it.

This *Nautilus* was now as much the Duncans', as anyone's, but could never claim any part of it.

Sara opened the hatch to the engine room, the turbine works all performing. She checked the rotation speed of the propellers, and their cooling. All was well, as she suspected, because she'd done work here also. A needle in a temperature gauge hesitated. Sara flicked its glass. It jumped, responding, and was right.

She settled on an iron seat that folded down from the wall, a relic of the old *Nautilus* that she'd never removed. And she listened, to the engines, and their power. Sara didn't cry, and wasn't going to. She just sat alone, her fingers absently turning General Sigel's poisoned ring on her left hand.

32

RESURRECTED

The first capture was Cincinnati, leaping a low fence, legs out-stretched, and Efrem holding on. The second was Efrem standing by the horses as they took water. The third, Efrem checking a saddle cinch.

It was after that capture that he looked up and saw Mr. Horace standing, suddenly, in front of him by the corral fence.

"Getting along well, are we, boy?"

Efrem tightened the cinch, but kept his chin down while speaking. "Yes, sir. Very well."

Horace said, "The President asked me to check, make sure your duties were to your liking, even though you're no longer in the telegraph room."

Efrem said, "Mr. Grant's a fine a man, and I'm liking my new situation quite well."

"Should I report that?"

"Yes, sir, Mr. Horace."

Horace stepped to the fence, offering one of the horses

an apple core, saying, "Efrem, you're very smart, and I'm rather fond of you. You're the youngest on staff, and you've done better than the rest. That says something."

After a lens adjustment, this was the fourth capture.

Efrem looked to Horace. "Sir?"

"You have a friend in one of the most powerful men in the world. That's quite a responsibility, for all of us."

Efrem nodded his agreement, trying to end Horace's conversation and get the horses bedded down.

"Yes, sir, Mr. Horace," he said, opening the corral gate and forcing Horace to step aside. "Like I said, Mr. Grant has been terrible good to me and my family."

"Did he give you a letter?"

Efrem led a paint pony from the corral. "Yes, sir."

Horace said, "And what did he say to do with it?"

"Give it to my grandma."

"And you did this?"

The pony snorted, and Efrem said, "Yes, sir. I did."

Horace managed a wrinkled smile, and patted Efrem's shoulder without letting his fingers touch him, saying, "You did the right thing, then. That's what I had to check on, make sure of that, while the President's away."

Efrem said, "Yes, sir. I've got the horses out three times a day, regular. Cincinatti, whenever he wants to run."

"Ah, very good," Horace said before buttoning his coat against the chill and walking back toward the White House's old war room. His stride, shoulders forward, and back bent, was the fifth capture.

"Five pictures, and not a one worth a glass of green beer."

Lime was walking around the side of the stables, checking the film in his camera. "It's too bloody dark, and that last one, you can practically see through him already."

Efrem stood at the large, open stable doors, holding the lead to the pony, and said, "Sir, if you mean Mr. Horace, he went back to the telegraph, I think."

Lime regarded Efrem. "You don't know me, do you, Efrem?"

"I've seen you, sir."

He held up his camera. "Photographer, and the President asked me to take some special pictures, if anyone started to bother you."

Efrem said, "Mr. Horace wasn't no bother. I worked for him."

"What did he want?"

Efrem led the pony to one of the stalls, hooves echoing on the clean concrete. "Just asked if I was liking my new job, is all."

Lime said, "Efrem, look at my tie."

Efrem turned, puzzled, then heard the small click from Lime's tie clasp. "That's fine wardrobe."

Lime said, "And I always wear it, so you'll always know me. If there's a problem, look for the brogues and forest greens."

He held up his camera. "Also, I'll be watching, from all around. The General's eyes, if you like, while he sails the skies."

"I've never had my photograph made. Could I have one for my grandmother?"

"Family portraits aren't a specialty, but I'm sure we'll find something to please Grandma," Lime said, rolling his eyes at the twelve-year-old. "My bloody God, you're taller than I am."

Efrem smiled. "And supposed to get taller."

Sara leaned into the bunk, mopping Fulmer's brow and face with a wet cloth before adjusting his intravenous feed. Jess had jury-rigged a rum bottle and a piece of rubber tube to drip milk into Fulmer's mouth so he wouldn't have to sit in crew quarters with "the ape in the corner what wants to chop my head."

The Whaler was still there, machete across his knees, as Sara wrapped Fulmer's blistered neck and chest with clean linen, and tied it off.

She wiped Fulmer's eyes clean, looked to the Whaler with, "My feeling is, you can't understand, but just keep watch, all right?"

He stared back, and nodded his head so slightly, the movement was almost invisible.

Sara said, "That machete, you wouldn't use it on me, would you?"

The Whaler nodded his head the other way. No.

Bach's Toccata and Fugue was a whisper that grew into a chorus, traveling the *Nautilus* from the organ pipes, through the passageways to every deck, and into the ocean. The crew gave a nod, and Jess rolled back on his bunk, laughing, passing the rum and gin to salute hearing it again.

But the Toccata was part of the ship: the music as important as the tons of brass, iron, and glass that were the *Nautilus'* shell, the sounds of the organ were its soul, and part of the legend, giving reporters one more thing to write about, and of course, they got it wrong.

Bach wasn't an obsession, but an experiment in the traveling of sound through water. Nemo found at the right temperature and depth, the lower, bass notes retained vibrations longer and traveled farther in the water, to the attention of whales and dolphins, who called back with their own tones and sea sounds.

He'd begun communicating with them with music, trying all types, played through a speaker attached to the prow, but it was Bach's classical sadness that made the underwater journey.

The organ he played was a rescue from a bombed church in

Slovenia, and the last thing on the *Nautilus* to be refurbished. The bench was threadbare, the keys stubborn, but Nemo's playing was as sure as his control at the helm, even compensating for a dead key by combining two other notes for one. Even damaged, the pipes responded with strength and volume, surrounding him with his music, creating an island.

The refrain accompanied Sara from the crew deck to the bridge. The bridge was dark, the ship's running lights washing back through the dome, showing the instruments locked off to their course, the wheel turning automatically.

The Phono's mirrors spun at high speed, throwing silver darts as an image came into view, and Duncan's voice was static from the speaker horn. His words were dim, a distant sound, but everything he said could be heard, and the expressions on his face, in pieces on the screen, could be read.

"Sara, my sweet, is that you? At last?"

Sara was close to the speaker horn. "Yes, Father, and I'm fine."

"Oh, God . . ."

Sara said, "I hear something—where are you? In your office?"

On the dirigible, Duncan looked to Grant, who gave his permission with the flick of cigar, for him to say, "We're flying, dear. My dirigible design. Things have changed quite a bit, the dynamics of the mission, I mean."

Grant said, "We've got to speak to Nemo on that thing."

Bach was everywhere around Sara, and she cupped her ears when she spoke, eyes on the broken image of her smiling father. "I'll fetch him, soon. But you'll be pleased. We actually captured one of the sea creatures described. The monsters that sank the British cargo ship. One of the crew is on board with us, and we'll get a statement, as well."

"Be cautious," Duncan said. "But that's wonderful-sounding news, dear."

"Nemo's doing as he said he would."

"The hell he is."

Duncan's face changed, as he was nudged aside by Grant, speaking directly to Sara. "You're not following the routes, making it impossible for us to track any progress. Reports not made. Do you know what happened in Norfolk after you sailed? Do you comprehend it?"

"No, sir."

"It's war, Miss Duncan."

With Bach playing, Sara chose her words. "The mission will be completed to your satisfaction, General."

"Too late," Grant said. "It's already gone to hell."

Nemo held onto a G chord for several beats, inserting a *Nautilus* key in the shape of a starfish under the organ keyboard. He stood, and Bach continued, floridly, the organ keys depressing on their own as if a ghost were playing: his ship doing exactly as he needed it to do.

Each note accompanied Nemo, every step from the library, through the *Nautilus* arteries, to his bridge, stepping through an access door he'd kept secret. Nemo stayed at the door, draped in corner shadows, as Sara continued into the Phono, to Grant.

"Sir, we have the evidence of the claims in the reports, but not the reasons why. These creatures, these monsters, are real. Not what was imagined, but something created."

Grant said, "That's a hell of a claim, Sara."

"The explanation is here, sir. In the ocean."

There was static from the horn, then Grant's voice, quiet,

almost beneath the electronic noise. "You recall your mission? What you are to do if I order it?"

Sara nodded, without speaking.

Grant's face on the spinning mirror screen was larger now, intimate and fierce. "When I speak to these leaders, I have to have evidence in hand to stop a full-scale conflict. That's the point. Give up your location, so Nemo can turn over what you've found, and I can present it. But this can't be someone's word alone, it's already gone too far."

Sara said, "He might refuse. We're bound for the site of another sinking, to get more information."

"If he refuses, I'll have that submarine, one way or t'other. You understand?"

"Yes, I do," Sara said. "I'll have to calculate our present position."

"Do it, then. And don't forget the second part of your task—"

"Believe me, I haven't." Sara repeated her words, "The mission will be completed to your satisfaction, General."

Over the horn, Duncan pleaded, "Sweetheart . . ."

Nemo was beside Sara without sound, so quickly she didn't even know it until he reached around her and shut off the Phono. "This report is finished, gentlemen. I will be the one to keep you informed."

The screen dimmed, and he turned Sara around in her chair to face him. "Miss Duncan, I'm aware of your split loyalties, but I will decide when and what to report of this voyage."

"Sir," Sara said. "It's my father, and I have to tell them something. There's a war above us, we have to prove to them we're doing our duty. And we are, that's what I told them."

"There's always some war." Nemo went to the helm, unlocked the settings. "And I have to prove nothing, I only have to discover. That's our destination, and purpose."

Sara said, "Things are getting worse since we sailed; time's running out."

"For yourself, or me? Don't answer yet."

Nemo's hands were now completely under the controls, fit to the gloves and sensors, just as Toccata and Fugue came to an end, the final organ notes sounding forever through the *Nautilus*. Then gone.

Nemo said, "I needed to hear the last of the Bach. Always remember, Miss Duncan, that I know everything that happens on my ship. As far as I'm concerned, you're again one reprimand away from being a stowaway, and being cast off."

In the dirigible, Duncan sat at the phone, head down, hands in his lap, hearing Nemo and his veiled threat to his daughter. His reaction was paralysis. Grant kept his hand on his friend's shoulder as they heard Sara say, "I have my work to do, Captain," before the signal died.

The first shock to Fulmer was opening his eyes. They were clean, not sealed tight with salt, and he opened them too wide, letting in everything they possibly could see. The second shock was that the light was cool, shadowed, and not the searing of white sun. He shut them again, then gradually opened, as if double-checking that he was alive.

It took him a moment, spitting out the milk from the back of his throat and yanking free of the feeding tube as he sat up on the iron bunk. His stomach and mouth tasted sour, but he could taste, and that was a relief.

He wiped his mouth on the sheets, trying to orient himself. The riveted walls of plate iron. The low ceiling, and the *N* above the hatchway to the main passage. He reached out, for the side of the lifeboat that wasn't there, then pulled himself back. Eyes closed, and gathering himself.

His hands went behind his head, laying them flat against the iron wall, fingers spread. Feeling the cold of the metal, the heads of the rivets. Recognizing something familiar, and knowing what it meant. Calming.

Fulmer leaned forward, the muscles in his legs fighting him, straining from their rest. He grabbed hold of the edge of the bed and pulled himself up, just making out the silhouette of the Whaler in the far corner, sitting and watching.

"Jesus—"

Fulmer shuffled, dragging a foot closer to the Whaler, who had leaned forward and lit a candle in a small holder beside his chair, throwing light against one side of his marked face and the machete across his knees. Fulmer stopped.

When Fulmer spoke, he reached for his words, finding them in the back of memory, and putting them together. Halting, as he said, "Those—tattoos—I think I know them—seen them before—but in the sun. I've been with your people, what do you speak? Is it—Swasi? I've been there—not dreaming, but really there, I'm sure. And done some drinking—shipped out from the coast, I think—"

"Enough," the Whaler said. "I speak the Queen's English when I choose. Mostly, I don't."

"Can you tell me where I am?"

"The iron boat."

Fulmer's eyes were on the ceiling. "Underwater?"

"Yes."

Fulmer was leaning heavily against the bunk frame, looking around the crew quarters again, trying to take it in. Jogging his own senses, saying, "A submarine. Is this the *Nautilus*?"

Whaler nodded.

"Jesus."

Now he sagged against the bed, a great weight suddenly pushing him down. "Did the Captain—Nemo, did he save me?"

"The Captain, he found you up top. More dead than alive. Brought you back."

Fulmer said, "Son of a bitch . . ." He let his voice trail away, then looked to the whaler. "You've been here the whole time?"

"Yes."

"Part of the crew?"

The Whaler said, "Yes, my brother, too."

Fulmer looked to the hatchway, the *N* above it knocked askew and smeared with stains of a shattered whiskey bottle.

He turned to the Whaler, "That blade, can I see it?"

His hand was out, for the machete to be passed to him. "Don't worry, I know it's yours."

The Whaler lay the handle, leather-wrapped, into the flat of Fulmer's palm, his skin still raw and blistered, some peeled back almost to the muscle. He winced as he gripped the handle, but tightened fingers anyway. More pain. He held the blade up, his arm struggling with even this much weight, but felt better holding it. Raising it. And sure he could bring the machete down, striking with force, if needed.

Fulmer used the machete to touch the cross-braces and supports of the passageway, their curves and shape distinct to the *Nautilus*. He tapped them with the blade, just a clink, as if to verify them, as he walked from one end of the submarine to the other. He counted the number of side passages, dragging the machete across them the way a boy would drag a stick across a picket fence. He paused by the engine room to glance inside.

Sara looked up from her checking of the pressure gauges. "My God, are you all right? When did you awake?"

Fulmer kept on, now holding the machete by his side with military bearing, walking toward the first set of access stairs.

Sara followed, "I don't even know your name . . ."

Then reached for the hand holding the blade. Fulmer turned, slightly pulling away, but never raising the machete directly to her, only tilting the vicious edge as she met his cloudy eyes.

Fulmer said, "No. Please."

She half-stepped back, letting him continue for the stairs and to the upper deck. Sara grabbed for the crew phone, trying for the bridge, and Fulmer stopped on the stairs, saying, "Please, miss, you don't want any part of this."

Fulmer continued to mid-deck, through the library where he opened Professor Arronax's journal of sea life, and ran his fingers down one of the pages to see his name listed as "being of particular help in the capture of the giant mollusk."

Fulmer said out loud, "Thank you, Professor."

He'd replaced the book, and tightened his grip around the machete's handle as he reached the farthest end of the deck, where it rounded into a cul-de-sac around a view port below the bridge, with Nemo's quarters to the side.

He stood before the white-and-gold-lacquered door, scarred by water and traces of gunfire, and used the machete's tip to depress the door's jeweled dolphin latch.

An arm went around Fulmer's throat from behind, locking at the elbow, yanking him backward and lifting him off his feet. He slashed with the machete, the blade cleaving against a wall, sparking off the iron, as the arm tightened, choking off his air.

Nemo said, "I didn't save your life for this!"

Fulmer dropped the machete, and Nemo relaxed his grip. Fulmer turned to face Nemo, and behind him, Jess standing on the stairs. Jess' pistol rested steady across the railing, barrel pointed at the center of Fulmer's chest or back, depending on how he stood.

Nemo said, "Mr. Jess, careful with your trigger, this is Mr. Fulmer, who was First Mate. One of my best."

Jess said, "He surely ain't that no more. Have a good nap, did ya?"

"He's currently a ward of the *Nautilus*," Nemo said, kicking the machete across the floor and keeping Fulmer's eyes on him.

Fulmer said, "I don't even know what the hell that means."

Sara said, "Somewhere between a prisoner and a guest. But I think better, a prisoner."

Fulmer looked back at Sara, standing on the other side of the curved staircase. He said to Nemo, "My intention was to give you a chance, Captain. My memory's spotty, but I'm aware you saved me, by bringing me on board."

"A fighting chance, by ambushing me in my cabin? You learned a lot of tricks with the vigilantes you rode with; that must be one of them, the fighting chance, after cutting a throat."

Fulmer said, "I didn't know who was waiting for me, how many guards you had. I imagined I was the one to get his throat cut."

Sara said, "You damn near did, by pirates."

Fulmer nodded. "A lot of that's lost, but I recall the one in the yellow scarf."

"He's dead. Thanks to the Captain."

Fulmer said, "That's another to add to our history, ain't it?"

Jess watched Fulmer's reactions: a man who seemed crazed, just holding himself up with all his strength, but still trying threats. Not gin-crazy, but something else. He watched Nemo's moves as well, in motion, and shifting his weight as he took small steps in the passageway, side-to-side, taking nothing for granted as to what Fulmer might do. There was knowledge between these men. Caution, as doctors at an asylum would approach a dangerous inmate.

Nemo picked up the machete, regarded Fulmer's injured, peeling face. "I hold no ill will that you escaped when I was captured. But I hold it against myself that I got us trapped."

"That's your burden," Fulmer said.

"But I need to know your attitude about the sinking of the Man O' War."

"Unchanged."

Nemo nodded to Jess with his eyes, who thumbed the hammer on the pistol, but saying to Fulmer, "You've actually been under arrest since you've been on board. If you're a danger to my ship, you'll be put in irons, or cast adrift."

"Your laws aren't new to me," Fulmer said. "I've been your prisoner before, the rest, what kind of threat is that to me?"

Sara said, "We brought you back from the dead, do you understand?"

"To do what, kill me all over again?"

Nemo said, "I know what you're capable of, Mr. Fulmer. And here we are, on my ship, with a task before us."

"You makin' me an offer, Captain?"

"You are the only survivor of that bizarre attack. I've been charged to find the motives behind it. You can be of use. That's why you're alive. Can you clear your mind, table your mania until the end of the voyage?"

Fulmer touched the electric scars on his chest, saying, "If you can."

Jess holstered the pistol, swallowing his curses.

"Miss Duncan." Nemo reached around Fulmer, handing Sara the machete. "See that the weapon is properly returned. I'm trusting you with this task."

33

THE SURVIVOR

The President's Aero Force Number One had found its route along the Atlantic Coast, staying to the first layer of clouds, moving in and out of their cover. The wind speed boosted the dirigible, its guidance systems keeping its flight sure. Over Fort Sumter, a starburst fired from a guard tower and filled the sky around the dirigible with shimmering color.

Maston watched through the arched windows. "There's a greeting from Fort Sumter, Mr. President."

"Every barracks on high alert," Grant said. "You think those boys'd be sending off skyrockets if they knew how crazy things were?"

On the Phono, Horace's voice was all halts and stammers. "I've never spoken into a machine like this before, sir. This is quite a new experience."

Duncan said, "Relax, Mr. Horace, you followed my instructions well."

"If I might, we should install these throughout the White House."

Grant said, "Then we'd never get any damn peace. What about the latest communications? What intercepts?"

"There's been activity between Prussia and Italy, but we haven't gotten all the telegraphs. They will be sailing to the meeting point, however. I'm expecting more notices in an hour."

Grant, at his desk, cut his cigar. "Keep us informed."

Horace said, his image splitting across the mirrors, "We have confirmation that your aircraft has made headlines in Britain and France, Mr. President. Front pages, with photographs. If I might say, well done, sir."

"Yes, you might."

Duncan shut down the device, spinning Horace away. His words were flat, worried, as he said, "They know we're coming, Sam. That's sending the message you wanted to send."

Prudent said, "Mr. President, we can have you at your destination in less than twenty-four hours."

He pulled the chains above him in sequence, adjusting the dirigible's angle centrally into the air stream. A smooth, imperceptible piloting move. Prudent flicked one of his lapel badges, giving himself credit.

Duncan said, "If Nemo doesn't complete the mission, we have other ways to send the message of our innocence. We've made the accommodation."

Grant said, "Not just innocence, that we as a nation share a common enemy with all nations, to band together to fight."

Duncan said, "Your speech is included, Sam."

Maston shifted a baseboard to one side, revealing a bomb rack loaded with several hundred grenades, the edges of the shells fluttered with colored streamers.

Grant said, "Those letter bombs will only take us so far. The leaflets are just another denial on paper."

Duncan said, "Delivered from this ship."

"All eyes will be on us, I know," Grant said. "Believe it or not, I want Nemo to come through, show the world you were right to put him to sea again. Because I don't want to have to engage a goddamn submarine and these other nations at the same time."

Grant took a miniature carafe from his desk, poured himself a short bourbon. "Because that's not a fight we can win."

Maston said, "Sir, there's a load of grenades in here with real punch, black powder grain, send a different kind of message."

"I hope to hell we don't have to use those. On anyone."

Maston said, "In case you do, they can be auto-loaded. A rain of fire, Mr. President."

"Your fighting skills have notched up some," Fulmer said.

Nemo said, "I had a good deal of unwanted practice."

They entered the laboratory, with Fulmer stopping upon seeing the spider on the examination table.

Nemo moved to it. "Yours isn't the first reaction like that this thing has had. Not that I can blame anyone."

Fulmer said, "But they're reacting to what they think that thing can do, not what it is."

Nemo turned it over, propping it up on its mechanical legs, and said, "Miss Duncan found this in your pocket."

He opened his hand, with the sliver of blue diamond in its center. Fulmer nodded, and Nemo closed his fist, then put the diamond into a test tube next to the sea spider and corked it. He inched the tube away from the spider's body, making sure Fulmer saw the separation.

"No worries," Nemo said. "I found that's the power source."

"Yeah, I figured that out, after I shot the hell out of about a thousand of those things."

"A thousand? Really?"

Fulmer said, "Sure seemed like that many to me."

"Can you tell me?"

Fulmer leaned against the examination table. "Is this where you did your work on me?"

"It is."

"I remember from when you set my broken arm. Elbow bent clear back. I was screaming murder, but it knit right well. No problems, except in the rain. Little stiff. That's when this was sick deck. Some time ago, isn't it?"

Nemo studied Fulmer, holding all back, and saying simply, "Yes, it is."

"And, I do remember," Fulmer said, "whose blood that is, Captain."

Nemo kept working. Had no response.

"So, I'm thanking you for this time, especially. My brains were mush, I know that."

"Be of use," Nemo said. "Tell me about this thing."

"I thought it was real." Fulmer leaned against the table, picking up a scalpel and poking the spider's steel mandibles. "Then it sprayed that green stuff. Burned Red's face right off his skull, others', too. The eyes lit up somehow, and when they walked, you can hear the machinery inside."

"What was your ship?"

"The *Mariner*, registered out of Brighton. Just a tramp freighter, I hitched on as a cargo rat. Hauling everything you could think of, but our hold was full of rifles. For India, I think."

Nemo let the mention of India sink between them, before he

said to Fulmer, "How did these things get aboard? Were they in the crates, or didn't you take care to observe?"

"The first ones I saw were perched on top. We busted out some guns, and didn't see any layin' in among 'em. They were pouring in through the portholes, though. And the deck. Like regular spiders, on webs. It takes two to three slugs for a dead-stop. I guess there's an engine you have to hit, or something."

"Do you see any in the water?"

"No, but they were all over the sides, crawling up." Fulmer took the scalpel away from the mechanical, turned it over in his hand. "Captain, I know you've seen hell."

Nemo said, "More than once."

"This was worse."

Nemo slipped on a pair of gloves, moved to a steel-and-glass tank on the opposite side of the lab. "Supposedly there are more than a half dozen ships that've gone through the same thing, all on routes around Brigand's Trench."

Fulmer said, "Jesus, another fantasy."

"Like your spiders?"

Fulmer said, "I don't call that anything but a good reason to drink."

Nemo said, "The feeling is all the sinkings are coordinated, and you've given me an excellent process as to how I might find out why."

"You've already taken the goddamn thing apart."

Nemo lifted a luminous jellyfish from a tank. "Hand me a glassed needle. On the tray."

Fulmer handed him the needle, looking around the lab at the fish swimming in their tanks, the monitors, and the large vaulted door.

"I haven't seen all of her, but you've made some changes."

Nemo said, "She certainly needed some after the cannon damage. Obviously."

He drew phosphorous fluid from the jelly's main sack with a hypo, carefully inserting the needle between poison ribbons. "Now, not more of this than you can spare."

He gently submerged the fish, waiting for its cap to undulate, then bloom its sides and swim to the bottom of the tank.

Nemo held the needle filled with the light-catching fluid, moved to the spider, and opened the belly cavity with tweezers. "It's an amazing piece of work, this thing. The interior's a combination of mechanicals and organic tissue. That acid it spits, self-generating through some kind of glandular system that's a variation on a poison rockfish from Australia. Hold it in front of you. Straight."

Fulmer took the spider, keeping it as far away from his face as he could, as Nemo injected the natural phosphorus fluid into its exposed belly sacks that held its venom and acids.

"A South African jelly," Fulmer said. "Always of the sea."

"Indeed."

"You were talking about something like this, years ago. Called it hybrid mechanics?"

Fulmer put the spider down on the table, almost dropping it, then wiping a grotesque feeling from his hands. "To help species of fish that were thinnin' out, artificially building their immune systems, give them a little extra fight. Someone beat you to the punch?"

"Perhaps, but with what intention? It will be a while working through its system, but if this creation swims, it probably has some sort of device that will take it back to its nest. The fluid from the jellyfish will allow us to track it."

Fulmer said, "To wherever in hell?"

"More appropriately, to whoever made it. Why did you fight

to hold onto this creation? You were delirious, and wouldn't let it go. You almost drowned with it."

Fulmer said, "Ship went down, lots of men dead, and I figured I needed proof of what happened. Who'd believe it? Sun baked my brain a little, guess that's all I could think about, not going to prison."

Nemo replaced the needle on the instrument tray. "The lessons learned from the battles lost."

Fulmer said, "You'd know better than me, Captain."

Sara lay in her top bunk, staring at the riveted metal of the *Nautilus*' ceiling, and feeling suddenly closed in. As Jess does. The other crew. She reached out, brushing her fingers across the iron, and tilted her head to the other men in the quarters. Asleep, snoring, and farting. But not trying to sneak their way into her bed.

She closed her eyes, felt something under her mattress. Sara felt under it, and came back with a small stiletto, and a note, "Sis—just in case."

She held the knife to her, smiling, and let some rest happen.

The Bach resounded almost the moment that Fulmer set foot on the bridge, as if an accompaniment. Jess was at the wheel, guiding the ship over a small section of coral reef, carefully ascending to avoid any scrapings. Or hassles.

Fulmer said, "He hasn't lost his touch, has he?"

"The Captain loves his music, that's for sure."

"Even if the rest of us are a little cool. I think it would have been nicer if he'd learned to play the banjo."

Jess gave Fulmer a nod and a smile, but held back as Fulmer

walked the bridge. Checking navigation instrumentation, examining the wires to the Phono.

Fulmer said, "Things are sure changed up here."

"You didn't bring your machett this time," Jess said, using the pronunciation from the African Coast.

"The way you said it, bet I can I guess where you picked that up. And that you're wearing that Colt."

"Americans always know their guns." Jess nodded. "And yes, I am, mate."

Fulmer said, "Funny, you calling me that."

"Actually, I didn't." Jess steadied the wheel, made adjustments through the glove controls. "And I never will. A slip of the tongue, part of me heritage, you know."

Fulmer showed his hands. "No offense meant. You're the first, and that's it. I'm still trying to get my legs back. But this is a beautiful ship. Amazing what he built, and he's done better with it since I stood where you are now. And those controls, they're different, too."

"I imagine most of it is," Jess said. "Your being here is cause to carry this Colt."

"You don't need protection from me, Mr. Jess. I'm just a rescue."

"Like in the passage?"

"Still sun-struck."

Jess said, "Well, just in case. To protect Sis, keep the horny ones in line. And protect me-self, so I can do my duty without interruption."

"That's how you get paid at journey's end," Fulmer said. He was at the standing switches and said, "What about the Maoris? I've been around, I could read those tattoos. There's a blood oath, right on the throat, with three slashes. That means three brothers, doesn't it? They gave me the machett."

"I know."

Jess was now in the captain's chair and said, "Used to be three, now only two. I took the other out with a piece of flat iron in a fight. Took his head down to his knees. He was having a go at me, it was fair, but they don't see it that way."

Fulmer said, "So you're surrounded by it, aren't you?"

He walked to the center of the observation dome, his eyes following the beams from the *Nautilus'* running lights into the splay of colors of the night ocean, saying, "Really is beautiful, and worth protecting."

Jess said, "It goes with the sea life, goes with being First Mate."

The last echoes of the organ cords still hadn't faded when Nemo laid out the sea spider on the examination table, keeping it on its back and working its eight legs. Back and forth, to all positions, pumping its gear and tube circulatory system with specialty wrenches made for the *Nautilus'* guidance systems.

The tools aligned perfectly, forcing the natural glowing of the jelly through the spider's joints. The diamond sliver was still in its test tube, away from the power cavity, as Nemo worked, freeing the pistons and engaging flywheels and gear works.

Finally, a hint of color traveled down a leg. Then another. The lab was dark, except for the new light coming from the mechanical, as all eight legs worked the phosphorus though the spider's system. And was recirculated, the essence of the jellyfish glowing brighter each time, creating a beacon.

34

BEASTS AND THE SEA

The Greek freighter seemed to have been cleaved in half with an enormous blade, the bow lying twisted into the ocean floor, sides and the deck cut through, the steel shredded as wet tissue. The stern was farther away, crushed by the smokestack falling backward onto it, pounding the midsection flat before catching fire; the shape of an open wound, cut from blackened iron.

An avalanche had buried most of the ship, leaving pieces of railing, some furniture, and even sailor uniforms caught between the wreckage and the sea shelf. An accordion hung from the bow, expanding and withdrawing with the currents. Sand, gravel, and plants continued to roll down the small mountain, onto the ship, for no reason other than to bury it further.

The remains of a few bodies were strung through the wooden railings, the bones of limbs, still connected, wafting about as fish darted around them, feeding on sinew or marrow, then schooling away.

Nemo was at the observation port, eyeing the freighter with a telescope. "Miss Duncan, here's the wreck, as you can see, please make note, but there's no obvious evidence of what caused it."

Sara, standing by him, asked, "Like more spiders?"

"Meaning, we've made visual contact."

"But those are burn marks."

Nemo said, "Melted scars, more to the point. Incredible heat. The midsection will always explode when the stacks are compromised, but this ship looks to have been put apart by a Frost Giant's battle ax."

Sara said, "That, actually, wasn't one of the causes listed."

"I'm surprised," Nemo said, refocusing the scope. "There's some movement there. Under the sand."

Sara said, "I see something; could be an abandoned telegraph cable, a creature pulling at it?"

Jess squinted from the control board. "Yeah, metal looking. Cap, is that some kind of deep-sea rig? Piece of a diving bell, maybe?"

Nemo took his place at the helm, his expression darkening. "We'll table that suggestion. Mr. Jess, all engines standing by. At full power."

The sand around the wreckage shifted, something under it rippling back and forth, snakelike. But made of steel. The polished top of the thing could be seen as silt and sand fell away, revealing giant sections of tubular steel, interconnected by what could have been veins and tissue, but was actually thick telegraph wire, wrapped in rubber sheeting. It whipped upward, leaving a long, deep furrow in the ocean floor.

Nemo increased the power with the glove controls, watching the indicators strain, the *Nautilus* engines turning but not engaged. "All engines prepared to reverse—that's prepare, Mr. Jess!"

"Aye, sir!" Jess repeated the order.

Sara said, "Captain—"

Nemo cut her off before the objection of not moving yet: "We don't have enough power built, Miss Duncan! I know my ship!"

Through the dome, the steel snake erupted from the sand, so huge it knocked part of the freighter's bow away. Tons of metal fast-spinning through the water, tossed with incredible force. The steel thing was followed by another machine-snake, and then another.

Sara watched the snakes as they drew back in unison, then were joined by two more. Metal tubes, wires, and pistons, interacting with each other as living things. Steel tentacles, snapping through the ocean, creating their own waves.

The movement of the polished metal tentacles was constant, pulling more and more away from the ocean floor, trying to free itself from under the ship. Its head, made of flexible interlocking plates, forming the artificial skull of an enormous squid and housing its impulse center.

Another machine, not an animal.

Buried beside the stern wreckage, the sides of the skull inflated, gathering water in rubber chambers, then jetted it out, powering forward, bursting from the sand and wreckage. Its tentacles snapped hold of the *Nautilus'* hull and pulled itself around it in a violent motion that rocked the submarine.

The observation dome was suddenly covered with one side of the squid's head, pressed against the glass, almost splitting it. An artificial eye roamed from its socket, the thing taking in all corners of the bridge.

Jess said, "Another beastie, made of scrap iron and bad intentions. Jesus save me, I'd believe anything now."

Nemo ordered, "Engine room!"

Jess leapt down the stairs, and from then on Nemo gave no verbal orders. He watched the thing, reversing engines only through

the helm hand controls, the crew below, scrambling at the shifting, setting gears in motion, resetting the speed.

On the bridge, quiet. Sara was about to speak, and Nemo si-
lenced her with a gesture, fixed on the eye and its iris. Moving in
and out, like the lens of a camera. Opening wider to absorb more
light, more visual information. Around it, the natural "flesh" was
stitched rubber cushioning metal plating.

The mechanical was strangling the *Nautilus*, acting on
command, pulling its body onto the submarine from the bow to
amidships, steel and piston tentacles wrapping tighter and tighter,
covering the view ports and gears locking. Digging into the hull,
as a real squid would crush an enemy.

Its body twisted, water bursting from its side as a geyser,
shifting its weight, to turn the submarine on its side, forcing it
over. Shaking it lifeless.

But it was a machine, fighting a machine. And if it could react automatically to what it observed, it could also react to the
sounds it detected. The *Nautilus* shook, the hull plates groaning
from the pressure of the steel tentacles squeezing the submarine's
frame. Bending. Trying to snap the iron.

Belowdecks, Fulmer charged from the crew quarters, raced
the passage, getting to the Exploration tubes. He knew deep-
water squids, and had fought them. He knew they would search a
prey for any wound or opening, push their tentacles in, forcing
through the flesh, to rip apart from the inside.

He also knew that the crew couldn't react that way to this
creature. It wasn't an animal, but a mechanical, like the sea spiders, and it had to be dealt with the same way you'd attack a tank
or a Gatling gun.

The Maori Whaler grabbed the machete from his brother
before throwing his weight against the hatch to the Exploration

chamber as a long steel tentacle exploded through one of the tubes. Glass shattered, and metal crumpled to nothing.

The Whaler slashed with the machete, as if he was cutting through thick skin and muscle. Bringing it down. Again and again. Hitting a thing of moving steel, whipping the air like a cat o' nine tails against a mutineer's back.

The blade struck. Cutting wiring between pistons. Hot sparks. The electric shock slammed the Whaler out of the dive room, tossing him as if he was nothing against the passageway wall. Dropping, in a long smear of blood, electric-burned hair and skin.

On the bridge, Nemo pulled Sara to him, speaking low. "Remember, it's not alive."

That's when he shut down all power.

The *Nautilus* was completely dark. The thing reacted as if the machine it was killing was dying, in its death throes. The tentacles tightened. Rivets on the hull loosening, then breaking from the hull like fired bullets. The submarine's iron starting to bend.

On the bridge, the view ports bulged, the seams giving way. Water tore around the ports. Nemo had been standing close to the glass, watching the steel move over it as a giant coiled spring inside a steel shell. Examining its construction, looking for vulnerabilities, even as the *Nautilus* began to scream.

There was the sound: that ricochet underwater, of more iron breaking from the hull, the ship's skeleton fighting the thing. Barely holding.

Nemo spoke in low tones. "I don't know what sensors that thing has, but your repairs, with the rubber skin, can you cut through it, get to the outer plates?"

It was the moment that comes to all crews at sea: that time during the crisis, when they work as one, all hands doing as they do best, brought together by death, not life. Nemo had seen it hundreds of times, faced it himself with death looming, the sailors who know their fate find extra strength, extend their abilities, as if having a final salute before the inevitability of a burial at sea.

Jess would spit and grin, taking a moment to think about it. He was in the engine room, bringing the reversed engines down, letting them cool, easing their power and checking all rods.

He ran the passageways as First Mate, making sure others bolstered the crossbeams with lumber supports, using torches and candles for light even as the outside iron shifted, the tentacles bending them, the corners breaking free.

The squid-thing pressured the hull; the *Nautilus* was withstanding. Barely. Taking the torture, even in pain. The ship, doing herself proud, and the crew, doing the same.

Sara, Jess, and Fulmer converged on the lab.

The only light was the flicker, a spatter of fire, coming from Nemo cutting through the side of the wall with a small iron blade, heated red in a metal smith's coal scuttle. Fulmer pulled the wall free, and Sara sliced away the rubber skin to reveal the outer iron plating of the hull.

For them, it was as if they were building a ship a thousand years ago, but their movements were in deliberate half-inches, with no words between them. The huge mechanical's reactions were to sense its enemy, and instantly rip the *Nautilus* in half, as it had the Greek vessel. Any sign of life, any movement, could be detected by the squid's mechanisms, so the *Nautilus* had to look like she was dying, tricking the mechanical to ease off its force. Then they could ambush the machine.

Jess choked. "You know better than I do, Miss, but this scares me dry!"

Sara whispered, "You'll be drinking soon enough," as the cardio machine was hauled to the wall opening.

Nemo still whispered, "Miss Duncan's addition of the rubber lining protects us from any escaping charge, but no direct contact with metal. If you're foolish, you're dead."

He attached the copper paddles to a support beam and the hull's outside plate, while Fulmer bared an idle power cable. Furious work, with instructions being nods, quick whispers, and pointings in the dark.

Sara lit a lens-focused candle and held it high as the power lines were pulled from the wall by Fulmer and cut open. From the passage, they heard ocean pour in from above. A section giving way.

"First Mate, has word been passed?"

Jess stood straight with a bolt of pride at Nemo's recognition, still whispering, "Yes, sir, Captain. All set below."

Sara moved behind the fish tanks, the creatures sensing and swimming furiously to a power grid. She connected the cardio cables, turned to Nemo. He faced the laboratory, the stretching operating theater, as Fulmer hefted himself again onto the wooden table, lying down as if for surgery. Waiting.

Another support beam screamed, the squid tightening, nearly breaking through.

Nemo kept back, away from the cardio machine and the copper contacts, feet off the floor, and turning to Sara. She had stepped up, also away from the floor, sitting on a counter next to a fish tank. No contact.

She used a broom handle, and threw the power grid control switch as Jess leapt from the table, pulling her back, away from a trail of water from the floor to where she was sitting.

The electricity arced as the ocean sprayed in.

Blue sparks exploded from the panel in a wild burst of heat, the cardio machine blowing apart as it sent electricity to the ship's hull and its beams at the same time. A swarm of blue-hot insects crawling through the *Nautilus'* metal guts and skin, making their way along the hull and ripping into the squid's metal tentacles.

The glass eyes became liquid behind their covering, the electricity traveling along the *Nautilus,* webbing across the hull, heating the water around it, and blowing apart each tentacle. Steel joints exploded, falling away from the submarine as the skull's pieces collapsed inside its rubber covering, becoming a deflated, burning balloon sinking to the ocean floor.

Followed by the other pieces. Steel and wire turning in the water, colliding with the wreckage of the Greek ship. Raising the silt and sand, which covered the thing again, as if it never existed.

Above it, the *Nautilus'* engines engaged, the lights flickering on at all ports and sides as it aimed for the surface.

In the laboratory, Sara leaned over, cutting the power switch with the broomstick. Jess dropped from his table. "Sorry I manhandled you, Sis, but you're too important to let go."

The final burst of power from the cardio ripped across the wet floor, tearing into Jess instantly. His spine stiffened, cracked, the surface of his eyes cooking black before his legs buckled and he collapsed on the laboratory floor.

35

REQUIEM

The waves have now a redder glow,
The hours are breathing faint and low,
And when, amid no earthly moans,
Down, down that town shall settle hence,
Hell, rising from a thousand thrones,
Shall do it reverence.

Nemo let the last of Poe's words settle as the canvas gunnysacks
were brought onto the *Nautilus'* forward deck. The crew stood
silent, covered by their own shadow, as the Maori Whaler and Jess
were wrapped one last time, the edges of the canvas stitched closed
with heavy twine, and bound once with a leather tie.

Sara stood between Nemo and Fulmer, wearing Jess' old
jacket, looking out at the miles of Atlantic that surrounded them,
the cold gray of the water matching the color of the gunnysacks
and the dullness of the sky. Everything was a shroud.

There was no music, nothing other than Nemo's reciting. The

Whaler's brother, alone by the conning tower, watched his brother's body lifted by the crew, before being gently rolled into the cold water.

He said, "They both wanted the other one dead. That's a sad desire, to come true."

The Whaler went below, as Jess' body was lifted, and followed the Maori into the waves. Jess floated for a moment, the ocean embracing him, before the canvas soaked through, weighing him down, and he was gone.

Fulmer said, "We are of the waves."

Nemo said, "There's the epitaph."

He started for the hatch, turned to Fulmer, "You're first mate. Miss Duncan, you'll be supervising repairs."

A Crewmen waited for Nemo to descend, then hoisted the last of Jess' clay rum jug, taking a swig and then passing it on. No words. After the drink, each crewman went through the below hatch, in their own silent ritual.

It reached Sara. She hesitated, but they wanted her to take a drink. As one of them. She did, and passed it on to Fulmer, the last in line. He downed the few, awful drops, then hurled the jug into the water. It landed, floating with the waves longer than Jess himself.

"If that rum tells the tale," Fulmer was still wincing at the taste, "I don't think Jess liked me too well."

Sara said, "He was my friend."

He touched Sara's shoulder, which she twisted off before walking toward the bow. Fulmer watched Sara, her hands deep in the pockets of Jess' jacket. Not wiping wet eyes, but staying fixed on the horizon, on the bleeding gray.

He said, "You can stay, but better be ready to swim."

Sara pushed her way around Fulmer, into the hatch.

————

The boy's brown arms went around his father's neck, and the man could feel the softness of his cheek against his. He pulled away from the hug, so his beard wouldn't scratch, and looked directly into his son's wet eyes.

Prince Dakkar said, "Don't fear."

The boy's mouth was open, in a smile, when the bullets tore into him, splitting his shoulder blades.

Nemo startled awake, lying on a tangle of sheets. The only light in his quarters was the glow around the edges of the family portrait. He splashed water on his face before moving to his desk and catching the breath he lost to his dream.

He opened his journal, and wrote one line: *Dearest Dear. Today I buried two.*

Nemo stepped onto the bridge, examining the splits in the observation dome made by the squid, now patched with hard wax mixed with ground glass. The steel frame had twisted, but held, and the walls had been spattered with ocean foam. But it had survived, and that's all Nemo could think about, surveying this bit of the damage.

Duncan's voice seemed to come from nowhere, calling out, "Come in, *Nautilus*! Sara, it's your father, can you hear me? Please, respond. Please."

Nemo bent into the receiver horn. "This is Nemo. We will report when I deem fit to do so. Nemo out."

He shut the device down. "My invention, and I despise it."

Nemo's words had just cut off as Maston lit the lamps lining the gondola's first deck. Prudent angled the dirigible's bow toward

the setting sun, the last of the orange splitting apart into evening. Duncan sat by the Phono, as if waiting for another word.
Another voice. His head bowed.

The gondola swayed, as if making a lazy turn on a river. Maston
set another lamp glowing, paused by a painting of the Battle of
Shiloh, the bloody charge, hanging beside a bookshelf of leather-
bound volumes.

He adjusted the gas flame to highlight the gold-framed artwork. "Mr. President, I love this painting, the courage of it. If I
had the money, it would be the only one I owned. But you should
be represented in it, I think. I only see General Buell."

"Good man, who saved our lives, what was left of them,"
Grant said.

"It turned the tide of the war."

"Cost a lot of men, and a lot of blood, and we were able to
push through the Confederate line, but Gettysburg was worse,"
Grant said, moving to his desk and sets of rolled battle plans.

"I wish to hell it wasn't here. That was a time I don't need
reminding of."

Duncan turned from the receiver horn. "There's nothing now.
You heard the voice, he won't give up a thing."

Grant said, "Nemo's on his own mission, and so are we. We
just have to pray that we can tie-up, so we'll be exonerated."

Duncan looked to Grant. "You were right, Sam. You said
traitors are like drunks, practiced liars who don't mend their ways
so easily."

Grant said, "Being right doesn't always bring satisfaction."

Maston faced Duncan. "Sir, I feel a little caged up here, but
you know I'm ready to jump in. At any time."

Duncan said, "It's appreciated, Mr. Maston."

Prudent brought the dirigible through a cloud bank, letting it
move around the ship as a white and flowing waterfall, the clouds

spilling around them, then separating with the motion of the dual propellers, revealing the Atlantic Ocean below.

Prudent said, "There's your view, gentlemen, and I will land you exactly where you need to be, by high noon."

Grant opened the telescope rack, and handed Duncan one of the long glasses, all polished brass. "Take a look, he's down there. Someplace. Sara, too. Just keep thinking about that, about her. And seeing her again."

Duncan said, "I never thought I'd hear you defending Nemo, or the *Nautilus*."

"Right now, I'm acting as a friend. Not the President," Grant said. "There'll be ample time for the other."

The *Nautilus* was a night predator, moving at mid-speed through an ocean bed, swordfish veering away from its jagged-iron snout and the lit ports that were the predator's fiery eyes. Bearing down, ready for an attack.

On the bridge, Sara welded the edge of the viewing port with the ruby beam from the laser rifle. The swordfish broke in front of her view, then swam off in quick, acrobatic moves, away from the needle of light.

Nemo stepped to the helm, checking the instrumentation. "How bad are the ruptures?"

Sara said, "I wish we had our repair dock at Norfolk."

"I believe that's gone in flames."

"Then Vulcania."

"Someday, perhaps." Nemo set the direction. "Can we sustain this depth?"

"You have to understand." Sara put down the rifle. "That anything I do will be a bandage on the wound, and we'll have to keep bandaging until we dock and put the ship back together properly. I think she'll hold, but there better not be any more mechanicals."

"I wish I could predict that," Nemo said.

"Me, too, because I surely couldn't take another, and I don't think the *Nautilus* can, either."

Sara held the rifle's bone-stock to her shoulder. "Even this would have been of little use against that thing. The polished steel, it would've broken up the beam shooting through the water, bounced off it like rain."

"I agree."

Sara said, "It's like it was created to fight you, to know what you had at hand to battle it."

Nemo said, "It was a surprise attack. I know about those."

She fired the rifle, melting the last of the lead stripping around the domed port, sealing the glass tight in its place, then looked to Nemo. "It won, though. That thing, whatever you want to call it. It attacked, and won. Killed those men, and won."

Nemo said, "This ship was saved, Mr. Jess, sacrificed. It goes with the pay and the rum. The sea's our home, our work, someday our grave. We accept it, so should you."

Sara let the rifle drop, putting it aside, and speaking quietly. "I guess you've seen more men sacrificed than I have."

"You'd be correct, but you already know those facts." Nemo moved to the navigation station. "You can't pride yourself on your complete knowledge of who I am, what I've done, and then be shocked when faced with it. You can't have it both ways, Miss Duncan, because that only reveals your deceptions."

Sara said, "I'm still here of my own accord."

"You're here because I allow it," Nemo said. "You wanted me to plot a course, and I followed my own, but getting to Brigand's Trench would bring us where we are tonight. Either course we followed of the sinkings, we'd be here. What do you see?"

Nemo guided Sara by the shoulders to the glass dome, the lights of the *Nautilus* cutting through a bleeding of rust, infecting the water from the remains of a battleship, its cannons tilting over from sections of exploded decks or scattered in front of the bow as blasted-apart scrap. Barrels half-buried, the guns housing thousands of fish and crabs, while the salt water feeds on the iron skin of a shattered hull and what remains of its bridge.

Sara said, "Yes, a warship."

"It is the *Abraham Lincoln*. What remains of it."

Sara's eyes were closed. "A hundred and twenty-five sent to the bottom, at your order."

"So, you do know. Well. And there's no mystery here, this is my doing. So, yes, I have seen more men sacrificed than you."

"And you were to hang for this."

Nemo said, "Until your father intervened. It's quite a bit different reading about something in the newspaper, and seeing it, drifting in front of you."

A shred of a tunic was pulled from a hold by the submarine's wake, caught up by speed, and dragged alongside. Sara looked away, shaking her head, aware of the sailor who was once inside the jacket. Of the idea of the men trapped in the *Abraham Lincoln* as it sunk. She had flashes of sailors sleeping and writing letters.

Nemo said, "As always, I gave them fair warning to abandon ship, but they refused. The *Nautilus* retaliated."

"Against what? A ship of innocents, who wouldn't give up their posts?"

"That craft was built for no other purpose than to end human life. It had to be eliminated. Look closely at the *Lincoln*'s hull: what do you still see there?"

The center of the hull was torn through, a gaping hole jagged on both sides, the tear in the iron matching the *Nautilus*' prow.

"We rammed her amidships," Nemo said. "It was Mr. Fulmer's brother who was officer of the deck, and gave the order for the sailors to remain on board, instead of abandoning ship. He was killed along with the crew, which is why, when this mission is over, Mr. Fulmer will kill me."

Sara said, "Your war against war. No matter what, people die. You justify your brutality like everyone else, like every institution."

"You're quoting me back," Nemo said.

"But there are penalties to be extracted, aren't there?"

"Now you have a dilemma, understanding the real prices to be paid for our choices," Nemo said. "You have quality Miss Duncan, but you're sounding more like an editorial, or a Pinkerton, rather than one of my crew."

Sara looked to Nemo. "What are you saying to me?"

"That on my *Nautilus,* I am law unto myself, and if I were you, I shouldn't test those limits."

Nemo turned away from the dome and the wreckage. "One day, above, in the so-called civilized world, I'll be the bloodied one. I know this, and so does your father, which is why I was chosen. Death by hanging weeks ago, or death, after the mission."

Sara said, "I don't know what choice I'd make."

"Your guilt about Mr. Jess is pointless. He was doing his duty, saving your life, and your insulation saved the lives of the crew. There are greater burdens waiting for you, Miss Duncan, so abandon this one. Sometimes it's preferable to be a mere stowaway."

It was a side passageway, with only a small view port, but Fulmer stood there, watching the tunic from the *Abraham Lincoln* drift by, turning in the water, before entering the laboratory. His hand went to the light switch on the wall, when Sara spoke.

"Don't put on the electric lights. Please."

Fulmer said, "All right, Miss Duncan. It helps me to see if my memory can still serve. The switch was over here years ago."

"It still is. I just can't see the room right now. Not with all the damage, and the rest."

Fulmer sidled his way through the strips of shadow from the scientific equipment, following glints of reflection from the maze of counters and glass tanks, to where Sara stood before the vault door.

As he moved, banging his shins, he said, "I understand, but think of the time when you can turn the lights on, see the memories, okay?"

Sara said, "I was told to report here."

"We've a special job. Nemo needs something out of the vault."

"Oh. I have the combination."

"So do I. It's the date his wife and son were killed by troops in Khamar," Fulmer said, dialing. "If he gave it to you in Hindi, that's his test. It means he has you all lined up."

"For what?"

"To stand with him on the *Nautilus*." Fulmer opened the vault lock, the works turning over. "For as long as she lasts."

Sara said, "I don't know if that applies anymore."

He pulled the door open, the weight of the thing rolling him back. He stepped in and lit the candle on the holder on the immediate inside shelf.

Fulmer stood for a moment, surrounded by the weapons, pictures, and uniforms. What he hadn't seen in years. He walked farther into the vault, to the Kraken, still sitting with its mouth hanging open, and the paper ships in its large, wooden belly, sinking.

He said, "I would've thought the old Kraken was for the bonfire."

"We got our map coordinates from that machine."

"I know it works, pretty damn well, I'm just shocked he kept it around. The Captain's not known for his whimsy. Did you use the coordinates?"

Sara said, "No. We didn't have to, he went his own way."

"No surprise. Is that how you found me?"

Fulmer reached around the side of the box, and turning a switch, brought the harpies back, flying and wire-swooping again over the tiny ships. He said, "As the First Mate, I'd say it's important to see those numbers. Know what y'all have been up to. Or not."

The Kraken's tongue rolled out, with the sinking information printed as before. Fulmer tore it off then rolled it into his pocket.

He said, "A little trick I learned from the fella who made it. That was right before he got shot in the head by the army when they seized the ship."

Fulmer pushed aside a rifle rack, revealing a cache of brass-cased torpedoes, brilliantly polished, and stacked like cordwood for winter. Beside them, boxes of fuses, primers, and timing systems.

Sara said, "I had no idea . . ."

"You still don't. Lend a hand."

Fulmer took one end of a torpedo, five feet in length, and hefted it as Sara took the other side. She reacted, thinking it would be heavier than it was.

Fulmer said, "There's nothing inside but a guidance system and a little powder to launch. No special deliveries. Yet."

Sara said, "You can imagine what all the newspapers would make of this bit of—"

They back-walked toward the vault door. "Hypocrisy? If Nemo followed his own philosophy, he'd have to turn these against himself?" Fulmer said. "I've heard it a thousand times, and worse."

"Do you think it so?"

Fulmer regarded Sara. "The business between the Captain and myself is our own, settled in our own time."

Sara said, "Very elegantly put, and very evasive. Is that you?"

They stopped by the door, the candle flickering down, the last bits of flame showing a stack of photographs on a shelf. The top one, a curling, sepia image of a young man with an idiotic grin and single-shot rifles resting on each shoulder. He sported no uniform, only ragtag clothes, and stood before a tramp schooner.

Fulmer blew out the candle. "Mind you don't trip with this thing. It can still do some damage."

The lab was fully lit as Fulmer and Sara brought the torpedo from the vault.

Nemo opened a small freezing cabinet beneath the row of aquariums. There was still a spatter of Jess' blood on the walls and scorch marks from the electricity.

Nemo said, "The missile goes to the old table; take the head from the casing. Lend a hand here, Miss Duncan. And protect them!"

Fulmer set to work, wrenching off the torpedo's top section as Sara wrapped her hands in an old bloody bandage from the table to grab hold of the steel box covered in solid ice. Liquid nitrogen spewed from the freezer, a burst of snow settling around the box, refreezing the moisture as it hit the air. Nemo cracked the ice around the edges, prying it open.

"A good suggestion," he said. "The tongs, then take out the torpedo's timing mechanism. You're the only one with hands small enough."

The surgeon's tongs went to Nemo, with Fulmer laughing as she suddenly jammed her hand into the torpedo casing and twisted the timing wires around her fingers.

Fulmer said, "You're like a pickpocket, trying for the first time."

"Well, am I doing this correctly or not?"

"Seriously. Easier touch." Fulmer was close to her ear. "He ain't kiddin' about being careful."

"I thought these were safe."

Fulmer said, "Any weapon can bite you."

Nemo pulled the sea spider from the freezing box with the tongs, the cold misting with it, saying, "That will house our friend, and we'll launch from second tube. Corrupt the threading between sections; we can't have any delay with separation after firing. Miss Duncan?"

Sara held up the timer. "All gutted, sir," she said as Nemo brought the frozen spider and placed it alongside the torpedo.

Fulmer said, "That's a good fit, Captain. This is pretty outrageous."

Nemo said, "That sometimes yields results, yes, Miss Duncan? The blue diamond, next to you."

Sara opened the test tube, dropping the diamond into Nemo's hand. "This is outrageous, and nothing I've ever seen."

Nemo said, "A month past, and I would have said the same, about any of these mechanicals, but we have dead men, and we're told, a world tipping over on itself, all because of gears and servos in the shape of God's creatures."

He inserted the diamond into the spider, seeing it draw power, but unable to move its frozen legs as intended. "Actually, given all of this, I don't think outrageous is anywhere near an adequate label."

Sara said, "I've studied every inch of this ship, and I didn't even know it could fire a torpedo."

Fulmer said, "There will always be secrets, Miss. This is its own world down here; maybe you should stop being shocked."

Before Sara could respond, Nemo said, "Miss Duncan's made contributions to this mission, that includes saving your life. You're the new First, but don't condescend."

The rest was done with pure military efficiency: the Captain and First securing the weapon's special charge, positioning the sea spider in the brass casing, as a delayed explosive would be. Levers were pulled in coded order, the torpedo firing tubes revealing themselves beneath the laboratory floor, splitting away at the dividing point between the new *Nautilus* and the Victorian surgery, as if the submarine were shedding its old skin.

Fulmer stepped into the divide, loading the torpedo into the breech firing mechanism and locking it off, all in moments. Expert and sure.

The laser rifle fitted to a sniper's tripod, with Fulmer aiming through the top of the observation dome. He slid back the power cradle, widening the beam. "How long will we be tracking this thing, Captain?"

Nemo was at the helm, checking speed. "I examined the device's every complication, found no markings of origin. So, a day, a week, a thousand years. Somewhere you need to be, Mr. Fulmer?"

Fulmer set his aim beyond the bow, tightened on the trigger. "No, sir. I'm playing the waiting game."

"The order, Miss Duncan," Nemo said. "Would you like to give it? It would be something specific to report to your father."

Sara was at her navigation post, blank charts posted in front of her. "I wouldn't know what to say, Captain."

"Torpedo-bomb lexicon isn't in common usage, perhaps a sign they won't be popular, but I doubt it. Mr. Rongo, open the right grating, for flooding."

The Maori Whaler stood his post, at the far side of the bridge, an enormous figure, his hands ready to take hold of the ballast rail switches or side-fin controls. He angled his head, acknowledging being addressed by his proper name, before throwing the levers, flooding the torpedo tubes.

The water rushing was a roar from belowdecks, brief, then silent.

Rongo said, "Flooded, sir."

"Miss Duncan?"

"Fire the torpedo, sir."

Rongo set the mechanism to work, and the torpedo to fire, the missile racing ahead of the *Nautilus*. Nemo upped speed, seeing it travel, then, "Aiming, Mr. Fulmer. Now!"

Fulmer shot. The laser beam hit the edge of the torpedo just as the top section blew apart, ejecting the spider into the water. Fulmer kept the beam on the thing as it sank, the ice melting, cut by the beam, freeing its joints. He kept the laser on it. The legs ground. Jerked to life, the machinery thawing. They began to move in mechanical unison, the eight pistons clawing at the water, outlined by the luminous jellyfish fluid working its way through.

The sea spider was a lantern in the dark. Under the laser light, the glowing thing began to swim, speeding instantly ahead. Darting around coral to open waters, with Fulmer taking the rifle barrel in any direction, never losing his target.

The spider's movements were quick, the legs balancing and propelling simultaneously, all guided by its internal mechanics, as Nemo predicted.

Nemo brought the *Nautilus* to cruising, giving the thing as much distance as possible, not to pull it back into the propellers or have its course shifted by the submarine's wake. His hands worked, as keys on the organ, always adjusting the glove controls and steering bar, according to the moves of the beacon ahead.

Sara said, "This truly is Goliath chasing David."

"More like chasing a prairie dog." Fulmer laughed. "I can keep it in sight, maybe as much as a quarter mile ahead, if it stays steady and the water doesn't fog. But I don't know what tricks it'll pull. Or it's supposed to."

Nemo said, "None of us do, but this is a fine test of maneuverability."

Fulmer said, "Until it leads us to a battle armada."

"Captain, what course do I chart?"

"You don't chart the progress, Miss Duncan, but our arrival. Our destination."

Sara had to ask: "And the mission?"

Nemo said, "Our destination."

The dirigible passed invisible through the midnight clouds, its lit windows showing as six stars moving in a row across the night sky with a hint of music behind them.

A map of the Atlantic was projected across the ceiling of the Gondola, with Grant studying the indicated positions of the ships arriving for the summit. As always, Duncan was at the Phono, ready to respond to the first sound coming from it. Anxious eyes behind bifocals.

Maston and the Guards stayed their positions, with Maston cleaning his pistol. The music came from a harpsichord box in the corner by the library shelves.

Prudent sipped tea, and said, "Gentlemen, we're right on course, right on time. And my thanks for the tea, Mr. Duncan."

Duncan said, "Least I can do for the pilot. Honestly."

"Down to my last cigar," Grant said, cutting it at his desk. "It's been a hell of a long time since I smoked this much. Mrs. Grant will kill me."

Duncan said, "She hasn't so far."

"Not that I haven't given her reason." Grant lit his last. "Or anyone else. If we raise Nemo, I'll order him to the summit, hand over whatever it is proving we didn't sink any ships, or behind the assassinations."

Grant stood, pacing the tight space of the gondola. "If he refuses, and he damn well might, that means we'll be facing a lot of enemies. But I'll have a frigate to do nothing but capture the *Nautilus*, and bring that son of a bitch to heel. Then hang him."

Duncan said, "The confrontation might be exactly what he wants."

"He can be gotten, and we'll do it again."

"I truly thought he'd cooperate, with all that's at stake."

Grant said, "We're beyond that, now. We can't second-guess."

"Indeed," Duncan said, bringing the pistol from his jacket, and shooting Prudent in the head, blood spattering the pilot's chair. Then, a shot through his lapel, blowing the golden balloons apart.

It was all in moments. Grant turning at the sound, with Duncan on top of him, pounding him down with the butt of the gun, steel-to-temple, while pulling the pistol from Grant's shoulder holster. Turning. Shooting a Rifle Guard in the chest with Grant's gun, then the second, blowing a hole into his throat, and his eye, still sitting before the sky windows, never getting off a shot.

Duncan stood before Maston, holding two pistols. The Rifle Guard's blood washed the lens of the map projector, casting the entire gondola in red.

Maston's own jacket was open, but his hand hadn't reached for the gun. There was still blank shock in his eyes, and he wiped blood from his cheek and the front of his jacket, rather than draw. Stunned by the academic.

"I know you're good," Duncan said, "and that's caused me a lot of worry."

The first shot was through Maston's heart; the kick pushing him back. Feet tangling. The next shots, Duncan alternating between guns, firing both, propelled Maston back, crashing him through the window and over the gondola's railing. And falling dead through the clouds.

"Sam." Duncan picked up the guard's rifles. "I wish to God we were still over Washington, and he landed on the steeple of one of your reconstructed churches. The irony of that would have been delicious."

Grant was on the floor, his back against his desk, looking up at Duncan. Eyes fixed as Duncan took off his glasses and crushed them under his boot.

"Amazing how differently people treat you, wearing those. Never a threat," Duncan said. "And you're speechless, Mr. President. This night proves that all things are possible."

36

THE *TERROR*

Horace had surrounded himself with telegrams and translatable notes, all before sending a message through the Phono in Duncan's office. He was pleased with himself, straightening his jacket and running his fingers over his few strands of sticky yellow hair, when he managed to get Duncan's image onto his mirror screen and hear his voice with clarity. It was an achievement.

"Congratulations on reading my instructions," Duncan said. "What telegrams, what are we to expect?"

Horace shuffled through the paper stacks. "Quite a bit. Most of these are more objections to an all-out war, with a hint of an invasion by Germany, through Mexico."

Duncan's image said, "Not hints."

"Mr. Gladstone's invited the president to board his ship, and to conduct affairs under the protection of England's flag. He warns this isn't strictly sanctioned by Her Majesty, but"—he held the telegram up to a lamp flute, squint-reading—"'You surely deserve a Marquess of Queensberry fighting chance.'"

Duncan was in the Pilot's Station, Prudent's corpse lying crumpled behind him, guiding the dirigible, and saying, "That's certainly news. On the other matter, make sure about any other messages going out. You know what I mean."

Horace came back on the mirror. "I do, indeed. Taken care of tonight. And sir, may I say what a privilege to be part of such a daring—"

Duncan shut the power, pulling the guide chains above him for rudder direction, feeling the great machine moving, bending the air to its needs. Taking pride in it.

Duncan reached down and pried away the one balloonist pin on Prudent's lapel that hadn't been destroyed by a bullet. Grant was at his desk, bent and watching, hands cuffed behind his chair.

Duncan wiped the blood before attaching the honor to his own jacket. "That conversation: did you get all of it, Sam? The man's a troll, but he's proved of some use, manipulating your White House information."

Grant said, "You're a goddamned traitor."

"At least. But I prefer visionary."

The hair around Cincinnati's bullet wound was finally darkening, and growing in more fully. Efrem covered the raised skin with salve that he smoothed out with his fingers, massaging the horse's muscles for the mixture to work its way in. He always stood still for this, swatting with his tail and bobbing his jaw, as if in agreement.

"You're the finest animal I've ever seen."

Efrem always said this, giving a bit of a pause each time, as if waiting for the horse to actually speak. But he said it, over and over, as he finished with the brushing, and checking the stall's water and oats troughs.

"Hard at work, as always."

Efrem scooped oats into a feed bag, looking up as Horace entered the stable, holding a lantern. He always checked around him as he walked, as if the stable floor wasn't cleaned every hour, and always scraped something off his soles that wasn't there.

Efrem finished with the bag. "Yes, sir. Lots of work, these animals."

"But worth it."

"I have an"—Efrem was reaching for it—"affinity."

Horace kept the lantern high. "That's good, Efrem, very good. Taking extra lessons?"

Efrem said, "No, sir. Mr. Lime said it, and I just recalled it."

Horace peered over the top of another stall, at one of the mares belonging to Mrs. Grant. "If I was impressed before, it's doubled now. That's two times more."

Efrem poured clean water into the trough. "Yes, sir. I know."

"Since there's nothing I can tell you, maybe you can tell me, again, about the Presidential message to your grandmother."

Efrem stepped back from the stall. "Sir?"

"The letter. Grant gave you. You lied about it."

"No, sir. I didn't. It was a note for my grandma."

"Saying what, exactly?"

"That Mr. Grant thought I was doing a fine job."

Horace was steps closer. "And what else?"

"Nothing."

"There was an envelope. Nothing else in it, just that note to Grandma?"

Efrem gave Cincinnati a last pat on the nose. "There was some money."

"Of course. How much? Don't be exact."

Efrem said, "A little. Nothing to a man like you."

He started for the back of the stable, toward the tack room.

Horace followed, keeping just enough distance, so if Efrem tried to run, in any direction, he thought his long, hopper-like legs could spring him directly in front, blocking his escape.

Horace said, "This is the right place for all these words of yours. They're all the shit of a horse."

Efrem was now at the back of the stable, standing by the open door to the tack room, edging for it, kicking away bits of straw, saying, "No, sir. It's all true. Mr. Grant will tell you."

"Grant will not be setting foot here again."

"What?"

"So you better let me know everything he said to you, and give me every message he passed," Horace said. "You're a lying little darkie, and you will not infect my future by holding back information."

The flash was sudden and bright-hot.

Bursting from the shadows of the tack room, followed quickly by another. Horace covered his eyes, as if to wipe away the moving purple floating in front of them. He stumbled against a stall fence.

Lime stepped around his camera and flash pan. "I should have warned you, but you should have bloody well told me what a villain you were. Would have made all of this much more convenient."

Horace grabbed his lantern and swung it wide, as if it were a broadsword, smashing the glass against a post, the oil splashing back against him. And lighting. The fire was quick, spreading across his jacket.

Efrem pulled a blanket from a stall, wrapping Horace, extinguishing the flames. Over before it started. Horace leapt to his feet, screaming, and ran for the stable doors.

"Jesus save me, I'm burning!"

By the corral, Horace spun around in one place, pulling at his scorched jacket, still screaming. Hysterical yowls. Another flash pan burst, as another picture was taken.

Lime walked from the stables, with Efrem beside him, and said, "You've been exposed for what you are, Mr. Horace. An insect. But you're not on fire."

"God, you don't understand!"

Horace dropped to his knees, then rolled onto his back. Around him, Guards with rifles climbed the corral fences, stepped from the shadows, keeping their guns aimed, four in a circle around Horace, and all less than six feet away. Horace thrashed. And screamed.

Lime howled, "Grant made preparations, but you're not bloody on fire!"

Horace cried, "You don't—I was to bring—the stable was to come down, with the boy in it, if he didn't speak! God, help!"

He finally tore apart his long coat, revealing a stick of dynamite in the inside vest pocket, the bottom stuck through a tear in the lining, snarled in fabric, and the fuse burning down.

Horace screamed, "The fire! It lit! And it's tangled!"

The Guards took a half-step forward, then raised their weapons and turned their backs as the dynamite exploded. Lime had made Efrem face the other way, placed his hands over his ears, and held them there.

Lime said to Efrem quietly, "I have to, must, get some pictures, but don't you be looking, boy-o. Don't turn around, go to your grandmother's. Run there."

The bombs fell from the sky. Dying sea birds landing on the decks of a dozen ships, under a dozen flags. Bouncing off railings, falling to the water, getting tangled in lines or rolling off the sails.

A few were targets for sharpshooters, ricocheted into the ocean or hurled from the decks in nets. The crews ready for an explosion that didn't happen. But other bombs were lodged into the deck planking, their crowns splitting open, revealing the paper inside.

Gladstone looked up from the bow of Her Majesty's Turret Ship *Captain,* to see the dirigible, with its flag, sailing through the highest clouds, the last of the letter bombs falling from an open hatch.

Gladstone read the message, then looked to the sky again. Trying to decipher what was written there, and more importantly, why it was written: a puzzle that couldn't be solved.

Around him, on the decks of other ships, some still a mile or more out, shots were fired in rotation, each gun with its own distinctive report and echo, identifying its country.

"That's the reaction to your message, Sam. Every country having a voice."

Grant, at his desk, still cuffed, said, "That assurance from me, now, would mean very little . . ."

Duncan moved to Grant, sitting across from him as he had many times in The Shop, and said, "It wasn't an assurance of non-involvement, Sam. It's a declaration of war."

"My God, what you've done."

The words were as heavy as the corpses stacked in the battle-fields where Grant had commanded. Where he had walked among the dead, feeling the blood seeping into his boots while giving orders to fight on, and assurances to the wounded. Not just a memory. Immediate, because the echo of the gunfire from the ocean was real. As was the pain; all the battle wounds opening inside of him, as if their healing had been a lie.

"You carry too much with you, Sam."

Grant said, "What do you think I'd be doing if I wasn't chained down like this?"

Duncan said, "Engagement makes a difference, doesn't it? The heat of the conflict turns you into something else. I saw it, saw you kill."

"Killed in war, never murdered."

"Nemo would argue that distinction."

Grant's voice was a growl. "Did he put you up to this?"

"I'm my own master. But you, sitting here, at my command, you're a ghost of who you're supposed to be. A broken soldier."

"You think so?"

Silence. That total lack of sound that happens after a life's been taken was the answer to Grant's question. He looked to the blood left by the guards, the glass Maston fell through. And then, he knew.

"Sigel, that was you."

Duncan said, "No."

Grant said, "Because you weren't there. And Norfolk? I watched you cower in the street, all those men and ships. And it was you, you son of a bitch."

Duncan said, "Your emotions, Sam, always your undoing."

He took hold of the back of Grant's chair, and pushed him toward the bullet-shattered glass of the dirigible's sky windows.

"I know you're a man of faith, men of war usually are. We're sailing close to the heavens," Duncan said. "But that's your sweet myth, not mine. Look up, Mr. President."

Grant's head was down, until forced up by the barrel of his own gun, pressed under his chin.

"Look up, and see what a true creator can do."

Grant moved his eyes, and they widened at what he saw, the reaction slipping out. "Jesus, Mary, and Joseph . . ."

The slope of the underwater dunes had been taken down by a hurricane that cleared the water as well. It was an enormous glass bowl, crystal blue with green, and absolutely calm, the *Nautilus* cutting through its center. A beam of red light spit from the bridge: the fire from a dragon.

Fulmer was leaning against the tripod, keeping the sea spider in view. He let the rifle tilt, while pouring no-label tar whiskey on his tired arm and rubbing it in as laudanum.

He stretched, then took hold of the weapon again as Sara stepped onto the bridge, saying, "Next time, invite me."

Fulmer fired, "You'd accept? I wouldn't. What about your calculations?"

"When we arrive."

"It's going to be damn soon," Fulmer said. "Take a look at what the Kraken put out. It's with your charts."

Sara unrolled the thin, paper tongue. "I've already done this, and Nemo rejected it. And here we are, Goliath chasing David."

"I'd watch that talk." Fulmer turned to her. "Look at the last coordinates. I've been at sea long enough to know we're almost on top of that spot."

"Is this, that place, that Brigand's Trench?"

"It's where we're supposed to be," Fulmer said, leaning off the rifle and pointing toward the spider, which was now diving for the ocean floor. "That thing led us here; so did the Kraken box. So, you tell me."

The hashish had amber streaks, was of good quality, and Top Knot placed it in his bamboo pipe with delicacy for a man with only eight fingers. He never stopped speaking the entire process, even when lighting.

"We're all dead, under this Nemo. You're forgetting what we've gone through? I'll have nightmares the rest of my life. Maybe the ones killed already, they're the lucky ones."

Rongo was sitting in his usual spot in the corner, wrapped by shadows. "My brother and I came to crew as a mission of mercy. And revenge. Now, they're both dead, him and that Jess. All I want now is to find my way home. *Kwenda nyumbani.*"

The rest of the crew huddled by their card table, Top Knot stretched out on Jess' old bunk, the smoke from his pipe building like a winter fog.

"You think crewing will get you there?"

One of them from the card table said, "I want to get paid. That's all."

Rongo's voice was deep and steady. "You say Nemo won't pay?"

Top Knot said, "We're fools to expect something out of this voyage. We don't know anything about it, except the number of dead. And the number of secrets. They want us telling about these serpents? No. Cut our throats, leave us tied to the bottom. Less trouble that way."

Rongo said, "Nemo would not give that order."

Top Knot lit the last bit of hash residue, letting it settle before drawing. "You know what he's done? How many he's left dead across thousands of miles of water? Why would it bother him with us? Or Fulmer? Better to go back to a humpback you harpooned, get the money from him."

Rongo stood. "I came here for one reason. That reason is done. Now, all I want is to get paid, get home."

Top Knot drew again. "Take a sand dollar."

"I don't believe."

"Then it does no harm. Come on, a man like you."

Rongo reached into a straw basket hanging from the bunk for a sand dollar. He turned the shell over in his palm: it was larger, with gray blooms. He dropped it on the table as if it was the pot for a poker game.

Top Knot said, "If there's angels inside, then you're protected."

One of the crew split it in half, tapping both edges on the table, for the smaller shells, the Angels, to tumble out from the dollar's middle. But there was nothing. Just dust.

Top Knot said, "You don't leave this iron boat alive."

The crew call sounded, ordering all to the bridge.

Nemo had given an "all stop" order that sounded through the ship as Rongo and the crew made their way to the bridge. The hum of the engines had calmed, and the *Nautilus* was easing into a drift.

Fulmer rubbed his arm and said, "As you predicted, the little beastie's found his way home. Maybe you have, too."

Nemo didn't respond, but took his place in the center of the dome, to see what was before him. The spider had dipped away, swimming on the other side of the ship, but it had led Nemo to this place. This thing, built from the ocean floor.

An enormous, double-door entrance in the side of an underwater mountain, with a large *N* at its center. Riveted, of dark blue metal and stone, it was wide and tall enough for the *Nautilus*, but had an ancient feeling, as if designed as part of a pyramid: a shielded fortress for the pharaohs, to repel any attackers from any time.

Fulmer said, "Miss Duncan, you wanted a place to dock for repairs. This looks pretty perfect, don't it?"

Sara's voice was all wonder. "I don't know what this looks like."

Darting from below the bow, the still-glowing Sea Spider swam for the entrance, the *N* spiraling open into a hatchway, and the mechanical thing vanished to the other side. The hatch closed as if it was never there.

"And there you are," Fulmer said. "Whatever the hell it is, it appears to be waitin' for us."

"Not for us," Nemo said. "Mr. Rongo, break out my diving gear."

Sara turned to Nemo. "Begging your pardon, Captain, but you need to think this through."

"You have no voice in this, Miss Duncan. Mr. Fulmer, the bridge is yours."

Nemo and Rongo had turned, starting for the stairs to the belowdecks, when Sara said, "You're putting everybody at risk! Your duty is to report whatever you find before more lives are lost. The safest place is from the *Nautilus*."

Nemo stopped, regarding Sara and this defiance.

She said, "I'm just asking you to remember what's already happened. This isn't a challenge."

Fulmer coughed out, "We could lob a couple of torpedoes, find out who's on the other side."

Nemo's eyes were on Sara. "I haven't made that decision, Mr. Fulmer. And if I'm willing to take a risk, then so are the rest of you. You're of my crew, that's what it means."

Sara said, "You agreed to certain conditions in exchange for your freedom! You said you'd find whoever's responsible for sinking those ships, and destroy them if ordered. If you don't, it's treason. Grant swore he'd hang you."

"I've already been condemned, that's a matter of record, but this other . . ." Nemo stepped in to Sara, threateningly close. "Was it your father who gave you all that information? You're confirming my worst doubts about you, Miss Duncan."

He grabbed her hand with Sigel's ring, pulling it from her finger, the gold ripping over a joint. "But then, I don't have to go to the gallows, as long as Grant has you as an assassin-in-waiting. Did he give you your orders personally?"

Sara said, "No, I am trying to stop this. Captain, if you make this choice, then it will solidify who you are to Washington and the world. Do you understand that we're facing this with you, but you're acting as if our lives are meaningless?"

"Is that what you would report to your father?"

"Everyone here risked their lives to bring us to this place."

Nemo said, "I'm aware of everyone's efforts."

"Miss Duncan?"

Sara turned on Fulmer's words as he fired two shots into the Phono, blowing it apart. Sparks and mirrors. The pieces were still spinning from impact when he said, "Sorry, Captain's orders."

"I am taking back my ship, Miss Duncan. Completely," Nemo said. "And all shall know what's behind this when I do. And what I do about it will be my own accord."

Sara said, "Whatever it is could destroy the *Nautilus*. And nations."

Nemo said, "My feelings about the world above are also part of record, but are you seriously suggesting that I'm somehow a conspirator in this, that I bear responsibility for these mechanicals, and all the rest of this destruction?"

"That is your signature on that structure," Sara said. "You have to prove you have nothing to do with this, by following the direct orders you were given. I know you have other, personal missions you've sworn to carry out, but this must come first, sir."

Nemo said, "You've just condemned yourself."

He turned to Rongo, just controlling his rage because of the reference to his wife. "Crewman! Miss Duncan is under arrest for espionage and mutiny. The law of the sea, Miss Duncan. You know about that, by now."

Rongo locked his arms into Sara's, completely trapping her. "Apologies. Miss."

Nemo said, "Lower deck. Mr. Fulmer, anything to say?"

"Our business is end of voyage, Captain."

On the lower deck, Rongo released Sara. "Stop your fighting."

"Where are you going to put me?"

Rongo said, "You want off this ship? To follow Nemo?"

Sara said, "To stop him, and save the ship and us."

"That's not going to happen. We're taking the iron boat. Save our lives. But if you want off, then I won't force you to be with us."

Sara stood in front of the Whaler. "How?"

"A diving suit. If we take the ship, we won't be here for your return, but maybe launch the silver ball. It's up to you. No matter what, you're still a prisoner. Miles of water holding you."

"We can't use the diving tube now; how will you get me out?"

Rongo said, "Can you cut your way through flesh?"

The Diver's Access was still twisted apart, the war with the mechanicals torn through the iron, steel, and glass of the room. Fulmer checked one of the manta-skin diving suits as Nemo took a bone-and-brass helmet. The *N* pike was leaned against the wall with other equipment, most of it destroyed.

Nemo said, "There's a purpose at work here."

"Give me the signal, and I'll torpedo the hell out of that purpose."

"It's still a journey of discovery, Mr. Fulmer. Let's see what we find, then we'll act. Or, you will."

Fulmer said, "Captain, I wouldn't be standing here if it wasn't for you. I know that. So, put a team together."

Nemo said, slipping on the suit, "An army of submariners marching off to war? I think that will be coming soon enough, Mr. Fulmer. Better I explore first, then we take action. Agreed?"

"Is that an order, sir?"

"Yes."

Fulmer handed Nemo his helmet. "Then, agreed."

"Keep a steady aim from the dome. I may not be able to use a weapon."

"Already done."

"You've been with me the longest." Nemo handed Fulmer the master key to the helm. "For now, the *Nautilus* is yours. If I die, you'll have your revenge, but remember why you signed on at the beginning. Use that part of your judgment to dictate your actions."

"Aye, sir."

Nemo stepped into the diving tube, and Fulmer turned all valves to fill it. He stood by, waiting. For an emergency, or a need.

The ocean rushing in, water rising above his eyes. This single moment, every time he is first surrounded by water, is Nemo's alone. It's when he becomes something else, a part of the sea. Even within a tube, before stepping from his submarine, or standing at the helm, and watching the waves through a port, covering his creation, as he angles the bow into a dive. That covering of water is his protection. His true home. It's also his immortality, as the newspapers declared him the one man who can live under the sea.

These were all flashes of thought, and feeling, as Nemo dropped from the *Nautilus*, knowing it could be his final dive. Thinking it, for a moment. He kicked his legs to bring him down straight, then settled on the bottom. He took it in, then started for the huge, metal doors, using the pike as his staff. A sea turtle glided by, making part of the journey beside him.

A light on the doors blasted on, turning all of the sea darkness into something blinding. This bizarre, pulsing light, casting rings of brightness through the water, as if a piece of the sun's been trapped, then released.

The *Nautilus* stayed in its place, neutral in the water, bow pointed for the giant doors and the beams of light. Challenging them.

Nemo struggled to move, trying to lift his legs, but couldn't. It wouldn't let him, the light holding his nerves. His eyes were paralyzed also. Held open by invisible clamps, the intense bright zeroed in on them like a hypnotist's pendant.

He knew this sensation, knew what this was. And began putting his mind someplace else. Removing himself from this world, this moment, to a time when mesmerism was part of his life.

On the bridge, Fulmer had taken the helm, the light so intense, the reflection slamming back at him, the controls and gauges liquid to his eyes: melting, but not melting. White obscuring everything.

Fulmer turned to Top Knot. "Get to the engine, and set for full reverse."

Top Knot said, "We leaving the mad dog to die?"

Sara pressed herself against a wall in the air-duct chamber, tight in the corner, not knowing who was going to come through the hatch.

Rongo entered with a helmet and suit. "This was the first of the iron boat that I saw. Like a bizarre, giant fish, but from some other time."

Sara pulled out the palates of the *Nautilus'* gills, tissue spilling, to the entrance of the water intake beyond. "One of Nemo's proudest achievements, having this ship breathe."

Rongo said, "So, it really is a living thing."

Sara said, "Yes, with just as many contradictions. Good luck, getting home."

"*Bahati nzuri na wewe,* dear *msichana.*"

She tethered her helmet so her head would fit through the small opening, pulled her diver's knife from her belt, and began slashing the walls of pink, artificial flesh that was the *Nautilus'* gills. She pushed her way through the cold, torn skin. Slime sticking to her as she made her way through layer after layer. Each one thicker, with more oxygen collected on its surface.

The sections reacted to the touch of the blade, quivering as she sliced more tissue, pushing to the next section as if she were a disease, working its way through a body, until finally getting through to the water chamber.

A massive wave rolled in. Sara scrambled for her helmet, crawling through the belly of the *Nautilus,* water powering in and out, until being pulled into the ocean by the water's force.

Sara knifed her body, swimming strongly away from the submarine, turning herself around, then landing in a circle of white on the ocean floor. Plants and silt burst around her as she landed and was enveloped by hypnotic light.

Shutting her eyes, she swam for Nemo, reaching him from the back, and taking his shoulders. Suspended in the water above him, but he didn't turn. Didn't respond. Sara floated, jostling for a reaction, but Nemo was immovable before the enormous doors. The continuous light.

The doors opened.

A wave of water erupted from behind the massive structure as if a dam were bursting, the doors opening inward, revealing two bright, red lights. Smaller and parallel, the lights blasted forward toward Nemo and Sara, as headlamps on a vehicle, coming at them with incredible speed.

It was sharklike, all of white metal, with the lights instead of eyes, a dorsal fin on the roof for guidance. There were skis on either side, and the exhaust of what could be hyper-steam engines protruded from the seamless, metal skin.

The vehicle roared through the deep water like it was air, coming straight for Nemo and Sara. Guided toward them, as the perfect amphibian, swimming and running simultaneously.

Nemo turned, completely aware, and shoved Sara aside, sending them both tumbling to the sand as the vehicle swooped close, making a wide, fast turn through the water, then racing back, its front section opening like an enormous, gaping mouth.

Nemo and Sara could only look above them, at this thing hovering. Descending. Pinning them to the ocean floor.

On the bridge, a burst of water exploded against the dome, wiping out the intensity of the white light. Fulmer leapt to the helm, looking out the view port, to see that Nemo and Sara were gone. The pike was falling as if it had just been let go, and landed in the silt.

Fulmer ordered, "Engine room! All rudders hard right and all engines full speed ahead!"

Within the vehicle, Nemo and Sara were suspended before a control panel that was nothing but a strip of glowing color, while water and sea life rocketed by the thick glass view port. The vehicle made a wide turn on its own, banking in the water, and came back, slowing its ascent, letting the cabin depressurize for Nemo and Sara to wake.

Behind them, hovering just above the ocean floor, the *Nautilus* engaged full power.

Fulmer pushed from the helm, trying to turn the enormous submarine, as the gray vehicle sped out of sight almost instantly. Fulmer could trace the wake of the thing, but it had aimed for the surface, side fins expanding.

Fulmer ordered, "Attention, all crew! Sound alarm! Surfacing now!"

The ballast tanks blew open, the *Nautilus* responding as a craft half its size, speeding upward, the bow tilted, with engines at full speed.

Fulmer was lurched forward at the helm, one hand in the gloved controls, the other on the steering bar. It was a different helm than he knew, but he could feel the ship. Feel its momentum, and reaction. Its life. Fulmer brought the sub hard-about, fighting to keep a trace of the vehicle in sight.

They broke the surface, the ocean bleeding away from the dome, the *Nautilus* balancing itself over the waves as the gray, sharklike vehicle skimmed across the water half a mile in front of them.

It bounced on the ocean surface, its bow pointed up.

It turned, spewing a wake, and kept going in a circle, faster and faster, until the side fins engaged, stretching out completely as broad, curved wings, lifting the vehicle from the water.

Fulmer watched, helpless, as it sped toward the horizon, then vanished behind a bank of clouds.

37

THE CITY IN THE SKY

The vehicle was moving so fast, turning in a pattern as it flew about the clouds, that it took Nemo a moment to get his bearings. The cockpit was completely dark, except for the strip of pulsating yellow on what seemed to be a control panel, but was without dials or indicators. The vehicle plunged, and came back, and Nemo's natural instincts were to control and steer, but he could only keep his hands by his side. The vehicle did it all.

Sara was next to him, still put out by the movements and intensity of the hypnotic light, but slumped forward, her hands on the panel, the yellow pulsations around her fingers.

Nemo had freed himself, let his mind take back his own thoughts and actions, but was waiting for the moment to strike. All of that had been hijacked when Sara tried to help, and then ended when they were pulled from the ocean by this thing that raced across the bottom, and was now flying beyond reach, none of which he could stop or steer. He despised being at the mercy of someone, something, else.

The clouds were shredded to flecks of vapor, his eyes adjusting to the view through the thick glass that surrounded the cabin of the vehicle.

He saw the City in the Sky.

A walled fortress, with four corner towers, each topped with a series of helio-copter-type blades at different heights. Balloons, in docking bays, balanced the sides, with the center dominated by a large aircraft landing port, where the President's dirigible was tethered, moving in its bay with the winds.

The vehicle flew in a wide pattern, wings banking, allowing Nemo to see, to react in wonder. There were no corners. The entire city, rounded at the edges, reminded him of the mosques and low buildings he had seen from one side of Africa to the other: that combination of places of worship, surrounded by military fortification. He knew whoever built this amazing place must have known those outposts.

But here, instead of walls and domes cooked and beaten by the desert, the buildings were of a clean, futuristic material, with a metallic gleam. Weapons turrets and pillboxes bordered the walls, and a grassy pathway leading from the main structure to all the others was the only evidence of plants.

It was all information; all a realization that Nemo had to take in, and the vehicle seemed to sense it, slowing and circling when Nemo needed it. Letting him assimilate. Connected to him, somehow, as the *Nautilus* was, but more sophisticated. Much more.

The vehicle whipped by the towers, its flexible wings bending on the air current like a bat's, then slowed to ascend into the center landing port, next to the President's dirigible. The doors puzzled-open, and Nemo's eyes focused, to a figure standing before the vehicle, silhouetted by a halo of bright sunlight.

"Welcome to a perfect world, Captain. My world."

Sara blinked her eyes. "Father?"

On the *Nautilus*, Rongo and Top Knot blocked Fulmer's way to the helm, with other crew standing by the doors, holding tall switches. Fists were balled, with attitudes bent forward.

"You're supposed to be at battle stations."

Top Knot said, "We'll return to stations, but only if we're getting the hell away from here. Now."

Fulmer said, "Those aren't the Captain's orders."

Top Knot said, "I know you had that to say, but we are giving new orders. This ship is bound for home. You, you can take us there or not."

"I have my duty. So do you."

Rongo said, "Don't do this, Mr. Fulmer."

Several of the men moved around the bridge, grabbing a sextant, instruments, or tools as weapons. One wrenched a lever from the wall. Fulmer stood his ground at the helm, trying for a stare down, but figuring the order to throw his punches. Dropping a big one first, so he'll block the hatch, giving him time to get away. Pub-brawl thinking.

Top Knot said, "Nemo's probably dead and we're not going to be, not now. And God knows what he's led us to. You crewed this ship when Nemo sank *Abraham Lincoln* with your own brother on board. Now's your chance to right that, Mr. Fulmer. You should take it."

Fulmer kept his chin down, nodding in agreement before laying a heavy fist into a Sailor, sending him reeling. The others attacked. Fulmer pulped a jaw, ribs broke under his fists, dropping the sea dogs, but they brought their clubs down hard. Pounding Fulmer into helplessness.

Rongo threw Fulmer across his back. "We kill him, then we'll hang for sure. Too much blood on this voyage."

Top Knot said, "Lock him in quarters."

Rongo hefted Fulmer down two decks, to crew quarters, dumping him on Jess' bed. Blood was pouring from his mouth and nose, and Rongo tossed an old towel, before locking the door.

Diving helmets off, Nemo and Sara stood beside the vehicle in the central landing area of the city, its whirring engine winding down, like a watch spring and its works.

Facing them were the towers with the turning blades, the largest at each corner of the platform, and smaller blades along the edges, with gas-filled balloons suspending the walls with heavy cable. Uniformed and armed Air Crew moved between the multiple buildings, carrying weapons or aero-tools. Not speaking, just going about their purpose.

Duncan was all polish and imposing demeanor, moving before Nemo and Sara, the lenses and mousy bent having completely vanished. He sported a military uniform of sorts, black with rows of gold buttons and braid, but claimed no country's insignia or colors.

Duncan allowed Nemo and Sara to study him for a few heartbeats before speaking. "Captain Nemo. My dear. This wasn't the way I wanted you to meet me, and this project. But we're here, and that's the important thing."

Sara couldn't believe what she was seeing around her— including the President's dirigible—or her father, with a stance, and confidence, she didn't recognize.

Duncan said to his daughter, "I know you're shocked," then to Nemo, "but I thought you'd appreciate that I used a hypnosis technique of your own culture, to guarantee calm travels."

Nemo said, "I wasn't affected."

Duncan took Sara's hand. "You'll feel fine in a few minutes."

Sara regarded him for another, longer moment, taking it in. Then slapped his face. Hard. Nemo created a barrier with an arm between them, but Duncan never flinched at the blow. He straightened, standing taller.

Nemo said, "Remember, she's your daughter."

"I do." Duncan looked to Sara. "And she doesn't even know her real name. The pity of it."

He signaled a Guard. "Take Miss Sara to the quarters with our other guest. We'll see each other later, dear."

More guards, uniformed and of all ages, seemed to come from nowhere, silently gathering around Sara and guiding her off toward the largest building facing the landing port. Then she was efficiently gone.

Nemo said to her father, "What's this business about the name?"

"Duncan is a dull, anglicized version. My family name is Robur, and it shall remain so. No more hiding, just as you chose Nemo, and it's become your legend."

"The word is who I am."

"And this place is my name. I told you once I learned a great deal from you. This is the result, the tribute to your inspiration."

Nemo regarded the gun turrets behind Duncan instead of his words, and walked to the edge of the landing area, bordered by a fence of chains. A gesture from Duncan and the power through the fence was shut off, so Nemo could look over the sheer edge, to miles of sky in all directions, and the ocean, miles below.

He could feel steam wafting back onto his face, created by a series of open pipes pumping vapor from all corners of the structure's base, creating the gigantic cloud hiding the floating city from the world.

Duncan said, "What you've accomplished under the sea, I've built in the sky."

Nemo stepped back from the edge. "That vehicle alone, is certainly remarkable."

"I christened it the *Terror*, striking at the hearts, yes? Capable of traveling on land, sea, and air at speeds of—"

Nemo completed, "Over two hundred knots."

Duncan said, "And what ignorant commander wouldn't be terrified by its action? Like the *Nautilus*, its mere existence gives power."

Nemo said, "You have power, Mr. Duncan. No doubt."

They were walking back toward the main compound as technicians fueled the *Terror*, checked its retractable fins, and sprayed the ocean floor from its tanklike treads. It was an automatic system, these men in uniforms, immediately tending to needs. Others were performing maintenance on the dirigible, while still others stood guard.

Nemo couldn't judge how many there were, but it wasn't his crew of old dogs: this was an elite army. Trained; moving as one to carry out orders, like the military units from several nations that swarmed the *Nautilus*, executing his men before his arrest by the United States, or the army from his own country, that killed his wife and children.

It was at this moment that Duncan was not Duncan anymore. He had changed before Nemo's eyes. As if the kindly academic, with the bursts of strength and humor, had been assassinated, and someone new had taken his place, proud of the killing of his old self.

Duncan was Robur, and he had given orders for all guards to keep their distance. That Nemo was an honored guest.

Robur said, "The *Terror*'s my *Nautilus*. Decades of secret research, the trial and error of manufacture. The results, well, you're the only one who can truly appreciate what I've done, gone through, for this accomplishment."

"This city's more than your *Terror*. If the vehicle's impressive, this place seems a marvel."

"Praise from Caesar."

"I'm overwhelmed."

Robur said, "You've created miracles. Many of them."

"Nothing like this," Nemo said. "The genius on display demands recognition."

Nemo's words were drained as they crossed along the grass path to the main buildings, passing under an archway that was identical to the one over the entrance to Vulcania. Every detail from his old base was recreated, including bullet holes.

"My exact memories," Nemo said.

Robur said, "A tribute to your struggles."

"There's much here to absorb."

"Captain, you'll have the time to see it all."

On the gun turret, the Lieutenant loaded an automatic pistol, handing it to a City Guard, while watching Nemo and Robur pass below, to the main building. Robur looked up to him as they reached the doors. Keeping his hand on his belt he extended two fingers in a silent victory signal. His fingers, though, pointed downward, meaning something else.

The Guard didn't push Sara, and she didn't fight herself away. It was all silence between them, when a prisoner is marched to their cell. When the door to her room slid open, she was hit with it: her childhood bedroom, duplicated. Toys, pillows, wallpaper roses, and chintz curtains, but around windows that were painted on the walls, with a view that was exactly her old backyard, as a still life.

The door rolled closed, and locked before she could turn around. Sara pressed her hands against the painted sky, as if a window would split open in the wall, then pounded with her fists. It was solid.

Behind her, a desk was stacked with her diary, and perfectly bound copies of *Alice's Adventures in Wonderland,* Dickens' *Our Mutual Friend,* and Poe's *Extraordinary Tales.* She opened the diary, and saw an entry on the first page: *Father and I, reunited.*

Sara's eyes settled on a dollhouse on a table in the corner. She remembered it, from when she was four or five. Not a dollhouse, but an odd, tiny doll city, built by her father, its distinctive shape exactly the same as the structure where she was. She remembered wishing her doll city could float to the ceiling.

"Seen this view before, have you, Sara?"

The voice was hollow, coming from behind the wall. Someplace.

"You owe me at least an explanation, girl."

Sara followed the sound, tracing it along the wall with her fingers, before an opening appeared before her. Beyond the opening, she saw into an adjoining room. Large, and sun-drenched.

President Grant sat before a huge window that was one entire side of the room, the glass braced with wood and curving at the center, to magnify the view. Bourbon and cigars were at hand, as was the library and artwork from the dirigible. Familiar comforts; other paintings and rolled-up rugs rested against the walls, as if the decorating had just begun, and Grant would be there a long time.

He faced Sara. "The last time I was in this chair, I was handcuffed. Your father released me into here, my plush cell where I'm supposed to die. As you well know."

Sara shook her head. "No. I didn't."

"Your father played me for a perfect fool; you played Nemo like Daddy's old fiddle. An excellent plan, bringing the two of us together, hopefully to destroy each other, leaving your father unchallenged."

Sara said, "I didn't know."

Grant opened a case full of fresh cigars, took one. "It's called the Joining of Enemies Gambit, and I've used it, in our final push against the Confederates."

Grant poured himself a drink, offered one to Sara, who took it. "I know espionage, as do you. Except I think you forgot whose side you were supposed to be on. Or, you never were. Clarify for me."

Sara measured her words. "Mr. President, I had no idea about any of this."

"Of course, of course." Grant sipped, eyes down.

Sara said, "We've been fighting the things sinking the ships."

"Who fought? Do you mean Nemo?"

"Everyone on the *Nautilus,* following your orders," Sara said. "Machines, made to look like sea creatures, but are actually weapons. Those insane reports, they're all true." She stopped herself, and the flooding words. "I sound like I'm the one who's lost their mind."

Grant said, "I'd say yes, if we weren't sitting in this insane place together. Nemo, is he for or against your father?"

Sara said, "I don't know. He's destroyed these mechanical things, but also led us here. There was a structure, it seemed to be waiting for the *Nautilus.*"

"Your father's?"

"After all this, I have to say yes, but Nemo didn't know. Part of the mystery, and he was going to solve it his way. I tried to stop him from leaving the *Nautilus,* but he was going to see the mission through, what was happening here. He was determined to give you your information, and be done with it. He said he was to die a free man, no matter what the outcome."

Grant said, "That, I believe."

Sara dropped into a corner, putting pieces together out loud, so she could comprehend them. "We're actually prisoners. My father actually did all this, built all this."

Grant moved to the wide expanse of glass, the enormity of the sky just beyond it, saying, "The shutters, they opened just before I called out to you. Like a magician's trick. Do you know why?"

Sara said, "The window they gave me isn't real."

"During the war, we'd release prisoners for rides outside the walls, show them the world they were losing, then threw them back into dark cells. The longing, it broke some of them, made them give up secrets, which was the damn point. Show us the world, then take it away. Can you imagine what never touching the earth again would do to you? It's brilliant strategy."

Grant crossed a Chinese rug, just as he had in his White House bedroom, to stand next to Sara. "When he pushed me so hard about Nemo, I read the Arronax diary. He couldn't believe what he saw on the *Nautilus*; what the hell would Arronax say about all this?"

"All the delusions, all the sailors' claims, and every one, the truth." Sara blinked at the intense sun spreading across the glass, wiped her eyes and nose on her sleeve. "This will make a hell of a report, sir."

Grant offered his handkerchief. "One that nobody'll ever read."

"You trusted me to do something about Captain Nemo, and I didn't."

"And why didn't you?"

"I became one of the crew," she said.

Grant's eyes overwhelmed Sara, but she stayed with him, meeting his look. "Are you going to kill him, and my father?"

"There's no question about your father," Grant said. "He was my friend, but traitors are to be executed."

Ocean-surface-level, and the *Nautilus* moved through far Atlantic waves, but listed to one side, the water pounding up against the observation dome as it dipped, the bow exposed above the waterline. The hum of the engines faded, and the submarine slowed, and finally stopped, its wake washing back as if it were swamped.

On the bridge, all lights were dimming out, sputtering, as Top Knot struggled with a frozen helm, yelling, "Check fuel! Maybe the wiring's been cut, but find out why the engines aren't responding."

Rongo said, "Because, she's not ours."

"You don't believe, but the sand dollar said you'd die on the iron boat. Well, you're making it happen."

Rongo grabbed hold of Top Knot's hand, smothering it with his own, and thrust it onto the small hidden port for the *Nautilus'* master key.

"Not ours. That's the difficulty."

In the crew quarters, blood washed over Fulmer's ears and down his back, streaks of red as he doused himself with a pitcher of water, the cold soothing the open wounds. He comforted his head with a towel, then felt for something. Around his neck. A small chain with a golden key shaped like a seahorse, hanging from it.

Just as Nemo had given to him.

Fulmer hauled himself to his feet, head still throbbing, and braced against the iron bunk before smashing the small side table with his heel, splintering the top away from the legs.

A long passageway, curving as an artery through the sky's center structure, displayed the entire floating city as a thing of beauty to Nemo, with one side glassed from beginning to end. Like the finer points of the *Nautilus,* the passage was protected by gods, but of air and sky, not the sea.

Jupiter stretched across the rounded ceiling, power ripping from his fingers, touching the windows as flakes of gold. Surrounded by the Egyptian god Horus, and the Mayan creator of the sky Tzacol: spiritual forces of sun, wind, and flight are montaged across the walls of all that Robur has built.

"How does one man do all this?"

Robur said, "As you did, in your Vulcania."

Nemo said, "But I didn't launch anything to the heavens, and make it stay. You've built flying machines, when we haven't begun to conquer flight. I built a submarine, improving on what we've already learned. And this city, is this to be your outpost, or do you want to rule a new society?"

"You spoke of a city under the sea."

"The last dream of a condemned man," Nemo said. "Talking to a reporter from a jail cell isn't the start of anything. What you've done here is part of a new world."

Robur said, "It is, and can make your city true, also."

"How?"

"In pieces. I launched in balloons, put it together like a puzzle. We could do the same, sinking each structure. Everything here was from a different factory, with government contracts. With my office, I hid the costs inside other projects. Reconstruction paid for most of this."

Nemo examined the walls with Chinese air gods casting winged spells around him. "Surely not wood or steel, you couldn't stay aloft."

"Paper, treated in special presses I designed," Robur said. "Even the windows, made of a liquid fructose, so a quarter of the weight of normal glass. You might use whale urine?"

"Too dark."

"No matter, with you, it would certainly come from the sea." Robur laughed. "The clouds shielding my city are steam from the power generators keeping us aloft. All the technology you'll see, you inspired it, Captain."

"You're giving me far too much credit."

"Never. This place is yours, too," Robur said.

Grant and Sara sat against the side of the room that jutted toward the sky, but the shutters for the expansive window were now closed, darkening the room with slashes of shadows like the bars of a prison cell. The diary from Sara's room was on the floor between them, open to the first page.

Grant said, "Everything."

"I don't know—I—my mother died when I was young, and I've spent my life in boarding schools. My father is a scientist and advisor, that's what I thought."

Grant held up his hand to stop her from speaking, and wrote in the diary: *Choose your words. Fortifications?*

"I don't know."

He wrote: *Troops, or guards?*

"I don't know that, either."

Grant spoke admiringly. "Your father disclosed nothing to you, about his incredible creation?"

"Not about this place. This is all a bizarre secret."

Grant said, "Your mother left your father a fortune."

"From silver mining, yes. And I went to great schools to study engineering on my trust. The first woman in most of my classes. You know that. You know all of it—"

Grant stopped Sara speaking again, and this time she wrote: *To when you asked me to kill Nemo.*

Grant wrote: *I am trying to find out everything about my enemy.*

Sara said, "That's not how I knew him."

Grant wrote: *He has betrayed millions, not only us. This is a chance to right a wrong,* and then said, "Not many get that."

Sara rubbed her finger, where the poisoned ring used to be, and said, "I understand."

"Do you really think they listened to everything we say?"

Grant said, "This is a new world, no secrets anymore."

Sara made a last entry in her diary that Grant couldn't read, and closed and locked it.

The Lieutenant held the box, and knocked on Sara's door with a light touch. When she answered from the other side, he had to unlock it and slide it open. She was standing directly before him, not allowing him over the threshold.

His manner remained as delicate as his eyes and accent. "Miss Duncan, my apologies, but this is for you. Hand delivery."

He handed Sara the box, and she read the card, another salutation from her father. Her expression didn't change.

She said, "What is this?"

"A gift."

"Of what?"

The Lieutenant half-bowed, and smiled, looking up at her. "Something beautiful, I'm sure."

Sara pushed the door, but the Lieutenant's polished boot held it open. "I'm the officer charged with your security. So any concerns you have, please feel free to speak to me about them."

"Will you leave me, with this door unlocked?"

There was only more of a smile. "Our meeting was a pleasure."

Sara shoved the door closed, heard the locks tumble before she pried open the box to see the dress inside. She looked at the card again: *The first of many gifts, your loving father.*

Beneath the city was the enormous man-made cavern housing the heart and nerves of Robur's creation: a space as large as the city itself. A sub-structured basement for all the machine and energy works, encompassing the city's whole length and width. And beneath this, nothing but free-falling sky.

Robur and Nemo moved through it on a motorized wheeled platform running on a narrow, miner's rail track. Circling among the generators and the rod works turning the giant propellers to keep the city aloft, Robur was a king surveying his kingdom.

"Between Heaven and Earth," Robur said.

They passed a generator, in its own domed container, with its energy source affixed to it, a small, glowing dome. A technician handed Robur a message, that he approved and handed back, their transport not stopping.

Nemo asked, "That spider device drew its power from a diamond sliver?"

Robur said, "We can draw power from any substance that's been pressurized, peeling away the energy onion, if you will. Diamonds work well, but any natural gem will do. Studying your power supply and engines was essential to me. The *Nautilus* uses the atomic structure of metals, a marked improvement over its storage batteries."

"I thought so," Nemo said. "That gold ingot will keep us underway for two years, at least."

"One gem in this system will double that time, perhaps more, and with no waste."

"You should have let me modify the *Nautilus*."

Robur said, "I thought about it, Captain."

Nemo said, "But then you would have revealed yourself."

The transport went onto a length of straight track, with the balloon works on either side as they were being repaired by uniformed crewmen, and inflated through gas jets, before attachment to the support chains for each of the city's corners.

Robur said, "Holding back on my knowledge has been the most difficult thing. What I did at the White House was like a Neanderthal with rock and flint, and they applauded me for it. Grant could be effusive in his way, but I always felt it was like applauding a cheetah for running."

"Or a cobra for striking?"

Robur said, "I don't mind the comparison, because you've been labeled far worse; we're natural conquerors. Like your *Nautilus,* my accomplishment here was inevitable. It is who we are."

"Your crew, they follow you, and never leave?"

"Rarely. Like the crew of the *Nautilus,* citizens of the world. You might even see a few of your old prison mates. We even house a few young ladies, so it's not all work. This year saw our first marriage, and birth. It's a city. My city."

They were now on a section suspended by wires over an open area to service the pontoons and steam system under the city's foundation. On either side of the car, a straight fall for miles.

Nemo said, "You've done more for flight than any man who's

ever lived, so I need to know what this is all about, beyond the hundreds you killed, for no reason."

Robur said, "Also inevitable."

The vehicle cleared the opening, stopping on its track before two large, gilded doors set against polished black stone. Robur stepped out, saying, "You and the *Nautilus* turned the Atlantic into a cemetery."

"For warships only, and always giving fair warning."

"Don't ever forget my knowledge of your record, Captain."

Nemo said, "I didn't push the world to the edge of war, I pulled it back. Stopping war is what brought me here."

"What brought you was insatiable curiosity, and my will. Nothing since we met has been by accident."

"The underwater structure?"

Robur said, "The *Nautilus'* new docking pen, built to its specifications, and for its total security. That was an invitation, and you accepted, sir."

Nemo said, "I was shanghaied."

"My God, that word's from the waterfront. You've always been a man of the sea," Robur said. "But now you can be a leader. I know you have a thousand questions, but you were brought here for a purpose. To join me as a master of the world."

Robur opened the golden doors with a brush of his hand, and Nemo stepped through them.

A pistol barrel poked into the crew quarters hatchway before Top Knot. Fulmer looked over from his bunk.

"You're holding back, and we need it. Now."

Fulmer said, "You're gonna have to speak plain, mate. I've had my head bashed in."

Top Knot stepped around the smashed side table, legs, and

busted pieces. He put a foot on the edge of the bunk to balance
the pistol across his knee. "You'll get worse than that. Nemo's
key, if it's not in the controls, the ship shuts down. He's got one,
so does the first."

Top Knot held out his hand.

Fulmer said, "Who told you all that?"

Fulmer looked over to Rongo, filling all of the hatchway. Fulmer shifted his body, but stayed lying down.

"We dock, you do anything you want, but we ain't being
around as a picnic for one of these sea monsters, whatever they
are," Top Knot said.

Fulmer sat up slowly. "They write songs about them; you don't
want to be in the verse about Nemo and his monsters?"

Rongo said, "You're being a fool."

Top Knot angled the pistol upward, directly between Fulmer's eyes. "Give it. Now. Or your brains feed the turtles."

Fulmer put a thumb under the key around his neck. "Only
thing keeping me alive, because I can run this submarine better
than you. But, that pistol's made me think. See—"

Fulmer wrestled a piece of the tabletop from under his shirt,
dropped it beside the bunk. "I thought that'd stop a bullet. I
must've been stinkin' to think that up."

It was enough for Top Knot to laugh. Fulmer whipped the
table leg from the sheets, swinging, smashing Top Knot's jaw,
knocking the pistol from his hands, sending him backward to the
floor. Fulmer grabbed the gun, leaping from the bunk and bash-
ing Top Knot's temple with the ball of his foot. Blood fountained
from his mouth as if he was coughing in his sleep, but he was
breathing.

Fulmer turned quickly, aiming at Rongo's massive chest. "It'll
probably take six to bring you down, so, if you want, I'll start
shooting, and we'll see."

Rongo didn't move, didn't raise his hands. "I don't like get-ting shot. I have been, before."

"You want to keep standing? Because unless we get on the bridge, she's gonna heave over, and we'll be upside down, trapped on the ocean floor."

Fulmer reached under the mattress and tossed Rongo a bone-and-brass breathing device, saying, "I crewed the *Nautilus* out of Vulcania, and I can smell mutiny a month before it happens. So can Nemo. We knew what you were going to do before you did. Put that on."

Fulmer kicked open a crate by the bed and took three amber bottles of milky fluid from a bed of straw.

"Nemo uses this stuff to operate with. Toss 'em like grenades, put everybody to sleep."

"And then what?"

"Right the ship, finish our mission, and you go home."

Fulmer still had the pistol in one hand and the bottles in the other, but couldn't read Rongo's expression. He read his tattoos: the three slashes for his brothers; the marks of killing a man in battle, with honor; and a marriage tattoo.

Rongo nodded, putting the breather in his mouth, taking two bottles.

The *Nautilus* was turning, the passageway tilting. More and more. Fulmer and Rongo stepped from the crew quarters as a mu-tineer charged a corner with a throwing ax, screaming for Rongo to get out of the way.

Slamming against the walls, trying to keep his balance, he threw the blade. The bottle was tossed. Shattered. The white-thick vapor burst into the air, choking the mutineer to the deck before falling him into unconsciousness, the ax having barely missed Fulmer's skull.

Fulmer and Rongo went for the stairs. Grabbing for a hold as the ship moved again. Lurching. A bullet ricocheted. Sparking off iron. Fulmer hurled the bottle at the mutineer who'd taken a sniping position on the second deck, hiding behind the hatch. He fired. Blasting the bottle. Soaking himself in fluid as it rained back on him. Instantly out, the rifle fell from his hands, and Fulmer caught it.

Up the spiral stairs, and breathing through their devices, Fulmer and Rongo were swimming through the thick vapor, wafting its tide away with their hands, and ascending to the bridge.

The crewman had the rifle butt poised, ready to crack the skull of anyone who came up the stairs. The vapor was first. Swirling white. He stumbled, taking a deep breath as Rongo's huge hands grabbed his ankles, yanking him hard to the floor.

Fulmer and Rongo were out of the hatch, had sealed it, before the crewman tried to stand.

Fulmer said, "You're stuck up the whale's ass, mate!" and shoved him over with a push on his chest. Rongo grabbed the gun, and spit out the breather.

Fulmer nodded to the observation dome and the waves crashing against it as the bow started tilting, up-ending the horizon, like a drunk who finally loses his balance.

"We've got to empty that ballast, mate."

Rongo went to the levers, and Fulmer inserted the power key into the control panel. Resurrection. Panel after panel lights, the submarine humming with renewed energy. The ballast tanks were opened, flooding outward, and the ship began to level.

Fulmer increased speed from the helm, and went to the crew call. "Attention, all hands that are still awake! This is Mr. Fulmer! I'm again at the helm, but make no mistake, Nemo's the captain of the *Nautilus,* and we'll follow his commands to the letter. I'm not hearin' any arguments so, all hands, stand by."

"All hands." Fulmer looked to Rongo. "I guess that's you."

Fulmer took the Kraken's tongue from his pocket, and set the *Nautilus*' direction for the final set of coordinates.

The sun's bleeding behind the city's man-made clouds spattered orange and red across the *Terror*'s silvered white. Nemo moved around the vehicle, running his hands across its sealed surface, finding no trace of the fins or the retractable tank treads when underwater.

"You helped make that."

Sara was standing feet away, in the new dress, with lace at the collar and cuffs. Her arms were tight around herself, fighting the wind and her breaking apart.

Nemo said, "So I've been told." He touched the *Terror*'s side, opening the vehicle. "You have a remarkable family, indeed."

"Captain, I had nothing to do with any of this."

"The eternal innocent."

Nemo ran his hands along the seats, the driving controls, which were now a flat, blank, gray surface. "From the moment your father stepped into my prison cell, every action I've taken has somehow been engineered."

Sara said, "But not by me," her hands brushing the dashboard, bringing it to glowing life.

At Sara's touch, Nemo stepped back from the *Terror*. "You seem to have a great deal to do with all of it, Miss Robur."

The wind increased, a storm biting from the North. The dirigibles and balloons strained against their anchors, shifting the City's platform, with the pontoons compensating: a waves-rolling motion.

"I've been denying President Grant's accusations all afternoon. I think he finally believes me. Truly."

Nemo said, "He probably needs to, but I'm my own man or I'm nothing. I think hanging's preferable to being a pawn."

The Lieutenant reached them first, leading the way from the main, with Robur behind him, boasting over the wind. "A fleet of my machines would complement the *Nautilus* very well."

Nemo said, "They're faster on the water than any Navy."

"Under the water and in the air. With the right commander, ten of these could rule the sea."

Sara interrupted, "Father—Mr. Robur—what are your intentions for me?"

"This isn't the right place, daughter."

Around them, aero-crews threw storm nets around the dirigible, tightened chains and tether lines. Windscreens unfurled like bunting, circling the city and blocking the main area from the storm. This all happened in minutes with Robur silently approving the efficiency.

Clamps fastened to the *Terror*'s treads, holding it to its launch pad, with Robur saying, "I'm still not satisfied with that system. I need the secret to your operating table, Captain."

Nemo said, "I would venture there's nothing you don't have, Robur."

"Perhaps, you're right."

Sara said, "In the middle of your creation, I think this is the perfect place to know if I'm going to be alive tomorrow."

Robur regarded Sara, the harsh cold hitting them both. "I saw to it that you received a brilliant education. My obligation to you in that sense is finished, though I hoped you would stay on, working beside me. Your quarters were designed for that."

Sara realized the Lieutenant had been staring at her, near-targeting with his eyes. She looked suddenly away, to Nemo, but said to her father, "And, what if I just can't?"

The wind from the storm was building into a sharp edge, cutting around the shields as Robur said, "That would be regrettable."

The frigates, iron-clads, battle vessels, and smaller gunboats formed a wide circle, all facing each other, and all flying their different national colors. Lanterns and torches outlined the decks, even as the boats dipped with the churning seas and the beginnings of the storm.

A blue flash of sheet lightning showed up the number of vessels, and their armed crews on deck. Grant observed through a magnifying pane built into the window that was one wall of the massive dining hall, figures of Zeus standing at both ends, lightning from their fingers aimed toward the room.

Grant turned away from the ships, saying, "Not a diplomat in sight."

"You're surprised," Robur said. "All belowdecks, cowering. They're not you, Sam."

"Don't use my first name anymore."

"I always honored your wishes, sir."

The City in the Sky's dining room was formal and formidable, as one would imagine a Viking dining hall. The walls and ceiling reaching out and up, forever. The only break in the structure was the dominating massive window where all eyes fixed. Robur and Nemo sat across from each other, as mirrors, with Grant and Sara placed at the full table, beside them. The lieutenant stayed at the door, smiling, in case of an attempted escape, or assassination.

Robur said, "The world's gathered to meet about you, Mr. President. They make a colorful target."

Grant said, "You're in the sinkhole; attack those ships, you think they'll give a damn about me? Hell, you know half of them believe I'm part of this chaos you created!"

Robur said, "But you are, because this controlled chaos was created by a member of your own cabinet. You're soaked in blood, Sam. Mr. President."

"I've never denied my past, but not this. Not what you're counting on. And my death means nothing. My head gets blown off, somebody else sits at the desk, and the first order'll be to come after you with guns blazing."

"How? By air? Or by water?"

Nemo had been fixed in his stare, and Grant turned to him. "You backing him up? Take on all the navies of the world?"

Nemo said, "I have before."

"And it didn't get you a damn thing but a death sentence. Maybe the world hasn't changed to suit you, but you two sons o' bitches are about to make it a lot worse."

"There's the firebrand, not the statesman," Robur said. "Who better than you understands you must destroy to rebuild, to re-create. I've offered the good captain something you can't. The oceans to cultivate as he sees fit. No more hunger, new sources of energy, control of the skies. A Utopia. Better than just a delayed hanging."

Grant stood, moving around the table as if he were in The Shop, surrounded by a doubting cabinet. "Won't work, never does. Each country wants something different, and they'll never kowtow to you."

Robur said, "After a month of coordinated assaults, they'll fall into line, and the new life we offer will seem like paradise. *'The art of war is simple enough. Find out where your enemy is. Get at him as soon as you can. Strike him as hard as you can, and keep moving on.'*"

"*The Art of War.* You appropriated the phrase, but the example is yours. Those are your words, Mr. President," Nemo said.

"Goddamn." Grant was beside Nemo. "Every instinct I had told me not to trust you."

Nemo's manner was unbreakable: "My mission was to find the source of your troubles, and I did. The path I choose now is my own."

Grant said, "The buccaneer and the madman: killing the world in order to save it."

Nemo looked to Sara, not Grant, saying, "There will be peace, and no need for men like you."

Grant said, "Believe it or not, Captain, that doesn't sound too bad to me. But it won't happen."

He took a cigar from his pocket case, bit off the end. "You've just declared a world war, and you'll both rot in hell for it."

Sara pushed back her chair and stood, carefully defiant, as she moved from the table, saying, "Mr. President, I'll be going with you."

"Sara?"

"Father, whoever, this is all beyond me. Everything is a lie. I can't think—can't be a part of it."

"My dear, below us are ships from twenty countries, and not a one sees things the way the other does. It's all perspective, so yes, it's all lies. Wouldn't it be the best to wipe that slate clean, and start again, and with you here?"

Sara shook her head, denying her father's words. Robur sipped claret, lost in thought. "I will give you some time. Escort Mr. Grant and my daughter to quarters."

Sara moved around the table, and Nemo grabbed her hand. "Consider carefully what your father's offering, Miss Duncan."

Sara pulled away and walked for the massive doors, where the Lieutenant stood, at smiling attention.

"One thing's clear," Grant said to him, "I know who the hell you are, boy."

The Lieutenant opened the doors with artificial flourish. "Mr. President, it might not seem so, but I'm flattered I made an impression."

Grant and Sara stepped from the room without giving Robur or Nemo another glance or moment. The violence of the storm shook the room; a clap of thunder was cannon fire into a steel drum. Like Nemo maneuvering a typhoon, Robur was unflappable, pouring out two more glasses.

Nemo said, "I want to see how you'll coordinate this attack."

"It will be our first masterpiece."

The Lieutenant stood at Sara's door, waiting for her to step through. She regarded him for a moment, studying the blue eyes, the boyishness.

"How many have you killed?"

"I'm showing you to your quarters, miss. That's all."

Sara said, "You've done all this bidding. He promised you something enormous."

The Lieutenant said, "My own Army. Now please step back, so I may seal your door for the night. I wouldn't want you hurt, or sleep disturbed."

The Lieutenant's smile was frozen. Sara took the step, and the door was shut, then locked.

The Lieutenant turned to Grant's quarters, and repeated the ritual, always with one hand on the dagger in his belt, saying, "General, if you don't mind."

Grant said, "I don't. Our time is coming, believe me."

"And believe me, it will be my honor. I have learned a great deal from studying you. And, sir, feel free to converse with Miss Duncan. Robur does not want you to feel like common prisoners."

The door shut, and was locked. Grant turned, moved to the large window, which was open again, giving a view of the storm clouds around them, and below, the ships.

Grant watched, and said quietly, "The art of war."

Sara sat on the edge of her bed, leaning forward, elbows on her knees. She looked about the room, the books and dolls that her father recalled, and then to the miniature version of the City she used to play with as a girl.

She opened her palm, and peeled away the tissue from the object Nemo had pressed into it. The poison ring.

38

FIRESTORM

A starless night for the *Nautilus* to surface a mile from the frigates, their decks lit with hanging lanterns, and small craft moving back and forth between the ships.

The submarine's engines pulled back and slowed, with Rongo in the observation dome. Fulmer stayed the helm, while crewmen climbed back to life, shaking the chemical grog from their heads.

Rongo said, "This is where we're supposed to be?"

Fulmer said, "It's the final coordinates that Miss Duncan had, Brigand's Trench not two miles away, and there's the armada. Where the hell else should we be?"

"You mean that boat that stole Nemo and her away."

"This was its direction."

"To the clouds that don't move." Rongo threw a thumb at the giant clouds, building on top of each other, suspended above the international flotilla. "There's the coming storm."

It was a demonic version of da Vinci's Vitruvian Man, finely etched in glass, and lit from behind. The perversion of da Vinci was a snake, with human arms, and it stared from the sides of a walled-maze of one sea monster after another, beautifully rendered, with all details of their artificial construction indicated.

"I attended the world exhibition; it was quite an inspiration," Robur said.

He was guiding Nemo through the assembly line of the fantastic nautical creatures. Mechanic-driven eyes, steel claws, brass teeth, and the artificial organs of monsters were laid out. There were Sea Spiders, with exposed pouches of acid ready for insertion, and what look to be giant wasps, stingers filled with poisonous fluid.

Hanging above barrels of whale oil, the giant manta ray was being rebuilt, half of its skin torn away, revealing its fused-metal skeleton and gear works. The center of the assembly line was a great trapdoor for the launching of flying creatures.

"The acid in the stingers can burn through the hull of any ship. There's no defense against a coordinated attack from my creations."

Nemo said, "Every single one, a perversion of nature."

"Why did you create the *Nautilus* as you did? Your design was to frighten your enemies as much as sink them. How many newspapers labeled you monster? Why not make them real, bring their worst fears, the idiotic editorials, the cartoons, to life?"

Nemo said, "The inspiration for the squid that almost destroyed my ship?"

Robur said, "It was damaged, that never should have happened, but you survived it. No one else could. The reaction from the governments when a mechanical attacks? Chaos, that I can control. They can't allow themselves to believe what they knew to be true, and don't know how to react, except to panic, then blame the United States for the atrocities, since none of their vessels were destroyed."

"Something you made sure of."

Robur said, "Very easy to manipulate with my influence; it also freed you from Libby prison."

He opened the trapdoor directly over the international ships. "The leaders of the world, waiting for death from the sky."

"Which we will provide," Nemo said.

"For a greater good. These are the very men who cheered when you were sentenced to hang; who better to sacrifice?"

Nemo moved to where the Sea Spiders were in bits and pieces, and said, "Everything you've done, every motive behind this, is tied to me?"

Robur said, "'I will bring these despots to their knees, and then we'll have a perfect world.' You said that in a letter you wrote to my office during the Civil War. Here's your chance."

Nemo stepped around the illuminated images, locked the door.

Robur said, "I'm offering you half the planet. Take it."

"The sea isn't yours to offer. I'm not interested in conquering the world, only living as a part of it, showing others the way, if they open their minds."

Robur said, "You're a sentimentalist. You keep memorials to your crew, which I knew you would use to follow my map. And an operating table where your son died, while you tried to save him. All over the *Nautilus* are signs of a genius, who won't step away from his past. It's an anchor."

"Like your daughter?"

Robur said, "Maybe we are alike in that way, but if you're going to join me, you have to decide."

Nemo grabbed one of the acid bottles, smashing it against the door, its material bubbling over and sealing them in. "You can't build a Utopia on a mountain of corpses. I hate war no matter who wages it."

Robur said, "Oh, the great hypocrite. So you'll prove your point by killing me?"

Grant was holding up the bourbon decanter, admiring the light flowing through the whiskey, and waiting for the door to open. The Lieutenant entered with a Cheshire grin. He didn't notice the paper door sliding, and the Lieutenant was silent in his entrance.

"Thinking of a last drink, General?"

Grant stood, his leg throbbing. "Thinking that I'd never left a wounded solider behind, until now."

"Never?"

"Never."

Lieutenant said, "If I might, sir, I'd much rather sit and discuss with you your technique in Norfolk. You know your weapons, and made admirable shots."

Grant said, "I didn't finish you off."

"Nor I you, at the White House stables."

Sara stepped in, through the small panel, and the Lieutenant didn't even turn around, when he said, "Miss Duncan, these cells are adjoined, as part of your humane treatment, but you're abusing the privilege. What the General and I have to do isn't for you."

He turned, suddenly grabbing her arm, and wrenched it, forcing a drop of the knife she was holding. His mouth curled open, to teach Sara the error of her ways, when she stabbed him in the neck with the side of General Sigel's ring, the tiny needle puncturing his jugular.

Sara punctured again, blood jetting, as Grant pulled back her hand, thrusting the General's ring close to the Lieutenant's eyes. There was recognition there, of the seal and decoration, before his eyes clouded blank, and he dropped, red soaked, to the floor.

Grant took his pistol and ammunition.

Robur moved behind the glass panels, his voice emanating from a creature's schematic. "I won't die here. These weapons will be put to use whether you join me or not."

"If I have to declare war again," Nemo said, "it'll be against you, without hesitation."

Robur was now behind the demonic snake. "No, not against me."

The glass panels shifted, as stage curtains open, exposing a large, egg-shaped object, more than six feet in length and translucent, with something moving inside. A sharp edge sliced the egg from within, whale oil gushing through the cut. The edge tore away, more pieces shredding, oil flooding. A birthing, as the thing freed itself.

The mechanical's claws were more than three feet, its stinger tail curled over its body, poised to strike, more than twelve feet when extended. Its multiple eyes were redesigns, and placed lower to the mandibles, accommodating a wiring system protruding from the front of its exoskeleton to receive operating signals. All of black metal, the scorpion moved as a natural one, springing forward on its legs, swiping at the air, and bringing down its stinger with amazing speed, belying its enormous size.

Robur said, "Its only function is to tear my enemies asunder. Imagine the useful panic."

Both of the mechanical scorpion's claws extended, body bending forward to strike at Nemo. The thing charged, its tail stabbing. Nemo dove from the stinger, leaping over a table, grabbing a long section of tubing, and swinging at the scorpion, in man-to-machine combat.

Metal claws came down, smashing a table, creature parts flying. Nemo rolled from the floor, swinging again, pounding the claws with wide, battle-ax slashes. Metal split, and wires tore. Electric sparks erupted. The tail swung around, whipping Nemo into a wall, punching him with its barb.

Claws snapped open, and moved with ferocious speed and force, catching Nemo's leg. He pulled it free, steel edges slicing deep, blood running in rivulets. Nemo twisted, got to his feet, brought the pole down again, between the metal claws, snapping it in two.

It was all of a single motion: Nemo jammed the bar into the scorpion claws, breaking their hinges, then batted the eyes of the thing with the other piece of the bar, dodging its tail, its massive body slamming him before he jumped onto its back.

Nemo straddled the thing, legs around its black-metal spine, the tail curling back to strike again, all pistons and servos whirring, as if the thing had a top speed gear.

Nemo kept pounding into the eyes with all his strength, shattering the lenses and breaking the skull plate. The whale oil for the mechanics poured out as a bloody torrent; the machine's tail, claws, and legs thrashed independently of each other in a mechanized spasm, tossing Nemo, claws and tail ripping the manta ray to pieces. Smashing the glass panels and reducing the assembly line to scrap, all in moments.

Nemo moved up behind the thing, and using scrap steel for a fulcrum, he pushed the scorpion over and through the open trapdoor, sending it spinning through the midnight clouds and crashing into the ocean, just missing the British warship.

What was left of the scorpion exploded on impact with the

water, becoming instant shrapnel hitting the ship's hull, and scrambling the crew to their battle stations.

Robur, standing in the middle of the wreckage, grabbed a Sea Spider's acid pouch, scattered across the room like broken eggs, their liquid eating the floor and walls. In near hysterics, Robur hurled a full pouch, just missing Nemo. Acid splayed across a piece of counter, melting it, the toxic smoke invading Nemo's eyes, sending him to the floor in blinded pain.

Grant and Sara moved down the corridor, taking each step with caution, Grant with the Lieutenant's pistol. They didn't speak, just kept moving for the landing pod, then stopped. A Guard stood at a bend, and so far there had been no alarms, no notice of them.

Grant had made sure of that. He and Sara had hidden the lieutenant's body without making a detectible sound. Except Sara's dress was heavy-streaked with blood, and all that needed to happen was one person to spy them. They moved up on the guard, with Sara raising the ring, but Grant pulled her hand down, stopping her.

For Grant, Sara's loyalty was proven, and he didn't want to put her through the ordeal again, even in combat.

Grant moved behind the guard, knocking him down with the butt of the pistol. Grant picked up his rifle, and then he and Sara ran low, staying tight to the walls, making their way to the landing port.

They held by the gateway, Guards and personnel walking the port, and securing the air vehicles for the night against gusts of wind and the jags of lightning.

Grant said, "Can you really handle that thing?"

"Sir, we would be a target in the dirigible, a low-flying one in this wind."

"Don't worry about the dirigible, I mean the flying submarine. You got it to run?"

Sara said, "I think so."

"Do better than that. Obviously, there's no way to invade or seize this place, so it's got to be turned to ashes. Yes?"

Sara nodded her acceptance.

"That vehicle's your escape. I'll cut loose the dirigible, it has grenades and bombs on board. I'll drop them, try to steer the hell out of here. If you can, get to the ships below, or the *Nautilus*."

"Mr. President," Sara gave her voice a lift, "would you call this a suicide mission?"

"I sure as hell would."

Grant saw the landing port as he'd once seen a guerrilla outpost in Ohio: small, with a closed perimeter, troops inside, and more possible, riding in from all sides. The landing port was the same to him, and the moves had to be the same to take it: quick, and sure, with eyes in the back of your head to ensure the surprise. He had only a few men with him that foggy Ohio morning; now it was Sara, and that was just fine, because her courage was real, and he knew it. Grant won in Ohio, and he was going to win this.

Grant had been chewing on an unlit cigar, and chomped down on it. His leg was numb, the pain from his back pounding him as he moved close to the windscreens, stabbing a Guard in the neck with the ring, bringing him to the ground with a hand over his mouth. Sara moved for her objective.

The *Terror* opened with a touch of Sara's finger, as if it were reading her. Grant watched her get in, praying the doors would close before the first bullet's strike.

The shot skimmed wild off the door, a searing ricochet. The

door shut as Grant brought up his rifle and began shooting, laying down cover on all four corners of the pad. Instant confusion, and time for Sara to get away.

The *Terror* lurched forward.

All rifles opened up. The bullets scraped and bounced off the *Terror*, the engine powering up and the treads spinning fast, throwing up pieces of the landing pad as it moved. The guards kept shooting as the vehicle roared from one side of the pad, skidded around, and roared for the other, always faster.

The shooting didn't stop. Grant stayed his position, picking off two Guards in the tower, letting them fall directly in front of the *Terror*, one bouncing off the hood, the other, fodder for its treads.

It gained more speed, racing for the edge of the pad, tearing through the chains and windscreens, then careening over the side. Free-falling, nose first, its weight turning it over on itself. The wind screamed.

Its wings engaged, folding out and locking into place, the side motors now on, balancing the *Terror* to pull it out of its nosedive. The plummeting, gray monstrosity suddenly had grace of flight, turning on its side to gain altitude, then sweeping toward the city, and away into the night sky, the last guards still firing.

Grant watched from the gondola view port, having slipped in during the gunfight. Alarm bells and sirens were sounding, shrill and loud, while Grant was on the floor of his office in the sky, finally lighting his cigar and feeling a twinge of pride before wiping the blood from his hands.

Nemo had found water to splash his eyes, even as blood masked them. It was a moment of cooling from the acid smoke, before Robur charged with the blade. Nemo, not able to see beyond a curtain of blurry red, turned on instinct, blocking Robur, smashing kneecaps, felt them split under his foot before dropping back to the floor. Waiting, with hands outstretched, searching blindly for a weapon. Feeling gears scattered on the floor. Nemo picked up two between his fingers and stayed down as he heard Robur stand. Take a struggled step.

He kept his eyes shut tight, clamped, as if that would ease the burning pain. It didn't, but he focused beyond it. Heard what he needed to hear, then let the gears fly from his hand, oil slick and spinning. Finding their target in Robur's throat.

Robur screamed, his words blood-choked as he pulled the gears from his flesh: "You won't defeat me the way you defeat everyone else! We're the same goddamned man! Killing me is your suicide!"

Robur's scream couldn't hide the sound of his arm, raising the blade and coming down with it. Nemo rolled, countering with a piece of jagged steel. The blades collided, bounced off, vibrating, and collided again. Nemo was up, moving, sensing Robur's moves. His blade sliced into his arm, but the jagged steel opened Robur's chest. Robur advanced, and Nemo met every slash, listening, then moving. Ignoring pain. Chopping at the air with the jagged steel, Nemo kept up the fierce blows to force Robur back, with Robur struggling to fight, trying to stop his own bleeding, and Nemo not retreating.

Robur lunged, fighting on pure rage. Tackling Nemo around the waist, and carrying them both to the edge of the trapdoor with their momentum. Nemo could feel the night wind powering up from below, feel the height, and kneed Robur in the chest, knocking him back, but he held on, pulling them both through the floor and Nemo grabbing. It was just a small piece of iron, keeping the trap open, now stopping them from falling.

The wind beat Robur as he dangled, miles above the water, fighting, his fingers tearing into Nemo's clothes. He cried out, trying to climb up Nemo's side, to get his hands around a piece of his City. To hold on, to anything.

Nemo held, trying to pull Robur up, while keeping his own grip. Robur's oil- and blood-slick hands slipped from Nemo's own. Nemo could only feel Robur falling away, into the darkness.

Sara moved her hands across the *Terror*'s control panel, the yellow light shifting from side to side with a turn, or intensifying with speed. She was flying the vehicle now, bringing it toward the water, searching for the *Nautilus*. She spotted it in the distance, the light spilling from its dome, throwing diamonds across the water around it.

She brought the *Terror* around, circling back, when she saw the figure. Falling. From the City in the Sky. She never saw her father's face, or his body destroyed, but she felt it, this terrible, sudden pain.

Sara increased the airspeed, and aimed for the bank of artificial clouds.

Rongo dropped his scope, turning to Fulmer. "That flying boat, I just saw it."

Fulmer moved to the laser rifle. "Coming from up there? Maybe we can spot it, find out where the hell the Captain is."

Fulmer fired the laser, the beam spreading out in the clouds, outlining the front part of the city in glowing strokes of red. The beam broke apart in the clouds, and Fulmer took his finger from the trigger.

"Christ on a crutch, that's one for the books."

"Yes," Rongo said. "Like the rest of this journey. Now what?"

"We prepare the torpedoes."

Fulmer dialed the death of Nemo's wife as the safe combination, opening the huge doors. He slid open the torpedo cache as
Rongo took one-half of the largest brass case.

Fulmer said, "Most of these were empty, so Nemo could use
them for underwater exploration and whatnot."

"But not this one."

"Not this one," Fulmer said. "He packed this one himself,
part of the *Nautilus'* self-destruction. If we're trapped, we fire one
of these out, take as many enemy with us as we can, and set off
another that's built in, so no one gets hold of the *Nautilus* again.
This one, we're going to fire."

Rongo said, "To destroy whatever's up there."

"Maybe the Captain too, but I'm pretty damn sure this is how
he'd want it. A little hell comes to breakfast."

"And the other bomb?"

Fulmer said, "Nemo's orders first."

Nemo hauled himself up over the lip of the open door, blindly pulling himself to the center of the room before standing. He doused
his eyes again, cooling them before picking up the long jag of steel
and feeling his way to the back of the assembly line and the rows of
whale-oil barrels, which were all shapes and shadows to him. Dark
gray and light gray, cobbled together with no meaning.

Nemo brought back the steel, the first blow rupturing the
first barrel, before prying through the tops and sides of the others,
letting the oil flood across the floor, soaking into the paper structure of the room.

In the gondola, Grant fit the last of the bombs into the delivery
cradle and settled against his desk, still keeping down from the

view ports. The gondola was dark, surrounding Grant with the boys who had died there not two days before. A thought, because it had been another battle, with another to come, but this one from the air, just as Maston had predicted.

Rifle fire tore the air.

The *Terror* circled the City, dipping close to the pyres and domes, the Guards firing wildly from the towers, letting the bullets bounce off the vehicle's skin and hoping one shot would bring it down.

The shootings were bursts of flame into the air, slugs tracing the dark, trying to follow the *Terror* flying off and then coming back in a taunting, dangerous move.

Grant kicked open the gondola's escape hatch, letting himself drop to the landing pad and moving behind the dirigible to the tie lines. The guards fired at the flying vehicle, moving in all directions. Grant didn't know if Sara was that skilled, or if the thing was out of control.

But she was keeping them from him as he cut the first tether line. Gunfire ripped the ground around him, and Grant spun, using the automatic pistol on the Guard tower, and another, charging toward him with a rifle and sabre. Grant shot him twice.

"Those are the only precise shots I'm hearing."

Grant turned to see Nemo, under the Vulcania wall, and calling out, "Robur's no more. If they knew it, they'd stop."

Bullets strafed as Grant made his way to the arch. More slugs tearing around him. He returned fire, then to Nemo, he said, "Did you kill him?"

Nemo said, "It's done, that's all that matters."

Grant looked into Nemo's eyes, which were solid bloodred, as if replaced with rubies. He said, "And all that he built?"

"There's genius here. If it can be saved, it should be."

A bullet tore Nemo's shoulder, exploding through, pounding him against his own tribute, smearing it with blood. The *Terror* dipped between the main towers, its air wake knocking Guards from their turrets. Falling to the ground. Trying to shoot at Grant, hauling Nemo to the dirigible.

Grant blasted the last tether line with pistol shots, slicing the cable clean, before pulling Nemo on board, the dirigible already starting to lift, tearing away its docking.

The *Terror* circled the City again, coming in fast as the dirigible rose. In the gondola, Grant was at the helm, with Nemo at the bomb rack. The propellers engaged, and Grant angled the balloon away from the city as more gunfire peppered the gondola's sides and roof.

The balloon sleeve tore with the gunfire.

The *Terror* moved in from behind the dirigible, as if it were going to land on it.

A Guard fired a small Howitzer from the middle of the pad, directly into the balloon, exploding it. The flames were instant, and engulfing. Hellish.

On the *Nautilus*, Fulmer saw the bright fire, and said to Rongo, "The rain of fire. Nemo's end of the world. Fire torpedo."

The torpedo burst from the *Nautilus*, shooting straight across the dark, toward the fire high in the night sky.

The *Terror* bore down on the gondola, a cable dropping from underneath, its sides opening as the paper city burned, whale oil exploding. Plumes of flame and smoke, devouring the paper city. The four support towers toppled, collapsing under their own weight, loosing the balloons that were swallowed in the hot curtain.

The gasses engulfed. Hellish.

The torpedo struck, and the night was turned to bright noon for a moment before all fell from the sky as liquid flame and burning ash.

Lime focused his camera, first on the waterfront and the scarred buildings with stacks of new lumber and paint before them, the workers all standing silently, some with their hats over their hearts. He captured that image before moving his tripod, to where the other reporters and photographers had gathered for their glimpse of the *Nautilus.*

The crowd lined the docks and the cobblestone streets for blocks, bleeding into curious miles. Fathers carried their children on their backs, and soldiers held others behind a barricade, all trying for a look.

People were five deep along the docks, with injured sailors and soldiers making up the first rows. Fishermen stood on their decks, but dressed in suits, all facing the *Nautilus* in its slip. The sides of the submarine had been draped in black bunting, with the *Terror* lashed to its stern deck by large chromium bands.

Sara, Fulmer, Rongo, and the crew stood by on deck with one of Nemo's tridents as President Grant addressed the assembled group: "Most of you knew Captain Nemo from the accounts in newspapers. He was the terror of the seas, and branded an enemy of the United States. Those were all sentiments that I shared, until we entered into a truce, to hunt a common enemy. And the Nemo that I came to know was an amazing scientist and a man of high principle who did not chart the easiest course for himself."

Lime put his tripod over his shoulder and pushed his way through, angling around everyone taller than he, to the man standing across the street, in front of the Old Confederate Post

Office, the scars from Grant's bullets still unpainted and unrepaired.

Lime said, "This is quite a tribute for a squirrely son of a gun like Nemo."

The man said, "Don't you want to hear the president?"

Lime said, "I've heard him before. And so have you. Maybe we should talk about that over a drink, maybe do a little business. Maybe."

"Sorry, I don't drink."

The man adjusted his dark glasses without a word and started walking, away from the open waterfront, and still hearing the echo of Grant's voice: "If he began this mission for the United States as a traitor, then he died a patriot. More than anything, he wanted to return to the sea, and that he did. I am here to salute the Captain, and wish him a safe voyage home."

Grant threw a salute, and a bagpiper played, as Fulmer dropped the trident into the water, letting it drift with the tide.

Flash pans ignited like fireworks, and the crowd cheered as Grant was escorted through. He leaned heavily on his cane, and was flanked by security until he was able to climb into his coach.

Efrem, protected by armor plating designed by Duncan, looked down from the driver's seat. "You have a special appointment, sir, and I'd like to take the horses for a run."

Grant said, "Whatever you think best, son."

Lime's flash pan burst as Grant climbed into the coach, both men exchanging a look.

Grant settled into his seat. Nemo didn't remove his glasses.

Nemo said, "I hate bagpipe music."

Grant said, "It's a tradition, live with it. Or die with it."

"Death is preferable."

"You have your wish. You can live or die anywhere you want."

Nemo said, "You'll honor that?"

Grant said, "That's my intention."

They rode for a moment, listening to the steady rhythm of the team as Efrem drove them. Nemo said, "He always called you Sam, but that's not your middle name."

Grant said, "I don't have one. The *S* was added as a moniker. It doesn't mean anything."

Nemo said, "My name doesn't mean anything, either. Anymore."

Grant nodded, and they rode, neither man acknowledging the thick file folder, marked Top Secret, on the seat between them.

NEMO RISING

FROM SCRIPT TO NOVEL AND BACK AGAIN

A kiddie matinee, with popcorn boxes and cups of soda flying overhead, was my introduction to Jules Verne. The movie was *Mysterious Island*, that grand and very loose adaptation of Verne's semi-sequel to *Twenty Thousand Leagues Under the Sea*, which featured that wonderful giant crab, created by Ray Harryhausen, and a mesmerizing Captain Nemo in the form of actor Herbert Lom.

I was about eight years old, and hadn't read any of Verne yet, but I knew who he was, thanks to monster magazines, comic books, paperbacks from the local spinning racks at the drugstore, and a series of record album adaptations of *Twenty Thousand Leagues, Journey to the Center of the Earth,* and *Around the World in Eighty Days.* There was even a dramatic record of *Twenty Thousand Leagues* starring Jonny Quest and Race Bannon (!), which I still proudly own.

I wish I could pretend my interest in Verne, and all that he created, had more sophisticated roots, but the movies and comic books touched the nerve that made me want to discover the real thing and sit down and read.

Discover would be the right word, as Verne not only predicted future technologies with amazing accuracy, he wrote his books to be about discoveries and the journey made, whether around the world or to the Moon. There is a sense of wonder about Verne's writings that often found its way into the best film adaptations, especially Disney's *20,000 Leagues.*

Wonder is something we don't see much in movies anymore, as the sense of media awareness has made even five-year-olds experts on popular culture. It's also led to a sense of cynicism, especially in fantasy films, that I wanted to avoid when I decided to write my own "loose" Verne adaptation: really, creating a new adventure by combining Captain Nemo with Robur the Conqueror from *Master of the World,* and hopefully capturing that feeling I had in that kiddie matinee decades ago.

Over time there had been a bit of studio interest, and even an option or two, but *The Return of Captain Nemo* as film or pilot was never made, and after more than a decade, and the prodding of author Miles Swarthout, the script became the outline for this novel. I kept to my original structure, but found discoveries along the way, including a major shift by focusing on the technology that Verne was so fond of, and pushing it further in the book, to the creation of the villain's monsters and President Grant's dirigible.

The following scene is the classic, and expected, battle between the *Nautilus* and a giant sea snake that's actually a multi-headed hydra, so a little mythology—movie and Greek—snuck into the old screenplay as well.

In the novel, this became the fight with a mechanical beast that, to me, feels closer to the spirit of Jules Verne, and the dreams he created during the revolution of men and machines. Or at least, it's a nod to all those crazy, wonder-filled adaptations that led me to the original works of this genius and all that he foretold.

```
EXT. UNDERWATER—THE SEA GARDEN
Nemo and Sara sack the last of the lobsters.
Behind them, in the darkness of a cave—

AN EYE OPENS
Then another. And a third. And a fourth.

NEMO AND SARA
Move around the edges of the "garden," harvesting
sea fruit. Sara grabs a bunch of seaweed that
SLITHERS out of her hand and swims away! She
starts. Nemo laughs. Sara looks toward Nemo,
SHOUTS SILENTLY TO HIM, as—

A SEA HYDRA
Swims from its lair. Double-headed. Body over a
hundred feet. The thing races for Sara and Nemo.
Two sets of jaws jetting through the water. Bearing
down. Striking.

NEMO
jerks Sara away from the snapping heads. A forked
tongue lashes her. Squeezes. Sara rips a knife
from her belt, slices the tongue deep. Blood
smokes the water. The snake whips in pain,
SLAMMING the two to the ocean floor. Silt EXPLODES
around them. A thick cloud rises.

INT. NAUTILUS—THE BRIDGE—NIGHT
The view ports are clouded blind.
```

FULMER
Engine room! Be standin' by with full
power!

UNDERWATER W/ NEMO, SARA, AND THE SEA HYDRA
Through the rolling silt, sand and blood, the
Hydra angles toward the sub. Nemo grabs one of
the marking stakes. The two heads come for him.
Nemo falls on his back, the thing passing just
inches above.

Nemo jams the iron stake into the sea snake's
belly. The *N* rips it. The creature SCREAMS, body
flailing. The hydra's tail SMASHES the *Nautilus*!
Flesh ripping metal.

INT. NAUTILUS—BRIDGE—NIGHT
The crew are SLAMMED into the walls. A crewman's
nose busts. The wheel spins. Fulmer takes hold.

EXT. UNDERWATER W/ NEMO AND SARA
Nemo grabs Sara, the snake circles the sub.

INT. NAUTILUS—DIVER'S HATCH—NIGHT
Water BURSTS from the hatch as Nemo and Sara roll
out. A SAILOR pulls them free, as THE HYDRA'S TWO
HEADS BLAST through the opening! Six feet high.
Snapping wild. One head SLAMS Sailor to the wall,
the other strikes at Nemo. Misses.
The Hydra's huge body imprisons it in the hatch-
way, as—

NEMO
dives for the weapons rack, grabs the laser
rifle. The snake lurches forward, snaring Sara in
one of its jaws, pulls her in. She struggles. It

clamps. Nemo tries to shoot. No power. Sara
barely SCREAMS. Lungs empty. Ribs cracking. Nemo
SMASHES her helmet with the rifle butt. Shark
bone and brass flying.

SARA
gulps air as Nemo PLUNGES THE RIFLE BARREL INTO
THE HYDRA'S EYE, bursting it. Hydra SCREAMS,
dropping Sara. Retreats back down the diving
hatch. Nemo SLAMS the hatch, makes it fast.

INT. BRIDGE—NIGHT
As Nemo and Sara charge in. Fulmer's at the
wheel. All eyes go to the view ports where
the giant belly of the sea snake can be seen,
coiling. Rope of flesh around the *Nautilus*.
Strangling it.

EXT. UNDERWATER WITH THE NAUTILUS AND THE
HYDRA—NIGHT
The two-headed monster constricts. Ribs and mus-
cles tighten. Rivets on the sub loosen and pop.

INT. NAUTILUS—VARIOUS—NIGHT
The CREWMEN react as the *Nautilus* creaks. Metal
whines. A seam above Jess SPEWS seawater. Starts
to bend.

INT. BRIDGE WITH NEMO, SARA, AND FULMER—NIGHT
The view ports start to bulge.

                    SARA
        What if we electrify the outer plates? I
        can siphon power directly from an arc in
        the laboratory.

Nemo regards Sara. Water tears around the
ports.

                    NEMO
        Get Miss Duncan anything she needs—!

The action of the crew is whip-fast. Moving.
Preparing for battle.

EXT. UNDERWATER WITH THE HYDRA—NIGHT
The *Nautilus* is completely covered by the
sea snake. The animal—blood flowing from its
blind eye—keeps drawing in on itself. Ever
tighter.

INT. NAUTILUS—LABORATORY—NIGHT
Sara and Jess haul the arc with the crude
cardio-cables from the lab.

                    JESS
        You know better than I do, miss, but
        this scares me dry!

                    SARA
        You'll be drinking soon enough.

INT. NAUTILUS—BRIDGE—NIGHT
Jess and Sara set the machine down. Sara attaches
the paddles to a support beam, while Fulmer bares
a power cable. They work furiously, and their
words collide as they speak on top of each other:

                    SARA
        Let's pray your little invention can
        save more than one life at a time!

                          JESS
        If it don't, we're supper for that thing!

                        FULMER
        Ya signs on, ya take yer risks—

                         NEMO
        A professional attitude, Mr. Fulmer.

Sara opens the main control panel, exposing the
power source. She gives Nemo a nod, he shuts the
main. Darkness. We can HEAR the crew YELLING
O.S. Jess lights a lens focused-candle for Sara
as she splices into the hot line.

A metal seam SPLITS. The sea sprays in. The
HYDRA'S ROAR FILLS the sub.

Jess shoves Sara into the captain's chair as
Nemo throws the main power switch. BLUE SPARKS
EXPLODE from the control panel in a WILD BURST!

THE CARDIO MACHINE'S
Electricity arcs onto the main beam; a swarm of
blue-hot insects crawling through the *Nautilus'*
metal guts and skin, making their way to—

EXT. UNDERWATER WITH THE HYDRA—NIGHT
The electricity TEARS FROM the sub's surface,
ripping the snake up the middle. Cooking it.
Boiling the four eyes before BLOWING the body
apart in an ACRID BLAST.

INT. NAUTILUS—BRIDGE—NIGHT
Rocked. Jess is thrown off balance. His hand
grazes a cross beam. BLUE POWER slams Jess—

Hellish—as he's hurled across the bridge, SHATTERED against the far wall.

NEMO
dives for the cable, rips it free. The blue arc sputters. Dies. And Jess folds over, dead.